Loretta Proctor was
English father and Greek mother who met in Athens
during WWII. She has written two previous novels,
The Long Shadow, set during the first World War in
Salonika, and *The Crimson Bed*, set in mid-Victorian
London. She also writes poetry and is pleased to be
a distant relation of Elizabeth Barrett-Browning.
Loretta lives in Malvern with her husband and
enjoys working in her beautiful garden. She has two
grown-up children.

BY THE SAME AUTHOR

The Long Shadow
The Crimson Bed

To Mary with love and thanks for all your support!

Middle Watch

LORETTA PROCTOR

Loretta Proctor

Copyright © 2012 Loretta Proctor

Loretta Proctor is hereby identified as author of this work in accordance with Section 77 of the Copyright, Designs and Patent Act 1988.

Apart from any fair dealing for the purposes of research or private study, or criticism or review, as permitted under the Copyright, Designs and Patents Act 1988, this publication may only be reproduced, stored or transmitted, in any form or by any means, with the prior permission in writing of the publishers, or in the case of reprographic reproduction in accordance with the terms of licences issued by the Copyright Licensing Agency. Enquiries concerning reproduction outside those terms should be sent to the publishers.

Matador
9 Priory Business Park,
Wistow Road
Kibworth Beauchamp
Leicester LE8 0RX, UK
Tel: (+44) 116 279 2299
Email: books@troubador.co.uk
Web: www.troubador.co.uk/matador

This book is a work of fiction and, except in the case of historical figures and minor factual details concerning their life histories, any resemblance to actual persons, living or dead, is purely coincidental.

ISBN 978-1780881-164

A Cataloguing-in-Publication (CIP) catalogue record for this book is available from the British Library.

Cover image with kind permission of Trinity House, Tower Hill London EC3 4DH

Typeset in 11pt Book Antiqua by Troubador Publishing Ltd, Leicester, UK

Matador is an imprint of Troubador Publishing Ltd

Printed in Great Britain by the MPG Books Group, Bodmin and King's Lynn

To Sara Jane Beven who gave me the germ for this story

Though inland far we be,
Our Souls have sight of that immortal sea
Which brought us hither,
Can in a moment travel thither
And see the children sport upon the shore,
And hear the mighty waves roll evermore.

William Wordsworth – *Intimations of Immortality*

Acknowledgements

Middle Watch was inspired by a chance conversation with a friend over coffee. Her life is one of those filled with constant dramas and some of this material gave me the idea for the commencement of this tale. But all authors will tell you that characters begin to take on a life of their own and Bridie O'Neill tells her own story. Perhaps there's some of mine in it too. In the Sixties I was once a civil servant working for the National Assistance Board at Archway and there really was a wonderful waitress called Queenie serving in De Marco's!

Visiting the many beautiful and historic lighthouses of England was a most pleasurable task. My thanks to the staff of these who helped with questions, particularly at Flamborough where I was given a most interesting tour. Lighthouses have a great fascination for us all; beacons of light and safety in isolated and stormy spots. It is good to acknowledge the heroic work done by the men who manned them until the late 20th century before remote control of the lantern was introduced.

The characters are all fictional and my use of well known lighthouses also coloured by imagination, so if there are any errors in the telling they are my own. However, I hope that nothing will detract from your enjoyment of the story.
Many thanks also to Trinity House who allowed the use of a beautiful photograph of Flamborough Lighthouse as the book cover. Their website *www.trinityhouse.co.uk* is worth visiting if you are a lighthouse lover. I hope this story will encourage more people to visit these wonderful places, part of our national heritage.

Thanks to Anna Rossi and Mary Cade for their helpful feedback. A huge thanks as always, to my dear daughter, Thalia Proctor, for her marvellous and professional editing and all her encouragement. And to my patient husband, John, who supplied a feverish writer with frequent cups of tea and coffee (and cake).

Spring 1963

I stood beside the heaped up mound of earth in the graveyard and watched the coffin carried over, lowered gently into the dark, empty hole in the ground. The vicar intoned his prayers for the dead, his voice mingling with the sudden angry wind that had leapt from nowhere, now raging through the ancient yews that surrounded the gravestones in the old churchyard. New graves with pristine white headstones surrounded me in this part of the cemetery. This wasn't some old man about to be extinguished from the world in that dark hole of death. This wasn't some ancestor with a lichen-covered gravestone and some exotic far-away date to intrigue the living. He was young; he would be forever young. It was all such a waste, so pointless and stupid. The angry wind echoed my angry heart.

But it's too late now. I didn't realise the dangers. Didn't understand how Middle Watch is a time when a man alone on a lighthouse in those wee small hours feels he's the only person in the world. A man awake and alone in the darkness of the night has time to think, and sometimes those thoughts turn towards revenge and hate.

PART ONE
EARLY YEARS: 1950'S

Chapter 1

Mealtimes were a torment. I was like the earthing wire in an electric plug, quietly diffusing the enormous tensions around me.

I was never sure what the ultimate quarrel was that made Millie and Dad stop speaking to one another. Since I was about eight years old, I found myself placed between them at meals, my two brothers opposite. They spoke to us, we kids spoke to one another but not a word passed between my parents. I was their mouthpiece.

'Ask your father if he wants any more potatoes.'

'Bridie, tell your mother, I've got more than enough.'

'Kindly ask your father to pass the gravy boat this way. He's had it next to his plate for long enough.'

'Inform your mother that it can hardly be called gravy. More like the remnants of the dishwater.'

'Bridie, tell that man beside you that he has never seen a bowl of dishwater in his life as he never stoops so low as to wash dishes.'

At first it was amusing to pretend to pass on these ridiculous messages but as I grew older it began to seem more and more childish. I simply sat in silence between them, a mere physical barrier. Sometimes I wondered if they would hit one another in their exasperation and whether one day I might be the recipient of their pent-up rage, killed by mistake, an unlucky punch bag.

Millie was jealous of my love for Dad. This had always created a wall between us. I called her Mother to her face though in my head she was always Her or Mean Millie. But Dad was Dad Joe and I adored him. Like a dog, I could almost smell him coming home on leave. I knew it with a deep instinct. Dad was in the Navy and often away at sea, yet I always sensed when he was coming back. Mean Millie would never tell me anything, but whenever I saw his familiar sprawling handwriting on a letter, I watched out of the corner of my eye to see her reaction. If he was about to come ashore, she would look up and stare out of the window with an exasperated little sigh. My heart leapt with joy when she did this. I knew then that he was on the way back and she was anything but pleased about it. I'd given up asking her when Dad would return. When I did she would get angry.

'What's it to you, Little Miss Nobody! It's no business of yours.'

But it *was* my business – Dad had taken me in as a baby and brought me up. As my real father lay dying, Dad Joe, who was his best friend, promised he would care for me and rescued me from being sent to unknown relations or, worse still, to a children's home. He was the most wonderful dear man in the world.

Millie never accepted me. She was the evil stepmother straight from any fairytale.

Even as a tiny baby, I knew I didn't belong to this family. I was the odd one out. Millie made it plain she had no love for me. What little she had was for her two boys. I was Little Miss Nobody in her eyes. I felt as if she watched me all the time with an expression of contempt and dislike, treating all my efforts to please with derision. It made no difference how hard I tried, nothing was ever good enough or properly done.

'You're such a sloppy, stupid child!' she shouted at me one day.

She had sent me straight into the kitchen when I got home from school and told me to make her a cup of tea. It had been a long, hot day. I was tired and longed to go up to my room and read a book, longed for a few moments peace away from her and those pitiless, inquisitorial eyes. But it was not to be. Anger bubbled up in me and made me clumsy. I mumbled to myself under my breath as I banged the kettle on the stove and grabbed a dishtowel from the oven rail. Set to work the moment I got home; set to work all weekend while she sat and read a magazine and polished her bright red nails! In my haste to get upstairs to my room for a precious five minutes, I dropped a cup on the kitchen floor while drying it.

'You're just as stupid as your mother! *She* had no sense at all. And you're the image of her.' Millie stood in the doorway, arms folded, towering above me.

She'd been in a bad mood since that morning. I suspect it was more to do with the fact that Mrs Hillman had called round at breakfast to cancel their Tuesday lunchtime outing, yet I always felt guilty as if in some peculiar way it was my fault. Feelings of guilt meant that I wasn't as sharp as usual that morning and spilt the cornflakes packet all over the breakfast table and floor. Well, that wasn't my fault. It was that idiot Andy, that hateful son of hers. He pushed my arm hard as I was pouring them into his bowl and grinned with malicious joy when Millie made me pick up every one.

'I don't want them in my plate, dirty things ... put them in yours,' he yelled, 'Mum, she's putting the ones off the floor in my plate ... tell her!'

And as always, she did so, giving me a slap for my pains.

'Oh, Mum, that's not fair. Andy pushed her,' Jim said in his laconic way but his effort to be reasonable made no difference. Andy was her baby, her little darling. She spoilt Jim, her eldest, but not in the same way.

So now, hearing the cup smash to the floor and my gasp of dismay as I hastily tried to pick up the pieces, she came over and stood there staring at me in her usual malevolent fashion.

'Stupid. Irish and stupid,' she repeated. 'That's the third thing you've broken this week. Thank God, you're not mine. Yes, it's time you knew it. I'd have been ashamed to claim you.'

She said all this while I was throwing the broken pieces of the cup in the bin. A shard of pottery had made a slit that poured blood and threatened to drip onto my white school blouse. I began to suck my finger but, at these words, took my finger out of my mouth and stared at her. It was the first time she had ever spoken of this.

'But ... then who *is* my mother?'

I asked almost pleadingly. It didn't surprise me to hear that Millie wasn't my real mother. Heavens above, I knew it instinctively and it made my heart glad to know for sure. But then – who was I? Why was I here if I had another family?

Millie made no reply to my question, just sniffed and tossed her permed head. It pleased her to think she'd broken my heart telling me she was not my real mother. The fact is I was jubilant about it. It meant I owed her nothing at all. However, there were now a hundred questions to answer and Millie was never going to oblige by saying more than she had already. She merely said, 'Hurry up and make that cup of tea and get upstairs and change before you ruin that blouse. School uniforms cost money. You cost money. I could have done without a burden like you in the middle of the war as well as trying to keep my boys. And now you cost more than ever to keep. Joe just doesn't understand, he never has understood.'

I ran upstairs once the tea was safely made and delivered. Flinging myself on the bed, I lay there, my heart pounding with shock and a peculiar joy. Over and over I asked myself, 'Who am I? Why am I here in this house?'

There was no way I could ask Dad Joe, as he was still away at sea. But I would ask him next time. Knowing I was fostered or adopted explained a lot and made the burden lighter, in a funny way. I could now dream of parents who were special and fabulous. Millie had hinted that my mother was Irish. That explained my deep chestnut-coloured hair and grass-green eyes. Not that I knew it at the time. I was far too young to know what any of it meant except that Millie wasn't my real mother, and that was the biggest relief of all.

The next time Dad Joe came home on shore leave, I asked him about it.

'Dad,' I whispered when we were alone for a brief moment, 'Dad, who is my real mother?'

He looked at me with his usual kindly expression, so different to Millie's hateful glare.

'What makes you ask that, Bridie?'

'Mother told me … I mean Millie Mother. She told me my real mother was stupid and Irish.'

He looked away and stared out of the window for a long while, various expressions passing over his craggy face.

'Oh, she would say that, she would malign the dead, the bitch. I knew she'd throw it at you some day. I suppose it's time, then,' he added, as if to himself.

'Time for what?'

'Come for a walk with me, Bridie.'

He had a serious look on his face and I wondered what he was thinking. I sensed he had something momentous to tell me. Taking his hand, I set off with him along the road until we came down to the quayside.

'Can we go down to the shore?' I asked. Whenever I saw the sea, I had to go close to it. It lured me with its sounds, the tumbling, rushing waves, the roar of its incessant motion. Frightening, majestic, terrible, it never stopped, it was never still, yet looking out over its vastness, I felt stillness in my soul. It was a paradox I would never understand. We shared this love of the sea, Dad and me, and would often come down here together – I sitting on the low stone parapet, Dad leaning against it, one arm about me, the other holding his pipe which he puffed with deep enjoyment. The smell of the strong, dark tobacco wafted about me and I snuffed at it with pleasure.

'Yes, let's go down,' he said and I stopped to take off my socks and shoes and follow him down the stone steps to the beach. My toes sank deliciously into the yielding, shifting sands. I ran as well as I could, stumbling and sinking in the softness until at last, I reached the flat, hard edges of the shore where the retreating waves had left a large margin of packed wet walkway.

Joyfully, I shouted and sang to the waves. Dad stood and watched me with amusement.

After a while, I ran back and we walked along the shoreline, stopping to greet familiar dogs.

'I wish we had a dog, Dad.'

'I'd get you one, Bridie, but Mother would never have an animal in the house. You know what she's like.'

'Doesn't Jim want one, or Andy?'

'Apparently not.'

Subdued, I looked out again at the sea.

We walked back to the steps. I put on my shoes and socks then Dad said, 'Let's sit down here for a bit, Bridie. There's something special I want to tell you, sweetheart.'

Climbing up after him to the bit of parkland at the top, I sat beside him on the wrought iron seat with its green-painted wooden slats, a present from John Barley to his dear, departed wife, Mary. I traced the letters of their names with my finger.

Dad knocked out the ashes from his pipe and put it in his jacket pocket. I felt a sudden feeling of dread, though I had no idea why. He seemed so solemn.

'You're not a baby any more,' he mused. 'You're almost a teenager now, and I feel it's time to tell you things you ought to know about, things about yourself, where you come from. So … now you know, don't you, Bridie, you know you're not my real daughter and Millie's not your mother.'

'Whose daughter am I, then?' I asked and began to bite the skin round my fingers, a nervous habit of mine when troubled.

He took my hands away and smacked them gently. I folded them in my lap and stared out to sea.

'Your father was called Bill O' Neill. He was my best friend; we both served on board HMS Winchester in the war. He was a great fellow, Bridie, always ready for a laugh. But when you were born, your mother died having you. She had some sort of rare blood condition and it proved fatal.'

I looked up at him and he took my hand in his, squeezing it affectionately.

'Was she pretty?'

'She was beautiful, Bridie. You're already getting to look like her, got her lovely chestnut hair and soft green eyes. Even her little freckles on your nose. Yes, you're like her a lot. But she died and your dad couldn't live without her. Just the week before when I was with him in Dublin he said, "Take care of Bridie if anything happens to me, Joe, promise." I can hear his voice even now. I wondered at the time what made him say that.'

'But how *did* he die, Dad?'

Dad Joe hesitated and looked at me for a long while as if pondering what to say.

'Well, let's say ... he died of grief.' He looked a bit worried at saying that as if he thought I might bawl or scream or something, but I didn't. I just sat and thought about it for a long time. His words were like a romantic story. It seemed to have little to do with me or my life. These unknown parents meant nothing to me. I felt no emotion at all. All the same, I wondered what they had looked like.

'Have you any photos?'

Dad looked relieved by my calm acceptance. He smiled and patted my hand again.

'One or two. I'll show them to you sometime. But don't tell Mother. She never liked your mum and dad, especially your mum.'

I wondered why, but had a feeling it was jealousy. Millie was always jealous of any woman Dad spoke to; jealous of all his friends come to that. She was a woman who demanded to be the centre of attention, no matter what it took.

'But *you* love me, don't you Dad?'

He looked down at me, his kindly face full of tenderness. He patted my cheek and pulled my ear gently.

'I love you like you were my own, Bridie. Millie refused to let me formally adopt you but it makes no difference. I'm your Dad now. I promised Bill. And I promise you.'

Dad later told me that both my parents came from Dublin. My mother's name was Maureen. He showed me the photos of them hidden in his wallet – the wallet he always kept on his person for Millie was a snoop who rifled through all his letters and possessions when he went away. Dad knew this and made sure anything he wanted to keep to himself went with him on his travels. Not that he was a man of secrets. He was an open, trustworthy person, his face craggy, warm and cheerful. His eyes were a bright blue in that tanned face. They were clear, sincere and honest, just as he was; not a handsome man but his face was strong and interesting. I could never understand why he had married Millie. He told me she'd been a beauty back then. The old wedding photo on the sideboard showed him smart in his naval uniform with Millie at his side, clutching his arm with one hand and a trailing spray of maidenhair ferns and roses in the other. I had to grudgingly admit she was pretty, in a 1940s sort of way. Her hair in the photo was longer and darker, permed into tight curls. She looked attractive and smiling, so different to the bitter, angry, middle-aged woman she had now become.

My real mother had an attractive rather than pretty face. It had character and strength about it. The nose was straight from brow to tip and the mouth quite full. Her hair looked lovely, thick and falling in natural waves to her shoulders. My father was the opposite, his hair dark, flopping across the brow and he was very handsome. I often asked to look at this photo when Dad and I were on our own and it was safe. When I was older, Dad gave me these photos and they remain my treasured possessions. I thought – I could have fallen in love with my real father if I'd met him in different circumstances. He was so beautiful.

So when Bill O'Neill appeared to me in later life in a different form, I fell in love with him all over again.

Chapter 2

Millie treated me like a servant from the start. As a very small child, she sent me to fetch groceries from down the road. It wasn't much to start with but as I grew older and stronger she asked me to fetch more and more. If the goods weren't what she wanted or not up to her standards, it meant a walk back again into town to exchange them. If I bought her a piece of lamb shoulder from the butchers, it had to be seven shillings and sixpence. Not a penny less or a penny more and not too much fat on it. I lost count of the times I had to traipse back with a joint and ask for another because the first one wasn't good enough. It was so embarrassing to have to go back again but it was either that or face Millie's wrath. One day she gave me such a list of heavy articles to carry that Mr Britten, the grocer, took pity on me and sent his boy, Alf, along with me to help carry the stuff.

'You're too young to send out for all this shopping,' he said, not looking at all pleased. It was nice to think someone was on my side.

Millie opened the door and seeing young Alf with me, holding some of the bags of spuds and things, was really angry. He had put his scarf round my neck too, to keep me warm, he said. I was touched by that gesture of kindness. People being kind always made me want to cry, it was such a rare thing. Seeing Millie's face, panic came over me. I tore off the scarf, flung it at the bemused Alf, and taking the bags, ran inside. Mille glared at Alf and told him to clear off. I think he'd rather hoped he'd get a tip, but that was his bad luck. She shut the door turned to me and gave me a slap.

'You can manage very well, you sly little thing. Luring young boys to carry your bags already, are you? I can see *you'll* come to no good. Far too fond of the boys already.'

I tried to defend myself. 'Mr Barrett said it was too heavy too carry. He said I was too young to carry all this stuff,' I said, rubbing my cheek. 'I'm not luring, Mother. I don't know what it means. He sent Alf with me.'

'You're such a liar, such a little floosie! God knows, your father sets you a bad enough example.'

'My father?' I felt confused. 'Dad Joe?'

'Don't you know sailors have a woman in every port? You think my precious husband is any different and able to keep his trousers buttoned up? Huh! He always had an eye for the women, did Joe.'

'I don't believe you!' I shouted. 'Dad Joe isn't like that, he isn't!'

Millie's temper was easily provoked and terrible. She went deep red in the face, a peculiar shade that began down in her neck and rose like some strange tidal wave of blood up to her cheeks, over her forehead until even her ears turned dark red. When that began to happen I always fled well out of the reach of a hard fist ready to smack my head or a thwack from the wooden spoon in her hand or any other object that she might grab and fling in my direction.

'You're as disgusting and argumentative as he is!' she screamed at me and grabbing an ashtray sent it flying in my direction. It splintered by my ear as I dived out of the door, quaking with her ferocity and hate.

Anything that was not in agreement with Millie's wishes and desires was construed as being stubborn and argumentative. I was not allowed a heart or mind of my own. She seemed to assume I would be a reflection of her in every way, know what she needed. I learnt to be so in order to survive. But she forgot, didn't she, that a reflection is your opposite face.

Maybe what pushed Dad Joe that bit too far was the day I broke my ankle. He could stand her harrying *him*, laugh about it even.

He was away so much he didn't really care. I asked him once why he didn't leave Millie, why he didn't divorce her but he said he didn't agree with divorce. He was Catholic and though he didn't attend Mass or anything, he still felt he'd made a promise to be with her till death did them part and he never broke a promise. I understood that, I was just the same, but I felt maybe God would be kinder to put them asunder now rather than let them live in such a farcical relationship. What I really wanted was for Dad to take me away or else for Millie to die.

The day I broke my ankle was a Sunday. A Sunday in January; cold, grey and miserable. Millie had sent me up to lay a fire in their bedroom as Dad Joe was coming home on leave that evening. They still slept together in a small double bed. It was just a habit, I suppose – the thing everyone did when married no matter what the relationship was like. Later in life, I looked back and wondered how they could bear to be so close at night when they never spoke to one another in the day.

I was always good at making fires and getting them going. I never needed to use a newspaper over the chimney to get a draught up. The trick was to make sure the wood and coal were really dry by bringing some in the day before, leaving it in the box near the fireplace where it would warm up nicely for the next day.

As I laid their fire, I thought about Dad and wondered if he was on the way from Portsmouth, or Pompey as he called it, where his ship had docked. I looked forward to seeing him and I knew he was always glad that I would be there first at the door, ready to hug and kiss him and welcome him home.

'My best girl, my little Bridie!' he'd say lifting me up in the air, even though I was nearly eleven, making me squeal with delight.

Millie would press her lips tight with annoyance and jealousy but she said nothing, never uttered a comment that she was glad he was home. Yet she'd attend with surprising care by making him a nice meal, getting the bedroom cosy, making the house extra neat and clean. But that was all. There were no words of love or welcome, no touch of hand or a little kiss or token of affection. The two of them simply stood and looked at one another for a few moments and then Millie would tell me to go and put on the kettle and make a pot of tea. Dad would pick up his kit bag and march upstairs with it, the boys following him, demanding gifts and treats. They were never disappointed.

Having laid the fire neat and nice, I got up, rubbed my blackened hands on a duster, and collected the coal scuttle to take down and refill. For a moment, I walked over to the window, put down the scuttle, and moving aside the thick cotton lace curtains, looked out over the rooftops towards the sea. It was only five minutes' walk away but we couldn't see it from here as our house was lost in a maze of streets near the town centre. Still, I knew it was there, could picture it and feel the thrill of it. Soon Dad and I would be walking down to the seashore and he would tell me some of the places he'd been to, his adventures and the exploits of his mates. I was so happy. A smile broke out on my face.

'What are you doing, girl, what are you grinning about?'

Millie had entered the room in her usual silent, sneaking, spying fashion. My heart leapt with guilt as it always did when she was around.

'Nothing. Just looking out of the window.'

'Looking at our private things is what you mean. I know you; you're nosy and always prying. Just do your job and get out of our room.'

This accusation was rich, coming from her, and I felt angry in turn.

'It's not me who noses into things,' I muttered.

She grabbed me by the arm, her face beginning to colour up alarmingly.

'And what's that supposed to mean?'

I tried to twist my arm away but her fingers dug into my flesh. I was already tall for my age and could easily push her aside but that never occurred to me. Her strength lay in her forceful personality, which held me in such a state of fear that it paralysed any actions on my part.

'Nothing, nothing ...' I bleated. She knew I was afraid and fed on the fear like some vampire, delighted with her power.

'Little tart!' she exclaimed. 'Always where you shouldn't be, always causing trouble between me and Joe. We were happy till he picked you up. You were a nasty little red-faced, screaming baby and you're a nasty child now. You're a horrible little thing, that's what you are!'

I fled past her to the top of the stairs, tried to escape her accusing face and voice, her upraised arm ready to slap me across the head. Stepping backwards, I stumbled and fell, rolling and bumping down the steps, feeling every tread catch at my spine as I went down. It was a peculiar sensation, painful and quick to end, leaving me with a feeling that I would never be able to save myself from anything; that all my life long I would be falling and falling into space in an effort to escape something evil.

The boys, hearing the commotion, came running out and stood staring at me as I lay still and twisted up at the bottom. Andy laughed. 'Silly cow! Get up.'

I was dazed but tried to get up and shrieked. Something hurt too much.

At the top of the stairs, Millie looked down on me from what seemed a great height. She folded her arms and looked upon me with utter contempt.

'Stop being a fool and looking for sympathy,' she barked, 'get up and get out, you rude, nasty thing!'

I tried again and howled with pain and fear.

Andy kicked me hard in the side and pushed me with his foot, 'Stop hamming, Bridie. You're such a blinkin' tragedy queen.'

Jim stared at me, frowning, and then bent down to look at my leg.

'She can't get up, Mum,' he said, 'look, her foot looks funny. I think she's broken something. We'd better get a doctor over.'

Millie almost hissed in exasperation.

'She brought it on herself,' she said as she marched down the stairs and took a look at me. I lay white and still and whimpering as quietly as I could though the pain was so immense I wanted to scream my head off. It seemed to dawn on her then that maybe I was really hurt, that Dad would be home soon and demand an explanation of events. In a funny way she was quite frightened of Dad who also had a temper though not like hers. His temper, though seldom roused, was cold and merciless once set in motion. He might not buy her story that it had been my fault, though he knew nothing of her regular ill treatment. She was always quite nice to me when he was around and I never said a word against her, there didn't seem any point. Nothing could be changed. To the young, their situation, however bad, seems inevitable and they just live through it, vaguely hoping that some day things might improve. I was the sort who kept things to myself and suffered in silence.

Jim picked me up, carried me into the living room and laid me on the sofa. I lay there moaning, gasping with the pain, and looked at him, huge tears brimming over, rolling down my face. His eyes flickered with a sort of compassion and I gave him a weak smile. I felt immense gratitude to him. It was the first time one of them had shown me any care.

'Better get the doctor, I suppose,' said Millie, looking at me with utter disgust. 'Trust you to cause trouble, just as Joe is coming home, attention-seeking little bitch. Andy, run down the road and get Doctor Barnes ... if he's in. It's Sunday as well.' She glared at me as if I had conjured the whole scenario on purpose to annoy everyone.

I began to feel I *had* done so and felt deeply unhappy. Now I couldn't greet Dad and we couldn't have our walk down to the sea. I began to cry again but not aloud; I just shut my eyes, letting the tears ooze out slowly, choking back my sobs.

Andy, also shooting me looks of annoyance and dislike, went most unwillingly to get Doctor Barnes. Luckily the doctor was in and said he'd come after his Sunday lunch. He did so in his own good time and I lay in pain till he arrived, wishing I was dead. He came at last and seemed to spend an age chatting to Millie at first, as if nothing was the matter at all and this was merely a social call. He was one of her cronies and I'd never liked the man. She always made sure she brushed her hair and put on her lipstick when he called round. He seemed to call round a lot but never when he was needed. At last, he deigned to come over and see me and stared at me as if I was some specimen in a glass jar, and not a very attractive specimen at that. Then he felt my leg, pronouncing I had probably broken a bone near the ankle and would have to go up to the hospital tomorrow to have an x-ray and a plaster put on. Meanwhile he set it as best he could. 'She'll be all right,' he said dismissively. 'It can wait till tomorrow.'

I wanted them to take me now but it meant a bus into town and no one would bother. If only Dad was here. He'd have insisted, borrowed a car or something.

Between Jim and the doctor, they got me upstairs, onto my bed and out of the way. I lay there while tears streamed down my face. Now I couldn't walk any more and I was frightened. Maybe I'd never walk properly again. It was better to be able to walk about and be normal even if it meant running about at Mean Millie's bidding than lying here incapable of doing anything.

Jim lingered a little and smoothed the blanket around me.

'Cheer up, old girl,' he said. 'I'll bring you up some comics and things if you like.'

'I just want to see Dad Joe,' I sobbed. 'I want Dad Joe.'

'He'll be here soon. Want me to read to you or anything?'

'No. I just want to be dead!'

'Don't be stupid. It's only a broken ankle. It'll get better. You heard what old Barnes said. You're young and it'll get better quick.'

'But I want to walk down to the sea with Dad Joe. I want to move about and it hurts a lot. I don't want to be up here all by myself.'

'I'll keep you company, Bridie. I promise, I will. Honest.'

I looked at him and saw how his gentle blue eyes were clouded over with an expression I'd not seen there before. It was a questioning. Not questioning me but something indefinable and troubling in his heart. I tried to smile. He sounded so kind and sincere and worried. He was the only nice person in this house when Dad Joe wasn't around.

Just then Millie yelled up the stairs, 'Jim! What are you doing up there, wasting time. Come down at once and help me with the dishes.'

'Helping Mum means I'll have to wash and dry,' whispered Jim, 'while Mum watches from her chair.'

'Don't I know it.' I whispered back, amazed at this traitorous comment.

'Look on the bright side, Bridie. You can have a rest for a change while *we* do the work. Andy won't be too pleased.'

'Andy won't lift a finger,' I said. 'Sorry, Jim. I suppose you'll get lumbered now.'

'Never mind. I *want* to see you rest, Bridie. I hate it when you work so hard. It isn't fair.'

'You're kind, Jim. You're really kind.' I looked at him with new eyes and with deep-feeling gratitude. He smiled and stroked my hair for a moment then scuttled off as Millie lifted her voice yet again, demanding he came down forthwith or she'd give him what for.

When Dad came in, I yearned to run downstairs to greet him but had to lie there, feeling weak and dizzy. He would be so upset that I wasn't there.

I heard his voice, heard him greet the boys and say, 'Where's my little Bridie?'

Millie passed some message via the boys. I heard Andy saying how I'd been stupid and fallen downstairs and hurt my ankle.

Dad came up straightaway and looked at me. He gave me a kiss on the cheek and stroked back my hair.

'What have you been up to, silly-billy? Going and getting your leg messed up. How on earth did you manage that?'

'Sorry, Dad,' I said feebly, 'so sorry to be a nuisance.'

'I'll say. Never mind, ducky, we'll make sure you're up and about again soon. I'll fetch you up a cuppa in a minute and a couple of aspirins. Then we'll have a little chat if you feel up to it. Lord above, you look so pale.'

He felt my ankle gently. I tried hard not to scream.

'Damnation! This can't be left till tomorrow; you could be lamed for life if we don't act now. That bloody doctor's useless, always has been. What the dickens has he done here? Is this supposed to be some sort of splint? He's no use at all. That doctor will never turn out unless it's to put you in the mortuary. I'll go down to the phone box and order a taxi. There's always some hanging about at the station. We'll get you sorted out and then it won't hurt quite so much, eh? You'll soon be right as rain.'

'Then we can go walking by the sea,' I said, cheering up a little.

'Yes, yes, we will,' was the hearty reply. 'Don't you fret. Dad's home again, my little lass.'

The words were like a balm to my soul. I felt safe and cared for now. Sometimes I had visions of running away to sea, stowing aboard his ship and begging to be a cabin girl or something. But those things happened in books, not real life. In real life I'd be sent home again or thrown in some juvenile detention centre or something equally awful and a triumphant Millie would say, 'I told you she'd come to no good.'

Chapter 3

Dad called the taxi and Millie stared in disbelief when it turned up at the door. But she didn't dare say a word. Dad had on one of his fierce looks that kept her mouth shut. Deep down she knew she'd been neglectful and so had the doctor.

'Can I come with you?' Jim asked, 'I want to ride in a taxi too.'

'Don't be ridiculous,' snapped Millie, 'you can stay here with Andy and me.'

She was angry that Jim was turning over to my side. Jim stuck out a lip and looked stubborn.

'Dad? Can I come?'

'No, stay at home with Mother,' Dad Joe replied. 'We may be a long while. Do your homework.'

Millie looked peculiarly triumphant as if she'd scored a point. She directed her look of anger at Jim now and that troubled me. I didn't want him to get in her bad books too. However, it felt really good to think I had an ally.

At Broughampton hospital, they set my lower leg in plaster and told Dad that I'd broken a small bone in the ankle but that it would heal well. Dad Joe sat with me, laughing and chatting with the doctor and the nurses in his usual cheerful way, helping me to forget the pains and aches. I loved having him there with me, liked looking at his nice lean, tanned face, the deep tramline wrinkles radiating from his eyes through squinting up into the sun when on deck. His face brimmed with character and, to my mind, was a book in itself filled with love and nobility.

'You had a nasty tumble, Bridget,' the doctor remarked,

surveying the bruises on my arms as he pushed my sleeves up, 'better take a look at your back as well.'

My back, where I had bumped along the treads, was also a mass of dark black bruising.

'They look bad but they'll soon heal; there are no abrasions. But this is a nasty mark.' He looked puzzled by a long scar across my shoulder, a dark red-looking welt where Millie had once hit me with a brass poker, the first thing she had snatched up in a fit of temper. I hadn't dodged her fast enough and as I'd been wearing a thin cotton blouse, it caught me hard and the wound had bled profusely, spoiling my blue top. That had upset me more than the whack for I had few enough nice things to wear. I remembered going to the bathroom and washing it as best as I could but it left a mark both on the blouse and on my shoulder which took some time to disappear.

'You do seem accident prone,' smiled the doctor but he looked a bit troubled. He shot Dad Joe a quick, suspicious glance. I felt hostility there and didn't want anyone supposing Dad Joe ever hit me.

'Oh no, that's an old one,' I said quickly, without thinking, 'that's where Millie got me with the poker.'

I regretted saying this at once. The doctor looked at me, puzzled.

'It's okay. We were just mucking about,' I shrugged. Thankfully, he assumed I was talking about some friend or sibling and looked reassured. He smiled and patted my shoulder.

'You youngsters should be more careful,' he admonished.

Dad looked hard at me and I knew he was making connections. I tried to smile then shook my head and shrugged again. 'Just mucking about, Dad,' I said lightly.

We were silent on the way home. Dad Joe had his arm around me but turned his head away. I could tell he was thinking a lot and it made me feel troubled. I wasn't up to talking either, the ankle hurt so much and the beginning of a thundering headache made waves of light flow back and forth behind my eyes like crashing sea waves. I longed be left in peace to sleep. Laying my head back on the cab seat, I watched the scenery flashing past as the cab sped along the main road. I hated orange street lights. They made me feel peculiarly sick inside so I tried not to look at them.

When we got home, Dad Joe settled me down on the sofa and I leant my head back again, feeling like a weary old woman. It was odd to sit in a sort of regal splendour like this, a rug around my legs, with everyone else doing the work for once; feeling tired and strangely detached and out of it all as if watching a dream being played about me. I could tell Millie was seething and fuming but she couldn't do a thing about it and that made me glad, oh, so glad! I had to work hard at keeping the delight from my face because I had a strong feeling that once I was better and Dad back at sea, there'd be hell to pay. So I looked suitably pale and woeful. It wasn't that hard. The dreadful aching pain helped.

Andy shot me looks of utter hatred when told to set the table.

'Why should I?' he demanded. His piggy blue eyes screwed themselves up as if in distaste. 'Ma, I'm trying to finish this meccano plane.'

'Well, someone has to help,' said Millie. 'I can't do everything and he ... ' meaning Dad Joe, '... isn't going to stir a finger, is he?'

'Well, Jim can help you,' said Andy. 'I've got better things to do.'

Jim, who was trying to do his homework in a corner, looked up at this.

'Oh, shut up, you twerp. You're younger, you can help Mum with the table. I'll wash up later. If you prefer, *you* can wash up. But you can do *something*, can't you. It's not Bridie's fault she's not well.'

Andy muttered oaths beneath his breath at this but flung himself into the kitchen and clattered about looking for the simplest things as if panning for gold dust. Millie produced a cloth, which he threw over the table with disorderly abandon, one side hanging far lower than the other. I yearned to set it straight. Jim looked at me and smiled a little as if read my thoughts.

'He's a twerp,' he murmured as if to himself, then went back to his efforts with algebra.

'Where are the bloomin' knives and forks?' I heard Andy shout and shook my head a little in amazement. They had all got so used to my doing everything. That stupid boy didn't even know where the knives and forks were kept. After a lot of barging about out there, he came back into the parlour looking sulky and cross. It was all I could do not to laugh, but I didn't dare.

The dinner was on the stove but even that normally welcome smell was making me feel sick. Everything made me feel sick. I looked over at Dad Joe who had kept silent during the table-laying kafuffle. He sat in his chair and puffed for a long while at his pipe, never saying a word to any of us. Suddenly, he stood up and said, 'You boys go and have a bath before supper.'

The boys looked at their father in surprise and indignation. Bath time was once a week when the kitchen stove was lit up for the hot water. Millie took first bath, then Jim and Andy together and me last of all in water by now grey and almost cold. Apart from this weekly dip, we washed in a bowl at the sink each night in turns. It was unheard of to have a bath any other day but Friday.

Andy ran into the kitchen to tell Millie that Dad had ordered them to have a bath.

She was so amazed that she came out and spoke directly to Dad.

'Friday's bath night,' she said, 'there's no hot water for any now. Have you gone mad or what? You know this isn't bath night.'

'Get the boiler going and they can have a shallow bath in an hour,' he said calmly.

'But I'm doing the supper now. Bridie, tell him I'm doing the supper.'

'Supper can wait,' said Dad and folded his arms and took on that set look that even Millie dared not argue with. He took up the newspaper and disappeared behind it while Millie stormed off to the kitchen, furious because I was lying on the sofa with my leg up and she had to ask Jim to get the boiler going. She gave me the filthiest looks as if she felt it all to be my fault.

In a way, I suppose it was. Dad had seen those bruises and marks on my arms and suspected they weren't all due to the stairs and my general clumsiness. He knew I was not normally a clumsy child, in fact a very careful and tidy one. If anyone was clumsy it was that fool Andy who was forever charging about like a bull in a china shop, breaking things and leaving a trail of devastation in his wake.

Now Dad's mind was working. He knew Millie's foul temper and I guess he wanted to check up and see if she beat the boys as well. So when they were at last in their bath, subdued and rather silent at this unexpected event, instead of shouting and fighting each other as they usually did, he went in to see them.

This was even odder and Millie had no inkling what he was thinking about. She looked worried and seemed to sense something was up, but she said nothing.

'Do I have to have a bath, Dad?' I asked when he came out, satisfied to find the boys were perfectly all right and had no more than the usual minor cuts and bruises and scraped knees one associated with any young fool at their age.

'No, ducky, you mustn't get that plaster wet. You'll have to wait till it's taken off, I'm afraid.'

I wasn't bothered as baths were hardly a pleasure in lukewarm or cold water, the disgusting grey suds from the previous occupants swilling around me. I felt cleaner when I washed at the sink.

'Ask your father if he's trying to imply that my boys are dirty?'

'Tell that woman that they're fine and clean, outside at least.'

Millie couldn't make head or tail of this answer but I couldn't help hiding a grin. Andy saw this and, when Dad's back was turned, yanked my hair as if to pull it out at the roots.

'Beastly brat!' he whispered, echoing his mother's language. He was going to be the same sweet-tempered person she was. I pitied any wife of his some day. He'd be like that drunk Mr

Treadman down the road whose wife was always covered in bruises and had a permanent black eye. Nobody seemed to do anything about it. The world was ruled by bullies.

'Yow!' I squawked and dug back hard with my elbow, but Andy had hopped it.

Dad had gone back to sea by the time I had the plaster cut off so I wasn't able to walk too far with him this leave time. I missed our private little chats for he never said much at home. He was always out at the pub with his local mates or off to a football match with the boys. Millie just got on with her life as usual: choir practice at church, meetings down at the local WI or jaunts with friends. She was always glad to see him off again. While he was around she was civil to me but I knew if he hadn't been there she'd have confined me to my room or made me get some work done despite the pain I was suffering as the ankle slowly healed. As it was she insisted I polish the brass and silver.

'You can sit at the table, can't you? Well, here's something to do instead of idling your time.'

'She should leave you alone,' grumbled Dad Joe looking up from his newspaper as Millie plonked the cleaning stuff in front of me and took away the riveting novel in my hands, flinging it on the floor where I couldn't reach it.

'Bridie should do some work, it's not good for her sitting there reading stupid books all the time.'

'Millie should try reading something other than *Woman's Own*. It might improve what little brain she has,' was the retort.

'Dad,' I said wearily, 'I don't mind doing the silver and brass. Honestly.'

Dad Joe and I made it down to the sea before he went, me hopping along with the help of a crutch, feeling a real fool.

'We'll just sit here a bit,' said Dad and we went over to our favourite bench, the one John had given his beloved wife Mary. We stared out at the ocean that lay before us, vast, white-flecked, endlessly rolling waves singing their luring sea-songs as they embraced the shoreline.

'You love the sea, don't you, Bridie?'

'I do love it,' I said, 'just like you do, Dad.'

'Yes, just like me,' he said. He remained silent for a while. All this week he had been like this. Never a noisy man, yet lately so deep in thought that I had a funny feeling something was brewing in him but had no idea what it might be. Nor did I like to ask him. He had his moments of turning inwards when he wanted for all his cheerful, jocular exterior. He always said he never liked to talk about things until he was sure of them.

'Well, we shall see,' he suddenly remarked, looking enigmatic. I stared up at him, saw a slow smile forming, and smiled too. Whatever was going on in there it made him look very pleased.

Life proceeded in its usual manner for the next few months. I was out of plaster now. Dad was no longer around to keep a watchful eye on me. As I had dreaded, Millie redoubled her efforts to be nasty. However, I had become so used to her she no longer worried me as much and my fear began to lessen a bit. I learnt to dodge her when I could and do as she asked without rousing her ire. Dear little Andy got more piggish, just like his mother, while Jim seemed kinder than ever to me – which was something at least.

We were walking home from school one day and Andy was hopping around in his usual stupid way, kicking at gates, throwing stones, dropping sweet wrappers in people's nice neat gardens.

'You shouldn't do that,' I said as he flung a stone that nearly hit a blackbird, setting the poor thing off in screeching protest and alarm, 'you'll hit someone and get in trouble one day, you will. You're so nasty.'

'I'll hit *you* first, beastly brat,' was his response and he went for my hair which he took a delight in pulling, generally informing me he hated ginges, not that my hair was at all ginger but a dark red-brown chestnutty colour.

I was used to skipping out of his way, practice having made me perfect at evasion in this family. The silly fat fool overbalanced and fell over and I started giggling, putting my hand over my mouth in an effort to suppress my delight. He didn't like that one bit. Like his mother, he went red in the face, sprang up, and went for me, dragging me round and round by my hair while I screamed and punched at him. He was younger than me by a year but taller than me already and though he was a slobby, gross brat, he was strong with it. I kicked at him, aiming for his goolies, and we ended on the ground in a real tangle of arms and legs.

Jim, who had been walking behind with some of his mates, came running up and disentangled us.

'Get off her, Andy, you stupid nit, what *do* you think you're doing?'

He dragged his shouting brother away, Andy yelling swearwords at me I didn't even dream he knew and covered my ears to hear.

Jim also looked shocked and gave his brother a smack on the face, 'Don't you use that language! Where d'you learn all that? Don't you let Mum hear you swear like that or you'll be for it.'

'Why d'you stick up for her?' muttered Andy. 'She's not our sister. She's Irish and stupid. Mum told me so.'

My heart skipped a beat as he said that and I went pale as a sheet. Jim looked at me and then pushed his brother by the shoulders in the direction of home.

'Get home! You're such a swine sometimes, Andy. She can't help it if she's not our sister. She's an orphan. We should be kind to orphans.'

'She's stupid and carrots,' Andy flung back as his last words. Then shrugging, he swaggered off down the road. My ankle was hurting me again, still not quite normal and the tumble hadn't done me a lot of good. I limped a bit but walked on in silence. Jim caught me up and walked beside me.

'So, you all know,' I said bitterly. 'You all know I'm an orphan. But my dad *was* a Naval officer, Dad Joe told me. He was his best friend. He *wasn't* stupid and my mother was beautiful!'

'I believe it,' said Jim, 'because *you're* so clever and pretty.'

I was astonished at this praise and lowered my head, unsure

what to say. We walked on in silence for a while. I still limped and Jim put out an arm to steady me.

'You're not really right yet, are you?'

'Thanks for getting Andy off me,' I said, refusing his arm. 'It's all right. I can manage.'

'You always do manage,' he said and I looked at him surprised. He almost had a note of admiration in his voice.

'I have to, don't I?'

'I know you're not happy,' he said, 'are you, Bridie?'

'No, I'm not happy!' I burst out, 'I may never be happy, not ever. Not till I can leave your house and I can't wait for that.'

'I can't wait to leave home either,' was the quiet reply and we both stopped then and stared at each other. It had never occurred to me that Jim might not like his home. I wanted to ask him what he meant, talk to him about it, maybe get some empathy between us but he pressed his lips together and marched on. I followed along behind him slowly, walking indoors to receive a smack across the face for messing up Andy's nice clean trousers in unladylike brawls.

'You vicious little cat!' screamed Millie. Andy sat at table smugly, eating a piece of bread and jam. I felt like ramming it down his podgy throat but said nothing as usual and took myself upstairs until Millie yelled up for me to come down and set the table for supper.

Chapter 4

I counted the days and weeks till Dad came home on leave. The last few weeks were more than usually miserable, partly because the weather was so awful that summer. School had broken up and I dreaded the days ahead. Rather than being allowed to go out to play, I was under Millie's baleful eye all the time, constantly set to work in the house, sent off to do shopping, peel vegetables, dust and sweep and iron clothes, allowing Millie to have the holiday instead. She sat in her easy chair, cup of tea beside her, the *Woman* magazine in her hand, thrilling herself with romantic stories and knitting patterns.

'I'd never have believed in Cinderella if I hadn't become her,' I muttered to myself as I filled up the boiler and got it going for the weekly wash. 'Will some prince ever come and rescue me? I doubt it. I doubt I'll ever get away from her. Ever, ever,' and a deep depression came upon me. I went mute and couldn't sing as I sometimes did to cheer myself up. I felt a constriction in my throat like hundreds of drops of unshed tears and a weight upon me like Buckingham Palace.

I was envious of Dad Joe sometimes. It was so easy being a man – you could get away and live life and do interesting jobs while women stayed at home or became typists, teachers or hairdressers and boring things like that. I wasn't keen on any of these options. I had no idea of what I thought I might do some day, some vague notion of being a singer or a writer or an actress floated past me. Silly ideas, likely never to be. Plus, I wouldn't have a clue how to set about such a profession. There was no inclination or love for performing and going up on a stage would have been anathema. It was all just daydreams, nonsense, and romantic pop music from the radio.

These days, I felt so sad that I switched off the radio unless Millie demanded it was left on. The songs grated on my ears. This stuff about love and kisses and all that was rubbish. I knew there was no love between Millie and Joe. Yet they must have thought they were in love once. It didn't last forever, it was stupid. Nobody I knew was in love. Everybody was hateful.

Yet it had to be said that Jim was becoming more attentive and friendly towards me these days. Occasionally he brought me home a magazine or gave me some of his sweets. I wasn't sure what to make of it really.

'You shouldn't spend your pocket money on me, Jim,' I scolded when he gave me a paper bag with aniseed balls and a liquorice cartwheel in it. 'You don't get that much.' Sixpence each didn't go that far, after all. Millie grudged giving me pocket money but Dad Joe insisted we all had the same. I seldom spent mine but tried to save it if I could – perhaps with some daft notion of running away one day, getting the train to some distant place well away from Broughampton and Millie.

'These days you're so sad all the time, Bridie,' Jim said. He tried to put an arm around me, but I shook him off – which was ungrateful, I suppose. For some odd reason, I didn't want him looking at me as if he was trying to understand me, to know me. It was all I had left; the defence of my own secret knowledge and thoughts. No one could own those but me. I didn't want any of them to know what went on in my head and heart.

'Okay, okay.' Jim sighed as his efforts at a closer warmth failed yet again. 'You can be so touchy sometimes. But you know, Bridie, I hate to see you like this. I like it when you sing and are cheerful. You're the only cheerful person around this house.'

'You think so?' I was amazed. I never ever saw myself as a cheerful person. I was always thinking deep things and thought I looked miserable and glum.

'I do. You sing, you smile and you work hard but never grumble. I hate the way Ma treats you sometimes, as if you are a skivvy. I hate it. I'll take you away when I grow up. I promise.'

'I'll take myself away.'

'But I'll look after you.'

'I can look after myself, thank you. I know how to do most things, better than any of you. I even know how to mend fuses and change plugs and things. Dad showed me.'

I rather liked mechanical things and thought it was interesting to be able to do all this. The fact was that Millie was hopeless at such matters and the boys no better. Millie, who had been to a grammar school, felt herself to be smart and above learning 'men's jobs' as she called them. She'd always done office work, even in the war. So it was rather nice when she had to call on me to do anything like that while Dad was away. My own little bit of power. I could have electrocuted her quite easily if I was as wicked as she was.

I suppose I didn't mind housework, even enjoyed it in a funny way; there was something quite satisfying about seeing everything look spick and span. The exercise was good for me and I was a lot slimmer than most girls my age. But I did long for something in life, an adventure of some sort. Life at this time seemed to stretch forth into a grey murky future like a mist rolling out over the sea obscuring everything, a shifting, shadowy grey wall of nothingness.

As I sat on my favourite bench looking out over the sea one day, I felt so miserable my heart hurt me, squeezing tight in my chest so that a feeling of faintness came over me. I think I passed out for a few moments and came to with the wind blowing hard on my cheeks. The kindly wind, fanning me back to life.

Before me the English Channel rose and swelled, the tide rushing forwards in huge breakers, foam spilling over the edges. Dad had told me how the sea could change from calm to turbulent in no time.

'When the foam breaks like that,' he said, 'it's Beaufort Force Seven at least and *that's* high winds. Enough to bend the trees and break a few dead branches and blow your brolly inside out. Force Nine'll take the slates off the roofs. Not comfortable at all. But I've been in worse, a Force Ten to Eleven when the waves are so high they crash over the ship and on the decks.'

'Weren't you frightened, Dad?'

'Of course not. I loved it. I love a good storm. Makes you think the Gods are busy up there, rolling their thunderbolts and chucking lightning at each other, almost playful. But then like everything, play can turn to quarrelling. I always see a really big storm as the weather gods quarrelling amongst themselves.'

'The weather gods quarrelling!' I loved this idea and looked out at the unruly breakers and remembered Dad's words. It made me smile again. Looking at the sea made me feel free for a bit, expanded my whole being from the miserable existence I led. Then I felt sad once more as I thought of going back to that house and the people I hated so much. Even Jim, nice as he tried to be, was Millie's son and that was enough for me. I couldn't bring myself to like him that much because out of the two boys, he looked most like her while Andy, as he grew older and lost some puppy fat, began to look more like Dad. And that really annoyed me. He was a caricature of Dad Joe who was a marvellous man while Andy was a pig.

The thunderbolt came in another form later that year. The next time Dad came home, we went out for a walk together before supper. He was in a splendid mood, laughing and cracking jokes though he told me none of his usual stories about where he'd been or what he had done. Still, it was wonderful to hear him so cheerful and I felt my spirits pick up at once. I wondered sometimes whether to say anything about how unhappy I was, but felt so insignificant a person, so unimportant in the scheme of things. Why should anyone care what a silly kid of thirteen felt or wanted? Maybe Dad Joe didn't care either and would think I was making it all up. It just wasn't in my nature to say what I felt or needed. I simply dragged on through life as if there was no other way, no other hope for me, as if the only sunny interludes would be Dad coming home now and then.

We walked back to have supper. I'll never forget that meal. It was fisherman's pie with apple crumble to follow. Millie was a good cook; it was one thing she never let me do and I know I'd have enjoyed cooking. She liked to get the praise for it herself, though I always did the donkey work of peeling and fetching and carrying and clearing up afterwards. These days, Jim helped me wash up at least and I enjoyed our chats while we did so. He would amuse me with stories of the boys and girls in his class; he had a way with anecdotes. It seemed to please him to make me laugh a little.

The food was especially good that evening and I enjoyed the meal, hungry after our walk to the sea. The sea air always gave me an appetite. To be fair, Millie never tried to starve me or anything like that. She believed in food and liked to see everyone tucking in with gusto. We were always expected to comment, praise and thank her for it afterwards. Fair enough. It *was* her only talent.

We were just in the middle of eating the fisherman's pie when Dad said to me,

'Bridie, tell your mother that I'm retiring from the Navy next month. It's the end of my service and I'm not signing on again.'

Millie looked up from a forkful of mash and ceased munching. She looked quite comical, her mouth almost open though she was too ladylike to let it fall open entirely. She swallowed quickly and said, 'Bridie, ask your father if he has gone entirely mad?'

'You can inform your mother that I am perfectly well and as sane as the next man. I've had enough of going out to sea and I mean to embark on another career.'

Millie put down her knife and fork. She couldn't bring herself to break the habit of years and look at or talk directly to Dad. She stared at me in anger. 'And might your father inform us what he proposes to do at his age, how he means to maintain his family?'

Dad was almost forty and that was middle-aged in those days. So we all stared at him and wondered what he could possibly do now. Wasn't he over the hill already?

Dad carried on eating and a faint smile puckered the corner of his mouth. He was enjoying his little bombshell. The boys looked over at us both, then at their mother. We were all waiting to see what came next. Everyone stopped eating except Dad. He continued chewing in silence then replied, 'I've made up my mind to accept the position of a lighthouse keeper. It's something I've always fancied doing; time enough they've saved us going aground in the Atlantic. It'll be near the sea but not in the same way as before. So suits me all round, it does. I've written off, had the interview at Trinity House, passed the medical and been accepted. I begin as soon as they have a Light for me to go to and that won't be long.'

I was both thrilled and terrified by this revelation. Did it mean he would leave us all? I couldn't bear the thought. But then he turned to me and smiled and his next words were, 'Exciting, isn't it, Bridie lass? I won't have to put up with that harridan of a mother of yours any more. She and the boys can stay here. And what's more I shall take you with me. If you'd like to come?'

At this I burst into tears. Uncontrollable sobs racked me through and through and I could do nothing to prevent them. I clung to Dad who hugged me and patted my back. When he let me go, some instinct made me turn and look at Millie. I saw the familiar red beginning to creep up her neck and just in time, I dived under the table. Her fist, aimed for me, hit Dad square on the jaw. His fork, which was on the way to his mouth with a piece of fish pie, was almost shoved through his cheek. He shouted in pain, flung down the fork and grabbed Millie by her ear. I had never seen them fight, get really physical. Blood was pouring out of Dad's mouth and Millie was screaming and writhing in his fierce grasp like an animal as he slapped her face repeatedly while the boys added their own howls of fury and tried to separate the pair. I stayed under the table. It was the first time in my life I had abandoned them to it and it was a lesson I learnt for life. Be piggy in the middle but not when it means you're about to be made into bacon.

True to his word, Dad began his service as a lighthouse keeper. The lighthouses were run at Trinity House in London, by the

Master and the Elder Brethren as they called themselves. The very first Master, appointed by Henry the Eighth, was Thomas Spert, captain of the ill-fated Mary Rose. Later, Samuel Pepys, the famous seventeenth-century diarist, became Master and the Duke of Wellington too – but now it was really a sort of honorary title. Winston Churchill had become one of the Elder Brethren. It all sounded very illustrious and Dad went up to London to see Trinity House, a splendid-looking place with huge rooms all ornately furnished, the like of which he'd never seen before. He was awestruck by their size and high, elaborate painted ceilings. The grand sweeping staircase was like something in a film and he'd almost expected to see Ginger Rogers sweeping down in a long white satin dress to meet Fred Astaire at the bottom and begin a waltz around the enormous hallway.

In the old days many of the lighthouses had been privately owned and used to charge the ships that went by them for the safe passage. They'd all been bought up over time and now maintained by Trinity House. Dad said it had a load of history behind it and he was going to look it all up one day.

Dad told the Brethren that he was married, that they had a house of their own in Broughampton, and that his wife had no wish to accompany him to various isolated spots. He was right about that as Millie screamed the place down for hours, telling him he was mad, he would ruin them all, and how were they going to live on the meagre pay he was going to get after he'd been an officer in the Navy? Our house was quite a nice one, nothing special but in a nice area. She was horrified that she might have to leave it and live in a cottage in the back of beyond or worse still a rented council house.

'You needn't worry,' said Dad. He was actually talking to her directly now so that was a bridge they'd managed to cross. 'Trinity House look after their employees. It's a secure job, which is more than you can say about a lot of other work I could have taken up with firms folding up all over the place. They'll give me the rent towards the mortgage here so you needn't move anywhere else and you and the boys won't go short. I'll have my naval pension as well and as for me, I won't be wanting much; nor will Bridie.'

'You can't take Bridie with you, it isn't possible. She can't live on a lighthouse,' said Millie and my heart sank. She didn't want me at all, she'd just miss her unpaid servant. I had to admit that the euphoric idea of going away with Dad seemed to melt under the cold stare of reality. If his rent was going towards keeping Millie and the boys here, where would I go?

'I'm taking Bridie,' he said firmly. 'I've got it all sorted out. None of your business. She wants to come along for the ride and so she can. You *want* to come, don't you, Bridie?'

I was speechless but nodded fiercely. I would die if I couldn't go with Dad. I didn't care if it meant living on a buoy in the middle of the sea.

As it turned out, his first posting was to a Rock Light way out past the Lizard. He was really excited about going and couldn't wait to get offshore. Dad was like me, he had to be near the sea or he felt something missing in his life. I wondered till the last minute what was to happen to me, but in the end learnt I was to pack all my things and we were to take a train to a place near Land's End where I would stay in one of the Trinity House Cottages with a Sheila Waterman and her children. Her husband was Principal Lighthouse Keeper on Longships, the Rock Light where Dad was to begin working as an SAK (Supernumerary Assistant Keeper) and she would look after me as if I was one of her own.

Before I left that hateful house, Millie came up and watched me packing my few things. She stood in the doorway with that baleful glare on her face and it made me clumsy as it always did whenever she was around.

'Just making sure you don't take what isn't yours,' she said.

I thought it best to ignore her. I was going away from her cutting comments, cruelty and nastiness. The mere thought made a little smile come to my face.

'Oh yes, you think you're getting away, don't you? You think it'll all be candy and roses from now on. I've done you good, one day you'll see it … you'll see! Made you a good housewife which is all *you'll* ever be fit for. You haven't even got the brains to do a Pitman course like I did. I was a secretary to Mr Tomkins, the Town Councillor, and he told everyone I was the best, the very best. And don't you ever forget that I took you in when you might have been a regular guttersnipe by now.'

'That's not true. I would have gone to my Irish relations,' I couldn't help saying, turning to face her taunts, 'I might have been a lot happier.'

'*They* didn't want you, your Irish relations. Got far too many brats of their own, haven't they? And all as poor as Dublin church mice. You've done well with us. Good food, good clothes, a *very* nice home, an education. And are you grateful? Do I hear a word of thanks or gratitude?'

She paused dramatically as if waiting for a response. My silence annoyed her. 'I thought as much. But you'll be longing to crawl back here soon enough. You'll never stand the lonely life out there. It'll drive you mad in no time. And Joe is going to forget you when he's off on those lighthouses. You're not his kid, why should he care? He's just full of bleeding heart sentiment, he always was, but the truth is he doesn't care about anyone but himself. He's going to leave you with some dumpy lighthouse keeper's wife by all accounts who's supposed to be taking care of you. She'll just pocket the money he gives her – the money that should come to his own family, damn him – and you'll be miserable. But then you always were a misery. Your father's daughter.'

'My father was an officer and brave,' I said, stung at last into replying.

Millie put back her head and laughed. 'Brave? He was a coward, a weakling. Faced the war but couldn't face life. He shot himself over that woman. She knew she had a blood condition. They should have been more careful, used precautions. But no, she was a Catholic like Joe. She wanted a baby, she said. And Bill O'Reilly – well, he let her do anything she liked.'

I stared at her. 'He ... my real Dad shot himself?'

She looked amused at my startled face. 'I see. Joe didn't tell you that choice bit of information, then? Wanted to gloss it over, protect you, in his sentimental fashion, I suppose. Yes, Bill O'Reilly sat down one night in his digs at Pompey and blew his head off. Nasty sight, so they say.'

Dizziness and nausea came rolling over me in waves but I kept upright and turned away. I told myself I'd think of it later, not now. Now I had to keep going till I could take my leave. Millie stood there a while longer. I neither looked at her again, responded in any way nor burst into tears, just calmly went on folding my clothes, putting them neatly in a suitcase. She eventually turned and left with a little trill of amused laughter. She wasn't fooled by my apparent indifference. She knew I was simmering with anger and pain and she felt delighted with her vindictive parting shot.

Chapter 5

'You'll love Sheila Waterman, Bridie, that I guarantee,' said Dad as we walked up Maria's Lane towards the four whitewashed Trinity cottages. The cottages were more like a row of terraced houses but they were stoutly built and roomy enough. They stood in their own patch of land surrounded by a low white wall to protect them from the fierce gusting winds that swept over the cliff tops. Each house had a private yard at the back with a door that led out onto little gardens where vegetables could be grown. On the upper front walls of the row of houses, facing towards the sea, was the red and blue Trinity House crest, *Trinitas in Unitas,* which meant 'three in one'. Something to do with the Holy Trinity, so Dad told me. From the houses you could see over the cliffs and way out to sea where the Longships lighthouse stood, grey, tall and sombre in the middle of its rock in the Atlantic Ocean. It was beautiful, the rolling grasslands and the rolling sea. My heart went out to it all in pure joy and gladness. But deep down I was still a bit scared. I said as much to Dad. I couldn't help wondering if it was a case of out of the frying pan and into the fire. Surely no one could be worse than Millie?

'No need to be scared, Bridie. Not any more. You'll love it here.'

'Millie won't come for me, will she?'

'No,' was the short reply, 'She won't be coming for either of us.'

The certainty in his tone relieved me. I began to relax and look around with real enjoyment.

My first sight of Mrs Waterman was her standing at the door

of the Principal Keeper's roomy house waiting to greet us. She was plump, comfy and motherly looking and my spirits rose. She had short, curly, grey hair, wore trousers, a loose knitted top and had on a pinny, one of those that looped around the neck and arms with floral patterns all over it. I liked the look of that pinny – it meant she worked and cooked and did nice things. Millie always wore a little apron when she was cooking, one of those frilly, useless things that hardly covered her chest. She always wanted to be seen in smart clothes, her hair done up and nails manicured.

'Hello, Joe – come right in, both of you. This is your girl, is it? Come in, my dearie. It's cold out there with the wind blowing so hard. It's always windy up on the heights here, but you get used to it.'

Mrs Waterman's voice was nice. There was a slight burr to it and Dad told me later that she came from Bournemouth way. The house smelt of baking bread and cakes and my stomach heaved with hunger. It was all so welcoming. Mrs Waterman smiled at my expression and put an arm about me.

'You sit there now, dearie. I'll make a pot of tea and we'll have some of these rock cakes, shall we? Would you like that? Thought so. And you, Joe?'

I was speechless at that moment. Totally and utterly unused to anyone apart from Dad Joe, and occasionally Jim, speaking and acting so kindly towards me. I wanted to weep and something welled up from deep inside me, threatening to burst forth in a torrent. I had to struggle hard to hold it back. Dad looked at me anxiously while Mrs Waterman was in the kitchen.

'What is it, love? Are you still afraid?' He took my hand and patted it. 'There's nothing to be afraid of any more, I promise.'

'No,' I managed to say, 'not afraid, Dad. Happy, you know. Happy …'

He understood and nodded.

'Well, no need to cry, then. Wipe your tears, all is well now.'

Mrs Waterman came back with a tray of tea things and she also looked at me, her eyes searching and kindly. She made no comment, simply handed me a cup of tea and a plate of fat, fluffy rock cakes. I could scarcely eat, choked up as I was with salty tears – a pity as they were so delicious.

Dad and Mrs W chatted away while I picked crumbs from my lap and placed them on the plate. She was putting Dad up for a bit till the weather calmed down and the relief boat could take him over to the rock light.

'It's just a spare camp bed which I've put up in the tiny box room,' she apologised.

'No problem,' smiled Dad. 'I've slept on worse in my time. It's only for a while anyway. Till I can sort out somewhere else to stay on shore leave. Not worth me getting too comfy, because this first year is training as Supernumerary.'

'What's that mean, Dad?' I asked, thinking it all sounded very grand.

'It's what you're called at the start, a sort of extra, roving hand. That way I'll learn all the ropes and get to understand what the life is like and I'll be moving about all over the place, maybe having to be off at a moment's notice to help as a relief keeper miles away up north or wherever I might be needed.'

'So you won't always be here,' I said, disappointed.

'Only for a little while longer. But you'll be happy with Sheila and her kids.'

I shot a look at Mrs Waterman who smiled back at me and nodded.

'The first year's the hard one,' she explained. 'Joe'll just have to get through that till he's made up to AK – that's assistant keeper – then he'll get a more permanent place.'

After we'd finished tea, she took me upstairs and showed me my room.

'I'm afraid you'll have to share with Susan,' she said apologetically.

The room was all done out in pastel pink and white, with pink flowered curtains and lampshades and two beds covered in similar multi-coloured patchwork quilts. It was beautiful. Later that night, I spent hours looking at all the different patterns and designs on it. Mrs Waterman told me her gran had made them for her and her sister years ago. 'I'm making a big double one,'

41

she said, 'for Susan when she marries. Helps to pass the winter evenings when my husband's away on the rock.'

'Is this really where I'll sleep?'

'Why, yes, dearie. Of course it is. It's nothing much, I'm afraid, but it's cosy.'

Having a pretty room, even a shared one, was the lap of luxury. Next to it was the bathroom with what seemed like incessant hot water as Mrs Waterman liked to keep the boiler on all the time. She said she felt cold if there wasn't a fire going. So I could bathe every day if I wanted to and not in someone else's soap and muck. Well, I felt I'd come to Heaven as a reward for being Cinderella so long. Dad had been my prince and taken me away. There was a just God after all.

After I'd unpacked my few things and had a brush and a wash, I came back downstairs to the sitting room. Mrs Waterman's daughter, Susan, had arrived home from school with a couple of other keepers' kids. She was a small, plump, fair-haired girl of about ten with a very pink dress on and pink bows in her hair. I was to learn that Susan wanted the whole world bathed in pink. She was very sweet and very silly and immediately began to fetch me down her favourite dolls and books to show me and introduced me to a little kitten curled up on her bed called Boo.

By now she had changed into a pair of monstrous fluffy pink slippers in which she padded around looking ridiculous. It made me long to laugh; I'd never seen such things in my life. However, I feigned interest and asked her questions while she rattled on about herself.

'My school's over there.' She pointed in the vague direction of the cliffs. 'It's on the main road to Land's End. I have to walk there and it takes ages. But I know all the shortcuts over the fields now. Where will you go to school, Bridie?'

'I don't know,' I said. 'Dad said something about my being taught at home by your mum. Where *will* I go, Dad? To Susan's school at Sennen?'

'No, no,' he replied, 'that's Infants and Juniors. The nearest secondary school is at Penzance and it's a long way to go. It would mean you boarding out there, not seeing me often at all. I don't think you'll want that.'

'I'd hate it, Dad.'

'You'll stay here, Bridie, with me and my son Ryan,' explained Mrs Waterman. 'He refuses to board out, does our Ryan, so I'm teaching him and you may as well keep us a bit of company. I was a qualified teacher, you know, before marrying. It's a shame to waste the ability.'

'How old is Ryan?' I asked.

'Fifteen. He'll be doing his O levels next year.'

I wondered what Ryan would be like and if he was a bully like Andy. I hoped not. Somehow I didn't think Sheila Waterman's son could be anything like that horrid Andy.

'You don't mind not going to a proper school then?'

'It sounds marvellous to me.'

This was a most interesting prospect. I had never liked the local school in Broughampton, thanks to Andy who, once he had discovered that I was what he called 'a charity child', went around telling everyone at school. Others, noting his habit of teasing and bullying, followed his lead and tormented me a great deal. I tried to ignore it and because I was always prepared to fight and be as nasty in turn, they gave up in the end and stuck to name-calling. Bullies get bored when their victims refuse to be passive and frightened. I was scared enough of Millie but that was because I was always afraid she'd turn me out or something and I'd have nowhere to go. These foolish boys and girls had meant nothing to me – they could only shout and be stupid and that hurt no one but themselves.

'You're nearly as tall as my Mum,' said Susan, staring at me when I rose to take some dishes in the kitchen. 'But you'll never be as tall as our Ryan.'

'I don't suppose I will.'

Ryan seemed to be the apple of their eye round here. Where, I wondered, was he? When would I meet him? The thought of being in close contact with a boy all day seemed a daunting prospect, wary as I was of all males except Dad and Jim.

Some time later that afternoon Ryan walked in and flung his coat down on a chair. He was tall and slim and dark-haired. I felt an odd sensation when I saw him for the first time; a queer sense of recognition as if I'd known him before and couldn't place where. I hadn't met him before but that was the feeling. His eyes were dark, serious, brooding. When introduced to me, he gave me a nod and a brief glance and then walked off to the table to get his tea. It was as if he didn't want eye contact with anyone. He just sat and ate and looked at his plate and seemed absorbed in silent thought. Mrs W fussed around him and Susan nattered on as usual and he took as little notice of either of them as he did of me.

I sat by the fire with Boo the kitten curled up on my lap and read *Great Expectations* while Dad and Sheila Waterman chatted together in the kitchen. They seemed to get on very well in the puzzling manner of adults whose conversations generally seemed quite pointless. Mr Waterman, the Principal Keeper, was over on Longships now, busy keeping an eye on his lighthouse, and he wouldn't be home for a while. Susan had at last fallen silent, mainly because nobody was really listening to her. She played with one of her dolls, dressing it up then flinging the little clothes aside and trying on something else. I had a suspicion this was just how she would be when she grew up: restless, silly, with no thought but clothes and how she'd look.

Ryan was another kettle of fish. I glanced over at him now and then from the corner of my eye. He remained seated at the table, hunched over some book that absorbed him. I wondered what it was but didn't feel at home enough to ask him.

However, I felt quite comfortable with his silence and didn't mind being ignored – it didn't trouble me at all. If anything, it was a welcome change from being the focus of everyone's dislike at Millie's. Except for Jim, he'd liked me in his fashion. Thinking of my old home made something grip me in the gut, hurting my insides. I couldn't bear to think of it. Instead, I looked round this cosy cottage, the chintzy cheerfulness of it, the high leaping flames of the log fire warming the walls with yellow light as the evening shadows began to gather in pools of darkness. I gave a long deep sigh of relief and content. Ryan looked up at this and for a moment our eyes met and held. I had such an odd feeling that he understood me, recognised something of my pain. This knowledge churned up my guts even more. However, he said nothing, looked away again unsmiling, and returned to his book. When he went off outside to the loo, I went over to the table and took a quick look. It was a book on astronomy. How interesting. My respect for him grew by the minute.

Dad at last got off to Longships as a relief keeper. I'd made up my mind not to ask him about Bill O'Reilly and his alleged suicide. Millie might have made it up just to be nasty. But what had Dad meant when he said Bill died of grief? How did a grown man die of grief? It was the sort of thing ladies did in fairy tales and Tennyson poems. A grown man *would* kill himself, wouldn't he? I longed to ask but never felt the time was right. One day I would ask but for now, I would put it away in the back of my heart and just be glad as could be away from Millie and Andy and Jim.

Lessons with Mrs Waterman, who insisted I call her Sheila, began in earnest and they proved to be most enjoyable. Special ones were set for Ryan who simply got on by himself while Sheila spent time with me, setting up books and tasks and helping me to write essays and do sums and things. It was so different being taught like this, so much more fun. I wanted to please, wanted to show Ryan I could be clever too. Sheila said she would teach me cooking and sewing while Ryan got on with gardening or carpentry. She was amused when I told her I quite liked doing boy's things and would like to learn carpentry too.

'If you want to, then you will,' she said. 'Ryan'll teach you. Won't you, Ryan?'

Ryan was seated by the window, reading. He looked up from his book and gave me a long searching stare.

'Only if she's serious,' he said.

'I'd be serious,' I said, offended. 'Of course, I would.'

'Don't know any girls that are,' he replied and went back to his book.

I felt miffed by this and made up my mind to be as serious as possible just to show him. I'd build a shed or a house or something. Girls could be just as good as boys if they got the chance.

Nothing was ever trouble for Sheila and she seemed to know just how to look after everyone, how to listen and deal with things. Being Principal Keeper's wife meant she had a responsibility towards the other two keepers' wives in the cottages around us. They all missed their husbands so much when they were off on a light and couldn't wait for the onshore leave, a month at home, and a chance to catch up with one another again. Sometimes leave might be delayed due to weather conditions and then the men on the rock couldn't come back. No boat would venture forth in crashing waves and high winds to take over the relief keeper. That was when some poor wife, especially if she was a new one, would come weeping and sobbing and saying how she missed her man and why was the sea so wicked and cruel to keep them apart?

Sheila would do her best to cheer them up, but I know she missed her Sidney just as much only she wouldn't show it. She had to put on a brave front for the others who considered her experienced and calm. It was a sign of hope that they too might eventually get used to it all.

'It's the weather gods,' I once said when Jean from the third house along came in wailing one evening. Her husband was a week overdue and her nerves were snapping.

Jean looked at me as if I was dotty so I said no more. But Dad was right. It was out of human hands and why they couldn't just accept it, I failed to understand. Sometimes they spoke as if the storms and the winds were specially sent to annoy them in their little lives. I thought that was daft then, but when I learnt a few lessons later, I wasn't so censorious.

I wanted Ryan to notice and take an interest in me but he

seldom spoke to me, always so silent, so very into himself. I was used to this because Dad was a bit the same but Dad also had a cheerful, sociable side and could laugh and drink and joke as well. Ryan never smiled or seemed to see anything at all humorous in any situation whereas I often thought life was a funny business, uproarious at times in its stupidity. Ryan was dead serious.

I was laughing hysterically one day over a P.G. Wodehouse book when he came in the room. He stood and stared at me till I felt those dark eyes burning through my head. I looked up in surprise.

'What's the matter?'

Ryan studied me for a minute as if I was a specimen in a zoo and then came over and took the book from me. For a moment I thought he was going to chuck it away but he just looked at the title, gave it me back and walked away.

'You should read it,' I called after him cheekily, 'it might cheer you up.'

He paused and turned again. In his slow, deliberate, quiet voice, he replied,

'I don't need your idea of cheering up, thanks. It's a flippant book. I don't read fiction.'

'Why not?' I said, annoyed by his rudeness. 'That's a stupid thing to say. Don't you like living in other worlds, seeing people and places through someone else's eyes?'

'It's not reality,' he said sternly. 'It's all make believe and romantic rubbish. All you girls like that stuff but my dad says it fills your heads with nonsense. I think he's right.'

I raised my eyebrows at this because if anyone looked likely to go the way of romance and nonsense it was his kid sister, Soppy Susan, with her pink frills and dollies that she dressed up incessantly. All the same, I didn't entirely disagree with Ryan. People did seem to live in an unreal dream bubble half the time. But for me reading stories was an escape from *too much* reality and that was something different altogether.

'You don't know anything about the real world,' I said heatedly. 'You've known nothing but kindness in your life, Ryan

Waterman, but I haven't – so don't begrudge me my little escape into fantasy now and then. Wait till life treats you as it has me and then we'll see.'

He frowned at this and seemed to think about it. However, he made no reply, just turned and marched out of the room and left me to P.G. Wodehouse. The book seemed to have lost its humour for me now and I read on feeling disgusted at its idiocy and in the end flung it aside and went for a walk.

Chapter 6

Longships Light was a stark and solitary grey granite structure with waves surging and pounding at its base. Thrusting up out of the sea were sharp, dangerous rocks and Dad told me that the seas round Cornwall were amongst the wildest, most storm-lashed coasts off Britain and that in the old days even the lantern had become submerged by the uprushing waters.

'Oh, Dad, does that still happen?'

'Not now, sweetheart. The tower's been rebuilt and it's safe as can be, don't you fret. But it's still pretty wild out there. There's not been such severe storms of late – not like they got in the Forties. Forty-Seven was the wildest year, they tell us – as I well know, being out to sea on HMS *Crossbow* at the time myself, right in the middle of it all.'

It sounded dangerous to me but as Dad said, he'd been through a lot worse in the Navy and this was a piece of cake in comparison.

It was such a beautiful spot where we lived – on a good day, we could see out for miles, though in bad weather we could see nothing more than the faint looming shape of Longships through the thick sea mists and listen to the muffled boom of the fog horn. Either way, I found it comforting to be able to see the lighthouse in the distance and know Dad was there.

'Let's go down to our little hidey place today, shall we Ryan … say yes!' said Susan one Sunday morning. She'd just come back from Sunday School and was raring to use up all that excess energy of hers after two hours spent singing hymns and listening to Miss Trevelyan natter on about Daniel in the lion's den.

Ryan was seated outside on an old wooden chair busy mending a fishing line. He looked up, a piece of thin twine between his strong white teeth and snapped it in half. He stared over at the horizon and gave it some ponderous thought.

'It'll be a good day for it today,' he said. 'Might as well, I suppose.'

I stared from one to the other. Was I to be included? And what was the secret place about?

As if reading my mind, Ryan stood up and said, 'You comin' then, Bridie?'

I felt a warmth inside at this casual inclusion in his plans. 'Where are we going?'

Susan skipped about, 'It's our secret place, our secret place! Come on, Bridie, you'll love it.'

She seized me by the hand and pulled me indoors, calling to her mother.

'Mum, we want sandwiches today. We're going on an adventure.'

Sheila was busy stuffing a chicken for Sunday lunch but didn't seem the least bit put out by the request.

'Ah, yes, its's just the day for it. You do that and we'll have our meal later,' was the cheerful reply.

From Trinity Cottages, we scrambled down the cliffs till we came to a tiny cove and a little sandy beach. There was a pleasanter and wider beach at Whitesands Bay, the long golden sands stretching for miles, but this little spot was superb, totally private and unused.

'None of the other kids know about this,' said Ryan with a look of secret pleasure. 'They want the bigger beach where they can muck around and eat ice creams. I don't want none of that. This one belongs to us; Sue and me and now you.'

'You don't mind my knowing it too?'

'No, you aren't the talking, telling sort.'

'No, I'm not. And I don't want to muck around either.'

'I reckoned you wouldn't.'

I smiled at this. In his way, Ryan really seemed to understand me. It was as if he knew me deep inside and I felt as if I knew him like this too. There were no words needed – a communication of the soul. That's how I saw it and it felt beautiful and oddly tender.

We spent a lot of time peering into the tiny pools to find crayfish and mussels washed in by the tide. Then Susan and I went for a swim while Ryan lay back on the rocks and stared up into the skies. I wondered what he was thinking about, his mind always occupied and interested in things. Later, I sat beside him, towelling my hair, looking out to sea, watching the flow of ripples on its calm surface. For a while he studied me with a detached air as I shook out my long chestnut hair and ran my fingers through it like a comb.

'Got nice colour hair. Like autumn leaves.'

It was said with cool appraisal, as one might speak of a piece of china, a picture or any inanimate object but all the same it thrilled my heart to hear it. No one except Dad Joe had ever complimented me on my hair before, rather it had been the butt of jokes and teasings. I made no reply, casting my eyes down with sudden surprised modesty. When I looked up again, his gaze and thoughts were already elsewhere.

I followed Ryan's eyes and looked up at the clouds.

'See them little thin 'uns, all wispy and soft,' he said dreamily, 'them's what they call mare's tails. Cirrus is their proper name. When they're all bunched up and white and bold they're called cumulus and they can get real towering and end up stormy. There's lots of other types of cloud formations but my favourite is at sunset when you get a mackerel sky of altocumulus, all yellow and orange where the sun sinks away underneath dark little bands of clouds swimming across the sky. I mean to learn all about it, what the weather means and what it shows.'

I was impressed and looked once more at the wispy trails of cirrus across the sky. Fairweather clouds, I always called them, but mare's tails was an even better name.

Amazingly, Ryan was chatty today and inclined to expound on his favourite subjects. I enjoyed listening to what he had to say and was glad he was in a good mood. It wasn't fair to call him a moody person for that implied emotions and changes. Ryan was always the same, really. Cool, quiet, withdrawn. Now and then he got onto something that appealed to him and then he'd talk the hind leg off a donkey. Susan was lying beside us, her eyes closed, drifting off to sleep. Perhaps she'd heard all this before.

'Tell me more,' I said.

'You want to learn about this stuff too, don't you?' he said, looking pleased to have an audience. I nodded and he continued.

'See, Bridie, I only like to read books on oceanography and meteorology. Nothing else is interesting to me but the sea and the sky. I can't read books about people, like you do. I don't much like people – animals, yes, but not people. It's the sea I love most of all, the sea and the sky, they go together like friends. Sometimes at peace together, sometimes fighting and storming at each other. I want to know what's in those heights and in those depths, especially right down there in the unknown, in the darkest part. I'm going to go deep-sea diving some time to see what's lurking down there.'

'But I think people *are* like that,' I said, 'they live in different layers too. Some on the top in the light bit where the sun shines; dancing and diving into the waves and playing like dolphins and flying fish. Then the others are in the middle: more ponderous and sensible and less frisky. And on the bottom, where there's no light at all, the monstrous people live and move in darkness and haven't any idea about the light and the sun and how life can be fun.'

Ryan looked at me in his slow, thoughtful way. 'You say some queer things.'

'No more queer than you,' I retorted. 'Millie is one who lives in the dark, her and her son Andy,' I added.

'Who's Millie?'

'My foster mother. Andy's her dear, baby son. *She* was cruel to me, really cruel and even Dad hated her in the end. That's why he took me away and left her.'

'Maybe she had a reason for being cruel; maybe she was unhappy.'

'No, Ryan. She just liked to make everyone else unhappy. I hate her and I always will. Andy, too. I hope they both rot in hell!'

Ryan almost smiled at my passion. 'I like people who know how to hate,' he nodded. 'It's not natural to love everyone all the time. Hate and love are funny things.'

'Do you hate anyone passionately?' I asked.

He turned his face away and stared out over the sea.

'A lot of people,' was the short reply.

'And do you love anyone?'

'No. Well – my mum, I suppose, but most people love their mums.'

'I love Dad Joe,' I said. 'He is my Prince. He rescued me from Mean Millie.'

'He's not your real dad then?'

'No,' I said, matter-of-factly. I had learnt to look on my story in this manner as if it had happened to someone else. 'My real father shot himself after my mum died having me. He loved her, you see. He couldn't live without her. I wonder if I'll ever feel that way about anyone.'

'You've had a good start in life and no mistake,' said Ryan, sitting up and looking at me. His voice had a sudden tenderness in it that sent a shock wave of feeling through my heart. I looked up at him as he sat there, on a rock just a little above me. He had on his serious, thoughtful look and there was a grim look about his mouth I hadn't noticed before. Suddenly he glanced down at me and smiled and that smile, so rare and unseen, was like a ray that lit his face. It made his hard dark eyes look almost sweet. I think it was then, when I saw that smile light his brooding, serious eyes with tenderness that I fell in love with Ryan Waterman.

'Could you ever love someone like that, Ryan?' I asked.

'What – kill myself over a woman? No flamin' fear. From all I hear and see, people are miserable together and miserable apart and marriage is all a lot of daft nonsense. Maybe I'll stay alone all my life. I mean to be a lighthouse keeper like my Pa. He can't wait to go off to his rock. He loves Mum and all that but he loves it best out there, just him and the other blokes, busy, quiet and peaceful like. I mean to apply as soon as I can and I know they'll take me on. I know more about lighthouses and how to mend the lights and how to maintain them than half the men on there. Wherever we've lived, Dad's always taken me up and shown me how everything works on his light. And we've been to lots of places.'

'Isn't it hard to make friends when you're always moving about?'

'I don't want any friends and neither does my dad. His friends are all keepers and their wives. We're like one big family in Trinity House. We look after each other, we understand the way of life.'

'It sounds a good sort of life,' I said thoughtfully, 'the idea of living in different places, having new experiences. I don't care about having friends either. I prefer to be alone like you do.'

It struck me then how alike Ryan and I were, though on the surface I was one of the ones playing in the light and frisking about and he seemed to be quite dark at times. But he was no deep-sea monster; he was just silent, intense and not prone to laughter at all.

Chapter 7

I sometimes woke at night and felt a foggy, uncertain anxiety grip my heart and would listen to the comforting, rhythmic sound of Susan's breathing to make sure I was in the pretty pink bedroom and not in that scruffy cream cell of a box room at Millie's. This fear would never leave me all my life. Millie was always just round the corner of my mind wherever I went. As soon as I realised I was safe in my room at the Watermans' house, I'd breathe a sigh of relief and snuggle back under the blankets and feel happy. I was always singing now, all the latest pop songs. When I helped Sheila with her ironing, I sang all the time.

'You're a proper little songbird, Bridie,' she remarked and added, 'such a cheery little soul you are and such a help to me. What a good girl you are!'

We had what Sheila called Domestic Science lessons in her kitchen and I progressed way beyond scrambled eggs and raised pork pies till I was allowed to cook Sunday roast sometimes. My Yorkshire puds were pronounced to be 'just perfect'. I couldn't wait for Dad's next leave so I could show off my new culinary skills. Above all, I longed to impress Ryan. He was so clever and full of interesting knowledge and I wanted to share it with him. Always somewhere in the back of my head was a memory and he seemed to be connected with this memory though I had no idea what it was.

He liked me, I felt sure of that, but he was not a person to show any feelings. Still I learnt to tell when I did something to please him even though his face remained impassive and he often said nothing, never even a thank you. I didn't need words – his softening eyes, his occasional smile were thanks enough and I wanted to bring that smile to his face as often as I could because it had this amazing transforming effect on his usual stern expression.

'You needn't have done that,' he said one day when I ran up to fetch a book he wanted. 'You're always fetching and carrying for everyone. Why, Bridie? You should look after yourself.'

'It's a habit, Ryan,' I said. 'Mean Millie always made me do everything for everyone, even her two boys. Hard to break old habits. But I *like* doing it for you and your mum. You're all so kind to me.'

He looked at me as he often did, studying me in a dispassionate manner, his eyes screwed up with thought.

'You're a funny girl, Bridie, and you're a caring girl. I don't think I've met as kind a girl before. But you're too eager to please everyone. There's danger in that. You need to know who *you* are, not what everyone else wants you to be. People'll respect you more for that.'

I listened and felt my old anxiety rise in me. Was he saying something nice or critical? I so wanted to please him but had to tread a fine line. I could see he didn't like being fussed over and would have to curb my enthusiasm but it was hard. I'd been bred to serve, to feel inferior and unwanted for too long. The only way I knew how to please was by doing things for people. I was also courteous by nature and knew when a door should be opened for someone or a seat in a bus given to an older person or a pregnant lady. These were surely common courtesies and I could never understand why everyone didn't do the same. The world would be a far nicer place if they did.

'It may be so, Ryan,' I replied, 'but I like to help folks. To put one's own needs before that of others is selfish. If people take advantage of it, then so be it. If they don't respect kindness and thoughtfulness, then I must put up with it.'

This brought on one of his rare smiles and for a moment his hand brushed my cheek in an affectionate gesture. 'You're too good for this world then, Bridie,' he said gently. 'You'll need someone to look after you one day. People are selfish and someone like you'll get crushed.'

'I've already been crushed,' I said, 'but I'm like a sponge. Wring me dry if you must but fill me with water and I bounce up again. And love's like water. You need it to live. Dry people are dead people inside. Millie was all dried out and no love left in her.'

'But she loved your dad once, didn't she? And he loved her. Why *did* she dry up, Bridie, that's the question to ask. Why did she dry up?'

When Dad had shore leave, he always came straight over to visit us. He'd found digs with one of the coastguard's families. These families lived in a row of tall Edwardian houses a little further along down Maria's Lane. So Dad was very close, though I sometimes wished there was room for him to live with us in the cottages. Mr Waterman, the Principal Keeper – or PK as he was known – naturally wanted his home to himself and his family though, of course, he and Dad were never on leave together, it was always one man off at a time, two men left to man the Light.

Mr Waterman didn't mind me living with them he said; he was glad Susan had a new friend. Dad had offered to pay rent, but all they asked for was some money towards my food and clothes. We were all hard up, lighthouse wages not being wonderful but the food on the Light was free and uniform provided so there really wasn't the need for much spare cash. I certainly didn't stuff myself with food like Susan nor was I interested in clothes or fashions. My old sweaters and cotton shirts with a pair of ancient jeans were good enough for me when life was spent scrambling about the cliffs or helping in the house and garden. Sheila. said I earned my keep as her little helper and that was good enough for her and Sid.

As for Sidney Waterman, he said I was a good girl and smiled benignly, a funny cracked sort of smile, when I made him a cup of tea and searched for his tobacco or his glasses. He was always leaving them somewhere strange.

'I'm used to having less space,' he said apologetically when I brought his spectacles down from the top of a bathroom cupboard. He'd left them in the toothbrush mug last time though why he'd put them there I had no idea. 'Used to my routines and my little room with one cupboard when I'm on Longships. Things don't get lost there.'

He always worried that nothing was functioning as efficiently when he was away from his beloved Light and would stand in the garden to make sure it went on at dusk at the exact time specified then get up at the crack of dawn to be sure it was extinguished. Sheila tended to be cross with him about this constant vigilance.

'You're supposed to be on leave,' she said, 'can't you pretend the damned light isn't there? Get Jed to take us into town so we can get away from it for a bit.'

Jed Tresconsin was the boatman employed by Trinity House to take supplies and relief to the lighthouse. He had a big truck too and sometimes gave us lifts to Penzance or the nearest town as we were miles from anywhere and no one else had any transport, though Abbi Simpson next door was saving up to get a little second-hand car. She couldn't bear the isolation and was determined to scrimp and save towards having some independence and mobility. Plus she wanted Patti to go to a proper grammar school once she'd got her eleven plus and that would mean going in to Penzance every day.

Jed it was who ferried the men offshore and brought them home again, a difficult process and a dangerous one, as the men had to make a jump for the landing stage onto what they called the Bridge and the exact moment had to be calculated and acted on or they'd end up in the foaming sea and possibly swept away for good. Coming back on leave was equally arduous and if the weather was bad the men couldn't get home sometimes for days or even weeks. They had to wait till Jed pronounced it safe to go over to the rock to fetch them and there was no way he was going to risk lives. But which *was* home to these men? I realised that Sidney Waterman had been in the service so long and on this particular light for at least four years that he felt Longships to be his home and almost resented coming onshore.

'It's time you went to bed,' Mr Waterman told Ryan the

other night. He'd been sitting up reading for hours and the light wasn't that good. 'You'll ruin your eyes, you will, my boy.'

'It's too early for bed,' protested Ryan, looking annoyed.

'If I says bed, it's bed,' declared his father.

'But Ma lets me stay up till ten thirty.'

'Well now, she ought to know better. Early to bed and early to rise makes a man healthy, wealthy and wise, eh? Isn't that the way? Haven't I followed that all my life and done well by it? Off to bed and as for you, you should have been abed hours ago, young Bridie. You're too easy on 'em, Sheila.'

Sheila raised her eyes from her sewing with an annoyed expression but said nothing, just looked over at Ryan and shrugged. He gave her a little wink as if to agree that while Dad was home, he was in charge and for his mother's sake her son wouldn't argue.

'Come on, Bridie,' was all he said and I followed him upstairs and we whispered 'goodnight' at our separate doors so as not to wake up Susan.

I realised then that it was hard for Sheila. She was in charge of the family for a month and then her husband would come home for a month and she'd have to defer to him again. Then he'd be off, with such apparent relief to get back it was hardly flattering for her and she had to take up the household reins again. He never interfered with the bringing up of Susan but Ryan was his beloved son and was meant to follow in his father's footsteps. It was lucky that Ryan by temperament was just like his father, entirely suited to the solitary life on a rock or tower. It was taken for granted he'd enter the service and I think Sidney Waterman rather hoped that some day he'd have his son's company on his rock.

Dad, as I said, had now found cheap lodgings with one of the coastguards, Arnie Roberts, who was a lively sort of fellow. Dad enjoyed Arnie's company and liked to get off to the pub and sink a pint or two, talk about his Navy days and the fact he was now a keeper. Some of the keepers got tired of being treated as objects of curiosity but not Dad. I think he liked being different and special.

He never failed to get over to see me every day though, taking me off for long walks on the sands or down to the harbour to watch the fishing boats coming in. I wanted Ryan to come with us on these walks but mostly he didn't. He said it should be time spent with my own dad.

'Dad won't mind if you come.'

'We can take walks any time, Bridie. You be with your dad. You'll have things to talk about that mean nothin' to me.'

I was disappointed but felt it fair and considerate on his part.

Dad would stop to chat to the fisher folk in Sennen, families that had been in the Cove for centuries. The men told us that they used to catch huge shoals of pilchards at this place since the sixteenth century till the turn of this one but now the pilchard had deserted the Cornish coasts where once it was so abundant. In late summer the haul was awaited with hope and enthusiasm, for a good catch meant the families in the Cove could pay their bills and have a little spare cash for things they needed. The pilchards were put in briny tanks to cure them and later packed away in hogsheads and kept in the cellars on the quayside. Even the women worked at packing and sorting the fish when a shoal was caught, paid by the day but glad enough of the money.

'Them huge shoals don't come no more,' said one of the fishermen. 'Them days is done. We're glad to live on mullet and lobsters and crabs now or whatever else we can get.'

I liked the fishermen, liked their tanned, weathered faces and honest, kindly expressions. Dad liked them too. They were his sort of men.

We walked up to the coastguard look-out high on the cliff and looked over to Longships.

'Sometimes I wave to you from the gallery when I'm offshore,' Dad said. 'Time you waved back, Bridie.'

'I never see you, Dad, it's too far away,' I said, indignantly.

'Have to teach you semaphore, ducky. That's how all the keepers' wives used to let their men know the news in the old days.'

He fixed the problem by bringing me home a pair of binoculars so that I could look over to the lighthouse and see him waving. Even looking through them I could only just make him out, a minute moving figure on the gallery. We arranged he'd try and be there to wave at about six o'clock in the evening depending on what watch he was on.

'No good my waving in middle watch when you're all fast asleep,' he joked.

Middle, or 'guts', as they called it, was between midnight and four a.m. and the loneliest of all the watches. Dad said some of the men found that watch the toughest of them all.

'I'm used to it from Navy days,' he said. 'Mind you, it was quite different being on a ship with lots of people still around and your mates all sleeping in their bunks. Out there on a lighthouse in the middle of the sea it can be inky-black with the wind howling at the panes of the lantern and rattling the deep set windows, while waves come crashing right up over the rock and banging on the walls as if asking to come in. It really feels as if there was no one else in the world and it's a funny feeling.'

'It sounds scary, Dad.'

'Aye, lass, it is in a way but I'm rather getting to like the drama – and even the loneliness. The PK loves it, he does. I swear he's glad if he's overdue coming home, he's so taken with this life. But then he's become obsessive about everything on that rock and between you and me he can be a stickler for things, a bit of a pain. I'm used to his sort in the Navy so it doesn't bother me. All the same, I hope I don't end up like him. He won't even put a hand on the brass stair rail so as not to mess up the polish on it. One day he's going to fall down them stairs and crack his flippin' skull. That's going a tad too far, don't you think?'

I agreed. I could tell Mr Waterman was like that; he was always tidying up after his wife who, though not sloppy, was more relaxed and comfortable with life and left the occasional book or newspaper about, umbrella in the hall or whatever. Mr W would tidy it all away and then she'd be looking all over for things. I did my best to keep an eye on them both during these times and produce items that had found their way into cupboards where they didn't belong. On the whole, I think we all felt a vague relief when he went off with Jed in the boat with his tin full of goodies baked by Sheila. Sometimes I contributed one of my famous hand-raised pork pies to the tin and Mr W said I'd have to teach Susan how to do them.

Knowing Dad was coming over to see us, I'd spent the morning baking him a pie and a fruit cake to take back with him. There was only one phone amongst the three cottages and Abbi from the cottage across from us had brought the phone over, plugged it in and said, 'It's for you, Bridie.'

I was surprised as I'd never had a call. We always knew when to expect Dad for he would come onshore when Abbi's husband went back. He generally came over to say hello first and then take his case and gear off to his digs where, Dad said, he could catch up on some sleep.

'Bridie,' said Dad, 'I'm going to give you a little surprise this time. I've got Jed to drive me to Penzance and that's where I'm talking from. I'll catch up on some sleep, then I'll be over with my surprise.'

'All right, Dad,' I said, but felt disappointed not to see him or get the chance to hug him and stroke the luxuriant beard which he had grown. He always looked so handsome in his keeper's uniform and cap and I liked to see him in it before he went home and changed into casual clothes. Mr Waterman always wore his uniform even when on leave. He was going a trifle batty, I reckon, and I think it worried poor Sheila a lot.

I wondered what Dad's surprise was going to be and felt quite excited. He'd begun learning from Mr Waterman how to make a ship in a bottle, a craft that required immense patience and skill. Had he finished it, maybe? If that was the surprise it would be interesting to see the finished result. There were ships in bottles all over the cottage but I firmly believed that Dad's would be best.

However, I had to be patient as Dad wouldn't be along now for a day or two. I put the pie and cake in sealed tins and set them aside for him. I knew he'd be pleased with those and proud of my new culinary skills.

Chapter 8

I had just gone for a walk along the cliff to look at the shearwaters and the storm petrels that had recently been visiting us and was strolling back to the cottages. It was a lovely morning, the sky as bright and fresh as if it was rinsed with laundry blue. Looking out to sea I could see thick solid cumulus clouds building up into massy towers of water and ice which would suddenly be over on us and pouring down rain. I was glad Dad had got back onshore before a storm brewed up. For some days the weather had been fine and warm, but now there was that sultry feel in the air and an eerie stillness that betokened no good. I hurried back home.

Ryan was working in the garden, turning the earth and digging out little early potatoes for our supper. Susan was seeing to the chickens that were scattering and running about and squawking fit to bust, trying to get them in the henhouse before the storm broke out. She was hopeless at catching them.

I stood inside the gate and watched Ryan as he dug, making it all look so easy and effortless. He was lean but very muscular and just now shirtless. I admired his strong young physique with pleasure. He glanced up and wiped his sweaty forehead and said, 'What you staring at, then?'

'Just watching you,' I said, 'no law says you can't, is there?'

'Don't like being watched,' he said, 'puts me off what I'm doing.'

'Sorry then,' I said with a shrug and turned towards the cottage. Then I heard the sound of a distant car and looked round. It was still a dot heading for the cottages along the lane. Nothing else was in sight – few vehicles ever came this way and this wasn't one I recognised. It certainly wasn't Jed's lorry and I wondered if Abbi Simpson had bought her new car and was coming home in it. That would be great for everyone because we could cadge lifts from her when she went into town. Jed wasn't always available when you wanted him and it was miles to walk before you could catch a bus and that only came once a day.

Ryan scooped up his can full of potatoes.

'Reckon that'll be enough for an army,' he said. 'Mum said dig up as many as I could. Who the devil's this lot coming?' He came over and leaned beside me on the gate to watch the approaching car. As it got nearer and started along the bumpy unmade road to the cottages, I recognised Dad behind the wheel and with a start of surprise began to yell and whoop with joy. He'd bought a car! But then I saw Andy sitting beside him, his pale, miserable face unmistakable and unforgettable. Out of the back window leaned Jim, waving at me.

I was struck with horror. They were coming to take me back to Mean Millie. I knew it and felt faint. I grabbed hold of Ryan and clung to him.

'Don't let them take me back,' I screamed, 'Ryan, don't let them take me back. I'll run away, I'll kill myself!'

Ryan put his arms about me and patted me awkwardly, unused to such outbursts.

'It's all right, Bridie. No one's taking you away. Calm down.'

Dad came puttering up in the old Morris and got out followed by Andy who already had a sneering look on his face. He had lost some of his fat and looked more like Dad than ever. Jim got out of the back and came over saying, 'Hi, Bridie, aren't you glad to see us?'

Jim looked at Ryan askance. I was hanging on to him for dear life and he still had his arm about me protectively. The two lads looked at one another in a funny, challenging way that I didn't understand at the time but one day would understand only too well. I too looked up at Ryan who loosened me and said, 'Well, greet your family, then. Where's your manners, Bridie?'

I wanted to run indoors to my room and lock myself in but years of self control took over so I stopped where I was, swallowing back that awful anxiety that always came over me in bad moments. Ryan stayed behind me and I felt a comfort from his presence. He seemed a bulwark between my old family and my new one. It was as if he was sending me silent waves of comfort and calm.

'Hi, Jim,' I said weakly.

Dad came over and scooped me up in his arms with a big hug that restored my fractured feelings. I ignored Andy, I'm afraid to say. I couldn't bring myself to look at my old tormentor and made sure I kept my long ponytail out of his way in case he tried any of his old tricks. However, he seemed oddly subdued in these unfamiliar surroundings and kept glancing around uneasily, looking at Ryan with awe, for tall strong Ryan looked at least eighteen though he was scarce sixteen. He had a serious, sober adult way about him, more like a man of forty sometimes.

Jim just looked uncomfortable as he gazed about him at the whitewashed cottages with their little gardens and nothing else but sea and sky behind them and barren, bleak plains of grassland rolling away before. He was all dressed up in his best clothes, smart as a bandbox, but then Jim always was a natty dresser like his Mother. I felt a mess in my old jeans and scruffy white cotton top and for some reason felt ashamed of Ryan still shirtless, arms akimbo, an unwelcoming expression on his dark, dour face.

Sheila came fussing out and welcoming everyone to step indoors. It seems she'd known all along about this horrid surprise. Apparently the boys had asked to come and see the lighthouse and where we all were living now so she, in her welcoming way, had said it would be lovely. I wished they *didn't* know where we were; wish we could have disappeared out of their lives forever. But they were Dad's sons after all. I couldn't begrudge his seeing them.

'Is that your car, Dad?' I said after a while.

'No, love, just borrowed it from a mate in town for a couple of days. I've plans to get myself one sometime so we can go trips and the like. Have to wait till I'm made up to AK though and get a bit of a pay rise.'

'What's AK?' asked Jim.

'It means Assistant Keeper. After fifteen years when some poor old sod dies I may be lucky enough to become a PK or Principal Keeper like Sid Waterman. I'm not in a rush about it. You have to start all over again in a manner of speaking, back on rock lights and towers and so forth, work your way back to where you were. More pay naturally but also more responsibility. Anyway it's a long way off yet. Got to get through this year as SAK first off.'

'Do you really work on that thing?' asked Andy, staring over at the lighthouse, far out on its rock in the midst of the Atlantic Ocean. It was a hundred and seventeen feet tall, Dad once told me. From this distance it looked like a toy, yet it was still imposing in its solitary grandeur.

By now the clouds had begun to move faster towards us as the stillness gave way to a rippling wind. The wind was moving the sea, urging her waves into higher peaks and troughs and it had begun to feel cold and damp.

'I do,' said Dad in answer to Andy's question, 'I love that *thing*, as you call it, whatever the weather. Mind, we've picked a bit of a rough day for your visit as it turns out, but it'll give you a sense of what it's all about out down here. Wind and waves and the cruel sea. Some days the waves come crashing almost over the top of the light. You get used to the constant drumming of it all, drumming away at the sides like it was asking to come in. It's a living, breathing being is the sea and we have to treat it like one, take note of what it's trying to say, skirt round its moods and furies and storms. Then be peaceful with it when it's feeling content and happy and still as glass. In a funny way, though, I enjoy its crazy days best. It's got an energy you can't describe.'

Andy shuddered and began to look as if he wished he'd never come at all. I fervently wished the same and hoped the experience would put him off ever coming again. He looked at me and said, 'You've grown taller, you have.'

I was almost his height now and that seemed to surprise him. He was not a bit the Andy I'd known back at his home where he was King of the Castle, backed by his mum and bigger and tougher than me. He almost seemed afraid, out of place, and my heart felt glad. Now he knew what it felt like not to fit in somewhere. I said nothing, however, just turned my back on him and marched indoors, followed by Jim who took my arm in a friendly manner and said, 'I think it's great here, Bridie, all this expanse of sea and sky. It feels huge and lonely and strange – but interesting.' He looked at me admiringly. 'You look so much prettier and happier. I can tell this place agrees with you.'

He bent and whispered in my ear, 'I can't wait to leave home, myself, Bridie. Guess what – I'm being sent off to a boarding school soon and Andy'll probably follow on. Our Nan has offered to pay the fees. She knows I'm keen to get on and make it to University. She reckons going to a good school to do my O's and A's will help me on my way. Thankfully, she's a bit of a snob and wants an academic in the family. I've got big ideas, Bridie. I'm not going to stay stuck in some seaside town all my life. I *want* to do really well, make you all proud of me. You wait and see.'

'That would be great, Jim. I hope it all works out.'

'It will.' His face had a determined look about it that I'd never see before. He'd changed a lot. I felt something in him was sterner, harder and in a way I found that interesting and attractive. I envied his sense of direction and certainty over his future. I had none at all about mine or about myself as a person.

'Yes, it'll work out. And Dad's grateful to Nan. He couldn't afford to send us to St Michael Bister himself. I'm not sure Mum wants us to go. She misses you too, you know, she often talks about you.'

'I wish she didn't! I wish she'd forget who I was and let me go,' I said with a shiver akin to fear. 'I've got nothing to do with her and I never want to see her again.'

Jim looked at me, shocked. 'I know she wasn't nice to you, Bridie, but you need to forgive her someday.'

'Why should I? I'm sorry, Jim, I never will forgive her and you can think what you like.'

He said no more on this subject. I went off to help Sheila prepare a huge spread for tea. The rain was beginning to torrent down in great, glassy sheets. We all crowded into the cottage and stared out of the windows at the flashes of lightning streaking the sky, waiting for the deep, solemn rolls of thunder. Dad loved it and stood at the door staring out to sea with the binos he'd brought me. The boys took turns looking through them at the tall lighthouse as it stood out there on its rock, waves lashing at the base, the whole structure looking as if it could be swept away any minute. Yet, it had prevailed for well over a hundred years and wasn't going to disappear that easy but it always looked alarming.

'Christ, Dad, I'd be scared out there,' said Andy and gave the binoculars back with a little shudder. He came in and huddled in an armchair, looking miserable and fed up. He was obviously looking forward to leaving as soon as possible. Dad said they would go back to town later on. He'd booked the boys a room at a nearby bed and breakfast and would take them back home the day after. I think Andy was looking forward to that more than anything in the world. However, he cheered up when Sheila called us over to the tea table, seized up sandwiches, pie and cake till his plate was full, then sat munching steadily and happily. I looked at him with disgust.

Jim was also quieter than usual, regarding everyone with a bit of puzzlement as if trying to fit us into some internal pigeon hole. He often looked over at Ryan and even tried to begin a conversation but it foundered swiftly on the rocks of Ryan's impenetrable silence and surliness. Ryan neither looked at me, nor anyone else, just ate a little, drank several cups of tea then took himself off to his room to study for his exams. I watched him go with envious regret.

Dad and Sheila laughed and joked together and I sat listening to them. Poor Sheila, I could tell she enjoyed having a bloke about and missed her old man. Then when he did come home, the miserable fellow couldn't wait to get back to his mistress, the lighthouse. I don't know how she put up with it. I decided she was a saint.

Susan was thrilled to have all these visitors, a rare enough event in our lives, and she chattered away non-stop in her soppy manner. Jim and Andy took little enough notice of her but she didn't seem to care. She was even daft enough to fetch her kitten to show Jim who was the only one polite enough to seem interested in her blether.

Sheila called her to help with the dishes after tea and brushed aside my eager desire to escape.

'Them's your guests as much as ours, Bridie,' she said. 'You must see to your dad and brothers and look after them. We're all stuck in for a bit but when the storm's passed your dad says he's taking you all out for a run and Susie's coming along too, if that's all right. Ryan says he's got too much work to do. You know him; he's never keen on company, just like his dad.'

'I can stay at home, and you go for the ride if you like,' I said hopefully. 'I don't mind, honest.'

She just shook her head at me in disapproval as if wondering at my peculiar lack of enthusiasm on seeing my family. But then she knew nothing about it for I had never spoken of my life before I came to live with her at the cottages. Ryan was the only person I'd told and he would never say a word to anyone else. I so wished I could stay with him. Just knowing he was there upstairs in his room was comfort enough. But I had to go perforce and sat in the back with Jim, Susan squeezed between us. She was delighted with the jaunt and full of her nonsensical chatter.

The storm had stopped and that wonderful sense of shining fresh wetness hung everywhere, dripping from leaves on trees, glistening on the vivid green grass. I let myself go in the joy of riding even an old jalopy like this Morris and looked out of the window trying to ignore Susan's constant poking me and exclaiming over something.

Dad took us into Penzance and Andy brightened considerably at the sight of civilisation, especially when we stopped for a

Cornish cream tea. I'd always wondered where he put all the food he ate, as exercise had never been his strong point, so I was surprised to hear him talking about rugby with Dad, telling him he was now in the team at school. The thought of Andy allowing himself to be shoved and pushed in a scrum and being brought down in a tackle was hilarious. He would certainly give back his fair share of shoving, swearing and bellowing and I could believe he'd guard the ball like a terrier with a bone.

Jim made sure he sat next to me in the tea shop and for once Susan shut up, her mouth occupied with scones, cream and strawberry jam. I nibbled at mine, sweet stuff not being my favourite food. Jim enjoyed his but he was never greedy, didn't live to eat like Andy.

'I like it round here,' he said after a while. 'Dad says they'll be turning his lighthouse over from oil to electricity soon, next year maybe, but he won't get the benefit of the change because he may get sent off somewhere else pretty soon. Will you be going with him?'

'I don't know,' I said. 'He hasn't mentioned it to me.' I felt annoyed that Jim knew all this before me. 'He did say in his first year he'd have to move about a lot. He's been on this rock light for three months so I suppose he's due to try a different one. Sheila says Trinity House like to test their SAKs and see what they can do, see whether they can really stick out the life. It's a sort of probationary thing.'

'I suppose Dad doesn't find it much different to being in the Navy, really. He's still on the sea in a way even if he's stationary and not moving about on a ship.'

'I think he finds it quite different,' I said, 'there's all that running up and down stairs. He says there's about three hundred of them in the tower. His legs ached like anything the first few weeks and now they ache when he's on land instead as he's got used to the stairs and forgotten how to walk on the flat. And then there's being all alone on a watch, especially middle watch in the early hours of the morning. He reckons that's different somehow, more lonely up there in the service room, even though the other two men are sleeping below him. I wish I could be with him, to chat to him and make him a cup of tea. I wish we were allowed on as well.'

'They couldn't have a *girl* on there.'

'Why not? Sheila said that in the old days keepers lived on the light with their families and she feels it was a much better, more normal sort of life for them all. It's crazy like this, husbands coming home for a few weeks and then spending the other four or more weeks offshore. You can't have a proper family life and lots of them get divorced. I'm surprised they stick it out, the ones that do.'

'It's a strange life. Dad always liked to do things different. Anyway, he's always been away from us for ages, hasn't he? *We're* certainly used to it,' said Jim. A trace of bitterness was in his voice and for a brief moment I paused to think how the boys must have been affected by Dad's long absences. It didn't just involve me; they were his sons. I felt a bit ashamed of myself for being so unwelcoming and unforgiving.

'I hope you get away to your school and Millie doesn't put her oar in,' I said, 'I hope for your sake you get away.'

'I will, don't you worry,' said Jim. 'It's my life, not hers and I won't let her stop me. Andy can hang round Mum if he likes, it's up to him.'

He swallowed the last of his scone and jam and some tea. Then he said,

'You seem awful close with that bloke you're living with there.'

'Ryan? Not close really. I'm not sure what you mean. He's not my boyfriend.'

'But you fancy him, don't you?'

I stared at him. It seemed an odd thing to observe and I wondered what he meant. So often people say one thing while underneath is another meaning altogether and you have to listen hard to their words or look keenly into their eyes to know what it is. 'I do *like* him, he's great. What is this? You being the stern older brother then?'

'Maybe. Someone has to keep an eye on you.'

Funny, that's what Ryan had once said. I have no idea why

these people thought I needed keeping an eye on. I felt perfectly capable of looking after myself.

'I'd be glad if you minded your own business, Jim,' I said. Wiping my mouth with a napkin, I rose and visited the Ladies for such a long while they sent out Susan to see what I was doing.

Chapter 9

It was such a relief when Dad took Jim and Andy to their bed and breakfast place and then drove me back to Sheila's cottage.

'You didn't enjoy seeing the boys, did you?' said Dad. 'And that's a shame, Bridie. I'd like you all to care for one another. The world's a small dark place sometimes and we need our friends and relations.'

'You left them, Dad,' I couldn't help saying, 'you don't act as if *you* need them much.'

He remained silent for a while after this and I knew I'd scored a point. It annoyed me being preached at by Jim and now even Dad. People should practice what they preach and to my mind neither of these two were in a position to take the moral high ground. Sometimes I couldn't help thinking that Andy and Millie, unpleasant as they might be, were at least truthful by just being their nasty selves without any qualms.

'I'm taking the lads back home tomorrow. I'll be over to see you in a couple of days, sweetheart. You are happy with Sheila, aren't you?'

'I *am* happy, Dad, unbelievably happy. You're not going to take me away yet, are you?' I looked at him as I said this, my face troubled.

He glanced over at me and shook his head. 'No, no. Don't fret, ducky.'

By now we had reached the cottages and twilight was coming on fast. The lighthouse lantern had been 'put in', as the men termed it, and the long white beam swivelled slowly around the wild, choppy seas. We both sat in the car and watched the light with emotion, a deep love for it and all it meant. It was comforting, this beam of light over the rough seas, an act of pure human kindness. The Cornishmen had long resisted having a lighthouse here because they made their living in those old days plundering the wrecks, even luring ships falsely ashore onto the treacherous rocks. And because of some mad ancient law that said they couldn't take stuff if there were survivors, they killed anyone who had the misfortune to crawl up on the sands from the stricken ships. Those were greedy, evil times. Then the lighthouses had been built and now ships were safe. Just knowing the lighthouse keepers were there to keep an eye out for any trouble was a great comfort to sailors in stormy weather.

'Always makes me think of *Jamaica Inn*,' I said, 'that was a brilliant book. How could men have been so cruel and evil, Dad?'

'No *could* about it, Bridie,' he said, 'Human beings have always been and always will be evil. We're the oddest animals invented by Nature. Good in many ways and evil in others. The point is *we* know the difference which animals don't. Animals act by instinct; they kill from fear or hunger, can't help themselves. We kill from greed and a wish to possess everything. And we know perfectly well we're doing wrong. That's the awful thing. We have a choice which way to go and mainly we go the bad way.'

'Have you ever killed anyone, Dad?'

'We all did in the war,' he said. 'I try not to think of it. I wasn't personally the one who sent off the torpedoes, but I *was* a part of it all and cheered as much as anyone when we scored a hit and sank a German destroyer or U-boat. To hell with the men on it, ordinary sailors obeying orders like ourselves – they weren't human any more, they were the enemy and we'd hit the enemy, got a bull's-eye. We all have it in us to kill others.'

I debated this. I hated Mean Millie and her son Andy with all my heart and might wish them dead – but could I actually kill them? I didn't think I could. Surely my conscience would trouble me forever if I committed such a deed.

'Anyway,' said Dad, 'to answer your question a minute ago,

I'm to be sent off after this leave to another light, a tower this time, right up in the North sea. That'll be a test, right out at sea without anywhere to be but in the lighthouse itself. Towers just come straight up out of the water, no landing stage, nowhere to fish or take a little stroll. You're stuck there till you get onshore and the weather's going to be just as rough up there, if not worse. May mean an extra week before the relief arrives.'

'Oh, that sounds awful, Dad, how will you bear it?'

'Have to see how I manage, won't I? Other men stand it and I'm sure I can do the same. It can't be worse than Longships ... bloody uncomfortable quarters there, I can tell you. Sid Waterman reckons it's the worst one in England but we all put up with it.'

'How do you get on a tower if it's right out there without a landing place?'

'They'll throw a rope down to the waiting boat and I'll be winched up to the light, then the outgoing keeper will be winched down to the waiting boat in his turn. Just have to hope I don't get hit by a wave and end up in the sea.'

'You will wear a life jacket?'

'I'll be in the Bosun's Chair, won't I? That's what they call the breeches buoy. It's all very safe and properly done, Navy style.' He smiled and patted my cheek. 'No need to be anxious, Bridie, it's being done all the time and I've climbed enough heights on ships and cliffs and mountains all my life. It will be exciting. We all love a spot of danger and discomfort, it's a bloke thing; life's too boring otherwise. Battling against the elements, fighting with Mother Nature and winning – that's the stuff of life.'

'Dad, you will be careful,' I pleaded. 'You've me to think of and the boys. Please be careful.'

'I will,' he promised, 'and you too. You'll be fine here and I needn't worry, I know. You're being taken well care of and seem to have fitted in like one of the family. Don't get too cosy, though. Sid Waterman may well have to move sometime and they'll all have to up sticks and go with him. I'll have to see what I can sort out with Trinity House when that happens.'

'Will that be soon, Mr Waterman leaving?' I asked fearfully. The thought of losing Ryan was the worst thing I could imagine. How would I bear life without seeing him everyday as intimately as if we were relations?

'Not for a while yet, I'm sure. Just be prepared, Bridie, that's all. We can't afford to get too attached to people and places in this job and you elected to come with me, little sweetheart. You chose your mad Dad Joe and his lifestyle.'

Dad came to see us a few times before leaving for the Northumberland coast and I knew it would be a long time before I saw him again. It was too far away for him to travel to see us often, though he promised he'd come down south when he could. Parting from him would have upset me once, but now I had new friends and new people about me so I accepted the separation with equanimity. The thought I might have to part from Ryan and Sheila sometime was one that troubled me a great deal. However, I said nothing of it and just made up my mind to enjoy each day with them as if it was the last.

It was a lovely summer that year and, looking back on it, one of the happiest of my life. The days were long, sunny and peaceful. I enjoyed the lessons with Sheila and learnt to cook well. Ryan even taught me how to cast a line and fish off the rocks – not that I ever caught much. I was better at catching crabs and sometimes I'd go down to the cove and beg a lobster from a fisherman down there, one that had maybe lost a leg or wasn't up to standard. Ryan taught me to make fish stock with the heads of the gutted fish we had for supper which I would then use to make a delicious fish soup with the crabs and crayfish I'd snared. They all went in the pot. Everyone said it was the best soup they'd ever eaten.

I felt great pride in these little successes and being accepted as part of the family. It was the first family I'd ever really belonged with. In some respects it was still a fatherless family, with Mr W so often away, but in his absence Ryan assumed the role of head of the household and Sheila often asked his advice as if he was a grown man. Ryan had never been a child, in my opinion; he had tumbled out of his mum as wise as Solomon. He was an amazing person in my eyes and I loved him fiercely and silently, with no possible hope or expectation that he might love a scraggy, red-headed fourteen year old in return. To him I was just a kid and a bit of a loopy one at that.

'Half your trouble is you feel too much,' he said to me when it was chicken day. Chicken day was when we took one of the fowl for supper, generally when Mr W was expected home or it was someone's birthday. Ryan and Sheila thought nothing of going out and grabbing one and calmly wringing its neck. Even Susan was capable of grabbing a chicken and would smash its head against a wall then bring it in to pluck. The plucking I didn't mind so much, the feathers all going into a big box to be used for refilling pillows and mattresses when they got too lumpy, but the killing part – no, I couldn't do it.

'Suppose you marry a keeper one day, yourself,' said Ryan, 'you'll have to get used to doing a bit of butchering and wringing a few chickens' necks. You might end up anywhere; nearest town could be miles away.'

'I'll cycle in or save up and buy a car and drive in and buy my meat from a butcher, thanks,' I said. 'Anyway, I'm not going to marry a keeper. I'll think of something more exciting to do.'

'Like what?'

The strange thing was that the future was never clear to me. I had no idea what I wanted to do at all. I would get my O levels and maybe stay on in the sixth form … and then what?

'I dunno,' I said, making a face. 'I suppose I *will* end up just a housewife. Millie always said so. It's her fault. It's all she taught me.'

'You say it like it's not an important thing to be,' said Ryan, 'which goes to prove you're still young and a fool. It's good for a woman to be looking after her home and her kids and her old man like my ma does. It's not a thing to be shamed about like so many girls seem to be nowadays. Don't you get like that, Bridie, don't you get all feminist now.'

'I'll try not to,' I said meekly, not too sure what a feminist was like.

'See ... life's sort of led you this way ... you'll make a pretty decent housewife one day. Like it's meant to be that way for you. Your fate. You can't go against your fate, you know.'

'I suppose not,' I replied, 'but I would like to do something else first before I settle. I'd like to be a teacher maybe, like your mum was.'

'Yes, I think you'd be good at that. You're patient and caring and I think you could keep kids in order. Kids need to be kept in order or they don't learn anything.'

I contemplated my choices in silence for a while. 'I dunno though, I'm not all *that* fond of little kids.'

'You'll be fond of your own, that's for sure.'

'Do you think so?' I asked dubiously. 'I'd like to be a lighthouse keeper but they won't take on girls any more, which is a cheek, I think. We could run it just as good. Dad reckons it's much easier now things have become electrified, not half the work it used to be and I'm good with electrical things. Girls ran a lighthouse in the old days, especially in the States.'

'Well, you're not going to be a lighthouse keeper,' said Ryan firmly. 'That won't happen, Bridie. Think again.'

'Oh well ... maybe I'll write a book instead. I'd like to write crime stories like Agatha Christie.'

'That's all a waste of time,' said Ryan scornfully. 'You'd be a sight happier caring for a home and kids. Writing's living in a dream world, that's what it is. It's making up things to be real that aren't real. Writing about murder, that's not nice at all. You'd have to think like a murderer, you'd have to imagine what would make him want to kill another person, get in his head and heart. Why should anyone want to spend time doing that? What sort of mind would you have to dream up stuff like that? Or reading it for that matter? It's not real, Bridie, and what's more it's sort of corrupting, to my way of thinking.'

'Corrupting?'

'Yes, like putting ideas in people's heads and making them get so they don't know truth from fiction any more. Makes them hard inside.'

'Is that why you never read fiction books?'

'Yes. I prefer to know about real things. Things like the winds and clouds and birds and the types of fishes down there in the deep.'

'But you said once that you hated a lot of people.'

'And so I do,' he said with passion. 'People can be so cruel to each other. I can't understand that sort of thing. Most folk are only interested in money and collecting lots of useless things, getting drunk and being stupid. I believe in a quiet, honest, simple life.'

'Are you really going to be a keeper one day?'

'Yes, I am,' he said and then he did something quite astonishing. He looked at me, his eyes deep and solemn, and took my hand in his. 'And one day you will be my wife, Bridie, so you'd better start getting used to the idea. You're the only girl I think I could bear to marry.'

Chapter 10

To say I was stunned by Ryan's words would be an understatement. He never said anything like this to me again. Neither was he in any way romantic nor any more or less interested in me than before. I kept repeating his words to myself for ages, telling myself I'd had a proposal at the age of fourteen and feeling amazed and thrilled about it, but in the end decided he was pulling my leg or I'd been dreaming.

I wanted to ask him what made him say that to me but didn't have the nerve. In the end I blurted it out and wished I hadn't.

We had gone down to the shore to look for crabs and mussels in the pools. As I poked and peered and enjoyed the feel of bare feet in the slimy ooze of the sand, Ryan stood and stared out at sea and then up at the clouds.

'Be a fair day,' he said, nodding like some sage old fisherman. I smiled at this and felt a sudden rush of love engulf me. He was so handsome standing there, the wind blowing his hair about his face. His beard was just beginning to grow in a downy manner and, as he wasn't shaving yet, it made a faint dark stubble about his chin. His voice had deepened almost overnight. He was a man now, I knew it. Had he ever been a boy?

As for myself, I still felt like a little girl, my dark red hair tied back in childish bunches. I wondered whether I'd get Sheila to cut my hair and maybe that would make me look a bit older and sophisticated but couldn't bear the thought of parting with my one and only striking feature. Sudden doubts assailed me. I looked at Ryan. Had he been teasing me? Was I really going to be his wife one day? He had always said he'd never marry. It was madness to suppose he had meant it.

'Were you pretending you wanted to marry me, Ryan? Or did you mean it?'

The words came tumbling out and I regretted them at once. I was always doing things I later regretted. He'd think me silly.

'I said so, didn't I?' he growled. 'I always mean what I say. You better know it. You needn't bother lookin' at any other boy either. You were sent here for me and no one else. Bridie, my bride. See? That's how it will be.'

He turned, softening his last words with a big smile. I felt myself turning weak inside. All the same, I didn't like the fact he thought he owned me and I'd not have any say in all this.

'Oh, and what if I don't want you, Mister Clever Dick? What if another boy comes along and I like him better.'

Ryan's face darkened and he seized me by the wrist. 'Won't be no other boy. I know you like me, Bridie. I know you do. You're meant for me. That's the way of things sometimes. Soon as I saw you, I was sure of it. And I'm not the marrying kind, as you know.'

'So I should feel pleased, should I? I should feel it a mighty honour that you've come off your pedestal and made up your mind over all this. Well, I've a mind of my own, Ryan Waterman, and you'd best know that as well. You needn't even *think* of marrying me. I'll marry whom I please and there's nothing you can do about it!'

I was in a right temper by now. I didn't have Irish blood and red hair for nothing, I can tell you. I flung down the pail and let all the crabs run out and marched off, leaving Ryan staring after me with a very sullen expression on his face. There were times when he really made me mad. Neither of us mentioned the subject again and I began to wonder if I really did love him at all or whether it was just a silly crush. But I ached with sadness inside. Loving is a very heart filling thing and I missed it.

When the opportunity arose at last, Dad came to visit us for a few days, a joyful reunion. I hugged him till he groaned in protest and then sat next to him and refused to part from him 'like a wee barnacle on a ship' as he put it. A delicious dinner was prepared by Sheila – helped by Ryan, of all people. He had decided to join in our Domestic Science classes for, as he said, 'a keeper has to be able to cook and there's no point in learning from anyone but Mum. She's the best,' which was true enough.

Sometimes I got the odd feeling that he and his mother were training me in all the domestic skills I might need. It was almost as if they had decided between them that I was destined to be Ryan's wife. I felt sure in my heart we would be together one day. In a way, the idea pleased me. It made the future clear; showed me the path I was to follow and who I was to be with. But at the same time a part of me rebelled and said 'no'. I wanted to see a bit of life first.

After the dinner was over, we all sat outside on benches in the balmy autumn evening and Dad lit up his pipe. Sheila lit a cigarette and smoked with him in a companionable silence. Her husband would never allow her to smoke and she would sneak off down the road for a quick ciggy when he was home so he had no idea of her habit. On the way back she'd suck a peppermint to get rid of the smell in her mouth and let the wind blow it from her hair. Soon as that peppermint smell came wafting in the house, I knew what she'd been up to and would smile to myself a little.

Ryan actually joined us for once and took a cigarette from his mum, lighting it up with such ease that I realised he had done this before. He savoured his cigarette with a deep, intense pleasure. It was the first time I'd seen him smoke. It made him even more grown up in my eyes.

Dad was in fine form and telling us stories about his new lighthouse.

'I love it on the tower,' he said. 'The other keepers are a friendly bunch, always cracking jokes and having a bit of a laugh. We had a lad come to join us, a holiday student fellow, but he couldn't stand the life more than five minutes and he was away in no time. He was a lazy sod, so no great loss. Our PK, Tim Wakefield, is a good bloke, been in the service for donkey's years, knows the ropes and isn't overly fanatic about keeping things so smart. Just enough to get by if an Inspector comes from Trinity House.'

'They come to inspect you?' I asked with some indignation.

'Oh, yes. You have to expect them any time as they like to try and surprise us, catch us out. But we get to know in good time as the other lights always pass on a radio message that he's on the way. We're generally one of the last on the list, being so far north so that gives us to time to get our finger out and polish everything up extra smart in good time. It's all part of the game, just like being in the Navy.'

'Who else is out there with you?' asked Sheila. She looked the picture of contentment, smoking her ciggy, blowing out smoke rings to amuse Susan.

Dad tapped out his pipe and put it away. 'Paul Harrison is the other keeper and he's a keep-fit fanatic, spends hours doing exercises in his room. He's thin as a rake. Best cook though; he makes a fantastic roast dinner and a lemon meringue to make your mouth water. Almost as good as yours, Sheila!'

She laughed and poked Dad playfully. I realised that they were flirting and this made me feel a bit uncomfortable. I hadn't got to the age yet when I could understand that adults could flirt happily without it meaning anything at all.

'Yes, I know Paul and Tim,' said Sheila. 'Sidney's worked with them both in his time. Nice easy going fellows, I recall. Glad you're eating well. Do you get much fresh meat brought over?'

'Only when the relief comes. They bring plenty over then. Mainly we live on fish – that's one thing we're never short of. I have a line out of the lower window and we reel up cod, haddock, bass, you name it. There's lobster pots too and nothing more delicious than fresh lobster or crab sandwiches at four in the morning! We have a great diet but not much in the way of fresh veg. Once we've used up what we've got we have to open tins, whereas on the light here they have a little patch on the rock and pots with herbs and lettuce, which is great. Most of all, I miss spirits and beer as they aren't allowed on the light so that's something you yearn for at the start. But it's funny how you get used to not bothering about it. There's too much to do, too much to occupy your time.'

'I would have thought it would be really boring out there all the time, right in the middle of the sea, nothing to look at,' I said, surprised.

'Boring? Never, my ducky, never. Heaps of things to do and see. The changing skies and seas and the stars at night. The stars, Bridie, just glorious in a sky so black that it's unreal. When you're up doing middle watch, you can walk out on the gallery and look up at them and they seem to go for miles up and around; limitless, galaxies beyond ours, suns and planets we know nothing about. And you are the only human being in existence looking at them, like some god just looking at Creation. That's how it feels. Yet you know you're not alone because far off you see another light round the coast, its beams circling the seas, and meanwhile your own light is turning, turning, different colours for the different danger spots. It's a magical existence in those moments with only the rhythmic sound of the sea crashing away below.'

He tapped out his pipe on the wall and reminisced. 'Saw a couple of sharks the other day, looking up at us as if they knew we were there and trying to say something to us. Heaven knows what's down there, right in the deep. I'd love to go deep-sea diving. Then there's hobbies – we've all got our hobbies. I've not quite got round to knitting my next jumper, but I might. Trouble is you get used to being peaceful and quiet like that and it's getting harder to come back onshore every time.'

I was troubled to hear this. I felt he would end up like Mr Waterman, yearning to leave us all and be back where there were no cars, chatty people, phones or modern appliances of any sort. I would end up like poor Sheila. Maybe he meant to send me to a boarding school like the boys and that would be awful. I couldn't bear the thought.

Ryan had let his cigarette burn to his fingers, so entranced was he with Dad's descriptions. His own father never spoke like this, wasn't a poet like my dad. And I could see that these words stirred his soul as much as they did mine.

'Ryan wants to go deep-sea diving,' I said, looking over at him, 'don't you?'

'Well, he will one day if that's what he wants. He'll get what he wants,' said Dad with a smile. 'He's that sort, is Ryan.'

I so wanted to put out a hand and touch Ryan. His eyes were full of longing and I knew what he felt as if it was me inside his soul. I knew he wanted to be out there with the sky and the sea and the stars. But more than anything, I wanted to feel him move towards me in some tender human contact, rouse himself from his private inner world. I wanted to touch him and hug him so much it hurt me inside, but I didn't dare. He seemed to dislike any such intimate human gestures. He would have thought me mad and crawled even deeper into his crab-like shell.

Dad looked very fit; all the running up and down the stairs kept him thin. He had changed in some subtle manner that I couldn't put my finger on. I felt he was further away from me and felt a sense of utter loneliness as if I too was standing on the lighthouse; an inner lighthouse. At times like this I understood Ryan so well. We both had this sense of isolation within us that nothing could change. We could be in a crowd and still feel this way. I admitted to myself that I did love Ryan. I loved him with every fibre of my being.

Dad had brought his five-masted ship in the bottle and presented it to me with the date he finished it stuck on underneath. *Made by Joe Bosworth, September 1954.*

I was thrilled with it and Sheila pronounced it a very good one indeed.

'You've certainly learnt that skill,' she agreed. 'Will you make more? Sid's made over two hundred and he sells some in Sennen and even taken them to a shop down in Penzance. It makes a bit of extra income.'

'I'll make a couple more for the boys but it's not a hobby I really take to,' Dad replied. 'I prefer to make things from bits of driftwood. I'll make you a mermaid someday, Bridie.'

'I'd like that,' I said.

I had a letter from Jim some days after Dad went offshore. He and Andy were at St Michael Bister's in Winchester.

I can't tell you how glad I was to leave Broughampton, he wrote. *Andy made a shocking fuss, silly nit, but Nan insisted we both went, said she wasn't going to be accused of favouritism (though I can tell you in private I am her favourite). Mum was pretty upset about it. Well, she's all alone now which I do feel sorry about, but I'm really enjoying it here and grateful to Dad. Andy isn't so sure but I think he'll come round. They have a great rugby team and he's interested in that. He's already lost weight now Mum isn't feeding him up so much so he's a lot fitter for playing. As you know, I'm more into the art and literature stuff. History especially. I like history and researching the past. It's great. The other boys are okay but I haven't made any special friends yet. Maybe you can come over and see us here some time? I'd love to show you round. You'd be impressed.*

'Like hell, I will,' I muttered to myself.

I had taken his letter and gone on a walk. It wasn't often I received a letter. Dad sometimes sent a few lines but he wasn't fond of communicating like that, he preferred to talk rather than write out his thoughts. Jim wrote well and had beautiful, elegant handwriting. He promised he'd write often and asked me to write back. I considered it. Maybe I might, after all. He was essentially my stepbrother and he had been good to me. It was mean of me to shun him. His mother's wickedness wasn't his fault and he couldn't help the fact he was the spitting image of her. And in a way I wanted news of them all; they were the only other family I knew.

As I stood reading Jim's letter, I saw Ryan coming along the cliff path and stuffed the letter in my pocket as he approached.

'That from your dad?'

'No, my brother Jim.'

Ryan face darkened. 'He's off to a posh school now, isn't he?'

'I suppose it's posh. It's a boarding school. Why? Would you want to go?'

He looked at me and a spasm of what could only be called horror passed over his face. 'Be with people all the time? Posh, poofy boys? I'd hate it. Wouldn't you hate it, Bridie, if you went to a girl's school like that?'

'I know I would,' I said. 'I'm so scared Dad will send me away too.'

'But you *can* start work at fifteen,' he said. 'You can get a job. *You* don't need any O Levels. What d'you need them for? You're a girl. You're going to be a housewife one day. My wife. I told you so.'

'Ye-es,' I said, 'But I'd like to do the things Jim's doing, history and art and literature if I was any good at them. Or maybe biology. That would be really good. That would be the only thing worth going for.'

'You don't want to end up like *that* poncey bloke,' said Ryan sharply. I looked at him in surprise. He seldom made any comment about anyone, especially such an adverse one as this. In a way I felt a bit cross to hear him run down my brother. I might run Jim down in my mind, but I didn't want anyone else to do so. Not even Ryan.

'He's not poncey,' I said. 'What d'you mean by that, anyway? He's not queer.'

'No, but he's kind of girly,' said Ryan. 'I don't like him. I don't trust him.'

'Well, it's not likely you'll ever meet him again, so I wouldn't worry about it.'

I turned away and walked on, feeling quite angry, though I had no idea why I should or why I felt a need to defend Jim. Only a moment ago I had made up my mind never to see him again and even debated not writing back to him. Now I felt sure I would do so, just to spite Ryan.

Ryan came after me and caught up, walking beside me. He said nothing but every now and then he glanced at my face. I kept it resolutely turned away from him.

'You're sulking,' he said.

'No, I'm not.'

'Yes, you are. Listen, I'm sorry to upset you over your "brother". Didn't know you liked him so much. Gotta learn to take the truth now and then, Bridie. He's a mean bloke and one day you'll find out I'm right.'

'Is that supposed to be an apology?'

'No. I don't apologise when I'm right. You're going to have to learn.'

'Why should I learn? What am I supposed to learn, Ryan?'

'What's true in life and what's false,' he said simply. 'And I'm the only one to teach you *that*, Bridie, not that poncey Jim.'

'Oh, are you!' I was even angrier now. I wanted to hit Ryan, he was such a smug bastard. I wanted to hit him hard.

'You think you know everything, don't you?' I shouted. 'You think you're dead wise and clever and all grown up now ... just because, because ... well, because you're growing a beard and read lots of brainy books. You're not someone easy to talk to, do you know that? Jim I can talk to, he's my brother ... sort of ... and that means something. You're not my family, so there. You don't understand what Jim and I have been through with Millie. *Your* mum's a lovely person ...it's easy for you to be honest and good. It's easy for you to grow up right. I wake up some days and I'm still afraid Mean Millie'll be there ready to drag me out of bed and hit me with the poker if she's mad at me or push me down the stairs. You know nothing at all about how nasty life can be, Ryan Waterman!'

I ran out of breath, hoarse with yelling at him. We stopped and stared at one another, there on the top of the cliff, silhouetted against the hazy autumn sky. A weird, intense feeling was running through me and I almost choked with it. Ryan suddenly took my arm, pulled me towards him and kissed me fiercely on the lips. Then, letting go, he strode off back to the cottages.

Chapter 11

As always, Ryan carried on as if nothing had ever happened. I couldn't understand what made him tick, which both infuriated and intrigued me. I loved him so much yet he remained cool and detached towards me. I wanted him to kiss me again, wanted to feel his warmth, hold his hand, hear him say he loved me or even that he liked me and that I was special to him. He said nothing of the sort but spoke as he always did about mundane matters or spoke not at all. Sometimes I hated him in equal measure to my love.

It was the loveliest Christmas that year. Dad came down to see us on Christmas Day. He said the boys had elected to go to Millie's for which I was deeply grateful. Ryan glanced over at me when Dad imparted the news, perhaps to see my reaction. He could see I was relieved and that seemed to please him.

Mr Waterman wasn't able to get off the light for Christmas Day. The weather suddenly changed and a gale Force Nine was blowing the waves into a frenzy so that he was compelled to spend a few more days offshore before the relief could come over. From all accounts he wasn't that bothered by it. Sheila. said he never did like Christmas much, thought it was all a lot of fuss and bother and eating too much.

'Can't wait to get back to work, can he?' she said with a sigh. 'Holidays mean nothing to Sid and we've never been away anywhere except the places where we've lived when he's on different lights. That way, we've been around from north of England to the south, from east to west. So far this is our favourite place and thankfully we've been here a few years now but who's to know how long that'll last? Trinity House are very good, they'll take account of the keeper's families and their problems but if a man is needed somewhere else then off he has to go, no question. Not that that would bother Sidney, he wouldn't fight against it. Sometimes I wonder if he's forgotten we exist over here. Even when he *is* here I get the feeling that if I stand still for too long he'll start polishing me.'

I was thrilled to see Dad and pleased to see the Waterman family welcome him with affection. Susan often hung around Joe; to my amusement she had developed a sort of crush on him. Even Ryan sat and talked with Dad, a rare thing by all accounts. He seemed to enjoy listening to Dad's stirring adventures. Joe had been around a lot, what with his time in the Navy and in the War. He was a restless fellow, I realised it now. Staying in one place never really suited him for long.

'Tell us about when you were in Cairo and how you fought with the Aussie in a bar over a lady,' said Susan, this being her favourite tale for some reason. For someone so soppy and girly, she had a strange penchant towards the violent activities of very masculine men. Maybe it made her feel safe if a man was proved tough. She liked to get Dad to roll up his sleeve and flex his biceps and show her his tattoos. I could just see the sort of bloke she'd end up marrying – a cross between Mr Universe and King Kong, but without the brains of either of them.

Sheila enjoyed fussing over Dad, seeing as her own bloke wasn't there. I felt sorry for her, she so liked looking after people and Sid Waterman just didn't seem to appreciate all the good things she did for him.

'We've made a specially big Christmas cake,' she announced to us all when dinner was over – a sumptuous dinner with chicken, mounds of roast potatoes, stuffing, home-grown parsnips, carrots and green beans. 'That way, Joe, you can take some back when you go off again, to share with the lads on your turn out there. There'll be plenty left for when Sidney get home. He loves fruit cake more than anything else.'

'More than his beloved light?' joked Dad. He knew Sidney well by now, having had to put up with his obsessive efficiency for three months.

'Oh, Lord, no. He loves his light more than anything in the world,' said Sheila, with a laugh. The smile faded swiftly and I knew that she was not happy deep down. Dad always cheered her with his stories and his good humour. He made it all sound such fun on the light.

'Nothing more intriguing than meeting so many different blokes. Just as you get to know their funny little ways off they go again and along come another lot of new faces. Or else you go back from leave ashore to find the company changed yet again. But *they're* all old hands and know one another pretty well. I'm still a new boy. I like meeting new folks all the time – suits me. Some like to chat a lot, others hardly say a word, some have lots of interesting hobbies, others just read the old papers brought with the last boat or do the crossword puzzles. One chap is mad on chess and I'm no mean hand at that myself so I always give him a game.'

'That'll be Amos Anderson,' said Sheila who was sitting cosily in her deep armchair by the fire, busy crocheting squares for another of her bedspreads. She never stopped doing something useful, even on Christmas Day.

'That's the one. He's a big chap! Must be nigh on six foot six. Makes me feel a dwarf and I thought I was pretty tall.'

'A big man in stature, but not in mind,' said Sheila. 'I hope you let him beat you. He hates to lose.'

'Aye, I noticed that,' said Dad, 'but I'm afraid I like to win as well. So I did beat him a few times, which makes him challenge me to yet another game. He could keep it up all night but I value my shut-eye and have to leave it in the end. So he always saves the game and corners me next time round and we have to finish it, willy-nilly. In the end I let him win just to get a breathing space.'

'There's men for you. Always competitive!'

'Oh, it's the way we are. Can't let ourselves get beaten.'

I'd saved up what little pocket money Dad gave me and had bought him a new tobacco pouch. His old one was wearing at the sides and he'd stuck it together with bits of black sticky tape, the sort electricians use for wiring. Shreds of tobacco kept escaping onto the floor and though Sheila never seemed to mind, I did.

'Honestly, there's enough here to roll a new cigarette, Dad,' I said picking up all the bits and pieces and putting them into one of Ryan's Rizla papers. Ryan had taken to smoking more openly now, even when his dad was around. Mr Waterman never said anything about it; in fact he began to offer one from his own packet or ask Ryan to roll him a fag now and then. Ryan told his mum he did it to cover the smell of her own cigarettes. He knew his dad would be angry if he found any of the women smoking. Sid seemed to think it was a masculine camaraderie thing and anyway, he always let Ryan do much as pleased.

I tried one once, lighting up a half smoked cigarette that Sheila had left in the ashtray. It tasted foul and nearly choked me. I couldn't understand how people ever got used to the nasty things and swore never to bother again.

'I'll get myself another pouch some time,' said Dad unperturbed when I told him off about it. I knew he'd never bother till it fell apart in his hands and it was time to sort it out.

It was such fun to go out Christmas shopping with Abbi from next door in the second-hand car she'd bought. It was a rattling, ancient old Ford that looked as if it might lose a door or a wheel any minute but as Abbi said, 'it did the trick'. Finding a special tobacco shop in Penzance, I got Dad some cherry-flavoured tobacco and a lovely dark brown leather pouch with a zip across it and a green tartan dog on the front. It was good to find something he needed, something useful and personal. He was really pleased and filled it with the tobacco straight away, throwing the old one in the wastebasket.

'You're a thoughtful lass, Bridie,' he said and gave me a kiss.

Scouring the bookshops, I'd found Ryan a secondhand book on Cornish sea birds.

I presented it to him, all nicely wrapped in Christmassy paper. He opened it up slowly, as if savouring the surprise, folding the paper neatly and taking so long I wanted to scream with the suspense. He had a lot of his father in him, did Ryan.

His eyes lit up on seeing the book and he gave me one of

those lovely smiles that made my knees turn to jelly every time. I wished he'd give me a kiss like Dad had done but that would never happen. Ryan was very private and hated shows of public affection. Instead, he was in a good mood all day and smiled at me a lot which I think was far better than a kiss any time.

'You really like the book?' I asked yet again and he would patiently say, 'Best thing I've had in years, Bridie.'

For Susan I got one of those books where you cut out dolls and various dresses, and change their clothes by putting the dress on the cut-out doll. She loved that sort of daft thing and it kept her quiet for a while after dinner which was a relief. For Sheila I bought a new tablecloth as she'd complained all the colour had gone out of her old one. So she was happy too. I felt very pleased with myself. My own presents were enjoyable, especially the lovely new fountain pen Dad gave me, but giving to others and having people pleased with me was my best gift. Ryan's gift to me I savoured most. He'd bought me a book by Daphne du Maurier called *Rebecca* and for someone who didn't think much of novels, it was a great choice. I was lost in it for hours.

'Had a boat on the cover,' he said laconically when I asked why he'd bought this particular book.

'I've always wanted to read it,' I said, 'how did you know?'

'I know you like that stuff,' he said with a shrug.

I was touched, despite his efforts at indifference.

The bombshell dropped early in the year. Sidney Waterman was home on his month's leave and he gathered us all together in the parlour and announced he was to be posted up north to be PK on Longstone Rock, the famed lighthouse where Grace Darling had lived and from whence she had performed her heroic rescue of the men from the wrecked *Forfarshire* steamer in 1838. I knew it was one of the bleakest and most dangerous spots of Britain, out there on the Northumberland coasts. It would suit Sid Waterman fine. The isolation wouldn't bother him at all.

'Means we'll all have to move,' he said. He lit a cigarette

he'd been holding between his knuckles and seemed very pleased with himself.

Sheila looked stunned. She knew it would be coming sometime but one always lives in false hope.

'If you're on an island rock, where the dickens are we to live?' she demanded. 'Ryan's okay, he's got his college in London all fixed to go to when he's done his O levels this summer and then he's off to the Army – but we've got Susan's education to think of, Sidney, I don't want to go up north again. It's cold and wet and awful. I'm a southerner by birth. Can't you have a go at Trinity House and ask for a land light this time? Surely you're due a land light? If you go up there we'll probably end up in some awful rented place in the nearest town or council flats or some such.'

'No use complaining to Trinity. They won't do anything about it, Sheila. That's where I'm to go, so go I must. It's my duty, isn't it? And it's your duty to follow on. They'll find you somewhere, don't worry. There'll surely be a place in Seahouses and you can get the boat over to see me now and then. Then the youngsters can all go to a local school instead of you teaching them at home. That'll be good for them, 'specially now Ryan's getting ready for his exams. It'll give you a break. It'll be a good thing all round, you see if I'm not right. You'll be less isolated in a town.'

'Well, let me tell you I've never felt isolated here. I've my neighbours and the kids with me. It's only a walk down to the Cove and I like the people down there, made some nice friends. I love it here,' said Sheila and I knew she was holding in her anger. 'I realise we'll have to move on; this cottage'll be for the next PK and his family now. But there's no way I'm going to Seahouses or anywhere else up north, Sidney Waterman, so get that in your head. We'll never see you at all. You'll be off to the Farnes when you're on leave looking at seabirds and whatever else. Maybe we'll go to my mother's place near Bournemouth for a bit till things are sorted out. We'll stay there awhile.'

Mr Waterman was taken aback by this and looked annoyed as he stubbed out his half-smoked cigarette in a saucer. 'Well, I want you *near* me, not in bloody Bournemouth. Ryan'll love going round the islands and seeing the birds and the grey seals, won't you, lad?'

He looked at his son and I knew Ryan felt torn by the idea. It sounded just the sort of place he *would* love. But his loyalty lay with his mother so he shook his head.

His father looked exasperated. 'Look, woman, it's a great place up there. You'll get used to it.'

Sheila made no answer, just looked upset. Susan looked upset too for her mother's sake. She didn't really grasp what was going on. Ryan remained as impassive as ever; he wasn't bothered one way or another. As for myself, I was terrified. What was to happen to me? Dad would surely send me to some boarding school amongst strangers and that would be awful. Worst of all I would lose Sheila and Ryan and even Soppy Susan. I loved them all so much and felt the future bleak without them. They were my family now.

Sheila saw my look of misery and put an arm about me saying, 'It's all right, Bridie, dear; you'll come with us if your dad is agreeable about it. You're like my own daughter now. You'll like it in Bournemouth.'

The relief made me laugh out loud. I was happy again. Ryan nodded at me with a faint smile and he too seemed pleased.

'No,' he said, 'we won't let you go to strangers, Bridie.'

I shut my eyes and felt a weight fall from me. It was the best thing anyone had ever said to me.

Chapter 12

In the summer of 1955 Ryan sat for his O Levels. He passed with distinction, hardly surprising as he worked so hard at achieving them. He had long ago decided to apply for an engineering course at a technical college near London. The day he left us was a sad parting. We all clung to him, sobbing to see him go.

'Leave off, women,' he said, 'you'd think I was going to the North Pole! I'll be back to see you in the holidays.'

'If you're like your dad, you won't,' said Sheila She was loath to let her son go but knew she must. Ryan was no Andy, clinging to his mum. He couldn't wait to be out in the man's world, couldn't wait to get to Trinity House after his National Service was done and apply for a lighthouse-keeping post. Trinity knew he was going to apply and he'd as good as got the job but Mr Waterman felt it would be a good thing for him to get some more skills under his belt. There was always the rumour that modern equipment would one day make the lighthouse-keepers redundant. Just a rumour as yet but a nagging fear for many who once thought they had a job for life.

Sheila had changed somehow. She seemed sadder and less contented. Everything had changed. I missed the cliffs, the expanses of sea and sky in Cornwall. We lived in Bournemouth now with Sheila's mum, a nice lady called Ethel Alcott. She was a widow and seemed to enjoy having the house full of people. I could see how Sheila had taken after her mother, the same round, pleasant face and plump, mumsy figure. Except that Ethel had hundreds of wrinkles; her face was like a well-used map of Britain. She was a kindly soul and made me feel just as welcome as if she'd known me all her life and I was a part of the family.

It wasn't too far to walk from her neat little semi-detached house over to Durley and Alum Chine, along the wooded cliffs with long sandy beaches down below that stretched all the way to Poole Harbour. It was beautiful but also a seaside town with all the attendant summer tourists, men with string vests and knotted hankies on their heads to protect them from the occasional bursts of sunshine, kids yelling and screaming over their buckets and spades and bored-looking mothers yearning for a cup of tea. Beach huts ranged most of the route along the beach at Alum Chine. I hated beach huts and the sort of people who used them. The sea wasn't meant to be a place for toe-dabblers. It was a place to be in touch with the elements in all their wildness and beauty. These people came to gawp; they had no real understanding or respect for that mighty watery world out there. They moaned if it wasn't non-stop sunny for the few miserable moments they chose to come and invade the shores. As if the weather gods cared about *them* and their pallid, flaccid townie bodies and the sudden fashion to be browned off like a Sunday roast! Anyway, who needed perpetual sunshine? I loved it most when the wind whipped up my hair and almost blew me into the waves; when I was the plaything of the elements yet totally alive, conscious, flowing with it all.

No, it wasn't the same as walking out in the early mornings from Trinity Cottages and finding oneself right out there on the cliff tops with a quick clamber down to our special little cove. I'd loved the isolation of it all in Cornwall, walking about on my own on the sands with just the sea and the sky and the sound of herring-gulls screaming over the cliffs and wheeling above my head in huge sweeping arcs; it made me feel real and myself, totally centred and at peace. As soon as I was with other people, I felt unreal, not sure who I was, trying to be someone they wanted me to be or imagined me to be.

Sheila wanted to go back to teaching at a college again. I was fifteen now and didn't need to go to school officially but Dad said he thought I ought to go back and do my O Levels.

'Oh, Dad, must I go,' I wailed. 'Couldn't I stay and help Ethel look after the house. Get a little job somewhere. Why can't I?'

'I don't want you abandoning your education so early,' said Dad. 'Look, it's only another year and by then I hope to be made up to AK. Maybe we can get a place where we can stay together for a bit. You'll want to be doing something with yourself some day. I don't want you blaming me that you aren't educated enough. I've done my best by the boys and I mean to do my best by you, too, Bridie. No, don't argue and sulk now, it's for your own good; you'll thank me for it one day. You're a bright girl and I don't want your abilities wasted. You deserve a good education.'

'Ryan says it's a waste of time for a girl,' I said mournfully. 'He thinks I'll just be a good housekeeper and wife.'

'Oh, does he?' said Dad. He paused and looked at me keenly, making me blush. 'Oh, *does* he?' Dad muttered again and lit his pipe and regarded me with interest. 'Well, Bridie, take no notice, he's just a lad and he's off to his college, then he'll be off to the Army. That'll open his eyes, that will. At the moment, he doesn't understand. He just spouts out narrow-minded stuff like his dad.'

'I thought you liked Ryan?' I said in surprise.

'I do like the lad,' he replied as he tamped down the tobacco he'd just taken from the lovely pouch I'd bought him. 'He's a good, honest, hard-working young fellow. He's born to be on the Lights, he is and he'll do well. But he can be very moody and withdrawn. That's a bad sign. Now you, Bridie, are getting that way too and that's a danger. I don't want you to get like that.'

'I don't want to be with strangers, Dad,' I said, nigh on tears.

'You won't be. You've Sheila and Ethel and Susan to come home to every day. But you need some companions your own age, need to get out of yourself more. You are going to school.'

And that was that.

The funny thing is I really loved school once I got used to it. I found that the other kids were interested in me and my background. There was no Andy there to set them against me or tease me and belittle me. I was almost esteemed. First of all the teachers put me in a lower class because they thought that, having been taught at home, I'd be as dim as a Tok H lamp. I proved them wrong, vindicating Sheila's wonderful teaching methods. My hand shot up in answer to every question and it was the other kids who struck me as slow, disinterested and dim. I was transferred a week later to a higher class and shone there too. I'd never shone at school in my life and it gave me a real impetus.

Susan was thrilled as she was always outgoing and enjoyed people. She was in her element at her new school and seemed so happy that when Mr Waterman said Trinity had found them a council house in Hull, Sheila wrote back saying she'd rather stay down south till Susan finished at school. (She didn't exclude me, she said, but she felt my Dad might have other plans some time), Mr Waterman replied that that was fine by him. I got the feeling even then that that marriage was over. A gulf wider than the Atlantic and just as cold separated these two people now. I knew the signs too well.

By the time I'd taken my O Levels, life took a different turn again. I contemplated taking a job, then wondered about doing A levels in the sixth form or college and maybe some sort of catering course. As always, I wasn't too sure what to do and dithered. Then it turned out Dad got made up to Assistant Keeper quite quickly and put in for a land light. He was always lucky, and there was a post available within the month in Devon, one of the keepers having died. Sheila said that, sorry as she was he was stepping in a dead man's shoes, it was sheer luck and no mistake to get chosen so fast and had he bribed the Elder Brethren at Trinity House or something? Dad smugly reckoned it was due to his impeccable service in the Navy as well as his time spent here and there as SAK in which he'd learnt the job in no time.

'Not that you have to be that brainy to learn all that stuff,' he said, 'it's a doddle compared to being in the engine room on a ruddy great destroyer. You just have to like cleaning, cooking and housework.'

Obviously there was more to it than that but in Dad's eyes, he'd fallen on soft times.

'Reckon even I could I do it?' I asked.

'Bridie, you could do it standing on your head. I'll dress you as a lad and send you up to Trinity for a job.'

Which I would have loved but Dad laughingly explained, just as Ryan had done, that it wouldn't do to let a girl live in such close intimacy with two or three men who weren't related to her. Grace Darling had lived at Longstone all her life with her family, reclusive and glad to avoid the frenzy of interest that had surrounded her heroic act. She had died soon after, poor soul, probably due to the shock of being the centre of attention and having to give away half her hair as souvenirs to Victorian hero-worshippers.

'Besides which the fellows swear all the time, every other word is effin' this and that. Not very nice for a young girl, eh?'

'Maybe I'd teach them better manners if I was there.'

'Now that would be hard work. It'd just break our hearts not to be blokes and cuss as much as we like all the time.'

' Huh! It just shows that men are uncouth beasts,' I said. I couldn't imagine Ryan swearing so freely, but who knew? Men seemed to become different creatures when there were no women about to keep an eye on them.

Dad asked me to go for a walk with him along the Chines and we set off in companionable silence.

'How do you feel about my new post?' he asked.

'I'm thrilled, Dad.' I added. 'I am coming with you, aren't I?'

He hesitated just the tiniest bit and I looked at him in alarm.

'Do you really want to come, Bridie? Start Point is right out in the wilds, right at the end of a headland over the English Channel. It's miles from anywhere. If you do come, they'll give me one of the smaller cottages there. That would be nice, of course but, sweetheart, I don't want to hold you back like this. You'll be leaving school now and may want to do something else, go somewhere else. I can't stop you and I wouldn't want to if you've other plans.'

I took a hold of his hands and looked him full in the eye. 'Dad, I've been looking forward to keeping house for you someday. I want to come, of course I do. I can't stay forever with Ethel and Sheila – it's a real squash in her little house. I *want* to come, Dad. I want to come so much!'

He smiled at my earnestness. 'Then you certainly will – there'll be plenty of room in the cottage adjoining the Light and you can housekeep for us both and I'll even pay you a little wage. That's fair, isn't it? And a great little housekeeper you are too, thanks to Sheila.'

'Oh, thanks to Millie as well,' I said with a grimace.

'She didn't teach you anything,' said Dad scornfully, 'she just bullied you, I know all about it.'

'How do you know?'

'Jim told me. Said she often beat you. I've not forgiven her for treating you like a servant while I was away and pretending to be all nice when I was home. The two-faced bitch. Only time I see her now is when I pick up the boys to take them for a day out in the holidays. She's as miserable and sharp as ever. What changed her so? She seemed such a nice kid when I first met her. A pretty kid.'

'She's still sort of pretty,' I said.

'No, not now,' sighed Dad. 'Oh, she's always smart, always well turned out but she's got a face to go with her inner landscape; harsh lines, down-turned mouth, angry eyes. She looks mean.'

'Mean Millie,' I murmured.

'What's that?'

'Oh, nothing.'

Just before Ryan left for college I asked him, 'Will you come to see us sometimes?'

'Seems I'll be busy in my holidays,' he said, 'visiting Mum and Susan, visiting Dad up north, visiting you and Joe when you go to Devon. When am I supposed to do all my studying?

But I'll try now and then. No promises though. Maybe I'll just give you a surprise one day.'

I gave him a curious look. '*Do* you keep your promises?'

He looked down at me from his height – for he had grown even bigger now and towered over me.

'Listen, Miss Bridie Bosworth, I always keep my promises. And you'd better keep yours.'

'Why, what have *I* promised?' I asked, astonished.

He grinned. 'That you'll be my wife, and no one else's. Mine. You hear?'

'I hear you, Ryan. But I'll only accept when you come to me some day and ask me properly. After all, this isn't exactly the sort of proposal a girl dreams about. I want bended knees and romantic moonlight – that sort of thing.'

'Well, mebbe I'll do that,' he said nodding. He smiled at my worried expression.

'You don't believe me, do you?' he said. 'You don't trust me.'

'I'm not sure you're serious,' I frowned. 'You can't be.'

'When I say a thing, I mean it,' he replied taking my chin in his hand and tilting my face up. I thought he meant to kiss me and went all funny inside but he didn't. He let my chin go when he'd contemplated me long enough.

Then he said, 'Are you still writing to that poncey brother of yours?'

'So what if I am?'

'He's not your real brother.'

'I know that,' I said, annoyed as always when this subject arose. 'You keep on saying that. Why?'

'Because he fancies you and because I can tell he's not a good bloke. Just watch him, that's all. I'll be watching him for sure.'

It never occurred to me that Jim might fancy me, as Ryan put it. I put this daft idea down to jealousy and a suspicious, misanthropic nature. It was a nice thought though because when someone is jealous of you it means they really care. As for the notion Jim fancied me – it was silly. I certainly didn't fancy him.

I carried on writing to Jim while he was still in the sixth form at St Michael's Bister and no Ryan was going to tell me I couldn't. I wasn't married to him yet. Jim's letters were chatty, sensible and normal, no sign of any special affection that was not brotherly by nature. He kept asking me to go over and see them when they went back to see Millie in their holidays.

'You needn't worry about Mum,' he said, 'she's not going to order you about any more. She's calmed down a lot. Anyway, you're sixteen now. Come over and see us as you're living so near.'

Naturally I ignored this request, so you can imagine my surprise when Jim suddenly turned up during late July in 1957 when he'd finished his A levels. He told me he had great plans for the future. He was soon due for his National Service call-up but didn't seem too bothered about that. He reckoned he would get out of it somehow.

I was still living with Ethel Alcott, waiting for Trinity to get the cottage at Start Point ready. Jim said he'd come over to Bournemouth for a day or two to see me before going over to his mother's place. I was pleased to see him, more than I thought I would be. As he stood at the door of Ethel's little house, I looked up at him in wonder, now a head taller than myself and more handsome by the minute. He was so different to Ryan, his hair fairer and his eyes a deep periwinkle blue like Dad's.

'Hi, Sis,' he said bending down to give me a hug and a kiss on the cheek. This was the first time he'd ever shown this much affection and I was warmed by it. It melted a barrier that I had put between us, though quite why I wasn't sure. It was nothing to do with Ryan and his daft notions, more to do with Mean Millie.

'Ethel, this is my brother, Jim.' I introduced him to the old lady who looked up at this fair handsome lad and went all soppy.

'Sit, down, dear, sit down. I'll put on the kettle and make us a nice cup of tea. Are you staying over at the Seaview Court? Good place, isn't it? How long you staying for, then?'

'Just a couple of days.'

'Oh, nice. Then you're off home?'

'Yes, for a bit. I mean to spend some of the holidays with a friend in London. He's going to show me the sights.'

'Ooh, lucky you. I've never been to London. Don't suppose I ever will now.'

She brought out a barrel of chocolate digestives and set it before him, urging him to partake. Jim had a soft charm and a smile that made women run about wanting to please him. Susan, who ever had an eye for the lads, was very taken with him and ran upstairs to change into her new jeans and put on some pink lipstick. I don't think Sheila even knew Susan had any lipstick. She'd probably nicked it from Woolworths and hid it in her bottom drawer with a few other forbidden items.

However, to Susan's annoyance, after we'd all had supper, Jim asked me to go out for a stroll and talk. He wanted, he said, to hear about my new life and what I was going to do. She gave me a bit of a dirty look as I put on my coat but I just shrugged and took no notice of her pouts. I vaguely felt that Jim was my property, not hers.

We walked down to the promenade and right along it to the very end, chatting about this and that. The wind was blowing and I kept pushing back my hair from my face as it whipped about me. Jim glanced at me when I did this, smiled and drew me into a more secluded spot. Here we stood and looked out over the sea for a bit, he leaning on the railings gazing at the far horizon.

'I've got such plans, such hopes, Bridie,' he said. His voice whipped away on the wind as if travelling to those far-off places where his heart seemed to be.

'What sort of plans?'

He turned and came over to me and sat beside me on a little wooden bench, our backs sheltered by a wall.

'I want to study law,' he said. 'I'm sure I've passed all my A levels, hopefully with a few distinctions. I don't mind hard work. Not at all. The harder the better – I love a challenge. And I'll sort out the damned call-up if it's the last thing I do. No way am I wasting my time square-bashing and being bawled at by some uneducated idiot of an NCO. I'll find a way out of that, you wait and see. It's the finances, though. Not sure how I'll do it but I'm damned sure I will somehow. When I want a thing, I want it with passion.'

I was impressed by this speech and looked at him with interest.

'I wish I could understand this passion to do something,' I said. 'I have no idea at all what I want to do. I feel such a dull person compared to you and Ryan. You both know what you want. I don't really want anything much, to be honest. One minute I want to be content and peaceful and run a home, but then sometimes – just sometimes – I really want to do something daring, break out and try a new life altogether.'

'You're not dull, you never will be, Bridie. I don't think you're dull at all.'

'But I am. I'm not clever like you or Ryan.'

'Ryan? Is that the glum fellow I met in Cornwall?'

'Yes, but he's not glum, Jim. He's ... ' I gave it some thought. 'He's sort of strong and silent. He's very deep.'

Jim looked at me thoughtfully. 'So you still have a thing for him?'

I let my gaze drop for a moment then nodded.

To my amazement, Jim seized my arm in a fierce grip. 'By God, you do, don't you? Dammit, he's a surly brute. What can you see in a fellow like that?'

He was shaking my arm quite violently. I pulled myself away and hit out at him, angry at this outburst. 'Get off! What *is* up with you! Look, it's none of your business who I fancy and none of Ryan's either. You two get on my nerves. Ryan thinks it's you who fancies *me*.'

'I do more than that.' His response was as fierce as his look. 'I love you, Bridie, I always have. You know that.'

'Oh – you don't! You can't! You're being silly, Jim. Just stop saying such things. I don't want you to be in love with me. You're my brother ...you're ... you're Jim.'

'But I'm not your damned brother, am I?'

His face, usually so sweet and fair, had darkened and he

gripped both my arms and turned me towards him. I actually felt a little afraid of him. His eyes looked like Millie's; their vivid blue piercing and frightening in intensity, filled with the desire to conquer and be in control.

I gave a little scream and broke away and began to run up the promenade. Jim set off after me. Catching up, he caught my arm again.

'Bridie!'

'Let go!' I shouted.

'Listen to me, damn you! I'm *not* your brother, d'you hear? I have as much right to you as he does.'

'You haven't any rights. Nobody has "rights" over another person! You talk as if I was a mare or a sack of potatoes or something. Let me alone, Jim!'

As I twisted about, I suddenly saw Ryan, walking along the road in our direction. I thought I must be dreaming. But it *was* him and he came running towards us.

'Let her go!' He echoed my words. Jim dropped my arm and we both stared at him in astonishment.

'Ryan? What …how …what are you doing here?' I stuttered.

'Come on a surprise visit,' he growled, 'and in fuckin' good time, it seems.'

He glowered at Jim who stood and stared back at him challengingly. The fair lad and the dark one standing their ground and me – as always – piggy in the middle. I gaped at them both and felt like a heroine in a book. Boring Bridie Bosworth, a heroine in a book.

'Go back home, Jim Bosworth,' said Ryan quietly. 'You got no business here.'

'I'll visit my sister, if I like. I've more business and more of a claim on her than you,' Jim retorted with passion.

'As a brother, maybe. But you aren't no brother, are you? You're no relation at all. And she's my girl, so don't go sniffing around her – or else.'

'Or else, what?'

'You'll live to regret it.'

'Oh, yes!' sneered Jim. 'You and whose army?'

'S'cuse me,' I piped up at this point. 'Do I get a say in any of all this?'

'Exactly,' said Jim, his hands stuffed in his pockets as if afraid he might give Ryan a poke in the eye. 'What *are* Bridie's feelings in this? She says I don't own her. You don't own her either, you great oaf.'

Ryan, normally so slow to arouse, lashed out at Jim and sent him sprawling.

'She's *my* girl,' he said, standing over him, his eyes dark and dangerous, 'she's going to marry me. So you keep off.'

'Oh, Jim, I'm so sorry,' I wailed and went to try and help him up but he shook off my arm with a petulant gesture and rose. He shot Ryan a look of pure hate. Ryan just stood, arms folded, a certain look of satisfaction on his face.

'Ryan, you bully!' I said, 'I'm not marrying you or anyone, so stop acting like this. Just say you're sorry to poor Jim.'

' "Poor Jim"! Fuck poor Jim!' snorted Ryan in disgust and, turning on his heel, strode off back to his grandma's house.

Jim looked at me and dusted himself down.

'You see,' he said, 'you see what I mean? He's uncivilised and stupid, too. Oh, Bridie, I'm glad you don't love him. That's so strange, his turning up like that. But it proved my point. '

'What do you mean, I don't love him?' I said, glum now as I watched Ryan's retreating figure. 'Jim, you'd better not come back to Ethel's with me. Ryan's here now and you two are not meant to be together in one room. And I want to see him so much. I'll come over to the Seaview Court tomorrow to say goodbye before you go on to Broughampton.'

'Don't bother,' said Jim in a huff. 'Go to your precious Ryan. See if I care.'

But he did care, I knew that now.

Ryan was seated at the table with a cup of tea when I got back. He looked up when I got in, his face expressionless, not returning the sheepish smile I gave him.

'*You* asked him over, I suppose,' was his morose comment.

'No, I did not. He wrote and said he'd be coming over for a

few days. If you'd said you were coming I'd have told him not to bother.'

'I wanted to surprise you all.'

'Well, you did that. Why do you hate Jim so much, Ryan? You must stop hating him. He's my only relation apart from Dad. I don't count Andy and Millie. I know Jim's not a real one but we did grow up together.'

'I'll hate who I like. I've told you, I don't trust him and certainly not around you. And what was he doing when I came up? Didn't look like he was being "brotherly" to me. Looked like a lot of other things. Be straight with me, Bridie. I can't bear it if you're not. If you'd rather have him, then say so. I agree, I don't own you. You must decide.'

I sighed. 'Look, I can take care of myself, Ryan. Jim and I were just squabbling over some silly thing. It was nothing, honestly. You know I love you. You know I do.' Tears came to my eyes and my voice wobbled.

He rose. Ethel and his mother were busy getting supper in the kitchen and Susan had gone out and wasn't back yet. He took me quickly in his arms and kissed me, holding me tight against his strong wiry body. I could feel him hardening as he pushed for a moment against my hips and it made such a strong ripple of longing flame up inside me that I wanted to marry him there and then. No one had held me, kissed me like this and it made me gasp. I knew there was no one else in the world for me.

'You're *my* girl, Bridie,' he said. His hand stroked my cheek with sudden tenderness and I felt myself melt as I stared up at him and saw the look of deep, profound feeling in his brown eyes. So different to Jim's frightening blue stare. I gave a sudden shiver at the memory.

Ryan pulled me closer.

'Don't be afraid of anything,' he said softly. It was as if he knew and understood what my thoughts were. 'I'm here; I'll always be here for you. Keep away from that fellow, Bridie. He's evil.'

Chapter 13

It was wonderful being out by the wild sea again. Start Point was situated on a lonely peninsula and had guided vessels through the English Channel for over a century. It was a beautiful circular building with a crenulated top and at nights it looked like some huge candle on an iced cake. I loved to see it silhouetted against the horizon at sundown, gleaming white in the sunshine or looming up in the sea mists like a ghost. Dad said that Trinity House planned to run the light by electricity very soon and that would make everyone's job so much easier. They wouldn't have to measure out oil or fiddle about with paraffin like many of the other lights he'd worked on but for the present the oil still had to be brought up the centre pole up to the lantern room and the lamp carefully lit each night.

The Assistant Keeper's quarters were close to the light with paths between and a wall enclosing them from the fierce roaring of the headland winds. The Principal Keeper had a larger dwelling a little further away. Little terraced plots of gardens provided vegetables and there were chicken coops and a pigsty too. The shifts were on a regular alternating basis over three days and then Dad would have off twenty-four hours. He could then spend the day at home, working on the garden, the evening by a cosy fire. But if there was a foggy spell then all the men had to stand by in case of problems.

I loved taking care of our neat little house and found the other keeper's wives friendly and pleasant and a good deal less neurotic than the ones at Cornwall. But then we all lived a far more normal life with our men coming home from work like anyone else.

'Not that we don't have our ups and downs,' said one of the women when I remarked on how nice and friendly everyone seemed, 'we had a right argy-bargy here once when one of the wives had tantrums over the fact that she felt she was doing more than her fair share of work looking after the chickens or the pigs or something daft. Stupid little things can set folks off, can't they? But this lot's okay. We all get on well enough. I mean, you have to out here in the wilds. Thank goodness things are a bit easier now the butcher calls on a Friday and we don't have all that hard work getting food like in the old times.'

I was also grateful that the postman brought us milk along with the post each day while the baker would call on Tuesdays and every fortnight a grocer would come along in his van with his goods and one could order something for the next time too. Otherwise it was a long walk to the next village over the windy headland or along the coastal path. Sometimes the PK would take us into town in his car if it was his day off, but that wasn't often. Mostly we relied on the local garage to send a taxi to take us all into Kingsbridge for a shopping trip, a real treat.

The PK's wife was called Mary Atkinson and after we'd been there a while, she couldn't contain her curiosity any longer and asked me, 'Bridie, why don't your dad let you get a job? You must be sick of looking after him. Don't you want to be with people your own age?'

'I'm perfectly happy, Mary,' I said. 'It's got nothing to do with Dad. I *choose* to be at home and love looking after him.'

'Oh.' She shrugged and gave me a look that said 'this girl must be daft,' but said no more. It *was* the way I liked to live and not because Dad was some sort of Victorian tyrant who made me stay at home as they imagined. I didn't mix with her a lot because, as Dad pointed out to me, she was well in her twenties with a kiddy and other interests. I was just a youngster in her eyes and a bit of an odd one at that, my nose always buried in a book. Books that she wouldn't even begin to think of reading. I might not have been at school any longer but I was certainly continuing my education. In my own style, that is – the things I was interested in and not what others wanted to stuff in my head and heart. I liked to come to my own conclusions through reading and considering, not be obliged to absorb and then learn to spout other men and women's opinions.

Looking back, I realise now that everyone was very curious about Dad and me.

'Is your mum dead, Bridie?' Walter Atkinson once asked me. Walter was a nice man, his face rough and wrinkled with being outdoors and having the wind hurl itself against his face so much. There was a look about all these men that was the same. Their faces were hewn as if from granite, hard, rough, weather-beaten, yet with great nobility and wisdom in their eyes. I thought they were all marvellous human beings and understood why Ryan felt they were the only kind of men he could trust, men of the sea, men with the wind and the waves singing in their blood.

'Yes, Walter,' I replied truthfully. 'My mum's dead. She died when I was born.'

He gave me a quick, appraising look and for a while he remained silent.

'Poor kid,' he said after a while. 'So that's why you're so canny with all the housework. You've had to learn young.'

'I learnt very young,' I said, 'but I enjoy doing it. It doesn't bother me.'

'I hope you're not lonely, lass,' he said. 'We all worry that you might be lonely-like when your dad's on the light, especially nights. Always pop over if you want a bit o' company. We'll be getting a telly installed, did you know that? Come over any time to watch with us. Don't be shy about it.'

I smiled and thanked him. It was so thoughtful and I knew his concern was genuine. After this conversation, he and Mary were kinder than ever towards me and Dad, thinking us poor lonely souls in a harsh world. They knew nothing of Mean Millie or anything else and as Dad never mentioned the past, except to talk about his Navy days, they kept their illusions.

Sometimes I would babysit for Mary and Walter if they wanted a quick drink together in the pub on his day off and they were grateful for that. I soon learnt to get the baby off to sleep, then curl up on the sofa with a book and enjoy the peace and quiet. It wasn't often that little Tony woke up, he was a contented little thing, and anyway, I didn't mind if he did, he was so cute. I loved to cuddle and kiss him, stroke his soft little arms and legs and sing songs till I put him back in his cot. Tony would lie there with his blue eyes wide open, listening to me, clutching my finger in his tight little fist, till slowly, slowly, the lids would droop – open again – and then finally shut tight. I'd sneak back downstairs and straight into Gaskell or Trollope, or whatever was the latest attention grabber. Television never had much appeal for me at that time apart from *Emergency Ward Ten* or funny old Sergeant Bilko.

'You'll never find a boyfriend living here in the wilds,' said Mary one day as she took Tony back from my arms. She gave me a sidelong look full of curiosity. Tony actually wailed when taken from me and held out his arms to come back.

'Tony can be my boyfriend,' I smiled. Mary didn't look too pleased that Tony wanted to come back to me and not to her.

'Not natural for a young girl not to get out,' she pursued, 'you ought to be making time off to go to the village hall. They have a dance every Saturday night – you could jive! An' there's the youth club and that. Wish I was single again sometimes,' she added with a sigh. 'I get tired of living here. Get really bored. Nothing to stop *you*, though.'

It was peculiar, her attitude. Almost as if she was angry that I was young, unencumbered and single but not making proper use of the fact.

'I don't think I'm the dancing sort,' I said with a sigh, 'and I do have a boyfriend, anyway. He's at college in London. That's why I don't see him much.'

'Oh. Right.' Now she seemed surprised. 'Will he visit you here?'

'I hope he'll come soon,' I replied and my eyes flew off to the horizon as if seeking him. Ryan was out there somewhere, doing something this very minute, but I had no idea what or with whom. I longed for him deeply and my heart travelled along the line of my eyes, along the paths and roads and buildings till it reached him wherever he was.

One afternoon, Dad came back from a trip to Kingsbridge and he had a little basket with him.

'Take a look, ducky,' he said.

I opened the basket and out shot a little fluffy ball of fur, straight across the room and halfway up the sofa before I recovered from my surprise.

'Oh, Dad, a kitten,' I said, thrilled to bits.

We named him Stevie, after the famous Stevenson family. *Treasure Island* and *Dr Jekyll and Mr Hyde* were Dad's favourite childhood books. The Stevensons were all brilliant architects and engineers who had built loads of lighthouses around the treacherous Scottish coasts. Robert Louis had tried hard to follow in his family footsteps but engineering just wasn't what he wanted to do. He wanted to be a writer. His dad was like Ryan in thinking writing a stupid pastime; he didn't understand the beauty of words. George Stevenson was creative in a practical manner but the creativity of mind and spirit eluded him. In the end Robert followed his bent and wrote his masterpieces and became far more famous than the rest of the Stevensons put together – which seemed a bit unfair as their achievements were pretty brilliant, really – but it made me think a lot about the permeating power of the written word which could be spread far and wide and influence so many.

Stevie was a delight and gave me such fun and laughter. We played hide and seek together and games with balls of wool. His eyes got quite wild with excitement when I dragged a toy felt mouse across the room. He looked so comical, I screamed with laughter every time. I forgot my age and was a child again, the child I'd never been. I'd almost forgotten about being a child, what with Millie and then sober-sides Ryan for company.

Dad made a few friends over at the local village and the fellows would set off for a drink in the pub or they'd all go out for a meal. Dad offered to take me too when it was to be a meal somewhere but I preferred to stay at home and read or play records on the gramophone. It *was* lonely some nights when Dad was off on the night watches. I always woke when he came in, no matter what the hour or how quietly he crept in the door; that instinct about his presence never left me and never would. I felt him coming long before the door opened.

Chapter 14

If Mary was waiting to see what my 'boyfriend' was like, then she had a long wait. In fact I suspect she didn't believe me and thought I was making it all up. I seldom heard from Ryan while he was at college. He wasn't much of a letter writer and, as we had no private phone, he couldn't ring. I walked up to the village Post Office every week to pick up any letters but he only wrote occasional brief scrawls informing me that he hated London and couldn't wait to get away from it even if it meant going into the Army. He had seen Buckingham Palace and Madame Tussauds and thought they were the ugliest sights he'd ever clapped eyes on. The only place that seemed to impress him was Westminster with its Houses of Parliament and the huge old Cathedrals. He liked the Tower of London a lot too but then towers always impressed him, even that horrid one with its dark, gloomy, history. The stones told tales, he said, they made him think about the cruelty and shortness of life – why he should want to contemplate such things was beyond me. He made a friend at college who owned a small boat and the two of them spent any spare time from studies going up and down the river from Greenwich to Hampton Court. Apart from this, he seemed to do nothing much to amuse himself. I could tell he was unhappy, that he pined for the emptiness of the sea and the skies, the winds and the wheeling, soaring birds, but he never grumbled He worked and worked, determined to get through college and make the most of it.

I do miss you, Bridie, he wrote, *but it's a long way to come and there's Ma to visit and all the fares and such. I can't afford it. But I will come, I will.*

He never did. I began to feel it was all a dream and that he had grown apart from me or perhaps even had another girl in London. That thought made me miserable.

Jim was a far better correspondent and kept me up to date with all his news and doings. There wasn't a hint in his letters of any of the conversation or upset we'd had that time he came to Bournemouth. I was glad, because I really did like him a lot and wanted us to be friends. I assumed that he had now accepted Ryan as 'my man' and left it at that. It had just been a bit of a crush he'd had, as they say. I began to look forward to his letters but never stopped longing for Ryan.

However, the day eventually arrived when Shelia Waterman, Susan and Ryan all came to stay with us one day in early August. Ryan had finished his training at college and was due to be called up for National Service. Dad was taking his month's leave though the only problem with living next to a land light was that you were always on call. So Walter got in a relief keeper, a fellow called Bob Crankshaw who lodged in their house for a few days while Dad at last enjoyed a little break from it all.

Life had become so quiet, regular and routine that it was almost a shock to have to think of other people and their needs. Happy as I was at the thought of seeing Shelia and Susan as well as Ryan, I wished he was coming on his own. I wanted him to myself. I wanted to talk about London and his life there. Longed to have him hold me against his strong body as he had done once before. That flaming feeling running through my body! … I wanted to experience the thrill of it all over again.

I prepared loads of delicious cakes and pies in honour of the occasion. The place was so clean that Dad reckoned he could eat off the floor. Stevie kept smelling the disinfectant I'd used on the tiles and puckering his little kitty nose in disapproval. Cats are amazing creatures, quick to learn and so intelligent. Unused to furry objects under my feet, I often tripped over him or else trod on the poor mite's tail. He soon got the message and kept well out of the way when he saw me scurrying about. But when

I sat down, he was on my lap like a shot, curling up into a small brown ball and refusing to budge.

I was in a mild panic while waiting for the visitors to arrive, standing by the window and often running outdoors to see if they were coming. At long last they emerged into sight as little specks, walking along the cliff path, laboriously puffing their way up towards us. I ran part of the way to greet them. This was my family. I really felt they belonged to me and I belonged to them and my heart swelled with joy, my face creased with broad smiles.

'Why Bridie, how you've grown, just in a year!' laughed Sheila, holding me at arms' length. She hugged me and bestowed a kiss on my cheek.

She had lost a lot of weight and looked happier and prettier than I'd ever seen her. I was really surprised. I'd never thought of her as other than a homely person, a mother figure. Now she had grown her brown hair longer, had it nicely permed and she was actually wearing a bit of lipstick, mascara and little tiny pearl earrings. I'd never even guessed her ears were pierced but maybe she'd just had them done. I was both pleased and amazed at the change in her appearance and seriously don't think I'd have recognised her if I'd come across her in the street.

Susan was as soppy as always and rattled on about her new school and her pals there. Her dresses were a little more sensible now she was a high school girl but her conversation remained as pink and fluffy as ever. She went dotty over Stevie and sat and played with him, chattering away non-stop even when others were talking. It would take a sledgehammer to shut her up, but as she never seemed interested in our replies, we all just ignored her and left her talking to the cat who remained attentive only as long as he got tickled and stroked.

As for my beloved Ryan; still the dark, serious, sad eyes, the slender muscular figure, the thick brown hair over his forehead brushed back by a lazy hand now and then. Still the rich strong, deep voice, slow in its syllables, a voice that made you want to listen because it remained unhurried and spoke sense. Yet he too had subtly changed. He was less withdrawn and silent now.

Companionship at college had done him good, made him more inclined to talk. When he arrived, we stared at one another for a few moments, then he bent towards me and gave me a swift kiss on the cheek. Not even a hug. As always, I felt unsure of myself and wondered if he really cared about me any more except in a friendly manner. He spent a lot of time with Dad asking him about the light he was on and life in the Navy.

As they chatted together, Ryan often looked over at me with that serious thoughtful expression as if summing me up. My heart quivered but I returned his look without flinching. I so wanted to be alone with him, to know whether his feelings were the same. Did he still love me and want to marry me or had it all been youthful nonsense? These questions burned in my eyes and seemed to sound in the air though I said not a word. Surely he heard the unspoken words, caught them as they winged towards him from my deepest heart? His expression gave nothing away and I wondered if I would ever really get close to him, ever understand him. I said nothing to interrupt the men's conversation, just sat by the fire and watched them both, or chatted to Sheila.

We had been discussing all the ordinary things in life for some time when she suddenly leant towards me in a conspiratorial manner and said, 'You know, Bridie, I won't be Mrs Waterman much longer, my dear.'

I stared at her and for a moment the two men also ceased their animated conversation and looked over.

'What d'you mean?' I asked stupidly. I felt confused.

'Well, it's simple, isn't it?' she said with a shrug. 'I started divorce proceedings from Sidney some time ago and he's not contesting it. I've had enough of the life we've lived and he doesn't seem to give a damn one way or another. I want to enjoy life again while I'm still young.'

Dad smiled at her. He didn't seem a bit surprised or shocked by this announcement and I wondered if he already knew. Susan continued to chatter away as usual as if her mother had simply stated what kind of weather it was. Ryan dropped his eyes and looked at the floor. I wondered what he thought of it all and whether he approved of his mother's action. As for myself, I didn't blame Sheila at all. I felt she had been wonderful to put up with Sidney Waterman all these years and agreed that it was time she had a life. She already looked better for it.

I made a lovely meal and everyone uttered their praises of my cooking except Ryan. I longed to hear his praise most of all but he said nothing, just ate it all in his slow fashion as if his mind was on more important things than food and drink. However, he must have liked what he ate; the empty plate was good testimony to my cooking.

Later on, when I suggested a cup of tea, he said quietly, 'Let's go for a walk over the cliffs, Bridie, you and me. We can have tea later.'

'I want to come,' said Susan at once.

'Let them have their walk, Susan. I'll borrow Mack's van and drive you and Sheila into the village for an ice cream,' said Dad. He and Sheila exchanged a quick look and I felt that they were conniving at something and blushed. However, I was quite excited at the prospect of some time alone with Ryan.

'Oh, goody,' said Susan, 'let's go.'

We all set off together, Dad ushering Sheila before him while Susan ran on ahead, all excited at the thought of an ice cream in the village caff. I noticed that Dad helped Sheila down the steps of the cottage with a peculiar solicitude and for the first time observed something in their eyes as they looked at one another. This gave me an odd sense of jealousy and uneasiness but I didn't have time to think about it. Ryan was calling me, so I waved them goodbye and followed him as he set off up the cliff.

For a while we walked along in silence then, without looking at me, Ryan suddenly asked, 'Have you missed me, Bridie?'

'No, not one bit,' I replied with a toss of my head.

He stopped and turned to stare at me. 'Not one bit, eh? Not one little bit?'

'No. I've been very busy. Why should I miss you? You hardly ever write.'

'I've been busy too.'

I made no reply to this and after a while he said, 'Anyhow, you know I hate writing letters. Useless at it. Doesn't mean I didn't miss *you* though.'

As always, the soft tone of his voice made me tremble. I capitulated and said eagerly, 'Did you? Did you really? I'm never sure, Ryan. Never sure what you feel, you're so close a person. How can a girl be sure when a man never tells her?'

'Bridie, you don't need me tellin' you romantic stuff all the time. You should trust me and believe in me like I do you.'

'I want telling sometimes. I can't read your mind, Ryan.'

He stopped and a slow smile spread over his face. He looked down at me and I up at him and I began to tremble.

'I need proof,' I murmured.

'Proof, eh? We'll see about that.'

We were well out of sight of the cottages, though anyone up on the light could see us. However, Ryan appeared not to care about that possibility. He took me in his arms and kissed me deeply as before, pressing and growing hard against me and my naughty desire to make him suffer – just a little – melted like the morning mists before the first sun's rays.

After a while we walked on again in silence and looked at the stonechats in the bracken and gazed out over the wall at the sea. Ryan's feet turned inevitably in the direction of the lighthouse, to its front door with the elegant archway and the Trinity House arms – *Trinitas in Unitate*, Three in One – over the top. All paths led there as far as he was concerned. The gleaming white towering structure rose up against the late afternoon sky; massive, solid and strong.

'Reckon they'll let us go look inside?' said Ryan.

'Oh, they like having visitors, breaks the monotony,' I said. 'Sometimes I go up to the gallery with Dad. I love to look out over the view. You can see for miles over the town and then out to the sea and the rocks. I wish I could stay up there with him and make him and his mates dinners in the little kitchen there and bring him cups of tea in the night to keep him awake. I know I go on about it but still don't see why women can't stay on a light and help out. Your mum said there were once women keepers; there was one at Cromer – and lots of them in America too.'

'You've got a thing about it, haven't you? Fact is, you want to be Grace Darling,' smiled Ryan, 'you want to be a heroine and rescue people in distress. It's your sort of thing, Bridie. But there's no place for heroines any more.'

'Well, maybe there is,' I said, rather cross at this sweeping statement. 'I'm learning to manage a boat and I know how to put up a sail now. Who knows when it may be useful?'

'Have it your own way. I'm glad you're learning to sail. We'll take one out on the sea together some day, just you and me, shall we, Bridie?'

'I'd like that,' I said, mollified.

The idea made me happy and my happiness showed. I turned my face up to him and looking down on me, he smiled his sweet smile, bent down and gave me another little kiss, then took my hand in his, swinging it a little as we walked along.

We came to the main door and Bob Crankshaw, the relief keeper, came down the steps to greet us.

'Comin' for a visit then, are yer, Bridie? And who's the boyfriend? I saw yer a-snoggin' there! Bet yer dad doesn't know you're a-courtin', sly lass! Come on in, the pair of yer.'

I blushed to be considered as 'a-courtin' and looked up at Ryan for his reaction. He seemed amused by Bob Crankshaw and said to him, 'Seems you've forgotten me then, Mr Crankshaw. Sidney Waterman's lad, Ryan? My dad brought me up a light he was on years back and you were SAK then, green as any of them.'

Bob Crankshaw came up and peered at Ryan and stepped back in surprise.

'By heck, it *is* Ryan Waterman, spit image of his dad an' all. Thought yer had a familiar look about yer. Come on in, both of yer, come on in and have a cuppa tea.'

We were ushered into the entrance hall and smiled at Walter who was seated in the office on the ground floor.

'Hi Bridie,' he greeted me,' any chance you can babysit tonight?'

'We've got visitors, Walter,' I said with regret. 'You could bring little Tony over if you like.'

'I'll speak to Mary. Thanks for the offer.'

He stared up at Ryan. 'You look familiar, lad,' he said, rising and offering his hand.

'Sidney Waterman's boy,' said Bob.

'Well, I never! Sidney Waterman's boy, He's up North now, I hear.'

Ryan nodded, 'Yes, up at the Faroes.'

'Well, I hope?'

'Well as can be.'

'And your mother?'

'Fine.'

Walter nodded and smiled and went back to his desk. I saw him mentally filing away the information that Bridie's boyfriend had come over at last. The news would soon go round our little community.

I let Ryan and Bob walk on up the stairs ahead of me. I liked to stand for a bit in the entrance, looking up the stairwell that spiralled in a coil around the bare white walls, the iron rail forming a rib to the steps scrubbed white as snow. The light of the afternoon sun fell through various windows along the walls, creating a warm golden glow on one side, deep blue shadows on the other. It was like the shell of some exquisite giant sea creature. In the centre was the huge pole they called the weight tube which was used to pull supplies up to the top. I heard Ryan labouring behind Bob, who ran up the stairs like a young fellow despite his age.

'Come on, lad – ye'll have to git used to the stairs, yer know, if yer ever to be a keeper! Eh, I could beat yer any day, yer land lubber, you!'

I followed on slowly, stopping for breath every now and then. How did anyone ever get used to climbing up and down these stairs several times a day?

When I said this to Bob later in the little circular kitchen with the kettle singing on the tiny stove, he laughed and said, 'I was in a light once wi' a lift put in, can yer imagine? I couldn't git used to the bloody thing. There was days when it was handy-like when you were in a bit of a hurry to git from ground floor up to the service room, when there was some emergency, like. But I'd rather walk the stairs, it's good fer yer. Keeps me slim, don't yer think?'

And he was indeed very slim, almost skin and bones.

'Don't come from not eatin', though,' he said. 'We likes our food, we do. I used to be best cook on the last light I was on. That was on Eddystone out Plymouth way. But the good thing on a land light is yer can git home when your shift's over for a meal wi' the family. It's more normal, like.'

One of the supernumeraries came to join us for a cup of tea. He took a packet of biscuits out of one of the little cupboards that ranged the wall.

'Ah, me favourites, Alan,' said Bob with a grin. 'If I'd known you had them hidden in there, they'd have gone long ago.'

'That's why I hid them,' said Alan.

Ryan took a deep interest in everything, looking round the neat sitting room with its quaint curved furniture, where the panelling shone with polish and all the instruments and equipment were neatly folded or put away.

'I'm a great one for polishin'. I'm always out there on the gallery shinin' up those windows and lenses all the time. I enjoys it. It's a satisfyin' sort of job,' said Bob proudly. 'I polish 'em like they was Army boots.'

'My dad would approve of you,' said Ryan with a smile.

'Oh ay, ole Sidney Waterman. He's a tartar for keepin' things shipshape, that he is. But he's never faulted me yet, not Bob Crankshaw.'

'How come you're not a PK yet, Bob?'

'No wish to be, that's why. Apart from the fact yer have to wait about till one of 'em drops dead or retires or summat. Dead man's shoes I call it. Job for life, int it? I'm fine as an AK, fine, free and no responsibility. Suits me, it does. Let someone other have the worry and the blame, that's what I says.'

After tea and biscuits, Bob took us up to the service room to see the optics. I loved being in this amazing room where the lantern was housed. The room smelt strongly of oil and paraffin for firing the lamp and curtains were drawn over some of the window panes in case the sun caused damage to the equipment. It was a magical instrument with its hundreds of concentric glass rings arranged about a central lens which collected all the light together into a single, strong, intense beam that would then be rotated so that it could be seen for miles. The lenses here were about six feet wide. They were enormous, like the multi-faceted eyes on a fly when you see it under a microscope but far more beautiful. I stood for a long time staring up at the glinting, sparkling glass rows while the men yattered on.

Leaving Ryan and Bob deep in a discussion about Fresnel lenses, prisms, mercury troughs and other technicalities that left me bewildered but which Ryan seemed to understand perfectly well, I climbed the little iron ladder that led through stout iron doors to the gallery outside. From there, I looked down on the keeper's cottages, the washing on the lines, the well-swept yards with their little pots of flowers and runner beans clambering up the walls. There was the pigsty where Bessie the sow grunted and snouted around. The lonely quiet of it all made me feel godlike. From here I could see the village in the distance like a haze of smoke on the horizon. A walk round the gallery and before me lay the still, calm sea, stretching out to the sky and melting blue into blue. Strange little clouds floated along and they looked for all the world like little puppies lying down in rows, little round-eyed smiling faces. Clouds were the strangest beings. They seemed to have a life, shape and personality of their own; they spoke messages to one sometimes and not just about the weather either. As I watched them float along, I saw the dog's faces change from little puppy smiles to horrid leers and then disintegrate altogether, the illusion lost; cloudy shapes that shifted and changed, impossible to pin down or understand.

It was a sunny autumn afternoon and the world was laid out at my feet; a glorious green and blue world of gentle beauty, soft breezes and the evocative cries of the seabirds near the shore. Life seemed incredibly wonderful just then. I saw Dad in Mack's little service van on the narrow road, snaking off in the direction of the village. Mary Atkinson was hanging washing on the line. I called down to Walter who had come upstairs and told him so; he laughed and came out and yelled over to her but his voice was lost on the breeze. However, some instinct made Mary look up at the light and seeing our distant figures she waved and we waved back.

Bob went back down into the kitchen, telling us to come down in a bit and have another cuppa. Ryan joined me at the gallery rail, looking out over the panorama spread below us.

'It's a good life, isn't it, Bridie? It won't be long before I apply for SAK. They'll take me on when I've done my National Service. I hope to join the Royal Engineers – makes sense, doesn't it? Dad was with them too. Then after my two years, I'll be free to follow my life's wish. Rocks, towers, land lights, I'll be round them all eventually, just like my dad. It's the life for me. I want nothing more.'

'Nothing at all?'

He grinned and put an arm about my shoulders, 'Apart from my girl, no – nothing else. We'll marry and you'll come with me wherever I go.'

I put my arm round his waist and squeezed him close to me and he made no objection. We stood there for some time looking out over the sea and the sky and felt the future reflected in its still peaceful calm. But even then that funny old anxiety trembled in my heart and whispered that, just like the clouds and the sea, the future could be deceptive and fickle.

Chapter 15

I was now seventeen years old, still wondering whether to go on to a college and take a course in something useful. I wanted to help people in some way and contemplated nursing but wasn't sure I could stand all the mucky side of it, the blood and bedpans. Secretarial work paid well but an office would be the death of me. The idea of being stuck in some impersonal business all day, typing out letters, having to run around for an unpleasant stranger who had the right to shout at me and tell me what to do – I'd had enough of all that with Mean Millie. No, the air of "dark-roomed towns" was not for me.

I was very much in love with Ryan but still felt we were not entirely committed to one another. He seemed so sure of me yet he hadn't even asked me to marry him properly or even hinted to anyone else that we were officially engaged. In a way, I felt trapped by the situation. I was in a limbo land of uncertainty that paralysed my freedom and actions. At the same time, I was entrenched in the quiet, regular life I now led; it was alluring in its simplicity and peace.

I loved looking after a home, cooking nice meals for Dad and taking care of things so that he could work hard, relax and have his pint at the pub with his mates now and then. There was time to read great tomes of books, think about deep and contemplative matters. Not for me the stuff teenagers seem to enjoy. I enjoyed pop music and thought maybe jiving could be fun but there was no one to go with and I didn't want to learn to dance with strangers. Not that I could see Ryan ever taking me to dances. The excitement of the Fifties was passing me by while I lived like a little nun. Waiting for Ryan. Waiting for something ... though I had no idea what it was.

This idyllic life couldn't go on forever. I'd become good at cooking and debated some form of catering and had visions of becoming good enough to open up a smart restaurant in a little seaside town like Lyme Regis or down in Cornwall. Pleasant dreams perhaps, but mere fantasy, a hopeful, unattainable vision like my old silly notions of being a singer or a writer.

Dad never interfered, didn't push me to go and find a job. He enjoyed having a reliable woman at home that wouldn't nag him as Millie had done. I revelled in being my own mistress, able to sit down when I wanted, work till I was tired, run the place the way I liked. But it was unfair to Dad: money was always tight as a good part of his wages went to paying off the mortgage on the house in Broughampton. He no longer got rent allowance now that we had a keeper's cottage. That at least was rent free and there was plenty of coal and other little amenities so we managed to live sparingly on Dad's small naval pension. Neither of us wanted much and were content, cheerful and happy with a spartan existence. I'd never known anything else; it didn't occur to me to be bothered.

Ryan came to see us just before it was time for him to set off for Merebrook Camp at Malvern, Worcestershire, where he was due to begin his six weeks' National Service training. When he arrived at the door he made me laugh by singing the recruit's lament, 'For gawd's sake, don't take me ... ' It wasn't often that Ryan was humorous and I was startled by his apparent lightheartedness. How could he be so cheerful when two whole years of his life were about to be taken away from him? One heard terrible stories about the conditions endured by the raw young recruits and there was always the fear of a posting to some unknown, unheard of, far flung eastern place. I didn't want him to go.

'I wish they *wouldn't* take you,' I said looking glum.

Dad Joe laughed too and said, 'Do you good, lad. You'll be so used to discipline, coming back to look after a lighthouse will be a piece of cake. And you'll be in the Royal Engineers with your skills and training. You'll probably have a great time.'

'Yeah, *really* great.'

'Get on. It does you boys good. I never regretted service life and I had a war to fight plus being involved in the bloody Korean blockade before my service ended. You've missed Suez, you're safe enough. But the Army – what can one say about the perishin' Army? Why didn't you try for the Navy? I'd have thought you'd be suited for it and they always need engineers.'

'No, thanks. I love the sea but prefer to view it from a lighthouse rather than a rolling ship's deck. Anyway, they want you to sign on for seven years. Bugger that idea.'

'Seven years!' I gasped, 'Oh, Ryan … that would be awful.'

He looked over at me, and grinned. 'See, you will miss me, won't you, Bridie?'

'Of course, I'll miss you, stupid.'

'Ah, you will too. And I'll miss you.'

We looked at each other for a few moments and felt a sudden sense of parting and sadness like a dark storm cloud blowing over the sun, blotting its light. I saw so little of Ryan and now I would see even less of him. How could we sustain our love like this?

'It'll soon be over.' Dad smiled as if reading our thoughts. 'Then Ryan'll be back home and straight off to a lighthouse. You'll have to get used to missing your man, Bridie.'

'All the same, I don't mind doing it,' stated Ryan, 'sort of feel it's my duty, really. We younger ones owe it to you fellows who fought the war and saved us all. We owe you. That's what I feel … so I don't mind doing my bit though it's not a lot in comparison. I just hope I don't get sent abroad, that's all. Don't like foreigners much.'

He might have seemed resigned to his fate but the thought of sober, reclusive Ryan with a group of young men joking and messing about and making a racket as young men do, made me dubious. However, *he* didn't seem to be worried. His time at college in London appeared to have loosened him up, made him more sociable, so perhaps this term in the Army might break down his silent barriers even more. But what would it do for me, creeping slowly further and further into my little nunnery?

Towards the end of the year Dad dropped a bombshell that was to change a good many things in our lives for ever.

'Bridie, lass, I've some good news for you,' he said.

He'd had a month's leave and gone off to Broughampton for a few days. He said he was going to catch up a bit with Millie and the boys and sort things out. He told me that Jim had done very well indeed and been accepted by Trinity College, Cambridge, where he would take Law. I already saw him as a barrister at the Bar with his wig and gown on and almost laughed at the thought of his laying down the law. Maybe he'd end up a Judge with all the red robes and the long wig though thankfully he no longer needed the nasty black cap on his table ready to sentence some poor bastard to the gallows. Poor Ruth Ellis had been the last to suffer that awful fate. However, the business of National Service loomed up for him also.

I don't want to defer it. I don't want to go at all, Jim wrote, *and I'm going to see to it that I don't.*

Apparently he managed to get that old crook, Dr Barnes, to write a certificate saying he had always suffered from severe asthma and was totally unfit for service. I gathered that Dr Barnes performed this helpful service for several of his friends' sons for a nice little fee. That was no surprise, but how Jim managed to believe in right and wrong yet was able to stoop to deceit like that amazed me. It did little to make me admire him. I thought of Ryan and his words about doing his bit and felt prouder and more in love with him than ever.

Andy was now in the sixth form, already showing signs of being a businessman and apparently dedicated to the idea of making pots of money. And he would; he had the flair for it. He used to sell all sorts of things at school when we were small kids; marbles, autographs, anything he could lay his hands on. He could always persuade some idiot to part with his pocket money. He seemed to know what people wanted and the right person to approach. There was no doubt he would do well.

As for Millie, Jim said she had changed a lot, gone downhill and taken to the bottle these days. He kept asking me to go and see her.

'She asks after you all the time,' he said. 'I think she's sorry now for the way she treated you and wants to make amends. Be a bit Christian, Bridie, go and see her, forgive her.'

Christian indeed! I cared for many people and helped whenever and wherever I could but I could not bring myself to forgive Mean Millie. The mere thought of her filled me with illogical, ancient fear. My heart still remembered her terrorising me and instinctively shuddered. Dad Joe was always saying I should go too, but I ignored the hints and pleas and made no comment. I made no comment in my reply to Jim either and wished they'd all leave me alone to make my own mind up. I brought Dad's attention back to his opening statement.

'What's the good news, Dad?'

'Millie is in a bit of a bad way but I've arranged for someone to come and help her out,' he said. 'We had a long talk about things and we've agreed to divorce. I should have done this long ago but I felt sorry for her. However, she won't want for money or help. Her mum died a month ago and left her that big house in Dartmouth so she can sell it or go and live there as she likes. We'll sell the house in Broughampton and some of the money from that will help out the boys at University. I want them to do well. I want them to do what they really want. I've no worries for Andrew; he's a money spinner, that boy, and has his feet on the ground. But I'm not always sure about Jim. He's a bit of a sensitive chap, an idealist.'

'Jim's very keen and works hard. He got his scholarship, didn't he? He's sure to do well, Dad.'

'Oh, he'll do well enough. He's a perfectionist in all he does, over the top in many ways, like bloody Sidney Waterman. I think he pushes himself too much at times. He says he wants to be a barrister but we have no contacts at the Bar and it's contacts you need to get on in that world. Still, he wants to succeed so maybe that desire will drive him. He always seems to charm the socks off people he meets so he'll be sure to make the right connections. It's *who* you know in that closed-in profession, not how good you are.'

'That seems to be true of anything one wants to do,' I said with a sigh.

'Aye, you're right, Bridie. Be thankful you're not ambitious. Your life will be more peaceful. Contentment is a rare thing, these days. Jim will never be content but must aim high and one day he may fall. For now he needs to have money to keep himself as he gets on. It's only thanks to old Gran Taylor that we could send the lads to nice schools. I'll say that for the old biddy. She always helped out there. Millie may help him out now she's better off but Andy's her favourite so who can tell? I'll make sure Jim's okay, though – I owe it to the lad. Things will be a hell of a lot easier when we sell the house and have a bit of spare cash to play with. We'll be well off at last, Bridie, do you know that? Life will be a lot easier.'

'Life's fine as it is, Dad.'

Dad looked a little sad and stared into the fire. Taking out his pipe, he opened up the pouch I'd given him all those Christmases ago and filled the bowl. He smiled as he looked at the pouch and the little tartan dog on it, now somewhat the worse for wear.

'You're a good kid, Bridie. You've turned out a treasure. You know, sometimes I look back and feel I've let you all down. I should have tackled Millie long ago, ended the farce of our marriage. But I ran away from it all the time, first in the Navy, then to the Lights. Now look at her, she's a mess. She might have remarried, been happier with someone else.'

'Why are you sorry for her now, Dad,' I said angrily. 'She's an awful person. She could have *asked* for a divorce. You wouldn't have refused, would you?'

He looked at me for a while in silence. 'Bridie, she's not so awful any more. She's sad. A bit of an old soak, I'm afraid. You know, she was an unhappy kid and I married her partly to save her from a violent father. He used to beat her daily and more that I won't repeat; you're too young to hear of it. He was a bloody sadist. I felt so sorry for her when I met her; she was a frail, pretty, sad little thing. I always feel for the weak and defenceless,' he added with a smile, 'which is why I took you on when you were a little mite left all alone in the world. I've been a good dad to you, haven't I, Bridie? I've done well by *you*.'

'You *have* done well by me, Dad, and I feel like you are my true father,' I said, tears welling in my eyes.

'Me too,' he said, 'me too, Bridie. I love you as my daughter and always will. You're a great lass and will make a great wife, whoever you pick upon.'

I lowered my eyes at this and smiled. Dad gave a low little laugh, 'Oh aye, you've picked on someone already, that I know, and so have I, Bridie.'

Startled, I looked up at him again. His eyes were merry and happy.

'What d'you mean, Dad?'

'This is the real good news,' he said, grinning all over his face. 'Been up to Bournemouth and asked Sheila Waterman to marry me when my own divorce comes through. She's finished now with that old misery Sidney Waterman, they're all sorted and separated and she'll soon be free. As soon as I'm free too, we'll splice the knot. Isn't that great news?'

It took a little while to sink in. I had my slow days. My first reaction was jealousy and possessiveness and I made a face.

'Ah, don't be jealous, Bridie, she's been like a mum to you and now she *will* be your mum – especially if you and Ryan get together as well. Won't it be splendid, all of us together as a family? I'll leave the lighthouse service and find a stable job and we can all live together by the sea someplace. I'm considering applying for a post as harbour master. If you and Ryan do get married some time, well then it's off to the role of keeper's wife you'll go! But that's your choice. Sheila's sick of it and frankly I'm all for a new adventures now.'

'I'm happy for you, Dad!' I said wholeheartedly and went over and gave him a hug. 'Sheila's a great person and I know you two care for each other. Of course, I love her as a mum and have thought of her as such for ages. Yes, let's keep her in the family! That *is* good news.'

Dad looked as pleased as Punch and I felt he had never seemed so happy. The crafty fellow! We'd both been courting the Watermans on the sly. It made me smile.

'Won't you just do one thing, Bridie, love?' said Dad. 'It'll please me a lot.'

'What's that then?'

'Go and see Millie. She wants you to go. Just the once before she leaves the old house and goes off somewhere. Just the once, Bridie.'

I saw that he still had compassion for Millie deep down: she was, after all, the mother of his two sons. His story about her unhappy childhood did little to stir my sympathy, so cold were my feelings towards this woman. But in fairness, I knew I was being as mean as she was in my way. How could I judge her if I in turn was so unforgiving? I decided that I would go and see her soon, lay our differences to rest. Then maybe the anxious feeling would go away and I would be free and happy to get on with my life.

Walking along Summerfield Rd, Broughampton brought on a strange feeling of *déjà vu*. Little had changed around here in these few years. The greengrocer, the butcher and baker still had their shops in a neat row at the end of the road. Alf, the lad who used to help me carry the huge bags of spuds and vegetables as far as he dared, was now serving alongside Mr Britten in the shop. He still took out deliveries but in a smart little Ford van instead of a bike with a basket on it. He had grown into a nice young lad of about eighteen or nineteen. He recognised me at once: 'It's the red hair,' he said. 'I'll never forget your red hair. No one else has chestnut hair like yours round here.'

We chatted for a bit about what was I doing now and that sort of thing. He looked at me with that appreciative glint I was getting used to, the way a fellow looks when he fancies asking you out but dare not.

'You going along to Mrs Bosworth's then?' he asked as I bought a pound or two of cherries and some flowers from him.

I shrugged. 'Well – reckoned it was time. She might be moving soon.'

'Really? Where's she going, then?

'Oh, I've no idea of that.'

'You going out anywhere after seeing her?' he asked hopefully, 'Could take you for a drink later if you fancy it. Talk over old times.'

What old times? We had no old times. But I smiled sweetly and said I was staying in Broughampton at the Red Lion and would set off early tomorrow to go home. I had a few other people to see, so 'no thanks' to the drink. Then I escaped when another customer came along and distracted him.

I walked down Summerfield Rd and looked at the houses. They hadn't altered very much. Dr Barnes' house was still there, looking exactly the same with its straggling rose bushes out front and tiny handkerchief patch of lawn that hardly seemed worth bothering over. It made me think of the time I fell down the stairs and broke my leg and how cold he had been; so disinterested in my fate beyond the necessary doctor's duties, horrid man. Oh, how lovely – the almond tree still grew in Mrs Maybank's garden! It used to flower a glorious pink every spring and was one of the few things that lifted my heart in those days; I would linger to stare at it while the blooms lasted, sorry to see the petals begin to fall. Millie had always moaned about it, saying those petals were a nuisance drifting into her garden, all over her path. To me, they looked like bridal confetti and I hated to have to go out and sweep them all up and put them in the compost bin. The old tree had grown a fair bit since then, its shade cast over the pavement and Mrs Maybank's tiny front garden. Nothing much else grew in that garden because of the tree but it probably suited Mrs Maybank who was getting old and wasn't bothered any more. The tree was worth a hundred boring red salvias, white alyssum and blue lobelia which decorated almost every garden border along the road; a burst of patriotic enthusiasm since the Queen's Coronation.

Other familiar hedges, mainly privet and holly with some flowering currants or mock-orange here and there, had swelled out, overhanging the road side like a pregnant woman's belly. An odd door or gate had been repainted a different colour but this was about the extent of any visible change. I had walked up this road so often with my bags of shopping and other errands that I knew every stone, crack, plant and weed in it off by heart. Now the road seemed dingy, tired and shrunk in some strange way. Of course, I had become bigger, but I knew it was subtler than that; gone was the feeling of weary dejection, the fear and the misery that had trailed with my footsteps up this road. I was grown up and felt elation at the thought that I was free of childhood passivity and intimidation.

I opened Millie's gate at number three. Here things *had* changed. Little weeds were growing in the cracks of the paving stones. Millie would never have allowed that. I'd have been down on my hands and knees prising out those offending weeds with a kitchen knife. The garden, once neat and tidy, looked untended and uncared for. She used to keep plants in pots by the door which it had been my duty to water daily. Now pots of dried up soil stood against the wall with straggles of plants falling over the edges that looked as if they had been there for years, desiccating slowly into stumps and dried brown leaves.

As I raised my hand to ring the bell, I felt a sudden jolt in my gut. I wanted to turn and run away. What was I doing there? I hated this place and I didn't *want* to see this woman. Why was everyone making me come to see her?

Be kind, I thought, she's alone now and abandoned by everyone.

Swallowing hard and breathing deeply for a few moments, I rang and the sing-song chimes sounded deep into the house. I waited a while and my hopes were raised. Maybe she'd forgotten and gone out. I hoped so with all my heart. But the door opened at last and there stood Millie Bosworth. I almost bit back a cry of alarm. She was gaunt and thin now and her clothes hung on her frame. She seemed to have made an attempt at smartening herself with a bit of lipstick and powder but looked unkempt and untidy, not the smart, clothes-conscious Millie of yore.

She stood there and looked at me for a while. No smile or welcome greeting came to her thin lips.

'Well, what are you waiting for, come on in,' she said and her voice was just the same if nothing else. I suppressed a yearning to turn and flee down the path but instead followed her into the house.

She went ahead into the living room and sat herself down in her old armchair, waving at the sofa.

'Sit down, then.'

Still the old tone of command, the way of acting as if I was nothing, no one, a servant expressly created for her use. My shackles rose. I wanted to scream.

I gave her the cherries and flowers. She waved them away.

'Put them on the table,' she said. 'Why did you get gypsophilia? You know I hate the stuff.'

How could anyone hate those dainty white flowers?

'I'm sorry, I forgot,' I said meekly as I put the unwanted gifts on the table and bit back tears.

She surveyed me for a bit.

'You've grown a lot,' she said, 'put on too much weight, I'd say. Your mother always had an ample figure and you'll take after her. And you still haven't cut that hair. Why don't you get a bit more modern like other girls and have a perm? It would look better. But you've always been an old fashioned little thing. I suppose *he* wants it like that. He always liked long hair on women.'

'Who d'you mean?' I asked, puzzled. Did she know about Ryan?

'Joe, of course,' she said still looking me over with that disparaging look she'd always had.

I ignored this odd comment and changed the subject. 'How are you keeping, Millie?'

'Oh, it's Millie now we're all grown up, is it?' she said. 'Mrs Bosworth to you, if you please, as I've never been your mother and thank God for that. I'm not well at all, as you can see, not well. My head aches all the time and I feel dizzy. My legs bother me and I can't walk that far these days. But no one gives a damn. No one rings or calls. Joe's abandoning me but then he did that long ago, didn't he? The boys are growing up and they've got their own lives now. No one cares whether I live or die.'

'I'm sorry you think that. I'm sure they do. Dad said he was getting someone to take care of you.'

'You know nothing about it,' she said dismissively. 'Joe is all talk, never does anything for me at all. The girl came for a day but she was useless. I don't want someone getting me out of bed at eight in the morning to *dress* me. I don't need someone to dress me or bathe me, I'm not that far gone yet! I want someone to cook and clean, that's all. I sent her off with a flea in her ear.'

Millie paused in her tirade and stared at me again. 'Go and put the kettle on,' she said, 'make us some tea, make yourself useful. You always were a lazy little thing. Make me a pot of nice tea. There's biscuits in the tin. You know where things are.'

Indeed I did. Little had changed but everything was a good deal neglected and not as Millie had once taught me to look after things. There wasn't much sign of cooking but the bin was full of empty tin cans and packets. How strange that this once fastidious woman should have slid into such a state of chaos and neglect. In a way it made me sad. I made the tea and put it on a tray with a doily, nice cups and saucers and a plate of biscuits just as in the old days.

I was always quiet about my tasks and as I came back with the tray I saw her taking a surreptitious little nip from what looked like a small flask of whisky. She hastily stuffed it behind her cushion and sat upright, pulling a cigarette from a packet on the table beside her.

'You pour,' she ordered and I obeyed as always.

I put the tea on the table beside her. When she picked up the cup her hand shook so badly that she almost spilt it. I pretended not to notice and sipped at my tea.

'So what are you doing now you've left school?'

I was nonplussed. 'Nothing yet. I'm just looking after Dad a bit and not sure what I want to do. I thought maybe some sort of nursing job, maybe even a cook. I like cooking and people say I'm good at it.'

'Come and stay with me then, cook for me,' said Millie. 'I'm not well and I certainly need some nursing. I forget my pills, you see. I need someone to cook, to talk to me and be here all the time, someone who knows me – not some stranger. You can come back here, have the best room. I know Joe's going to marry one of his tarts in Bournemouth, oh, I know all right. And he won't want you in his little love nest then, that's for sure.'

I put down my cup and for a moment felt the barb penetrate my skin. But I was determined not to let her get to me.

'As it happens,' I said with a forced smile, 'we all get on very well together. I know the lady he wants to marry and she's a wonderful person. Like a real mother to me. So you needn't be worried on my account.'

Millie's face went as sour as a lemon at this and the thin lips puckered up.

'Oh, a nice little scenario,' she sneered.

'And I'm going to marry her son, too,' I added, 'when I'm a bit older.'

'Are you now? Very cosy. And all live together in the Old Woman's Shoe, I suppose? Very cosy.'

She tipped her ash on the floor and I almost went to pick it up but stopped myself. She turned her face towards the gas fire and seemed lost in thought for a bit. I stayed silent and looked around at the familiar furniture and fittings. I felt a little sick in the pit of my stomach but in some ways I was beginning to enjoy the verbal battle. I felt myself up to her little games now and wasn't going to be beaten by them.

'But who's to take care of me?' said Millie softly. Her knee was jumping up and down in a strange, nervous manner, a habit I'd never seen in her before and she put out her cigarette only to light another one immediately. 'I'm getting so ill, I can't sleep at nights, you know. I dream things, frightening things. I need someone with me, don't you see? Come back and stay with me, Bridie.'

'Why do you want me back?' I asked puzzled. 'We never really got on, did we? You never seemed to like me at all. Why do you want *me* of all people to come and stay with you, even if I wanted to – which I don't?'

'What d'you mean?' Her tone was full of indignation. 'I always liked you, took you in as a baby, put a roof over your head and food in your mouth, taught you to be a good housewife. Then you go off with Joe and leave me. How could you take my husband from me after all I did for you?'

'After all *you* did for me?' I was so stunned by this that I almost choked on my tea.

'Didn't I take you in, feed you, clothe you?' she demanded.

I put the cup down. 'Yes Millie, you did all that but you never gave me a moment of love, not a kind word or a smile. That's real food, Millie, a smile and a hug. Sheila Waterman gave me all that and good food besides and an education. You gave me nothing but misery and fear.'

My heart was beating with the courage it took to say all this for Millie was one of those people that created a dark, frightening aura about herself, hard to combat. Her face went deep red and for a moment I wondered if her famous rage was about to explode and got ready to dodge the tea cup that she picked up with a fierce expression on her face. If she did throw anything at me I was prepared to walk out without another word.

'Don't even think about it,' I said with equal ferocity and rose to leave.

She put the cup down hastily and fished out the whisky bottle from under her cushion instead.

'Don't go,' she whined and took a swig. 'Don't leave me alone, Bridie. I always feel safe when you're here. Why did you have to go and leave me?'

I sat down, astonished at this revelation.

'You felt safe with me around? I was only a kid. You had two big boys. You felt safe because of me?'

'Yes,' she said.

'Safe from what?'

'From him!'

'Who, for goodness sake?'

Her eyes had a queer look in them. The woman was half mad as well as drunk. How could I hate this pathetic creature? She was falling apart before my eyes.

'I'm well off now,' she said suddenly, changing her tack. 'Come and live with me and I'll leave it all to you, Bridie. Think of it, you'll be rich. You can do what you like. You don't have to marry to get away from *him*. You can have a career, be a doctor, a nurse, whatever you like. And look after me.'

'I don't want your money, Millie,' I said, 'that's yours and the boys. Help *them*. They've always been your dear little boys, haven't they? Get Andy to come and live with you.'

'He won't come,' she replied, 'and it's not the same. I need a girl with me.'

'A servant, you mean,' I said, beginning to lose patience with her weird ramblings.

'A daughter,' she said.

'Oh, Millie, I would have gladly been your daughter if you had let me,' I sighed, 'but you never did, did you? God, you're a strange soul.'

Hearing the compassion in my voice, she redoubled her whining efforts.

'I wasn't always kind,' she admitted, 'but you were always such a difficult, ugly little thing. Joe spoilt you, you know, he always did. But I knew why, I knew why. And in the end he took you off, all very cosy. And then the boys left and I'm alone and afraid he'll come in the night like he used to. Don't you see?'

I didn't understand her at all. She was rambling and drunk. She couldn't possibly be talking about Joe – half the time, he hadn't been around and if there'd been any sex between them we'd all have heard it through these paper-thin walls. Then in a flash I recalled Joe's veiled remarks about her father and how violent he had been ... and more ... he had said. I was still a sheltered young girl and understood little about sexual matters and my imagination found it hard to grasp what Millie was saying but I felt a sudden sense of horror. I came over, knelt beside her and put a hand on her arm. She shook it off indignantly.

'No one will come in the night, Millie,' I said gently. 'No one will come and hurt you. I think you're speaking of the past. Dad said your father hit you sometimes. But he's dead now, isn't he? There's nothing to be afraid of.'

'My father was wonderful!' she said sharply, sitting bolt

upright. 'He adored me, I'll have you know. I was his "little missus", that's what he said to me. And he gave me presents all the time. What are you insinuating, you nasty little slut! I'd just like to know how you managed to get Joe away from me. I'll bet he was into your knickers in a flash and you got those legs wide open soon as you could, maybe even before you both left. You always were a little slut, walking off with him, leaving me in the house alone. Just like your mother, just like your mother. Joe always fancied her and for all I know, you're *his* daughter!'

I fell back from her, horrified at her words.

'Oh, my God, you're crazy!' I said and seized my bag and coat and began to leave. She jumped up from her chair with sudden alacrity and grabbed my arm tightly, just as she used to when I was a child.

'You're not going away again!' she screamed. 'You're to stay and look after me now. You have to stop him coming in the night! You've come back to me, Bridie O'Neill! Stay with me. Leave Joe alone ... why can't you leave him alone? He's found another tart, don't you see? All men are bastards. Stay with me and you'll be rich.'

I shook her off as if she was some foul, clinging animal.

'I don't want to be rich, especially with your money, Millie Bosworth,' I said. 'You're sad, do you know that ... sad! You should see a psychiatrist.'

'I'm lonely, Bridie,' she whimpered. 'Don't you care? Doesn't anybody care?' and suddenly all the temper and violence left her and she began to sob, her gaunt frame shaking and heaving.

'I don't care,' I shouted. 'Millie, I just don't care what you are or what happens to you. You've been evil to me and I'll never shake you off. You'll haunt me all my life. I'm going now and I shall never come back again. Goodbye!'

And with that I walked from the room and out of the front door. She followed me and stood yelling disgusting obscenities about me and Dad as I hastened down the road. Some of the neighbours popped their heads out at the hullabaloo but I didn't give a damn. I was getting out of that house and away from that evil, mad woman forever.

Chapter 16

I got back to the Red Lion and flung myself on the bed, trying to still my nerves. I wanted to leave there and then, but there wasn't a train back to Totnes that night, so I ate a solitary meal in the lounge bar and half wished I'd taken up Alf's offer for a drink to while the time away. That night I cowered beneath the covers, terrified that Millie would come after me in some way. It was nonsense and I knew it, but she'd really shaken me. I'd gone there meaning to forgive her, put the past behind us, establish some sort of human rapport despite everything and put all my old fears to rest. Now I was more afraid than ever, filled with dread.

'I hope you die, you old bitch!' I muttered to myself fiercely. It was wrong of me to think such things but I couldn't help it. I couldn't help the hate and disgust she aroused in me.

Next day I took the earliest train home to Totnes, waited an age for a bus to Stokenham and then walked down the winding country lanes and along the coast path that led along the mossy undulating crest of the headland towards Start Point. It was a long walk but I felt happier already, the fresh sea breeze blowing away my foolish fears and restoring my spirits. The wildflowers were all out on the cliffs and looking down to the bays below, I saw oystercatchers wading in the mud and even a seal basking on the rocks. How good it was to look over the rolling ocean and put these things into perspective. Before me, drawing me along the steep upward path, was the brilliant white of the keeper's houses and behind them the towering lighthouse set against a vivid blue sky. I felt that joyful feeling of being home where I belonged. Dad was off duty, luckily, and seeing me approaching hastened out to greet me.

'Why, Bridie, I thought you'd stay on there a bit longer, see some of your old friends maybe. Why didn't you ring Sally Wainwright at the garage and let us know what time you were returning? She could have brought you in the taxi, save you all that walk.'

'It's all right. I needed to walk and think a bit,' I replied.

He kissed me on the cheek. I was glad to see him but some of Millie's horrible notions and ideas had tainted me. I felt slightly ill at ease with Dad Joe all of a sudden and didn't greet him with my usual warmth.

He sensed something was up and led me indoors, peering at me anxiously, then disappeared to put the kettle on the hob while I took off my coat and gloves.

'So what happened?' he said as he brought the mugs over and put a plate of chocolate digestives on the table. 'Something's up, I can tell a mile away. You look pale as a ghost, Bridie. What happened with the old girl? She say something to upset you?'

'She's mad, Joe,' I said, my voice trembling, 'she's quite mad. She said some horrible things. I just upped and left her. She's changed all right. For the worse.'

It was the first time I'd called Dad by his first name and his eyes flickered to show he'd noticed, but he made no comment.

'What sort of things did she say?' he asked with a worried look.

'Things about you and me,' I said and burst into tears.

Dad banged his fist on the table in anger, making the mugs rattle, and then came over to me and hugged me hard.

'She's always been saying stuff like that, Bridie. And you *know* there's not a shred of truth in any of it. I've always thought of you as my own daughter and I always will. You know that. Have I ever treated you differently?'

I felt too hurt and tired to know anything just now and drew away from him for a bit. He gave me his hanky and looked troubled.

'Shit,' he said feelingly. 'I should never have let you go. I hoped you'd do the old harridan some good. She kept banging on about how she needed you, how she missed you and how she liked you. I began to believe it myself.'

'She's always *hated* me,' I said, 'and all she wants me for is because she's gone paranoid about something, thinks someone is going to come and get her. I'm not surprised she's scared; she's such a hateful person. All she wants me for, Dad, is to keep her ghosts at bay and slave for her as I used to do. You don't know the half of it because I've never let on. You don't know the half of what I went through.'

'My poor darling lassie. I believe you did suffer. And I wish I'd been there to spare you some of that. But Millie, she suffered a lot as a kid herself,' said Dad. 'It's warped her mind and the drink hasn't helped. I still can't help feeling sorry for her but she's her own worst enemy. If she'd been kinder and more loving, you might have gone to care for her, mightn't you, Bridie?'

Suddenly this question made me feel very angry. There was an assumption behind all this and my eyes opened up to it in a flash.

'If she'd been like Sheila,' I agreed, 'of course I would. I would look after Sheila, no matter what she got to be. But I hate Millie and I never want to see her again. So don't ask me again and tell Jim not to ask either. Just because none of you know what to do with her you think simple, sweet, little Bridie O'Neill will step in and be her carer. Were you trying to get rid of me, is that what it was? Now you're getting married and leaving this place? Did you think, all of you, I'd be happy to forgive and forget and solve all your problems over Millie, keep her quiet so you could all get on with your lives and be happy? Did you? Well, you can go to hell, the lot of you!'

I stormed out and went up to my room to weep with grief and dismay.

After a while, Dad came up and stood at the door.

'Bridie ... '

I refused to look at him.

'Oh, Bridie,' he pleaded, 'she's poisoned your mind and heart. Forgive me, sweetheart, for sending you to her. Of course it isn't because I want you to go. Sheila and I love you dearly and want you with us when we leave – if you want to come, that is. Maybe you've got plans of your own. We'll support you whatever you decide to do. I can afford to send you to college now if you want. Believe me, Bridie, please believe me!'

I looked at him and there were tears in his eyes and sadness in his voice. I felt all my old love rise up and ran over to him and we hugged again.

'Did it ever occur to you, sweetheart, how tongues might wag if you and I stay together alone now you're a young woman?' he said when we had made a fresh mug of tea and sat downstairs together again.

'No Dad, why would it?' I said, angry at the thought. But Millie's accusations still rang in my ear and I knew my happy ignorance was now destroyed.

'Sadly, you're not my daughter, even officially. I never even got to adopt you properly – Millie wouldn't let me. Obviously you don't look anything like me. Bridie, you've turned into a beautiful lass and you're nearly nineteen. People will start to say things, not just Millie, believe me. We couldn't have gone on like this much longer. We'd have had to think of something. As it happens, Sheila and I met up and really love and care for one another. We'll get on splendidly together, I know it. I'm due a bit of happiness at last as well as you. And that makes it fine for you to come and be with us as long as you want or till you and Ryan marry. I confess I did think you might want to stay with Millie a bit and it was selfish in me to persuade you to go. But I do feel sorry for the poor foolish woman. I always have.'

'I know, Dad,' I said with a sigh. 'You're a good man. I think Ryan is right. The world is full of strange and horrible people.'

'Not all, Bridie, there's good folks too in equal measure. Good and bad, that's what we're all made of, even inside ourselves. We can't pretend any of us are angels.'

'But some of us are really evil,' I said, 'and that's what I'm afraid of.'

I never felt quite right with Joe again after this. It's hard to explain but my encounter with Millie made me feel a sort of separation in my heart from that whole family, even darling Joe who had always been so kind to me, my saviour, my prince. Now I needed another prince to take me away. If I went to live with Joe and Sheila once they were married, the situation would be different for us; in a peculiar way it would revert to what it had been before with Millie. I'd be piggy in the middle again. My life was always about being in the middle, watching others battle on either side of me, trying to keep the balance and the peace. Though I knew that Sheila would never treat me like Millie, I would be there between her and Joe and his affections would be shared and maybe she'd get jealous too, who knows? I wasn't a kid any more, he'd said as much himself and I'd seen a flash of that look in his eye when he mentioned how pretty I'd become. Suddenly I knew I couldn't be with him any more. I didn't belong with Joe now.

I went to my little treasure box and opened it up. There were few enough things in there: letters from Ryan and Jim, a letter to Joe which he gave me to prove that I wasn't his daughter as Millie tried to make out. The letter was from my real father to Joe telling him that my mother was expecting a baby and already three months gone.

'How could I have been your dad?' Joe had said. 'I was in Gibraltar at the time and had been there for six months already. Millie always accused me of sleeping with Maureen. I loved her very much but as a friend. She and Bill were my best friends. Don't be corrupted by what Millie says, her mind's a cesspool.'

There was also a really old locket with red-gold hair in it – I have no idea whose, perhaps a grandmother whom I would never know anything about. Then there was a chased gold cross and Mum's wedding ring which had been taken from her on her deathbed. There were also the two faded black and white photos of both my parents and one of their wedding, my mother looking so pretty with rich thick ringlets of hair like mine, Dad still in Naval uniform. Joe had said her hair was a lighter red than mine, more apricot than chestnut.

Bill O'Neill's face looked back at me and I gasped to see

how much Ryan resembled him: the lock of hair over the brow, the slender bony face, the dark, intense eyes. This was a revelation. It was the reason why Ryan always felt so familiar and why his strong features always tugged at my heart with a desperate longing like an animal crying out for its mate. It was the need to fuse with something that as it turned out was actually a part of myself. In a funny way the shock of this discovery gave a little blow to my intense love for Ryan Waterman. It wasn't him I was in love with, it was my father. And like my father he was a long way away and almost as inaccessible. My heart cried out for something closer and warmer, more real and feeling.

I decided that in future I would call myself Bridie O'Neill, even if I married. I'd been left alone in the world and alone I would remain, come what may. I would be my own person henceforth, dependant on no one for my existence. Something inside me hardened into a core, a belief in myself that came from within and needed no one's approval.

Life carried on as usual on the surface. I spent it musing about what to do now. Maybe I would go to college after all, somewhere new and far away, and learn some cooking and catering skills, perhaps eventually go for a job in some seaside hotel. At least then I'd be near the sea and have accommodation and some pay. I'd be independent of all of them, the whole lot of them, start a new life. I put this to Joe, who said it was a very good idea and I would surely become a famous cook one day. I could tell he was thankful that I'd finally got a plan. Yet I still procrastinated and life went on the same as usual. I needed a good shake up and it wasn't long in coming.

After a couple of months we had a telegram from Jim. Millie had had a stroke and no one knew about it till a neighbour got worried about the milk bottles piling up on her doorstep and called the police. They broke down the door to find her dead in her living room, clutching a whisky bottle.

I felt nothing but relief to think that she had left this world at last and would no longer feel like a threat to me. I was even glad for her because her troubles were over and, hopefully, she would be at peace wherever she was now. God would surely judge her with more kindness than I had.

Joe was grieved, more grieved than I had expected. He really sobbed when he heard the news.

'Poor Millie!' he said over and over, 'poor, unhappy, Millie. You've been an unhappy woman all your life.'

He took out the photos he had of her – a couple taken at their wedding – and sat for ages that night looking at them as if trying to resurrect someone who had existed only in his mind. He remembered a Millie I knew nothing about and I couldn't share the grief he felt. However, I agreed to go along with him and attend her funeral in Broughampton Municipal Cemetery.

It was a quiet affair; few people from the neighbourhood attended. Dr Barnes was there but he'd always been one of Millie's cronies. I said nothing to him, didn't even acknowledge the man. When I hated someone, I hated them and that was that. I wanted to shout out loud what a crook he was, what a bloody awful doctor and why were people being so respectful and polite to him just because he put Doctor before his surname?

Sheila came too and took Joe's arm very comfortably. She hugged me, I hugged her back and smiling, admired her nice engagement ring. She and Joe did seem very suited and I was truly glad for him; glad he had found a warm, caring woman at last. They could get married all the sooner now they didn't have to wait for his divorce. Andy and Jim were there of course and they were probably the biggest surprise for me as I hadn't seen either of them in at least two years and they had both changed a lot.

Andy was now slim, tall and handsome, no longer the awful podgy brat of his youth. He came over to me of his own accord, shook my hand rather formally and was very affable and pleasant.

'Bridie, you look smashing,' he said and actually gave me a peck on the cheek.

'Thanks,' I said. To say his attitude surprised me was an understatement. We chatted a little about the usual inconsequentialities of life.

'I used to be ghastly towards you,' he mused. 'sorry, Bridie, for all that stuff. Do you forgive me?'

'I suppose so. Your family always seem to need forgiving.'

He grinned. 'I look on our tough stance towards life as a virtue,' he said. 'In business you need to be tough, but not in private life. I've learnt to separate the two. I intend to be a bastard in the workplace and an angel in the bedroom.'

I smiled and nodded but thought that Millie's tough stance had hardly done *her* any favours or helped her much in life. But then Andy hadn't had the rough start to life that she'd endured, leaving her permanently damaged.

He introduced me to his current girlfriend, Liz, a pretty, bright-looking blonde of about eighteen or so with a hard face. I didn't take to her but then what did it matter? I would probably never see her again and Andy seemed happy around her. He told me he intended to try for a place in the RAF when he got called up.

'Better food, less to do and you're not so likely to go and fight anywhere,' he said with a smirk. I smiled with faint politeness and decided I disliked him as much as ever.

It wasn't long before Jim detached himself from a group of relations whom I'd never seen or met before and came sauntering over to see me. He was even more handsome, well-groomed and charming than ever before. Women's eyes, young and old, swivelled and followed him wherever he went.

'Oh my God, Bridie!' he exclaimed, taking my hands and surveying me, 'you are simply gorgeous, my dear. How great to see you after all this time. I kept meaning to come over and see you at your new location. You and Dad will choose to live in these far flung, out-of-the-way places. Why didn't you come over and visit me as I asked you *many* a time, bad girl!'

'I didn't want to,' I said simply. He looked taken aback by this directness then smiled, raised my hand and kissed it. All very nice and sophisticated.

'We've a lot of catching up to do, you and me,' he murmured. 'Letters say little of one's real thoughts and feelings. I mean to understand you better, Bridie Bosworth.'

'My name is and always has been Bridie O'Neill,' I said, my voice cool and steady.

Jim looked at me keenly then laughed. 'I see. Hints of rebellion? Hints of growing up round here? Fair enough, Bridie O'Neill it will be – though not for long, I suspect.'

'Long enough and maybe forever,' I said. 'Even if I marry I mean to keep that name. It means more to me than you could ever understand.'

'But I do understand,' his face was suddenly serious and the old caring, compassionate Jim looked at me again. 'And if you marry me, you *can* keep that name forever if you want. I'm not that attached to Bosworth myself. Though I mean to make it a famous name; then you might change your mind.'

There he stood, suave and grown up and full of confidence. He was well on the way to doing well for himself with or without his father's help. Millie's money would now be shared between him and Andy which would help pave both their careers. Their mother had done them both a favour – she had done us all a favour – by dying. But what the hell was he on about, talking about marrying me? Everyone seemed to assume they could take me over like a parcel from the Post Office. He stood there all cocksure, the image of Millie. That alone would always make me feel an instinctual dislike for him.

'If I marry anyone, it'll be Ryan Waterman,' I said, my voice cold as ice. 'But it's okay. I know you're only joking.'

His face darkened suddenly, the lips drawing thin just like his mother's.

'I wasn't joking,' he said, 'but I very much hope that you are. Why would you want anything to do with that brutish, uncaring, uncouth recluse?'

And with these words he strode off towards the group he had just left without a backward glance.

Chapter 17

In the spring of 1959, Joe and Sheila spliced the knot, as he put it. The wedding took place in Bournemouth and Sheila looked really nice in a cream-coloured suit and a big bouquet of creamy freesias and maiden-hair fern in her hand. Joe, with his hair and beard neatly trimmed, was all smart in a new navy-blue suit. Tall and upright, he looked the Naval Officer he had once been. Susan was bridesmaid to her mother and looked sweet in a frothy pink organza frock with false pink rosebuds in her hair. I had declined to be a bridesmaid and I think Susan was rather pleased to hog that particular limelight. The couple made their vows at the Registry Office and after they had signed the register we all went off to the local inn to have a wedding breakfast.

Joe had left the Lighthouse service now and got the post he'd applied for as Harbour Master, managing a fishing harbour up on the Yorkshire coast. The post came with a lovely old eighteenth century house situated on the quayside. He was to be responsible for port maintenance, the allocation of berths, piloting and moving cargo and fishing ships in and out of the harbour. He was delighted with the new job and Sheila said she was delighted with her new home.

'I've never felt settled enough to get a nice home going. Now I've even got a little garden and can grow vegetables, bushes and all my favourite flowers. I can settle back and enjoy life.'

Susan had left school as soon as she was fifteen and opted to stay with her grandmother, Ethel Alcott, in Bournemouth rather than join the newlyweds and start yet another new life. She had found a job as a junior trainee in a hairdressing salon called

Mandy's in the town centre. She was proving to have some talent in this direction, having practiced for years on her dolls.

'Let Mandy cut your hair, Bridie,' she urged. 'You've got lovely thick hair and it would look great if she cut it in a nice modern style.'

'I like to keep it long,' I retorted. 'Keep those scissors of yours away from me. I know what hairdressers can be like once they get near you with a pair of scissors. You end up half bald.'

'Oh, rubbish! You'd look so much nicer; modern. It's old fashioned done up in a French plait like that. Cut it to your shoulders at least and have flick ups. That would look great.'

'I'm happy the way I am,' I said firmly and she subsided but still eyed me hungrily as if she couldn't wait to practise her own cutting skills on my thick mop. She'd got herself a boyfriend already, which didn't surprise me – a sixteen year old lad from Barrington's cycle shop next door. It was Tony said this and Tony said that all the time till I grew sick of it. All her conversation centred on Tony, the happenings at her salon, women's magazines and the soaps on television.

Ryan got leave to come to his Ma's wedding and, as her own father was dead now, took over the role of giving away the bride. He came up towards the Registrar's desk, his mum on his arm, looking proud and pleased, ready to hand her over into Joe's loving care. I'd never seen Ryan in a suit before; he wore a smart dark grey one with ease and elegance and I thought how he wasn't as playboy handsome as Jim and Andy had turned out to be, but had looks that were far more interesting, full of character and even a certain nobility. He suited formal clothes and always looked good in his army uniform though it had taken me some time to get used to the loss of his thick dark floppy hair, now reduced to a crew cut.

I wasn't surprised Andy declined to come to his dad's wedding. I suppose it's hard seeing your dad re-marry within a few months of your mother's death, whatever she may have been like, and Andy had always seen the best of her being the favourite. He sent a telegram and good wishes and a present and that was it. I could tell Joe was disappointed about it but, let's face it, he *had* abandoned the boys during their formative years. He couldn't expect them to feel much in the way of sentiment for him. As for myself I felt deep relief that Andy and his hard-faced girlfriend weren't coming. He may have appeared to change but I didn't quite believe it. Do leopards change their spots?

Jim, however, had promised to turn up in time for the wedding breakfast and this made me feel anxious. I was worried there might to be another confrontation or hostility between him and Ryan and didn't want Joe and Sheila's wedding day marred by anything unpleasant.

When I saw Jim arrive at the Ship and Anchor, where the feasting was being held, I glued myself to Ethel Alcott and her cronies who were having a preliminary sherry in the lounge. I hoped he wouldn't spot me too soon and meant to be very cool and distant towards him. He looked around when he came in but I bent down to fiddle with the hem of my dress so he missed me and went on into the saloon bar where some of the men were already gathering and ordering their drinks.

Jim was seated a way off down the table, next to Joe and Sheila as befitted the eldest son. Ryan was placed next to me as we seemed to be considered a couple by just about everyone. Thankfully, Susan was seated near some younger member of their family and well out of earshot. When the gong was banged and the meal announced, we all trooped into the dining room and that's where Jim caught me up, his eagle eye ever on the watch.

'Are you avoiding me, Bridie O'Neill?' he asked. His voice was slightly slurred and gave away the fact that he had downed a good few shots of whisky while waiting. He studied me with approval. I looked very smart today in a dainty blue frock, cut a little low in the neck, tight at the waist and with a full swirl skirt, fresh white flowers in my hair. He'd mainly seen me in plimsolls, scruffy jeans and sweaters when I was at home. I knew I looked good and many glances had come my way from the young men around me. I decided I rather liked dressing up now and then.

'Why should I avoid you, Jim Bosworth?'

'Don't even try. I'll always find you, Bridie. God, you've grown so pretty. You were such a skinny little thing. Now, well … ' his eyes dwelt on my nicely rounded bust and I shifted a little uncomfortably. I didn't like him looking at me like that and didn't like the smell of the drink on his breath. He changed the subject, sensing my embarrassment. 'So – our dad's found himself a woman to appreciate him at last. Aren't you glad?'

'I'm very glad,' I said. 'They both deserve to be happy. Sheila's a lovely woman.'

'Not exactly an oil painting though,' said Jim disparagingly.

'Oh, come on, looks aren't that important, Jim. Warmth and love are more important.'

'Well, yes, but looks as well make the perfect combination. In the end it's good looks in a man or woman that win the day. People will always choose the good-lookers over the ugly ones in any situation. I mean to make use of that fact when I become a barrister.'

'You think you'll sway a case because of your looks?' I asked amused.

'I know I will. It sounds vain but it isn't, Bridie. I'm not claiming the good looks, it's not any thanks to me. I was born this way, came from a good looking mother – just as you do. I merely mean to make use of it as an asset.'

'Has it proved an asset so far?'

'It has with the girls,' he grinned.

'Not with all the girls.'

His face went serious, 'I hope that doesn't mean you?'

'Looks aren't important to me. I prefer a caring heart. But that has nothing to do with it, has it? What I think of you isn't the point as you're my brother.'

'I'm not!' he replied with some heat. 'It makes me so mad when you say that. You're calling yourself Bridie O Neill now, aren't you? So, you don't want to be thought of as part of our family? That's proof enough. How can you say I'm your brother? We were brought up together for a bit, that's all. So are lots of people. All the more reason to be attracted to each other as we know and understand one another so well.'

'I don't think you understand me at all, Jim.'

'I do, Bridie, I know better than anyone what Mum put you through. I always felt sorry for you and wanted to protect and help but didn't quite know how. I was just a kid myself. I wasn't scared of Mum but I didn't know how to deal with her, not then. She had a fierce temper.'

'Don't I know!' I said with feeling.

'You do. And I want to make amends to you, Bridie.'

I stared at him and then laughed. 'You don't need to make amends, Jim, it wasn't your fault. I understand fully that you didn't know how to help. You couldn't do anything about it. It was up to me to stand up to her and I never really did. If I had, things might have been different. But I was a coward, Jim. I just did what she asked and was afraid of her most of the time. I was a passive fool. I wouldn't be like that now.'

'You were a child and she terrorised you. How could you fight that as a child? Run away? Where else could you have gone? It wasn't cowardly, Bridie, it was self preservation and we all go in for that.'

'Don't, Jim – don't talk about it any more. I want to put it behind me, bury it with Millie and never think of those times again.'

He put a hand on my arm and his touch was gentle and compassionate.

'I won't say another word about it. Anyway, I want to talk to you about what you're planning to do now Dad's married and going off to Yorkshire. I'll bet you've made a load of interesting plans. Are you sitting with me?' he asked as he steered me towards the table.

'No, I'm with Ryan,' I replied and at that moment up came Ryan looking daggers at Jim. Jim let my arm go and the two young men stood stiffly, staring at one another.

'How are you?' asked Jim very formally. He put out a hand but Ryan didn't take it.

'Fine.' was the brief reply. Taking my other arm, Ryan led me off to sit beside him at the table. I looked back at Jim, grimaced and shrugged my shoulders. His face in that moment looked dark and mean. God, he was like Millie when she was thwarted by someone! I was glad I'd looked back and seen that expression. It reminded me of the reason I could never take to Jim despite those amazing good looks.

Ryan said not a word, just held my arm tightly as if afraid to let me go. We found our places and sat down beside one another. I smiled at him and he returned a look full of feeling, took my hand under the table and squeezed it hard. In a way I rather liked this silent, undemonstrative passion. Ryan was never a conversationalist so we spent the soup course in silence, I making occasional conversation with some middle-aged auntie of his sitting on the other side of me. After the soup plates had been cleared away, Ryan bent towards me and said softly, 'Bridie, I'm almost done with the Army and I've got a place as an SAK. They reckon I'll get on the rock light where my dad is Principal Keeper. He was moved to Wolf Rock a few months ago and I'll be joining him there in September. I think that will be a turn up, don't you? Having Dad as my boss!'

'That's great news, Ryan!'

'Reckon they're doing it on purpose to try me out. Hope I live up to Dad's expectations. I bet he'll lead me a dog's life. He has a reputation does Dad and he's bound to be harder on me than the others. But I'm prepared for it.'

'Oh, you're tough, Ryan, and determined to do well. Nothing seems too much hard work for you. God knows you're as much of a perfectionist as your dad in your own way. He'll be a good training ground and I know he'll be proud of you. Is he keeping well?'

'Yes, he's fine and glad to know Ma's happy with someone that makes her feel safe and secure. He's not an ogre, you know. He's a good bloke is Dad, just a loner like me.'

I said nothing to this but wondered in my heart if marrying Ryan would mean that I'd end up feeling sad, insecure and lonely just like Sheila had been.

Ryan seemed to sense my thoughts.

'I won't be like him, Bridie,' he said. 'I'll look after you and I'll be *glad* to be home with you. I miss you *now*, don't think I don't. You needn't worry that I'll turn out like Dad.'

'You always read my mind, Ryan,' I smiled. 'How do you do it?'

'Because I know you inside. I read your eyes and know what's in your heart – and that's because I love you.'

He almost whispered these last words and I wasn't sure if I'd heard them right. But I could make no response just then for at that moment the speeches began and we were all distracted by bad jokes and the usual wedding day innuendos. I glanced over at Jim and saw him looking very bored, occasionally whispering without much enthusiasm to a young girl seated next to him and slugging the wine back like a good 'un. She seemed to be trying hard to win his interest but he was not responsive at all. When he looked over at me he didn't smile. If anything he looked tired and fed up.

Later on, when the guests had left, Sheila and Joe went off in the old Morris to their new home where they were to spend the night before setting off for a few days in the Lake District. After seeing them off with heaps of rose petal confetti thrown about in happy abandon and old boots tied to the fender rattling along the roadway, the rest of us went back into the inn to sort ourselves out and collect our bags and other belongings.

Sheila's mother, Ethel Alcott, had put me up again since Joe had left the service. Joe had lodged in a room at the Ship and Anchor while waiting for the wedding to be arranged and his new job secured. I felt so sad leaving behind my dear little cat, Stevie, but cats love their homes, not people. So I left him to the new keepers who were to occupy the cottage where I had known such happy times. They had a little girl who was thrilled with her new pet and promised faithfully to take good care of him. Stevie had given me great happiness and comfort and I cuddled him till he got restless and broke away. I watched him saunter off and jump up onto his favourite wall where he liked to sit in the sun and warm his whiskers.

'Goodbye, Stevie,' I whispered, 'goodbye, innocent childhood.'

A wave of sadness washed over me. It was the end of yet

another chapter of my unsettled life.

Jim came over to me as we waved our goodbyes to the happy couple and said, 'I hope to see you soon, Bridie. We've left it far too long to meet up again. I'm nearly through at Cambridge, finals will be next year and I mean to get a first, nothing less. I mean to do well, Bridie, make you and Dad proud of me. I've bought a little flat in London with my inheritance – well, it's only a couple of rooms really but it's all my own. I shall be there all summer. Here's my address and phone number. Call me up and let me know what you decide to do with yourself. I've got a few contacts and may be able to help you get settled. Come to London, Bridie,' his voice was winning and pleading, 'do come. It's the place to be. You'll love it there and I'll show you a good time. Take you dancing, to films… you act like an old woman sometimes. You need to let up, be the young girl you are. A modern girl, not one that's old before her time. Money's not such a worry for me any more, thank God. I can help *you* out if you need it.'

'This is how I am, Jim. I don't care about films and dancing and all that.'

'Maybe you should. Maybe it's just what you need, Bridie, before they make you settle down in some cut-off, lonely existence miles from anywhere.'

I smiled. 'I suppose you're right, I need to find out for myself. Thanks Jim, I'll let you know. I might come, I really might. I do want to do something else … something different, see the world. But don't offer me money. I can sort myself out. I'm not afraid of hard work.'

He smiled at me. 'I know you're not. You're an amazing girl. Come Bridie, come. I really urge you – you're wasted here. And I don't want to lose touch with you – little sister,' he added mockingly.

'That's right. Just think of me as your sister and we'll be fine,' I smiled.

He looked exasperated. 'You haven't still got a thing for that miserable, sour-faced bloke? I don't understand why. You don't owe him anything. I know they all think you two are going to marry but he's not for you, Bridie. You've lots of spunk. You don't want to be buried in some out of the way place while he pisses off and leaves you alone doing what he wants to do and to hell with your life. I can show you a different life. Come and see. Don't be as passive with him as you say you were with Mum. Remember this, Bridie – remember my words of warning.'

He wavered drunkenly towards me, aiming for my mouth, but I turned my head and the kiss landed on my cheek. Just at that moment Ryan approached us.

'You going at last?' said Ryan in a sour voice.

'Ryan!' I exclaimed. I'd never heard him be so offensive to anyone. He was always abrupt and blunt but he was never really rude.

Jim just laughed a funny little laugh.

'You won't win, Ryan Waterman,' he said enigmatically, turned on his heel and weaved his way to the door.

'Won't I though?' Ryan muttered. 'You drunken sod, you wait and see.'

I raised my eyebrows in disgust. Jim had a point. Was I to let Ryan bulldoze me like Millie had done? Treat me like Sidney had treated Sheila? My heart went a little further towards steel.

As I collected my handbag and cardigan, Ryan negotiated a lift for us back to his Nan's little semi near Durley Chine. He was to spend the night on the bed settee while Susan now had the room she had shared with her mum all to herself. I had a tiny box room, where even Stevie would have found it hard put to find some space to curl up, and where I was always knocking my shins on the wooden corners of the bed. However, it was adequate for the time being till I sorted myself out and decided where exactly I would go and what I would do with myself. It was a strange time. I felt at crossroads in life with many paths lying out there beckoning. Which to take? My old uncertainty rose in me but I had a feeling that somehow all would be made clear if I just waited for the still, small voice to murmur my future in my ear.

After we had all changed into more comfortable clothes and

had a spot of tea, Susan went off to meet her Tony while Ryan suggested a walk along the promenade to me.

'Off you go, you love-birds,' said Ethel, 'get yourselves a bit of fresh air. Be another wedding soon, I reckon.'

I smiled uncertainly at this but agreed a walk would be a lovely idea. It was a delightful spring day and the afternoon sun was pleasantly warm, shining a sharp yellow on the sidewalks and the white walls of the houses. We strolled along in companionable silence, my spirits uplifted at having Ryan to myself and also because Joe and Sheila were happy and Mean Millie was no more.

We sat down on a bench and Ryan lit a cigarette.

'Joe tells me you want to go to a college, Bridie,' said Ryan after a while.

I watched him smoking for a bit, admiring the rise of his sharp, high cheekbones. 'Yes, I want to learn about proper catering. I want to learn something useful and get myself out and about a bit more, find myself a place to live. I may stay here in Bournemouth, I'm not sure yet. Depends where I find a suitable course.'

'But you're already a great cook,' he said, puzzled.

'Well, you learn more than just cooking. You learn about how to run a hotel or a restaurant, how to lay tables properly, shop for the right things, and deal with staff and how to see to the business and book-keeping side. It might be useful one day.'

'Can't see why. You won't need to run a business married to me. You'll have kids and you'll come along with me wherever I go, won't you?'

I picked at the white freesia still in my jacket and twirled the half dead flower in my hands. 'Ryan, why does everyone assume I'm going to marry you? Seems everyone has decided my fate for me. Don't I get a say in this?'

'But you love me, Bridie, and I love you. What more is there to say? It's so simple and right and meant to be. I knew it as soon as I met you and you but a gangly kid.'

'Oh, thanks.'

He sighed and took my hand in his. 'I'm not the sort for

posh words and speeches, Bridie, you know that. I can't say such stuff easy. I only know what I feel – feel in my heart here.'

He put my hand on his heart as he said this as if to let me feel it beating beneath his jacket and I was touched by his words.

'My heart's open to you – wide open,' he continued. 'It tells you the truth of what it feels. I feel such deep love for you. It's like I know you through and through and down and up. I have a lot of love to give, such a lot of love. You're my girl, I know it, and you always will be. You know it, too. You saying you don't love me any more?'

My own heart moved out in a wave towards him at these words and I reached out and touched his cheek with my hand.

'Ryan, I do love you just the way you're saying and it's good to hear you say all this at last. I love you so much it hurts and the separation is tough enough already. It's something I've had to get used to and always will, won't I? But maybe you should have said some of these things before, not taken me for granted like you have. I never heard all this from you; you never even said you really loved me. And things have to be said sometimes. I wasn't sure and that's made me try not to love you too hard case you let me down in the end, in case I was dreaming.'

'You aren't dreaming, Bridie, and that's the truth. I'm mad for you. Always have been. But it wouldn't have done to show it when you were a kid. People would have said I was up to no good. Your dad would have whacked me one and mine too. So I had to keep quiet, don't you see that?'

I fell silent for a bit and a strange sense of regret came over me.

'Maybe we met too young,' I said sadly, 'maybe it's too late now. It's hard to explain but I feel a need just for a bit – just for a bit, mind – to be myself. To be Bridie O'Neill and not what everyone else wants her to be. I thought I was content with a simple life – well, I was content, but now something's stirring in me. A need for change and action and experience. I want to go to college, improve my education, learn to fend for myself. I'll have to learn to do just that if we do marry for you may be away for ages. I know the lonely existence of a keeper's wife. I don't mind it, don't get me wrong. I like the life and doubt I'd ever get bored for I enjoy my own company. But I want to see the world a little, the world beyond the keeper's cottages and the lights. I feel so ignorant.'

He looked at me askance. 'Ignorance can be bliss, Bridie,' he said. 'Knowledge isn't all it's cooked up to be. It can be a dangerous thing. May make you all dissatisfied and miserable where you were peaceful and happy before.'

'Well, Eve will taste the apple, like it or not,' I smiled. 'I want a bite of the apple, Ryan. Ask me to marry you properly in a year's time and then we'll see. By then you'll be an AK and you'll have had some experience. You may want to spend your life on an ivory tower but I'm not so sure I want to any more. Don't take me for granted, let me have an identity of my own. Not just as your wife, Mr Waterman.'

'You've been getting into all this bloody feminist stuff by the sound of it,' he said in some disgust. 'It won't make you happier, Bridie, you mark my words. You've changed, you have. What's changed you? Is it that bastard Jim Bosworth? He's always had his eye on you, I know it. Smart bastard, with his Cambridge accent and all his fine ways! I saw how he was eyeing you up. He's lucky he didn't get another sock in the eye but I wasn't going to play up at Mum's wedding.'

'Well, I'm glad you didn't! And stop swearing like that, Ryan. I've never heard you go on like this. It's not Jim, it's meeting Millie again that changed me,' I said. 'I faced fear and anger and hatred and all the bad things in me and I have overcome them and in a way, I've found my real self.'

'I don't understand. You seem harder and not the sweet, gentle kid I knew.'

'All the more reason for us to wait then, Ryan,' I said. 'In a couple of years you may not feel the same about me nor I you. We were kids when we met and now we're both grown up and naturally things change.'

'Hell, Bridie, I thought it was all so sure and certain and mapped out,' he said disconsolately. 'Look, I'm asking you now, marry me and come with me and forget all this college stuff. I'm off to the rock light soon and we'll get a flat in the nearest town and you can maybe take up something there, get a local job or something. Parting now and then's not always so bad, you know, it keeps love fresh, keeps a marriage from getting stale and boring. Don't look at Mum and Dad, they're different in nature but we're so alike you and me, we understand each other really deep. It could be like a honeymoon every time we meet. There's grandeur in that. Oh, Bridie, I want you to come with me, want to be sure you're mine. If you go off like this on your own anyone may get you before me. I can't abide that thought. You're *my* girl, d'you hear?'

These last words stung me to anger and I rose and began to walk on. He came after me, taking my arm and looking into my face.

'Now what?' he asked. I shook him off.

'You don't *own* me, Ryan. Don't you understand? I want to be myself for a bit, not just someone's wife. Let me go and ask again in a year's time. I'm still too young to marry. I don't want to be a mother yet, have lots of kids. I'm not ready for it. *I'm* the sensible one, not you. I've never known you so carried away! Look, you may feel different as well, meet another girl. How do I know? It's a risk we'll both have to take.'

He let go of my arm and walked along in silence beside me. I could tell he was angry. When we came to the end of the promenade we stood and looked over the sea. The tide had come in and the waves, rippled by the faintest breeze, were moving in delicate rhythm, lapping against the bulwarks and sides of the promenade. Little fair-weather clouds scuttled along the sky like busy people off to the shops. It all seemed so peaceful, unlike our stormy feelings.

Ryan turned to me miserably. 'You won't be happy, Bridie,' he said again. 'You won't be happy without me and a quiet life. It's the way you are and I know it. I know what you are better'n you do yourself. But be free if you must and I'll be back in a year and a day, like a fairytale hero, you wait and see.'

He turned and took me in his arms as he had never done

before, kissing me passionately and feverishly, and we kissed for a long time. Feelings, desires, longings flared up in me and I breathed hard, burying my face in his jacket. He held me tightly and said, 'See, you want me like I want you, Bridie. Why are you so stubborn, damn you?'

'A year and a day,' I said breaking away from him and we walked home in silence. I was *not* going to be passive. I already felt miserable but there was no turning back. My mind was made up and Ryan would just have to go along with it or go away.

I felt so sad when the time came for him to leave us. We hugged one another for a long time, speechless, forlorn, and he looked at me before he left with a deep, searching look that seared my soul. I wondered why I was making us both so unhappy. What was driving me like this? Wouldn't it just be simpler to give in and go along with Ryan, flow with the current like an unmoored boat? But I couldn't. Some spirit of self preservation made me feel a desperate need to flow against it, to swim upstream like a salmon and find my way back to my own true self.

PART 2

'Oh, London Town's a fine town and London sights are rare,
And London Ale is right ale and brisk's the London air.'
' London Town' John Masefield

Chapter 18

London. All blazing lights and shops and traffic and scurrying people flying about like a load of bees whose hive has been disturbed. It was almost too much for me when I got off the train at Waterloo. The noise of chattering, restless, moving people, trains coming and going, announcements over the tannoy, the rattle of luggage on trolleys – it all hit me like a brickbat in the face. I wanted to turn tail, run back and get a job in Bournemouth instead.

Why had I ever listened to Jim? He had kept writing since Joe's wedding, urging me to come and join him in London. His persistence wore me down in the end and I began to consider the idea as a possibility. And now here I was.

'You'll love it, Bridie,' he kept saying, 'you'll never want to leave.'

But I didn't love it. I felt terrified of so much noisy humanity and stood rooted to the spot, jostled by people who were used to all this and who knew just where they were going and why. No one took any notice of me at all except to give me an impatient look as they bumped into me, wondering what sort of a fool I was, standing there as if turned to stone.

Jim came running down the platform towards me. I was deeply relieved to see his familiar face.

'Oh, Jim!' I exclaimed. Seeing my look of consternation and dismay he laughed, then caught me up in his arms and hugged me.

'Bridie! Don't look so scared. It's fine. You'll get used to it. Then you won't be able to bear to stay in all those lonely spots you lived in for so long. Bit of a shock at first, I know, but I'm here. You're not alone.'

He was so sweet and caring. I felt a sense of comfort and trust in him. After all, he was family – almost. Picking up my two cases, he called a porter to take them out to his car.

'You've got your own car?'

'Bit of an old banger, really, But she gets me about. Vital when I'm in Cambridge, saves no end of train fares and hassle. I'd have driven down to get you from Bournemouth if you'd let me. Why wouldn't you let me?'

'I wanted to experience the train journey,' I laughed. 'Joe paid first class for me and it was so nice and comfy. I had a little meal in the buffet car and felt quite posh. Never done any of these things before, Jim, it's so exciting. Where do we go now?'

Jim was all cheerful and pleased with himself. He took me by the arm and gently steered me though the crowds until we reached his car. 'I found you a room,' he said. 'Alice, a friend of mine from Uni, told me about it. Her mother's really rich, owns houses all over the place and does single lettings in Archway. It's not the best of areas, I'm afraid.'

'That's kind of you, Jim. I wouldn't have known where to begin.'

'No problem. I'm here to help you. I told you so. This Archway place will do for a bit. And then we can go and look for something more salubrious.'

'Mmm ... .' I smiled and looked suitably grateful but wasn't keen on all this 'we'. It sounded as if *Jim* was trying to take over my life now. However kind all this help was meant to be, I was stubbornly determined to make my own decisions. All the same, as we drove through what appeared to be endless miles of streets, all looking alike, shabby, grey and ugly, I was relieved that I didn't have to negotiate all this on my own.

Just looking around this busy city made me feel homesick. I longed for open spaces, the crashing sound of the sea, the funny sight of oystercatchers wading in the mud and the wailing cries of the gulls over the rocks. The only sea round here was made up of people surging to and fro, lapping round every corner and every street. What was I doing here? My heart sank within me.

Ryan was right – I would never get used to this horrible place. However, here I was and I must make the best of it, see if I could find work and save enough money. Then I might decide what to do with my life and where to settle for good. Oh, but it would have to be by the sea!

We arrived, after what seemed an age of manoeuvring round noisy, traffic-filled streets, at a tall thin terraced house in a busy main road. The gaunt, forbidding houses stretched in a row along the road with little yards separated from the pavement by low stone walls in front and stone steps leading to shabby neglected front doors. We walked up the flight of steps to a double front door that was once a royal blue but now cracked and peeling. Taking the keys from his pocket, Jim let us into a dark, dreary, uncared-for hallway. The walls were a grimy beige and some kids had scribbled on it as far as they could reach. A public phone box was attached to the wall, surprisingly still intact. There was a nice square floor of mosaic tiling, but the same couldn't be said for the stair carpet: thin, spotted grey, held in place by brass runners that hadn't been polished in years.

I thought of Sid Waterman and what he would have to say if he saw such neglect. He would have this lazy lot polishing those rails and painting the walls too. As we climbed up the narrow stairs, we passed other closed doors, many of them looking scratched and scuffed. On each landing there were two rooms and a sash window that looked down upon a small fenced-off back garden. The garden was just a tumble of weeds, mainly rosebay willow herb growing in wild pink profusion but it was the most attractive sight I'd seen up to now.

I already hated the place; its bleak, dingy Victorian atmosphere was depressing and claustrophobic. Jim seemed oblivious to the decay around him and kept rattling on about all the sights he meant to take me to see.

'You've got to see Buckingham Palace, Madame Tussauds, the Tower of London and Hyde Park, have a ride on a bus and on the Tube. Bet you've never even been on an escalator. That's the tourist stuff, of course. After that I'll introduce you to some of my friends and we'll go to some nightclubs or boating on the

Thames … '

'Whoa!' I exclaimed. 'All in good time, Jim. I need to look for a job first before I can afford all this.'

'Oh,' he said, 'you'll be my guest. It's my welcome to London, little sis.'

Using another door key, Jim let me into a large room overlooking the street. I was disappointed not to be overlooking the garden but Jim told me the rooms at the front were bigger and anyway he had to take what was on offer. He dropped my bags with some relief for the stairs were steep.

'Feels like you've brought half of Bournemouth with you,' he groaned as he sank down onto the bed. Lying back, he flung his arms out, wiggling his aching fingers.

'All my worldly possessions. Mostly clothes and none of them much good. Thanks for bringing the cases up. You're quite the gent nowadays.'

'I always was,' he grinned. 'I always will be.'

'Then stop lying all over my bed and let's put the kettle on. There is a kettle here, I hope.'

He bounced off the bed. 'Must be. Let's have a look in the cupboard.'

We found a much-used tin kettle and gave it a good rinse out. I felt suspicious of the level of cleanliness in this place, being used to sparkling glassware and mugs that weren't coated in tannin. Luckily Jim had some matches in his jacket pocket and he got the little gas stove lit up and put the kettle on to boil. Then he rinsed out the mugs while I unpacked the tea and sugar.

'Haven't got any milk,' I said.

'There's a little shop on the corner,' said Jim, 'I spotted it coming up. I'll nip down and get a pinta for you.'

While he was off on his errand, I looked around and took stock of the room. It was a fair size, bigger than I'd been used to in the cottages and certainly bigger than Ethel's box room. The ceilings were high and it might once have been quite an attractive room. It was reasonably well kept, the cream paint looking quite fresh and new. However, I made up my mind to scrub the place from top to toe before I even unpacked. There was a drum of Vim under the sink, some green soap, a dustpan and brush and a few scourers. The last tenant had left a bit of washing up liquid as well. That would do for a starters.

Jim arrived with the milk, a packet of biscuits, some butter and a loaf of sliced bread. He'd even thought to get a tin of corned beef to cut up for sandwiches.

'Good thinking,' I said. 'I'm getting peckish.'

'Student sustenance,' he smiled. 'We live on corned beef, baked beans, bread and biscuits *ad nauseum*. I can do better than that now, thank goodness! It's weird having some spare cash for once in my life. I feel really rich but I'll have to be careful. Money doesn't last forever and thankfully I do have some summer work lined up.'

'Your money won't last at all the way you're proposing to spend it. Nightclubs, taking me around and all that – London flats and cars…'

'I need somewhere to live and transport is always useful. I hate waiting about for buses in the rain. Hate waiting for anything really. I can't wait to finish my degree and get a pupillage in London with some famous barrister. I've been pulling strings like mad lately and may have some good news when I next see you. It's never too early to get oneself with the right set, you know. I want to do exceedingly well, Bridie, exceedingly well.' He said this with a fierce passion in his voice.

'What's so important in doing well?' I asked. 'Frankly, I just want to be peaceful and happy.'

'My dear, you're a girl. Girls aren't ambitious as a rule, though they should be. Men have to be, you know. I want success, Bridie, I *need* success. I want to prove something to myself as well as to others. Show them I'm better than they are; a force to be reckoned with.'

'Isn't it just sibling rivalry? You want to do better than Andy?'

'Oh, Andy,' he said dismissively, 'he only thinks about making money – and he will, damn him. He's always had the gift for it and has no principles of any sort. I'd like to do better than him, naturally. I *was* Mother's little darling, you know, till Andy got a bit older and began to lay on the charm and hypocrisy. He's always been a liar and a cheat and kept Mum buttered up for his own ends. And she fell for it, poor fool.'

For a moment Jim looked pensive then went on in the same passionate yet oddly distant tone of voice he sometimes used. It was as if a voice spoke through him at times, using him as its mouthpiece. Where that voice came from within him, I had no idea, but it often scared me.

'I believe in justice, Bridie, that's why I want to go for criminal law. I want to see the evil people of this world behind bars. Pity they gave up hanging from the gallows. I want the victims and the innocent to walk free and safe. Isn't that a nobler desire than wanting to grub about for money all the time? Money is great. Oh, yes, it's a key to a lot of things but in the end it corrupts and rules you. No, it isn't money I'm after but justice, seeing justice done.'

These words all sounded very moral and high-principled and yet to my ears there was an almost chilling intensity in his voice that spoke more of a crusade and desire for power.

'Sounds like you want to play God, Jim,' I said. 'You make me think of that Lewis Carroll rhyme ... "I'll be Judge, I'll be Jury, said cunning old Fury. I'll try the whole lot and condemn them to death!" '

Jim's face relaxed and he laughed. 'I shall only be a barrister, not a Judge. But if I believe in my client, I shall do all I can to persuade a jury. The *power* will be in my ability to put forth what I believe to be right and the rest is up to the system.'

'All the same, I can just see you as a judge, one day,' I said. 'Then the power *would* be yours once the verdict was returned. The power over a man's life. Just suppose he was innocent of the crime? I would hate that responsibility.'

'No, I prefer the power of the advocate – the power of words, Bridie, the power of persuasion. We can do nothing about miscarriages of justice. They do happen, of course, but a man can appeal, can't he? The British system of justice is the best in the world and I trust it implicitly. But a barrister uses ...

persuasion.'

I stared at him and he looked at me in a funny sort of way as he said this. My heart leapt a little and suddenly I felt uncomfortable. I was tired and really wanted him to go so that I could get on with my cleaning and settling in. Putting down my mug of tea, I suppressed a yawn.

'Jim, I'm dead beat. I really need a rest now.'

He got the hint and rising, said, 'Right, I'll get going. I'm afraid I don't have a phone in my flat yet but here's my work number. I've got a fantastic bit of work for the hols, real bit of luck. I'll pop round tomorrow night to be sure you're okay and settling in and tell you all about it. Maybe take you out for a meal or something.'

'There's no need,' I said gently. 'I'm not a baby, Jim. I'll find my feet in no time. You don't need to molly-coddle me and I don't want you to either. I really want to do something for myself. Not that I'm ungrateful for all your kindness and help. It's great to be welcomed. It's great to know you're nearby. But let me be for a week or so. I need to sort myself out.'

'Okay, have it your way.' He sounded disappointed. I didn't care. I was tired of everyone running my life.

He came over and gave me a little kiss on the cheek. I smiled, opened the door and almost pushed him out. He seemed reluctant to leave but that was tough. I'd just sat down with a deep sigh of relief when he was back, knocking on the door.

'What is it?' I asked irritably.

'I almost forgot to give you the keys,' he said, 'put them back in my pocket by habit. Sorry. I really am going now.'

'Bye, Jim!' I said firmly. His face clouded but he went at last and I leant against the door until his steps died away on the stairs. Then looked about me.

Why was I here? I felt a sudden feeling of dread in the pit of my stomach but put it down to nonsense, tiredness and overstrained nerves. Here I was and must make the best of it.

Chapter 19

Shaking off a heavy tiredness, I set to work cleaning the place to my satisfaction. Though never as finicky as Sidney Waterman, I'd been trained to keep things spotless first by Millie, then by Dad. I couldn't live anywhere that felt crawly so I dusted and scrubbed and made everything gleam then felt more comfortable. Unpacking my few goods, I hung the clothes up in the old wooden wardrobe in the corner after checking for moths. Joe had framed the pictures of Bill and Maureen O'Neill for me and I set them up on the chest of drawers along with one of Joe and Sheila at their wedding and a big, blown up photo of Ryan actually smiling and looking relaxed. I must have caught him on a good day when I took that photo. These were the few people I loved with all my heart. I smiled and kissed Ryan's photo as I set it up.

'Miss you already, my darling,' I murmured. For a long, unhappy moment my heart ached with longing. It would be ages before I saw him and no way to communicate, even if I wanted to. He was on his Light in the middle of a storming ocean and I in my little room in the midst of a sea of strangers. I envied him. *He* was where I wanted to be. So why was I here? Why had I, in my own way, cut myself off from those I loved just as Ryan did whenever he took up his lonely sojourn on a lighthouse far from humanity? I had no answer for the question except that deep down we were so alike, Ryan and I.

I looked for a long time at the pictures of my parents. They still seemed unreal to me; unknown people who had once lived and breathed, whose scent, whose voices and faces and expressions I would never know except in dreams where they sometimes haunted me. Yet, these two unknown beings were in my blood and bones, my form and nature came from them. It was strange to imagine this and in that moment I felt a vast sense of loneliness. I would never know where I sprang from, not ever know true parenting. An orphan from birth, an orphan for ever in life. I could do nothing else but support myself and do everything for myself. How could I really trust anyone else, however kind they seemed?

Sheets and blankets were provided and they seemed clean enough but I had a good look over the bed before re-making it, scared by tales of bed bugs and the like. Nothing strange seemed to be lurking in there despite my repeated banging and thumping so hopefully all was clear. Everything appeared reasonable and I began to feel a little happier.

There was no time now to make it to the corner shop. That would have to wait for tomorrow when I would buy some food. I'd have to make do with the bread and butter, corned beef and biscuits for today. How thoughtful Jim was to have bought these for me. He was so sensible and helpful. It was foolish of Ryan to think Jim still had romantic feelings for me. Jim must have met loads of attractive girls at Uni by now. He had mentioned one … Alice? I wondered if I would ever meet her.

Looking round, I felt that my new abode looked pale and drab. I longed for a touch of colour, some flowers perhaps. Remembering the vivid colour of the rosebay out in the garden, I wended my way downstairs. On the bottom floor, I saw a long corridor that led to a big, stout, bolted door with a key in the lock. Unbolting the door, I stepped out, thankful for some fresh air. It was late in the day and the sun was beginning to set; songbirds were singing their vespers in the few old but leafy trees that managed to grow between the rows of terraces where all the little tiny gardens backed onto one another. They provided a row of arboreal green that softened the harshness a little. The garden, if it could be honoured with such a name, looked quiet and peaceful and I felt a sense of refreshment just standing there listening to the warbling trills of the blackbirds and robins. It made a change to hear songbirds rather than noisy, shrieking gulls.

Despite my love of order and tidiness, I rather liked a little wildness in a garden. There was a big rampant hydrangea in a corner, its bluey pink blossoms turning to a papery brown shade. A buddleia had seeded itself into a crack in the pavement and was still covered in deep purple flowers. The fiery pink of the rosebay made a beautiful contrast. I began to pick some of the tall stalks and tried to break off branches of buddleia but it was hard work as I hadn't thought to bring any scissors with me. I made a bit of a mess pulling the woody stems apart. So intent was I on my task that it gave me a shock when I heard a voice behind me.

'Wot you doin' 'ere?'

I jumped half out of my skin and turned to see a little old fellow watching me from the doorway. He looked at least sixty or more, his face thin and shrivelled, surrounded by longish white hair with a flat cap atop. His frame was bent and he leaned against the doorpost stiffly as if his joints were playing him up and he needed the support. Baggy, ill-fitting trousers were held up with braces and armbands kept up his sleeves. All the clothes looked far too big for him as if they'd come from a jumble sale.

'I'm picking flowers,' I replied.

The old fellow wheezed with laughter as if I was saying something comical. 'Them ain't flowers, them's weeds, gel.'

I looked at the vivid pink blooms in my hand, 'Far as I'm concerned, mister, they're flowers and I'm putting them in my room.'

'We called 'em fireweed, those,' stated the old man, gesturing towards the rosebay. 'Y'know why? Because in the War they allus grew on bomb sites or where there'd been a fire. I should know. I used to be a fireman. And these 'ere would all spring up and cover the ground fast as you please. And ain't they the colour of fire an'all? Nature's a funny business. And 'ere's you wantin' to pick 'em for your room. Daft, I call it. They won't last five minnits; weeds don't like to be picked. Me little gel used to pick stuff like that and bring it in and in five minutes they was all droopin' and then she'd bawl 'er bleedin' 'ead orf.'

I couldn't help laughing. 'Don't worry, I won't bawl,' I said. 'I know they won't last but even a few moments of colour will cheer me up.'

'You ain't from these parts, that's for sure,' said the old fellow, peering at me. 'Can tell you've a different way of speakin' but I can't place it. What room you got?'

'Up at the top, in the front.'

'Oh, yeah, used to be a young fellow there but 'e upped and went, couldn't pay 'is rent, they said. Wonder what 'appened to 'im? Most likely took to the streets. Some of 'em do. Bad lot 'e was, glad 'e went. I can tell you ain't gonna be 'ere long.'

'How can you tell that?'

'Bleedin' posh, in't you? Pickin' flowers an all. Daft. Wot's yer name?'

'Bridie O'Neill.'

'Wouldn've put you as Irish,' he said in some surprise, 'you sound too posh to be a potato-eater.'

'My parents were Irish but they died long ago,' I explained politely. 'What's *your* name?'

'They all calls me Dixie. Dixie Dean, that's me.'

'Nice to meet you, Dixie.' I made to go past him. He released himself from the doorpost and stood aside reluctantly. He could have nattered on all day, having nothing else to do. Poor, shabby old soul.

'I lives down 'ere,' he said, 'in that room wot looks over the yard. That's why I saw you out 'ere. Wondered what you was up to.'

'Maybe we could tidy it up together some day,' I suggested, 'put some proper flowers in the ground.'

'What for?' he said with contempt, 'nobody gives a damn. What's the point?'

'It'll make me feel happy,' I said, 'and who knows, if we make it nice, then others may like to come out here too. That would be good, wouldn't it?'

'For a bright lookin' thing, you can be really daft,' he said again, 'but then the Irish always are daft. Soddin' potato eaters.'

I said no more but walked up the stairs, knowing his bleary eyes followed me. I sighed. Were these to be the kind of fellow tenants I would have to endure? My mind was made up, though, despite Dixie Dean. I would get round to tidying up the scrap of garden and make it a nice little retreat for myself if no one else.

I went to bed early and slept a good part of the next day, exhausted with the travel and new sounds, sights and smells. The street traffic kept me awake for a while but I eventually got used to it and went off into the deepest sleep I'd had for ages. Rising late next morning, I went down to the bathroom on the second floor to have a bath, wash my hair and make myself feel neater and fresher. Then off to Preston's corner shop for food and other necessities. There was an oven and a little fridge provided in the room I rented and over that a deep cupboard for dry goods. Putting away my few bits of shopping I studied my purse. Joe had given me fifty pounds to 'tide me over' as he put it until I could start earning. It was a princely sum and I was grateful for it. It crossed my mind to put it into some sort of bank account, or maybe the Post Office savings bank. It wasn't a good idea to carry all this cash around with me.

Not being in the mood for cooking anything clever just yet, I baked a potato for lunch with lots of butter and some peas. I really was being a 'potato eater' now as that old fool downstairs had called me. How rude people were here in London! As I ate, I wondered just what sort of job I might go for and how I was to set about it?

Realising I'd forgotten to buy those vital items, toilet rolls, which as I discovered were not universally provided in the loo on the second floor, I set off again for Preston's corner shop. As I came back indoors, I met up again with old Dixie Dean. I swear he was lurking behind his door and waiting for me. He seemed a lonely, miserable old soul so I said 'Hello' politely when he popped out of his door on hearing my steps.

'What you up to now?' he said, looking with interest at my grocery basket.

'Just shopping. I need to eat.'

'Well, some of us is lucky then, ain't we? Hardly manage a bite on the dole, do I?' he said, looking mournful.

You old scrounger, I thought but I asked, 'Aren't you retired, then?'

'Retired? They laid me off at the factory years ago. Ain't been able to find nuffin' else, 'ave I?'

'I thought you said you were a fireman?'

'So I was when I was younger. That was in the War, that was. But I lost me leg in a h'accident, din' I? So I'm disabled now. See ... ' and he rolled up his trouser to show me the false leg. It made me shudder.

'And I'm on the dung 'eap, ain't I?' he added. 'They think they're doin' me a favour givin' me a few bob a week from the National Assistance. Me, what risked my life daily to save folks – that's what I get for it.'

'If I want work, where do I go?'

'You got to sign on at the Labour Exchange. Queue up with all the others. And then get treated like a bleedin' pariah by them Civil Servants. Like it was your fault you ain't got a job. They're supposed to take so many disabled on these firms they sends you to but they always think of some excuse and get shot of you after a bit. Tried 'em all, I should know.'

'I have to *queue up*?'

'Yeah. They'll sign you on, give you a few jobs to try for and give you an immediate payment to tide you over, like.'

'Oh, I don't need payment, I've enough to manage on for a bit,' I said.

' 'Ave you now? You've got a bit o' cash, 'ave you?' His old eyes narrowed and I wished I'd shut up. It didn't do to be innocent here in London.

'Just a little bit,' I said hastily, 'till I start work.'

'Some folks is lucky, then.,' he snorted.

'Where's there a High Street?' I asked.

'Archway Road or Junction Road's the nearest. There's a tube station in Junction Rd as well. You planning to do more shopping then?'

'No, just getting my bearings.'

'So where you from then?'

'Down south,' was my short reply. He was a nosy man and I didn't trust or like him. I clammed up and my face must have expressed my annoyance. Picking up my bags, I began to walk upstairs.

'Be like that,' muttered the old misery and went back in his room, slamming the door behind him.

When upstairs I found I hadn't locked the door when I went out. I just wasn't used to taking precautions of this kind but realised there was a need to be careful here. It was not like the coastal cottages where you could leave your door open without fear of thieves.

Still feeling tired, I sat on the only easy chair and lost myself in an interesting book but must have dozed for the next thing I heard was a knock on the door.

Hope it's not that horrid old man, I thought, shaking myself awake, and went to answer it. I might have guessed. It was Jim standing there, looking very smart, brushed up and handsome.

He looked me up and down. 'Get dressed, Bridie, I'm taking you out to dinner and won't take no for an answer.'

I blinked but let him in, yawning profusely as I did so.

'I'm not awake properly.'

'Lazy little thing, aren't you?' he said, giving me an affectionate peck on the cheek.

'No, I'm not! Just tired. It's all so strange and new.'

'Of course,' he said, 'of course it is, Bridie. I understand. That's why I want to treat you a bit till you get on your feet. I've something important to tell you that you'll be really pleased to hear.'

'What's that?' I asked, all agog for the news and a lot more awake than before.

He grinned and put a finger to his lips. 'Not telling. Not until you are all dressed up and we have a nice meal in front of us. So get going,' and he gave me playful shove.

'I'm not dressing with you here.'

'Let me decide what you're going to wear,' he said, 'then I'll go and wait in the car for you. I've parked outside the front door.'

'Why do you want to decide what I wear?'

'Because I know where I'm taking you and what's expected there.'

I had to admit to being intrigued and a little excited by all this. He chose a soft blue flowered cotton dress, about the only smart thing I possessed.

'You haven't got much, have you?' he said disparagingly. 'Really you need something more dressy for where we're going but this will have to do.'

I felt a little crushed and seeing my look of dismay he laughed and took my hand in his. 'I reckon I'll have to take you to the Nag's Head for some shopping at Jones Bros. You need some smarter clothes now you're a Londoner, Bridie. This stuff is fine for the seaside but not here.'

'I will, Jim, but it'll have to wait till I earn my first week's wages.'

'Ah,' he said mysteriously, 'that mayn't be so far away.'

'You're making me very curious. Tell me!'

Jim tapped his nose and shook his head.

'You've improved this place already,' he remarked, looking around, 'even flowers. Damn, I should have thought to bring you flowers. I'm slipping. My apologies.'

'It's okay, you don't have to bring me flowers. I got those – weeds, really – from the so-called garden downstairs. There's a weird old fellow lives down there who popped out of the woodwork and gave me such a scare. I didn't like him very much but he seems a sad old soul. I scared him in return by saying I meant to tidy up the garden a bit. He thinks I'm really nuts.'

'Well, ignore him. Do whatever it takes to make the place a bit more pleasing. All the same, I've high hopes of getting you out of here soon. I don't mean to leave you here for ever; it's only a stop-gap situation.'

I looked around. The place was already feeling a little more cheerful and it was cosy enough.

'It's cheap here and I think I'll get used to it in time. There's a lot more room in here than I had at Ethel's place. I'll stay as long as it takes, so don't feel bothered on my account. I have simple needs, Jim. I'm used to not having very much.'

'That may be so, but things can change. I'll make sure it doesn't take long,' was the reply. I looked at him. I didn't like the way he seemed to assume he could control my life – no 'by your leave or may I?' – just like Millie had done. I couldn't help but wonder what was in his mind at times, what lay behind the pleasant, charming façade. His nature wasn't uncomplicated and easy to read like Ryan and I felt there was more than a hint of deviousness about him for all his bonhomie.

Jim went downstairs to wait for me in his car. I dressed and made myself look as nice as I could. I had no jewellery except for a little silver necklace that Joe and Sheila had presented to me on their wedding day as a memento and a delicately chased silver bracelet, which had been a parting present from Ryan. He had inscribed our names inside it – *To Bridie with love from Ryan* – and it felt like a talisman against evil. I wore it all the time. Putting on the necklace, I looked at my reflection in the little mirror over the sink and decided it would have to do.

I went downstairs to find Jim standing by his car, smoking a cigarette and looking a trifle impatient at the time I'd taken.

'I've booked a table for eight o'clock,' he said, grinding the cigarette beneath his heel and opening the car door for me. 'We have to drive into London and park somewhere. It's getting harder and harder to find a parking space these days so we need to get going, Bridie. What took you so long?'

'All right. I didn't know that, did I?' I was annoyed at being bustled about this way, being a slow sort of person who hated to hurry too much. Jim was like a whirlwind, always dashing about and in a rush. What was the point? As Ryan always said, we were only rushing to our coffins.

'I met the old boy you mentioned,' said Jim. 'He gave me a very queer look, muttered a lot then shambled off into his filthy den.'

'I think he's lonely, poor soul,' I said. 'He told me he was a fireman in the War. I feel sorry for him.'

'You're far too kind. You'll have to get a bit tougher, Bridie. London's for survivors, not weaklings.'

I regarded him with some surprise. 'I think I could call myself a survivor, Jim, don't you? I'm no weakling.'

He glanced over at me for a moment before turning his eyes back to the road.

'You're right, that was a stupid remark. No, you're not a weakling, Bridie, and that's what I admire about you. I can't abide silly, fluffy women who play at being helpless.'

We remained silent for the rest of the journey. I was caught up with taking in the passing roads and changing scenes. Today things seemed less frightening and I noticed how fine some of the houses looked as we began to move further into the city. There were lots of open spaces, commons and parks. It wasn't as crowded a city as I'd thought at first and had a lot more natural beauty in it than I'd expected. We made our way towards the West End, where, Jim assured me, there was always fun at this time of night.

'The City's dead as a doornail now all the office workers have gone home. The business part is in that area around St. Paul's because that's where the mighty Old Lady of Threadneedle Street is. The good old Bank of England in other words. The only busy area at this time of the night is Fleet Street where all the newspaper offices are. From there you'll come to the Temple. I shall take you and show you the Inns of Court soon. I mean to have my chambers there some day and be a famous barrister. You wait and see, Bridie. We'll be rich.'

'We?'

'An expression,' he said looking at me with that humorous sideways look that I found rather attractive.

We toured about some time looking for a parking space, at last finding a slot in some leafy square. "Fraid it'll be a bit of a walk,' said Jim. 'D'you want me to call a taxi?'

'Heavens, no, a walk will do us good. That's what legs are for.'

I enjoyed the walk in the fresh night air. The neon lights were just beginning to twinkle and turn. I was amazed and enchanted with Piccadilly Circus with all its flashing signs and coloured lights. Eros fired his perpetual love arrows from his plinth in the centre of the Circus and traffic flowed around him non-stop. I stood and stared until Jim pulled me impatiently away.

'Come on, table's booked and it was a hell of a job to get one. We can't afford to be late or someone else will have it.'

He led the way down some steps into a restaurant below street level called The White Bear. It seemed an odd name for a restaurant. I had never been to a place as posh as this and felt a little overawed as well as underdressed. Most women wore sparkly or sophisticated evening numbers, the men were all in suits, some even in formal dinner suits with bow ties. A waiter glided forward and took us to a table. Music was playing softly somewhere, lights dimmed. The atmosphere was seductive and the smell of food delicious.

Jim pulled out a chair for me. I sat down and took everything in, almost open-mouthed. I was relieved to see that nobody was staring at my shabby little cotton dress.

'Do you like it here?' Jim asked, looking around with a sigh of satisfaction. 'I've been told it's the place to go if you are anyone. It's a bit pricey but my theory is you have to start as you mean to go on. That's the only way to attract the sort of people and attention you want.'

'I don't particularly wish to attract attention,' I said, 'but I can see you might need to if you're so determined to succeed.'

'I *am* determined to succeed,' he replied, 'you're right. Ah, here's a menu. Do you want me to read it out to you?'

'I think I'm capable of reading, Jim,' I said, astonished.

'Sorry. I mean it's in French. I can speak it quite well but I don't think you've learnt the language, have you?'

I put the menu down and surveyed him. 'As it happens, I did French at school. Not a lot but enough to get by. I'm not the ignoramus you seem to assume, Jim.'

He took my hand but I withdrew it at once, offended.

'Bridie,' he said cajolingly, 'I apologise for being so dense. It's just that I thought as you spent such a lot of time at home with only Sheila to teach you, you might have missed out.'

'As it happens, I didn't miss out,' I snapped. 'That's the mistake they made when I went back to school again but I soon proved them wrong. Shelia taught us very well and I've had time to read my socks off which is more than a lot of kids my age ever do. I read medical books, books on nature, geography, history, psychology, religion and all the classics, French literature, Italian literature, Russian literature … not in the original language, I admit, but still, I've read them. Frankly, I'd say that I'm a good deal better educated in some things than you are because you've admitted yourself you never read a lot. I'd say my general knowledge is probably a great deal better. You have specialised and so have a narrower outlook.'

Jim listened to me in respectful silence. 'I'm sure you're right.'

'But I don't know much about music,' I conceded.

He brightened up. 'That's something I do know a lot about. I learnt to play the cello at school. I love that instrument, it has such a deep, emotive tone. I'm not much cop at it but I can do a passable rendering of bits of Bach or Haydn's cello concertos.'

'Do you still have your cello?' I hadn't realised he was musical. It warmed me to him because I wanted so much to learn about classical music and a man who understood about music was something special. What little I'd ever heard was of the popular variety, the old favourites on the radio, just snatches really that made me long for more.

'Yes, it's my prized possession,' he said, 'I never had one of my own at home. Would you like to hear me play some time?'

'I *would* like that.'

His face cleared suddenly and he smiled at me with delight.

'Then I'll start practising as soon as I can and play especially for you. For you, Bridie.'

There was a sound and intensity in his voice that made me feel quite odd inside, a lurch around the stomach as if he had thrown something at me and caught me unawares, out of breath.

I took my eyes away from his and quickly put my mind on the menu.

'That would be nice, Jim,' I said as calmly as I could.

We ordered our meal, Steak Diane for Jim and veal escalope for me. It was all served elegantly, sautéed potatoes and delicious vegetables all in separate dishes, not flung pell-mell onto the plates. I took an interest in all this as I still had some idea of going in for catering. 'This is well served – I like this place,' I remarked.

'It's not bad,' Jim agreed.

'Is there a college I could apply to round here?' I asked between mouthfuls.

'What sort of college?'

'I want to study catering. There must be lots of colleges here where I can do that.'

'There's the North Western Polytechnic in Kentish Town. They may do something like that. No idea. Catering's not exactly my subject. Kentish Town's only a few stops from Archway on the Northern Line.'

'I'll find this place then and see what's on offer. I realise now that I haven't thought this whole thing through properly, just rushed off without a lot of preparation,' I said with regret. 'My hope is to be taken on somewhere for the autumn term. Or maybe find a night class of some sort and work in the day. I'll really will have to start earning, maybe doing something in a café to start with. It seems I have to go and sign up at the Labour Exchange. That's what Dixie Dean told me.'

'Aha, but that's where I come in with my little surprise,' said Jim, looking gleeful. 'You're not going to waste yourself in a café, for God's sake. Or queue up for hours at the Labour Exchange. What a ghastly thought! I have a far better proposal for you. I've been offered a summer job, a sort of pre-pupillage, so to speak, in the chambers of Sir Simeon Grantham QC, no less. I have real hopes he might become my sponsor. Do you know who he is?'

'Not a clue.'

'He's one of the biggest barristers there is just now. And because his son shares my rooms at Cambridge, I've had the marvellous luck of getting this close to the big man himself. David, that's his son, is helping out in Chambers during the summer hols and suggested to his dad that I could be useful too. Sir Simeon agreed I could come along and get some experience, isn't that smashing of him! Think of it, Bridie, if I make a good impression I may even manage to get a pupillage through his recommendation after I graduate next year.'

'I'm very pleased for you, Jim, but what on earth has all this got to do with me looking for a job?'

'I'm coming to that. Don't be so impatient. While I was there today, I heard them saying they need a new filing clerk as the old one has gone off to get married and won't be coming back. So I thought of you at once.'

He beamed at me as if he was handing me my winnings on the Grand National.

'But I don't know anything at all about office work, and what I do know, I hate,' I objected.

'It's easy, you'll soon pick it up. Just filing papers and stuff. It's not that well paid but it'd be a damn sight more than you'd get waitressing in a café and a lot less exhausting too.'

'I'm sorry, but office work is the last thing I want to do, Jim. I'd sooner get less money and help in a café or restaurant, meet amusing people. It's all I'm really any good at. The thought of being stuck in an office with lots of papers and desks and cabinets and stuffy legal people is not my idea of what I want to do. At least working in a café, I'll get some catering experience, I may even be allowed to do some cooking and it'll all be practice.'

Jim looked astonished. 'You don't want to work for Sir Simeon Grantham? Are you mad? And, Bridie, Middle Temple is such a marvellous place to be, full of history and atmosphere. And it's close to the Embankment, has lovely gardens, you'd love it there. Plus it would be an honour to work for such a brilliant man even if you don't have that much to do with him; an honour to be near a man who has done so much for the legal system. He's an inspired lawyer.'

'No,' I said, simply and firmly. 'I couldn't care less about the man. I've never heard of him and he means nothing to me.

People are only famous to those who care about what they do. Neither am I interested in the Law. I believe in justice and fairness and all that but I'm not sure the legal system always works that way. God's law, that's what I believe in. And His law is simple. He says all you need to do is love one another and all the millions of laws man has to make to protect himself would be unnecessary if we stuck to that, because no body would want to hurt or steal or be mean to other people.'

'Hmph! That sort of utopian world will never come about, Bridie, as you well know. There's been two bloody awful wars and if anything things have got worse for most people. Certainly, the crime figures are no better. In fact, they say there was less crime during the War.'

'That's hardly surprising considering half the men were fighting in it and the rest too busy to get up to much mischief. It just goes to prove men will always have to fight and make a nuisance of themselves,' I retorted. 'No, Jim, I know the world will never be filled with love but it's a nice thought and one to aim for.'

'Never filled with love? You believe that, Bridie? It's filled with love all the time … for me.' He looked at me seriously and I felt a little flutter again. His expression was frankly admiring. It unsettled me.

'You know, there's not many girls I know who are both intelligent, feminine and beautiful,' he said, 'but you are, Bridie. You're *all* that and it's some combination in a girl.' He continued to stare at me, his eyes on my mouth. 'And did you know you have the loveliest lips? I'm going to buy you a nice lipstick.' He paused and looked away as if he couldn't bear another minute of the way his ideas were going. 'God, I must put my mind elsewhere.'

'Please do!' I snapped. I didn't want to encourage him in this line of thought and didn't feel happy about the raw look of admiration in his eyes. 'That's kind of you but I don't wear lipstick. Ryan doesn't like it and neither do I.'

'*Ryan?*' He almost snorted in disgust. 'What would that misanthropic recluse understand about a truly feminine and intelligent woman? Didn't I warn you not to let him rule you?'

This was rich coming from Mr Manipulation himself but I didn't want to offend Jim too much. After all, he'd been good to me and was treating me to this slap-up dinner. So I swallowed any retort and looked down at my plate again. After a while, he said, 'You will change your mind about coming to work at the office, won't you Bridie? Think it over for a few days and don't rush into anything stupid. You can't afford to pass this by, you know. It's a great offer, really it is.'

'I don't need to think about it, Jim, the answer will always be no.'

His face clouded. 'Are you doing this to annoy me? Is it just that you don't want to work in the same place as I do?'

I contemplated this for a bit. 'No, I'm not trying to annoy you. I'm really grateful to you for caring, for trying to help me. Other people would think me mad not to accept your help. But Jim, don't you understand that I want to be left free to try and sort out things for myself for once in my life. Don't you see that? Don't you see how I need to be free of all you men for a bit – you, Ryan, Dad, everyone. It was you, after all, who told me to stand up for my own needs and not be passive and controlled by others.'

The shaft went home. His face turned a dull red. I saw Millie looking out of his eyes and for a moment shrank away from him. He was so like her and sometimes the same cold, unfeeling, demoniacal stare looked out at me.

I felt a little nervous on the way home but Jim's intense mood had switched and he made no more amorous comments. We just talked about this and that and all the while I knew he'd expect me to ask him up for a coffee and I really didn't want to do that.

He parked outside my door, then followed me as I went up the steps and got out the front door key.

'Is it okay if I come up for a bit?'

'Just for a quick coffee, Jim. I want an early night. Got lots to do tomorrow.'

'Sure, just a quick coffee,' he smiled.

He followed me up the stairs and we entered my little room. As I got the coffee on the go, Jim flung himself on the sofa and looked round, taking it all in properly for the first time. Out of the corner of my eye I saw him staring at Ryan's photo with a hateful look. When I looked over at him, he shifted his eyes from it.

'You don't have my picture in your little gallery, I see.'

I put his coffee cup beside him on a little table.

'Well, no,' I admitted, 'but then I don't actually have a picture of you.'

'I have one of you,' he said and began to sip at the coffee, staring at me over the rim.

'Do you?' I was surprised. 'Which picture's that?'

'One we took with all of us when Dad brought us to his first lighthouse, Longships, or whatever it was called. We had a Cornish cream tea together. Don't you remember?'

'I suppose so, but that was ages ago.'

'You haven't changed much.'

'I've actually changed a lot,' I said.

'Inside maybe, but not outside,' he said.

I nodded. 'Maybe.' We both fell silent for a while. I wished he would go. I felt so weary.

'You will think about coming to work with Sir Simeon, won't you?' he said, putting his empty cup down at last. 'Honestly, you'll find it easy work and enjoyable and you'll meet some interesting people. I want you to meet nice people, Bridie, not café riff-raff.'

'It's very good of you to take such an interest in my welfare,' I said with a wry smile, rising to see him off with a sense of relief.

'It's because I care about you,' he said. I put a hand up as if to shush him and he seized it and kissed it with fervour.

'Get off!' I said, pulling my hand away. 'Jim, stop being silly like this. I'm *not* your girlfriend so don't behave as if I was. I'm your sister, remember? Look, I'll think about the job but make no promises. I want to find my own way.'

'God, you're hard work!' he grumbled. 'Most girls would be

thrilled with such an offer.'

'I'm not "most girls".'

'No, you're not. Maybe that's why you're so damned interesting and attractive.' He stared at me for a long while. I returned his look. A silence fell between us laden with unexpressed feelings. Then Jim sighed and took his leave without even a goodnight peck, much to my gratitude. He was like a smouldering volcano; for the moment mere rumblings, but ready to blow up at any time.

Chapter 20

The next day I rose early. After breakfast I got out an A-Z of London and studied it. I needed to find the nearest Labour Exchange and would have to ask someone in a shop maybe or in the street. I also needed to find my way to the Polytechnic Jim had mentioned.

Putting on a smart navy skirt and pale cream blouse, which made me look efficient and capable, I sallied forth. On the way out of my door I bumped into a young, dark-skinned man coming out of the room next to mine. He raised his hat and apologised politely. I hadn't seen many West Indian people before and the sight of so many in London fascinated me. I'd heard they'd been asked to come over and help boost the post-war work force. He looked a nice person, older than myself, maybe twenty-five or so. I couldn't help staring at him but he seemed used to it. Feeling ashamed I said quite candidly, 'I'm so sorry to stare at you, mister. It's rude of me but I'm from the country and haven't met a dark-skinned person before.'

'Seems most people here haven't,' was his response. 'We don't get made that welcome either.'

'I'm sorry to hear that,' I replied, 'but I haven't felt very welcome here myself, so don't feel alone. It seems London isn't a hospitable place.'

The young man smiled and offered me his hand.

'I'm Luke McGraw. I see you've taken the vacant room next to me.' His voice had an accent but was cultured and educated. I wondered what he did for a living and why he was obliged to live in a dump like this.

'Bridie O'Neill. Pleased to meet you, Mr McGraw. Yes, I'm your new neighbour.'

'Well, Miss O'Neill, *I'll* welcome you to Portdown Road if no one else will.'

I smiled. 'Thanks – those are the first kind words anyone in the house has said to me. That old fellow downstairs is really rude.'

'What, old Dixie Dean? He's harmless enough, just nosy and a bit of a scrounger.'

'Mr McGraw, do you know where the nearest Labour Exchange is?' I asked tentatively.

'Oh, yes. Everyone here does. Most of us haunt the place. Just go right out of the door, follow Portdown Road to the end and you'll find yourself in Holloway Road. You can get a bus from there to the Labour or walk, just ask anyone.'

We parted smiling. To think a foreigner was the only person to welcome me here. I didn't count Jim who wasn't a stranger.

I eventually found the Labour Exchange, a dark, forbidding Victorian building. I pushed through the swing doors and went into the waiting room where I saw a great many people seated on hard uncomfortable chairs and more standing. There seemed to be an awful lot of them, their faces tired, dispirited or just plain bored. A receptionist took my name, gave me a form to fill in and then pointed to the back of the room.

'Have to wait a bit, 'she said brusquely. 'It's a busy day on Fridays.'

As she turned away, I heard her remark to a colleague, 'Another perishin' Irishwoman. Why can't they stay in their peat bogs?'

I began to discover that having the name O'Neill was not such a good thing round here. Almost every other name called out was Irish. The place was crawling with 'potato eaters'. I stood and waited for what seemed ages. No one offered me a seat though plenty of hale, hearty men were seated, some with their feet up on another chair. I tried to brush off the feet of one of these men but he swore at me and looked so threatening that I backed off.

'Better not cause trouble, dear,' whispered a woman standing behind me. Specially him. He's just out of the nick, he is.'

'How do you know?'

'Well, unless you've been on the bleedin' moon, you'd know as well,' was the reply. 'Everyone here knows Piggy Daniels.'

I looked at Piggy Daniels and felt the name suited him.

'What you starin' at?' he demanded but I said nothing and swiftly turned my eyes away. It seemed best not to get involved.

After a while another nasty-looking fellow came over to me and struck up a conversation of sorts. His hair was long and matted and looked as if he hadn't had a wash in weeks. How could he hope to find himself a job looking like this? At first he smiled at me with discoloured teeth and weasel eyes and mentioned the weather, the economy, the shocking shenanigans of the government who put good men like himself into this unemployed plight and then touched upon the stupidity of the 'bleedin' bastards' who'd thrown him off the site he'd been labouring on.

'Doin' my bleedin' best, I was,' he said, scraping at his teeth with a dirty, much used cocktail stick (heaven knows where he'd found that).

'Why did they throw you off the site?' I asked.

'Punched the foreman, didn't I? So would you if he kept tellin' you you was dead useless and not even fit to kick with his nice new boots – when *you* ain't got no bleedin' boots, new or otherwise. Day in an' day out he cursed me and told me how bleedin' useless I was. Kick a dog when he's down if you must but in the end the worm turns.'

I tried to make sense of his mixed metaphors but understood that he was an angry man. In a way I almost felt sorry for him. Seeing some flash of sympathy in my eye he then tried to find out where I lived and offered me a drink 'after I'd been sorted out.' I smiled feebly and said I was grateful for the offer but no thanks. The smile disappeared and so did all pretence at being nice. Looking at me sullenly, he said, 'Suit yourself, you fuckin' bitch,' and wandered off to another part of the room where he stood picking his teeth and glowering at me silently.

I felt lonely and afraid. I hated this place. There were other women there but they all looked at ease, some laughing and chatting with the men and giving as good as they got. I had no idea how to function in this environment. It was like being in another country. I watched appalled as one man, a huge burly-looking labourer, began to shout and swear at the desk clerk and make a rumpus. I could see why all the staff worked behind an iron grille. It had seemed so unfriendly but now I saw it was for their safety. Eventually the manager came out of his office and told the man he'd call the police if he didn't shut it and the fellow subsided and allowed himself to be escorted from the premises muttering and swearing as he went.

'Why's he making all that fuss?' I asked someone next to me.

'Ain't givin' him no more dole, I expect,' was the laconic answer.

When my turn came, I approached a desk and spoke to the job officer behind it. He was a tired-looking elderly man, brusque and disinterested, probably wearied with years of sitting there dealing with abusive, difficult customers. He filled in the form, barking questions at me, not even looking up.

'This the first time you've signed on?'

'Yes.'

'What have you been doing since you left school? I see you've got four O Levels.'

'I've been keeping house for my dad ... oh, and baby-sitting.'

'Bit of a waste of education, isn't it? Why don't you go for an office job? It'll be better paid than a restaurant.'

'I *hate* offices, that's why. They deaden the soul.'

The officer wasn't interested in souls, just facts. 'If you're used to housekeeping, you could try a job in a hotel ... chambermaids are always wanted.'

'I *definitely* don't want to do cleaning work.'

'Well, you're mighty picky, Miss O'Neill, if you don't mind me saying so.' He sounded cross but I didn't care. I wasn't going to do what he wanted me to do just for the sake of it. I was sure I would find what I wanted eventually.

'I want to be in catering. That's what I want to do.'

'So you want to cook or serve in a restaurant.'

'Yes, but a café will do if there's nothing better.'

'Not much in the way of *restaurants* round here, more pubs and cafés. You'll have to travel to Camden Town for decent restaurants and most of them are owned by Greek Cypriots.'

'I don't mind who I work for.'

'Maybe not, but they'll mind you. They always employ family, hardly ever outsiders. Close lot they are. Well, there's De Marco's, round the corner. I haven't heard they need anyone but go there and ask for Queenie. She's been serving there for years and you'll be hard put to match her. She never writes a thing down but remembers what every single customer wants. Frank De Marco's the owner, but Queenie hires the staff. And there's also O'Reilly's fish and chip place in Junction Rd. He wants someone to wash up and help in the kitchen. Here's the addresses – off you go and see what you can do and don't be so picky. Oh … I suppose you want an IP first.'

'What's that?'

He actually looked up at me in surprise.

'An immediate payment, of course. It has to go to the EO to authorise it – so you'll have to wait again.'

'Well, I don't need any payment,' I said, to his astonishment. 'I can manage for a little while longer on my savings.'

The officer regarded me as if I had just stepped off the moon.

'Hear that, Vera!' he called out loudly to one of his colleagues, 'got a customer here doesn't want any money!'

This remark produced a great deal of amusement amongst both staff and nearby clients. I turned bright red and gathered my papers together, stuffing them in my bag.

Still looking highly amused, the officer turned back to me and said 'Okay, well, get yourself off and if you don't have any luck you'll have to come in again and see what else is on the cards. Next please.'

I thanked him politely but he had already waved over the next applicant and didn't give me a further glance. I felt almost inhuman in this place, a name on a conveyor belt of names:

English, Scottish and Irish names, African names, Cypriot names.

I went off to find the famous Queenie at De Marco's. She was a pleasant woman in her late thirties, plump and motherly. She looked me over and shook her head.

'You'd do fine, dear, but I've just hired a couple of new girls only the other week. Give me your name and phone number and I'll let you know if one of them goes. Can't always rely on these local girls, they can be a lazy lot. You do look willing. Shame, really. I'd like to help.'

'I don't know the phone number where I live.' It hadn't occurred to me to take note of the pay phone in the hall. 'I just moved in, you see.'

'Well, this is our number.' She handed me a card. 'Ring here in a couple of weeks and see what's going on then. I'll bet my boots one of these girls will have upped and left or spilled soup over someone.'

I liked Queenie and the restaurant too, which looked clean and well run. I left with regret. What bad luck! A fortnight. Could I wait that long? Dispirited and already tired, I went to see O'Reilly's fish and chip shop but the mere look and smell of the place and its owner put me off so I didn't even stop to ask about the vacancy. I didn't mind starting with the washing up but something about Mr O'Reilly gave me the shivers and fish and chips weren't exactly the sort of cuisine I had in mind. I went straight out of the place and wandering down Junction Road found another grotty local café where I ordered spam fritters and chips, the cheapest thing on the menu. The food was greasy and heavy and felt like a lump inside me afterwards because I ate too quickly. I hadn't eaten much for breakfast in my eagerness to get going.

After my meal, I walked back down Junction Rd and found Archway Underground station. It was the first time I'd ever seen an escalator and I stood at the top of the moving staircase in trepidation, afraid to put a foot forward. A few people brushed past me until a young woman took me by the arm and pulled me on with her.

'It's not going to eat you, dear,' she laughed.

It was weird, this sensation of moving without my doing anything. The nice woman guided me off at the bottom as well. I thanked her and she smiled and hurried on her way. Everyone seemed in such a hurry; it made me feel quite dazed at times. I managed to manoeuvre the Underground and arrived at Kentish Town where I asked around for the Polytechnic and was directed to an austere building with a pillared portico. Here I was to be disappointed yet again. The woman in the office informed me that all the catering courses were booked up for the next term.

'You'll have to try again in September and book up for next year,' she advised me. 'Sorry, dear. Your teachers should have advised you about that.' But how could my poor teachers have advised me on any career move when I had no idea at that time what I meant to do? It was my own fault and I felt a fool.

On my return to Portdown Rd, I went slowly upstairs. I was sure I saw old Dixie Dean peering out of a crack in his door but ignored him and he didn't come out. There was something malevolent about the old man and I was determined to avoid him. There wasn't a sign of anyone else. I looked at the door next to mine and felt a sort of warmth that the nice West Indian man lived there. He at least had been friendly and helpful. Queenie was the only other person who had treated me like a human being with feelings and sense. I was upset at the way people spoke about the Irish. It was a mean and nasty world out there.

Entering my room, I sank down into the armchair and gave myself up to gloom. Eventually, I put on the kettle and then looked around me. My senses had been fine-tuned since childhood to anything out of the way through my fear of Millie. Something felt different about the room. I couldn't put my finger on it but odd things seemed to have been slightly moved; a drawer was very slightly open, something I would never do. I had a thing about shutting cupboard doors and drawers properly. And the photos looked wrong. A couple of photos had been picked up and then put back but not carefully enough.

It made the hairs stand up on the back of my neck. Someone had entered my room when I was out, but how? I had locked the door behind me. I took a good look around but nothing was missing. There was little to lose. My necklace was still in its box on the chest of drawers. Thank goodness I'd taken my money envelope with me.

Chapter 21

Something vague and frightening haunted me that night. I kept dreaming of Mean Millie and how I was grown up but she was still there in the house behind a door and if I was to open that door, there she'd be, staring at me with her awful manic eyes. It was so terrifying that it made me wake with a scream. My heart was hammering away and I felt as if I couldn't breathe, as if I was going to die. It was a horrible feeling. I sat up in bed, panting and clutching at my chest.

Morning light was filtering in through the window. It was about five thirty, too early to get up. Unable to sleep again, I lay there growing more and more uncomfortable and fidgety. In the end I gave up and went downstairs in my dressing gown, a towel draped over my arm, to have a bath. It was such a pain, having to lock the door every time I wanted to go to the loo or have a wash when I had lived in serene peace and trust these last few years.

No one was up yet in the house though the plumbing made enough racket to wake the dead. At least the Ascot boiler over the bath worked and the water was piping hot. I felt a lot better for the soak and crept back quietly to my room. Making myself a cup of tea and a piece of toast and marmalade, I took stock of my situation. It was far too early to go out job-hunting so I lay back on the bed with a good book and lost myself in another world for a little while until I dozed off. When I woke again it was seven fifteen. The sound of someone shutting a door close by woke me and I guessed Luke McGraw was going out to work. I wondered what he did for a living. Surely it must be a decent job for someone as well spoken and nice as he was?

After making another cup of tea, I sat at the little wooden dining table and debated what my next move might be. It might be an idea to go around all the newsagents seeing if there was anything on their notice boards. Or simply pop into every café and ask if they needed staff; even washing up would do to start with.

As I washed up my own dishes a little later on, there was a knock on the door. Who in Heaven's name was calling at this time of the day? I wasn't even properly dressed, still in my dressing gown and nightie.

'Who is it?' I shouted.

'It's the phone for Bridie O'Neill,' said a voice that I didn't recognise at all. Opening the door, I saw an unkempt youngish woman with a baby on her arm. She glanced swiftly about the room as she spoke, curious eyes taking in the details.

'Didn't recognise your name but the bloke on the phone said you lived up on the top floor. So you'd better get down there quick.'

'Did he say who he was?'

'No. Just said to get you. Sounded posh though.'

I followed her down the stairs and picked up the receiver, which was lying on its side by the phone.

'Yes?'

'Is that you, Bridie?'

'What is it, Jim?'

'Look, I had to ring. Someone else is after the job I told you about. I want *you* to have it, Bridie. If you get yourself ready, I can come and pick you up and bring you here for an interview. You don't need the formalities, I'm sure Miss Forbes will see you on my say so.'

'How do you know she will and who the hell is Miss Forbes anyway?'

'She's Sir Simeon's secretary, of course. She interviews any new staff. I've known her for a little while and I feel she would be fine about seeing you and I know she'd like you. You're a million times better than any of the half-baked girls I've seen working here.'

'Jim?'

'Yes?'

'Haven't I made it clear that I don't want to work in an office, not your office or any office?'

He sighed in exasperation. 'Bridie, you are so bloody stubborn. What does it take to make you see sense?'

'Swearing won't do it, that's for sure. Sorry, Jim, but even if it kills me, I'll wait till I find a job myself, a job I want to do.'

'Have you had any luck so far?'

I hesitated. 'It's early days yet but I've enough to manage on so I can take a little time. I mean to go around job-hunting today. I feel lucky somehow. Something will turn up. And I mean to move out of here as soon as I can. I really don't like this place, Jim.'

'Well, don't do anything rash. Let me help you find something better.'

'Thanks. I'll let you know next time I want to breathe,' I said with some sarcasm. He was the stubborn one, not me. He just couldn't get it in his head that I wanted to go it alone. Maybe he was right. It was silly of me when I was a stranger in a strange city. Friends were valuable and Jim had been wonderful but there was something in his claustrophobic interest that made me want to break away even if he offered me Buckingham Palace to live in.

'Don't be like that, I'm only trying to help!' he snapped back. I could sense the anger rising in him but when he spoke it was with an effort at his usual charm. 'Look, I worry about you, Bridie; you can be so trusting and innocent. London can be a dangerous place.'

'I'm getting less and less trusting by the minute. Look Jim, this call's costing you the earth. You'll run out of change.'

'I'm on the office phone; it's okay.'

That didn't strike me as very okay but I let it pass.

'I'm going to go out right away and look for work,' I said. 'It's nearly nine-thirty now and time I was on the go instead of nattering to you. You wouldn't believe I was up at six. I've done absolutely nothing.'

I wondered whether to tell him of my strange feeling of the night before, my intuition that someone had entered my room. He would think me crazy if I said it felt as if Millie had been there.

'You're off now, are you? I suppose you'll be out all day. Do you want me to pop over later in the evening? I leave the office at five. Do you want to meet me then?'

'Oh, all right.' I gave in, worn down as always by his insistence on doing me good. 'I'll meet you later. Call after six.'

'I will,' he promised, 'and don't worry about anything. It will all work out, wait and see.'

I smiled as I put down the phone. He meant well, but he was getting to be a real nuisance. I turned round to find old Dixie Dean standing behind me and almost screamed with fright.

'Have you been listening to my phone call!' I yelled, infuriated and shocked. He backed away a little and put out a hand as if to ward me off.

'Bleedin' 'ell, don't take on like that. I was just poppin' out me door to see what the wevver was like, that's all. Wot you bleedin' gettin' worked up about? Can't a bloke see what the wevver's like wivout some banshee Irishwoman yellin' at 'im?'

'Listen,' I said, my eyes flashing with anger, 'I may have an Irish name and Irish blood and I'm proud of the fact. It's better than your mouldering, mangy Cockney blood. But I've never been to Ireland in my life so stop going on about it. You know nothing about me, you nasty, creepy old man.'

Dixie muttered angrily but said no more and went back into his room, slamming the door after him.

'Good for you, gel,' said a voice and I saw the woman who had come to tell me about the call standing on the landing above me. 'He's a right nosey old sod, he is. He *was* listening in, he always does. Needed a good telling off – I loved it,' she added with a snigger. Smiling at me in a friendly manner she disappeared back into her own quarters as the baby within lifted up its voice in sudden lament.

It seemed everyone round here was into each other's business but then I was used to that from living in the keeper's cottages. That had been a closed little community too. I shrugged and told myself to stop being over-sensitive.

Returning to my room, I got ready for battle. Dressing quickly and seizing my handbag, I took off as at once. Time was being wasted by Jim and his calls and silly old men with nothing to do but be a nuisance to their neighbours.

It was a long, tiring and fruitless day. I tried various cafés and even pubs to see if they would take me on. I was eighteen but they said I looked too young and naïve for pub work so I knew they'd never let me serve behind the bar. I offered to wash up or do the eggs and chips or even cleaning but they all shook their heads.

'No experience,' they said.

'Yes, I have. I've looked after a house since I was a kid. I've loads of experience and can cook really well.'

'Yeah, that's all very well but you've no experience of pub work. It's a rough area round here. Lots of drunks and Irish layabouts. You don't look like you can cope. Sorry, love.'

'I could just stay in the kitchen. No one will worry me there.'

An amused laugh, 'Wouldn't bet on that either.'

The cafés all had their quota of staff and moaned that they were just about managing to keep going as it was. Sorry, they couldn't take on any more people. Goodbye.

Nobody seemed to want me. Nothing in the world would induce me to go back to the Labour Exchange and see what was on offer there. That impersonal, bureaucratic place and its rough clientele gave me the horrors. Maybe they were right. I hadn't hardened to this new world enough yet. I felt like a tender plant that needed time to adjust to the big cold world beyond the greenhouse.

Never mind, Bridie, I told myself. *I'll walk about every day till I find a place. Someone will want me. I won't give in to Millie.* I had meant to say Jim and felt my heart miss a beat when Millie's name came back to mind. Millie was dead and gone. I'd seen her buried, hadn't I?. Did I believe in ghosts – I wasn't sure.

Somehow, I believed in Millie's ghost. She wasn't the sort to lie quietly, vampires never did. And she *had* been a vampire, sucking my energy and spirit from me day by day. Was she still at it from beyond the grave? Had she bitten her son and transformed him too?

He wasn't a vampire though, was he? He had charm, of that there was no doubt. Sometimes I felt a little afraid of him but had no idea why. I put these difficult thoughts aside. I was hungry, that was my problem, nothing else. No wonder I was hallucinating. I'd only had a piece of toast all day and now my insides were trying to chew themselves up. I pictured a nice pile of potatoes and fried eggs and bacon and hastened back to what I laughingly must term as 'home'.

I spent the afternoon reading but, getting restless, I went downstairs to the little garden and surveyed it. It wouldn't take too much work to clear it up and make it better. There was a little circle of paving slabs in the centre and I pictured a sundial on it. Then maybe some flowers in the corner by the fence, not the buddleia and hydrangea corner, nothing else would grow there. A little seat would look nice too.

Walking down to Preston's corner shop, a marvellous emporium where one seemed able to buy almost anything, I purchased a small trowel-and-fork set and returned to the garden where I began to dig out weeds with a will. It was a pleasant and enjoyable task – simple tasks always made me content and I felt the happiest I'd been since arriving in London. I even sang to myself a little. Looking up, I saw Dixie Dean staring at me from his window and waved to him cheerily with my trowel. He scowled back and disappeared from sight but I didn't care about him. I had found something good to do and I would do it for my own sake.

After an hour's work, I surveyed the plot and it already looked better. I formed a little compost heap of weeds near the buddleia; they would soon rot down. I decided to leave in the rosebay; it looked so colourful and pretty. Why call it a weed? It was beautiful when in bloom.

The back door opened and the lady with the baby came

through and stood looking at my work. She had the baby in her arms and it looked a pink-cheeked, cheery little thing, its eyes wide open with astonishment at being in the outside world. The woman herself looked about thirty, care-worn and tired but pleasant enough. Her hair was pulled back by a rubber band into a stringy ponytail and her clothes were scruffy and worn but the baby was clean and well-dressed. That showed she cared for something other than herself.

'This looks nice,' she said approvingly. 'Time someone did somethin' like this. And you've only bin here a minute or two. Good for you, gel. It's always up to us. Them bleedin' men never get off their backsides to do anythin' useful. My bloke certainly won't. I've said to him, make a bit of space down there so I can put Lonny out in the garden – but he never stirs an inch.'

'Well, I like doing it,' I said, 'and I'm going to save up and get a little garden seat and a sundial and make it really nice. Then you can put Lonny out here and sit and watch him and put your feet up a bit.'

'Oh, that's likely, I'm sure! I ain't got time for that. I've got to go to work three days a week so his lordship can sit on his backside and collect the dole. He's supposed to be laid off sick but there's nothin' wrong with him, just bone idle. So, no sittin' about for me. But the idea's nice.'

'What work d'you do?'

'Cleanin'. In the local pub.'

I wondered which was considered as the local pub as there seemed to be one on every corner but asked no more. Cleaning for others was definitely not something I fancied unless desperate.

'My name's Betty. What's yours?'

'Bridget. Everyone calls me Bridie.'

'Glad you're here, Bridie,' Betty said, 'but take care. You look a good kid and it's tough round here. We have to keep an eye out for one another, us girls.'

I had a good wash down in my little sink after all that hard work and got ready to see Jim. I wasn't sure if he planned to take me out again so I dressed less formally in a creamy cheesecloth blouse and a skirt with a floral print that was not as severe as my morning outfit.

After six there was a knock on the door.

'It's open,' I called.

Jim entered swiftly, shutting the door behind him. 'You should always keep it locked,' he reprimanded me. 'You're in London now. Anyone could walk in.'

This comment reminded me of the feeling that someone *had* come in and again I wanted to speak of it but hesitated. It sounded so silly now and I knew I must have imagined it.

'We're meeting up with some of my friends at a pub in Hampstead,' Jim said cheerily. He was always full of beans and wanting to be on the go. I don't know where he got the energy from. 'Have you eaten?'

'I had a nice big lunch,' I said, 'but I'm ravenous again. I did lots of work in the garden, come and see.'

'I will, I will. Get ready then and we'll stop off and find somewhere to have a meal.'

'Don't I look alright like this?'

He looked me over for a few moments then smiled, 'You do. You look lovely. I'm proud of you, you know. You could look stunning in a sack.'

'Get on! You're such a charmer.'

'I mean it.'

'Jim, you say nice things to all the girls.'

'Not all the girls,' he said and looked as if he was about to say more but I changed the subject.

'Okay, I'm ready then. Now come and see what I've done in the garden.'

I took him down to see my efforts and told him of my vision of how the garden would look in the future. My enthusiasm amused him and he patted me on the back.

'You've worked damn hard,' he said in admiration. 'You're a marvel. Definitely deserve that dinner.'

As always, I caught a flash of old Dixie Dean, standing well back from the window now but observing us nonetheless. Best to ignore him, I thought. Just a nosy old man, as Betty had said.

'What is it?' asked Jim, sensing something.

'Just that old fellow,' I sighed. 'He's always watching me but I think he watches everyone. Hasn't anything else to do, I suppose.'

Jim stared angrily at the window.

'He'd better be careful. If he bothers you, let me know and I'll speak to him, scare the life out of him. I can even get him evicted if I want, I've only to speak to Mrs Townsend.'

'No, no!' I was horrified at the idea. 'He's done nothing wrong. You can't evict him, he has nowhere else to go. What reason would this woman have to evict him even if she listened to you?'

'She'd listen all right, if I spoke to Alice.'

'Alice is her daughter, you said?'

'Mmm.'

And your girlfriend maybe. How you like to use people just like your mother. Set them against one another.

We had a pleasant little meal in De Marco's where Queenie was still on duty. She seemed to work all hours of the day and night, always cheerful and on the go. As the man at the Labour Exchange had said, her memory was prodigious; she never wrote anything down but recalled names, tables, orders to perfection. A very impressive lady.

'I hope I'll be as good as Queenie, one day,' I murmured to Jim. Our meal was brought to us by one of the new waitresses while Queenie presided from a distance making sure all was well. This evening, Mr De Marco himself graced us with an appearance and served behind the little bar, dispensing drinks with a cheerful Italian grin and occasionally bursting into fluid song, which amused me but seemed to annoy Jim.

'Stupid man,' he muttered, 'why doesn't he go back to Italy and his gondolas.'

'It's nice, Jim. He's cheerful. That's nice, isn't it? I like to sing when I'm cheerful too.'

Jim looked at me and smiled suddenly.

'Yes, I remember,' he said. 'You used to do the ironing and sing all the pop songs. I used to enjoy listening to you. You were better than the radio.'

'Was I?' I felt rather flattered by this compliment.

'But it's different with him,' Jim added looking over at the owner, his eyes critical and hard again, 'De Marco's a restaurateur. He should maintain a little dignity.'

I looked at the little, oily-haired man behind his bar, whistling cheerfully as he polished glasses and poured out wine. 'I see no lack of dignity. He seems a nice man and Queenie is just amazing. Yes, I'd enjoy working here. I hope one of these girls leaves. I'd be tons better than her any day.'

'If I get my way, you'll never be in this position,' said Jim looking sulky. 'I can't for the world imagine why you'd even consider such an idea.'

'Because I want to run my own restaurant one day,' was my firm reply, 'or maybe a little boarding house by the seaside. I *need* to learn, Jim, and there's only one way. Start at the beginning.'

'I acknowledge that. I too will have to start at the beginning. But my aim is higher than yours, Bridie. I intend to be a barrister, to have a profession. You, my dear, are selling yourself short.'

'Rubbish! If someone didn't run places like this, do the cooking, the accountancy and all the rest, we wouldn't be sitting here having this delicious meal now, would we? Where would you be then, Mr Barrister? You'd have to cook for yourself, heaven forbid! Let's be honest. In your line of work you will only exist because of other people's mistakes and tragedies, trying to get them out of the trouble they've as like as not created for themselves. What's so much more wonderful in that? Why should that be considered superior to feeding and caring for others?'

'I shall be helping the course of justice,' he said, looking cross, 'a noble pursuit.'

'Hmmm. And I shall be helping the course of rest and

pleasure. If more people enjoyed themselves and relaxed over life there might be no need for people like you at all.'

He looked angry but did not pursue the theme any longer and we finished our meal in silence. Sometimes he had no sense of humour at all.

After our meal, we went on to a pub in Hampstead, near the posh house where Mrs Townsend lived. Jim made a point of driving down to the Vale of Health to show me the tall terraced villas there.

'There's a big garden at the back,' he said. 'It's got huge rooms and goes up four floors. That's just one of her houses,' he said. 'She owns houses and flats in France and all over the place. Do you know that D.H. Lawrence used to live round the corner in Byron Villas? He was here with his wife Frieda. Lots of famous people lived here. It's worth a bomb, this place. And, of course Keats lived in John Street. I'll take you to see his house someday, if you'd like."

It was a surprise to see such a different area of London with its attractive well-kept houses in quiet, wide, tree-lined streets. The vast, sweeping grasslands of the Heath were a mere walking distance away and then there was the charming village-like atmosphere of Hampstead itself. It was hard to believe that the Great Metropolis had encroached this far and swallowed this lovely place in its gigantic maws.

'It makes me think of Little Nell in *The Old Curiosity Shop*,' I mused, 'and how she and her father sat up on Hampstead Heath and could see London in the distance.'

'Yes, that's right. In Dickens' time it was a mere village from which one could view St. Paul's Cathedral and the smoke of London from Parliament Hill,' said Jim, 'but it's managed to retain its charm. It's another of those places I'd like to live in but can't afford just yet. But I will.'

We entered the saloon bar of the The Olde Bull and Bush of music hall fame. I looked around with some trepidation. I seldom went to public houses back home. The village ones were sleepy little places where only the drone of local conversation and the clunk of beer tankards on the bar accompanied by, 'nuther o' them, please landlord!' was to be heard; a request accompanied by the whistle of darts and the clatter of dominoes and skittles. Here the air was thick with smoke. Not a pewter tankard in sight but beer glasses for the men, fancy cocktails for the ladies and ashtrays clogged with dog ends and half-smoked cigarettes. The atmosphere pulsated with noisy activity as friends greeted one another or dashed back and forth to the bar to order fresh drinks. Glasses clinking and the sound of nasal vowels replaced the soft pleasing burr of countryfolk speech.

Jim introduced me to some of his student friends. They were pleasant enough young men and women but I knew I could never get on with them. They were all clever, witty, urbane and talked and drank a lot. To my mind they talked nonsense. It was all about earning lots of money, cars, property, who was going out with whom. Gossip mostly. In their company I felt shy and tongue-tied as if I was stupid and had little to say to any of them. Yet I felt in my heart I really knew and understood a lot more about *real* life and the things that truly mattered.

I sat sipping a gin and orange. It seemed the height of sophistication to me and after a couple of these, found the effect was mellowing. I began to relax a little and watch everyone with amused interest. A mousy-haired, unremarkable looking young man dressed in blue jeans and an open shirt came up to me after a while, smiled and offered to get me another gin. It didn't seem a good idea, unused as I was to drink and I said so.

'Come on, another won't hurt, my dear. I gather you're James's little sister, fresh from the countryside.'

The manner in which he said this sounded mocking but his smile was genuine and he seemed pleasant enough.

'Oh yes, I'm James's little sister.'

'Sorry, kid, didn't mean to sound patronising,' he said with a laugh. 'I'm Tom Shanklin. And your name … ?'

'Bridie O'Neill.'

He looked puzzled. 'Ah, you're married?'

'No.'

'How come you're an O'Neill then and not Bosworth?'

It was none of his business and I felt like saying so but managed to hold myself in check. He was just being friendly. Probably not the least bit interested really, just making small talk.

'I'm adopted. O'Neill was my father's name.'

'Oh. I see.' He didn't really. His interest had moved down to the curves of my bosom where his eyes lingered for a few moments. I wanted to cross my arms over my chest and wished I had brought a cardigan with me. It was horrible to have men stare like this. I wasn't used to it and it felt ill-mannered and invasive.

'So,' his eyes moved back to mine and he stared at me thoughtfully as if weighing me up, 'so you're all alone in the big wicked city then, Bridie O'Neill?' He stooped and peered into my face. 'Green-eyed Bridie?'

'Isn't everyone?'

'Clever remark,' he said approvingly, 'very clever. Yes, we are all alone when it comes to it. I *think* these people are all my friends ...' his eyes roamed disparagingly around the set of flushed, excited faces at the bar. 'I *think* I've got friends – but who are one's friends? This lot would stab me in the back at any moment if it suited them.'

'I hope not. I hope someone is your true friend.'

'Huh!' he laughed cynically. 'I doubt it. And where you came from, do you have friends?'

I thought of Ryan, Joe and Sheila. 'I do. They're still there, still my friends ...' my voice trailed off and I lowered my eyes to hide the sudden uprush of tears.

'But you're here. And missing them. So why *are* you here? Why are any of us here? I had good friends back in Northampton, where I come from. But I haven't seen them in years and doubt they even remember me. Nor would I want to remember them. You grow away from people. You'll be just the same. You'll turn into a sophisticated, permanently sozzled Londoner and wonder why the hell you ever bothered with the stupid bumpkins you left at home. Parents included.'

'I won't forget anyone!' I said indignantly, 'I'm not like that.'

'Aren't you? None of us are to start with. I was just as wimpish and pathetic as you are now, homesick and all that rot, when I left home for Cambridge. Then I came to work in London and bless me. Forgot my roots as happily as you like. Now I wouldn't go back for the world.'

'But you admit you're lonely.'

'Did I say that?' He smiled suddenly and leant towards me, whispering in my ear in a conspiratorial manner, his eyes shifting swiftly to one side and back again as if afraid of being overheard. 'Well, I won't be if you come along with me now, pretty green-eyed Bridie. Fancy coming back to my flat with me? I'll teach you *all* about London ways.'

I stared at him and his leering face and shuddered. 'I'd sooner go home with a rattlesnake,' I blurted out.

To my surprise he gave a great laugh. 'Playing hard to get, eh? Oh, how I love 'em like that.'

At this moment Jim came over and I turned to him with relief.

'Keep your hands off my little sister, Tom Shanklin.'

Jim's voice was jocular but his eyes were hard and nasty. I was relieved that he was ready to protect me. London was indeed a dangerous place for the unwary and innocent. I was about to ask if Jim if could take me home but Tom stood up, grinned and offered to get more drinks all round.

'Glad to see you're keeping an eye on your *sister*, Jim. She's a cute, fiery little number. Just my type. Love redheads – they're *hot* stuff, baby.'

'Stupid fool,' said Jim as Tom sauntered over to the bar to get the drinks. 'Ignore him, Bridie. He's all talk and hot air. Was he bothering you? I could see you looked uncomfortable.'

'Thanks, Jim. You rescued me. He was getting suggestive.'

'The hell he was,' muttered Jim. 'I'll sort him out one of these days. Still,' he turned and waved his hand around the bar, 'on the whole, they're a bright, amusing bunch and useful too. They've all got posh daddies and I need friends with connections like that.'

I smiled without enthusiasm. I didn't give a hang about Jim and his connections. In fact, I disliked them thoroughly. Suddenly I wanted to go home. My real home. I yearned to be out of this smoky, noisy public house and in the free fresh air but even if I stepped outside it would be into a street full of cars and people. For a moment, I pictured waves crashing up to the seashore and heard the mournful wailing of the gulls on high and it wrenched me inside.

A girl entered the saloon bar and looked around. When she caught sight of Jim, her face brightened and she came sauntering over. She was very blonde, very pretty and wore a very short skirt that revealed long slender legs.

'Oh, hell, Alice is here!' groaned Jim and rose as she came over. 'I thought she was on bloody holiday.'

The girl flung her arms around his neck. 'Jim, darling, I haven't seen you in *ages*!'

'Whoa, Alice, mind my drink, old girl.'

'Oh, to hell with your drink! Haven't you got a kiss for your Alice?'

'Our little Alice,' grinned Jim, 'always got a kiss for her. Haven't we all?'

So this was the ubiquitous Alice whose mother owned the tenement I shared with the other unfortunates. I watched her with interest. She was so modern and fashionable. Her lips were painted a luscious dripping shiny pink, her long oval nails the same colour and her hair was a suspicious shade of gleaming platinum blonde. Compared to this film star vision, I felt dowdy and countrified in my cheesecloth blouse with only a little powder and lipstick – and even that was the cheapest available from the counter at Woolworths.

'And where's Mummy now?' asked Jim as she settled herself on his knee without giving me as much as a glance or a 'hello'.

'Oh, she's away in Nice with her latest boyfriend. She didn't want her little baby girl along, now did she? She's scared he'd take a fancy to me instead if I went too. He's half her age, the silly cow.'

'He'll have to meet you someday, Alice, then what'll happen?'

She smiled suggestively. 'Ah, what d'you suppose? But Mummy will kid herself he adores only her. She's such an idiot over men.'

Jim laughed, 'Runs in the family then.'

Alice didn't seem to notice the insult. She draped herself over Jim and then noticed me gaping at her.

'What are *you* staring at?' she asked, her face and voice hard and aggressive all of a sudden.

'Alice, could you sit over there and behave,' said Jim trying to disentangle those clinging arms from his neck. 'This, my dear, is my sweet little sister, Bridie, just arrived in London. And Bridie, this is Alice,' said Jim turning to me now that he had managed to set the pouting, clinging Alice down on a seat.

'Your sister?'

'Indeed. I *told* you she was coming.'

'I don't remember,' said Alice and surveyed me once more with some suspicion that slowly turned to a faint astonishment. In her eyes I looked the country bumpkin and she relaxed. I was obviously not worth considering.

'So where are you from?'

'Bournemouth.'

'Oh. The seaside. So why have you come to London then … seaside is nice, isn't it?'

'Not when you have no work,' I replied.

'And what work would that be?' Her voice was dismissive as if she thought a bumpkin like myself couldn't possible be fit for anything of interest.

'Bridie's going to work in Grantham's office,' said Jim smoothly. 'All in good time.'

I frowned at him and Alice laughed. 'Well, *she* doesn't look too keen on the idea. Is she living at your place then?'

'No, I'm not!' I snapped.

Alice widened her eyes. 'All right. You don't have to bite my head off, only asking.'

'Just shut up, Alice,' Jim said. 'It's no business of yours what Bridie's doing.'

'Charming. Well, you and your little sister can do what you please.'

At this point, Tom returned with the drinks, which he set out on the table.

'Seems she's not really your sister, after all,' remarked Tom who had been listening for a few moments with an air of detached amusement.

'What d'you mean?' asked Alice, her eyes darting around our faces.

'Because she's adopted.'

Jim stared at him. 'How d'you know that?'

'I told him,' I sighed.

'So she's not your sister, really.' Alice turned to survey me with intense care. I felt myself turning pink under all this scrutiny. I could see she was jealous and angry and felt the hostility pouring at me from those pale blue eyes. Jim, however, laughed as if he was enjoying the scenario and leaning towards me, kissed me lightly on the mouth. I drew back, startled and glared at him. Tom laughed too and Alice glowered.

I'd had enough of it all. Rising, I picked up my purse and walked off towards the door and into the cool, fresh night air.

Chapter 22

Jim came running after me almost before the door of the public house had swung shut. I was standing on the pavement wondering where to get a bus or train back to Archway.

'Where are you going? What's the matter, for goodness sake?' He came up to me and took my arm. I shook him off.

'Why are you so angry?'

'Because you're behaving like a fool,' I said furiously. 'Jim, you play with people. I'm not in your game so don't play with me.'

'I *wasn't* playing with you. I don't understand what you mean, Bridie. Can't I give you a little peck but you storm off as if the banshees were after you? What are you planning to be a nun or something? Did Tom or Alice upset you? Ignore them. They're idiots both of them. And yes, I do use *them*. That's all they're any good for.'

'They are people, Jim. Alice seems to think you're her boyfriend and she's jealous. I understand that. I'd feel like that if Ryan had another girl, I know I would.'

'That bloody Ryan of yours! Can't you forget him? He's off on his lighthouse in the sea somewhere and I'll bet you are the last thing on his mind. Just forget him.'

'I can't.' A little sob escaped me. 'I can't. I want to but it's hopeless. I keep seeing his face, hearing his voice, missing him.'

'Then why the bloody hell did you leave him and come here – come to me, Bridie? I had so hoped you had seen sense at last and come to me.'

I turned at that and looked at him, surprised. 'I didn't come for your sake, Jim. What gave you that idea? I came because …' I paused and stared at the road full of noisy traffic rushing past.

'Because of what?'

'I don't know, Jim. It was as if I had to be myself. Find out who I really am and what, if anything, I can do. I want to be able to use my own ideas, talents – if I have any. I'm not sure I have but I want to find out. Not be dependent or belong to anyone at all but myself. I can't explain.'

'Well, it makes no sense.'

At this moment Alice came teetering out of the pub on her high heels and came towards us. She flung her arms about Jim and staring sullenly at me she said in a wheedling tone, 'What's going on, Jamesie? Why are you out here in the cold? Come back in and finish your drink.'

He pushed her aside with an air of contempt. 'Go back in, Alice, I'll catch up with you tomorrow. I'm taking Bridie home.'

'Why? Can't she get the bus?'

'I am perfectly happy to get a bus,' I said angrily and turning on my heel began to walk off again.

Jim came after me and caught me by the arm.

'Take no notice of that silly cow,' he said. 'Come on, let me take you home now. You'll not get a bus or a taxi from here for ages and you'll have no idea how to get back. Will you allow me to do that, at least?'

'Alright.' I felt mean. He was always so protective. 'Look, thanks, Jim. I'm sorry. I know I'm being difficult but I can't help it. What about Alice?'

'She's got her own car. Or she'll find someone else to take her home. It's all one to me.'

He took me home and dropped me off at the front door, making no suggestion about coming upstairs, much to my relief.

Perhaps this little squabble did the trick because Jim stayed away for a while. I managed to ring Joe and Sheila from the call box down the road. I didn't want that nosy Dixie Dean listening in to all my private calls.

'How are you managing, love? We've been worried about you, me and Sheila. Are you settled in somewhere?'

'Yes, Joe, I've got a room to live in and I'm still trying to find a job but I know something will turn up.' I tried to sound as cheerful as I could.

'Well, Jim will look after you, so you know you're not alone out there.'

'No, no, I'm not alone.' If Joe only knew!

'And you're okay for cash, aren't you? You've not spent the money I gave you on dresses, now have you?'

'Of course not. As if I would. You know I'm not interested in fashion. Joe, how's Ryan, have you heard from him?'

'Yes, we had a letter a few days ago. He seems well.'

'Did he ask after me?'

There was a slight pause and my heart sank a little.

'He says he misses you badly, Bridie, and doesn't know why you left. Well, I understand why you did – he and Sheila think you're crazy. But then they would, they've never been the adventurous sort, either of 'em. Anyway, he says he wants to write to you so give us your address, lass.'

'I miss him too, Joe. I do. Tell him to write, I'd love him to write.'

I gave the address and after some more chit-chat found myself running out of coins and had to hang up. The conversation did little to improve my despondent frame of mind. I walked back to the house slowly, went up to my room and lay on the bed staring at the ceiling for a long time till I eventually drifted off to sleep.

A day later I had a call from Tom Shanklin.

'Hiya, green-eyed Bridie,' he said. There was a little laugh in his voice which sounded attractive. I was so surprised to hear him that I remained silent for a while.

'Are you there?'

'Yes. Where did you get this number?'

'Followed you and Jim home the other night and popped in the hallway and took it down. Good sleuth, eh?'

'But why? Why did you go to all that bother?'

He chuckled. 'You know what, Bridie, you're so naïve that it's refreshing. I wonder if you're for real.'

'Oh, I am. But I'm a country bumpkin, not a smart Londoner.'

'Mmm ... but you do have a sharp tongue. That's real enough.'

'So what d'you want?'

'Come out for a drink with me tonight?'

'A drink. Where?'

'In a little club I know. Jazzy music, you know ... that sort of thing.'

I was still surprised. I couldn't believe someone was trying to date me. It frightened me a bit because I'd always felt so secure in Ryan's love that it hadn't occurred to me anyone else might 'fancy' me. Especially a smooth townie like Tom Shanklin. I tried to recall his features and what reaction he'd inspired. He hadn't impressed me. I thought of Ryan. He'd be furious. I thought of Jim, he'd be even more furious. These two were a deal too possessive. There could be no harm in having a drink out with someone. I made up my mind.

'All right.'

Tom sounded jubilant. 'I'll be round at eight.'

I was unsure what to wear to what Tom had called a 'jazzy club.' In the end, I put on a simple dark-green flared skirt. With this I wore a neat embroidered white shirt tucked into the waistband emphasising a small waist of which I was unduly proud. I made sure the shirt was demurely buttoned up. I didn't much like the thought of Tom's eyes roving to my cleavage and hoped no one would notice the white bra straps under the thin cotton cloth.

Tom knocked on the door of my room at ten past eight. I went out to meet him, firmly closing and locking up behind me. I didn't want to invite him in and hoped he wasn't expecting to come back for a coffee and a snog – though I suspected that was precisely what he intended. Now that I saw him standing before me, his eyes narrowing as he watched me lock the door, I wondered if I was doing the right thing going out with a man I'd met only once. I knew nothing about him except that he was a vague friend of Jim's from Cambridge. He looked me over for a few moments and I felt myself begin to blush. Did I look all wrong? Weren't my clothes the right ones?

'Do I look all right?' I enquired anxiously.

'You look fab, my love.'

He made no more comment and I followed him out to a waiting taxi.

I had no idea where we ended up but gathered it was somewhere in North London. We'd passed road signs indicating King's Cross on the way but none of the other names meant a great deal to me. The club was situated down some battered basement steps. I could hear loud music emanating whenever the door opened and people entered or left, laughing and chattering as they carelessly pushed past. Looking up I could see the dense crowding of tall, Victorian houses looming up around us. It made me feel hemmed in. An anxious sensation in the pit of my stomach, a sense of fear and inadequacy in such a milieu, made me pull back a little. Tom sensed my reluctance and taking me firmly by the arm steered me to a table where another couple were already seated. They acknowledged him with a half-hearted wave. I didn't particularly like the look of them either.

The air was thick with smoke which immediately entered my lungs, making me choke. Some jazz musicians were perched up on a small stand at the back of the room belting out old favourites and a lot of furious jiving was going on in front of their platform. The lights were a peculiar harsh red in which smoke wafted in sulphurous pink fumes.

'Oh this is Hell,' I declared. 'Tom, I don't like it here,' and turned as if to go.

'Hey, hey, hey,' said Tom, taking my arm again in his strong grip. He bent his tall body and peered into my eyes. 'What don't you like? It's a great place. Everyone who's cool comes here. The music's great, isn't it? Sit here. This is Gill and her bloke, Kev. This is Bridie, pals. Be nice to her while I get a drink. What d'you want, Bridie?'

I sat down and gave it thought. 'A coke or something.'

'Well, we'll start with a coke or something and then a stiffer drink or two later, eh?' He winked at Kev who winked back. 'Got to loosen these girls up a bit.'

'No, it's okay. I'll stick to coke. I only drink a little.'

'A little. You were knocking back the gins yesterday. You're funny, you are. You make me laugh, you know.'

He weaved his way to the bar and I looked around feeling decidedly out of place. Gill looked me over with a brief and not very flattering glance, stretched her face into a watery smile and then turned her attention to her boyfriend. She was a thin girl, her dark hair puffed out in huge waves and curls. Her eyes were long and narrow, almost Mongolian, the lids coated with a fantastic turquoise eye shadow that matched her turquoise top. I was rather fascinated by her lips which appeared to extend from one side of her jaw to the other, thickly crayoned in pale pink. In contrast to her astonishing appearance, astonishing to me anyway, the boyfriend, Kev, was a tall, unattractive, brown-haired young man with acne. However, she seemed enamoured of him, fondling his free hand, keeping her eyes glued on his face as if every fleeting expression was of importance to her. He sipped at his beer and allowed her this apparent adoration while slightly turning away and tapping his foot in time to the music.

The music was pleasant enough. I knew little about jazz but recognised some trad numbers I'd heard on the radio. My feet also began to tap and I smiled at myself. I really had to stop feeling paranoid about everything but learn to relax and take it all in. After all, I had wanted to come to London, experience the big metropolis and all its ways.

Tom returned, handed me the coke and set down his brimming glass of brown and mild.

'Here's to us,' he said with a grin, 'here's to some fun, eh, little green-eyed Bridie?'

I forced a smile and sipped my drink. Tom drank his beer as if he was a dying man in a desert.

'Bloody good that was,' he sighed after a while, wiping his lips.

Kev nodded his approval. 'Empty glasses, eh? *That's* no bloody good. I'll get us another round. You okay, Gill?'

'You can get me a gin and orange.'

'And you? You okay?' Kev asked, turning to me and looking at me a little more closely. I lowered my eyes at this sudden scrutiny and nodded.

'I'm fine.'

Gill looked sharply at Kev and seemed annoyed at his sudden interest. I sighed. Was this going to be another of those silly encounters with an insecure jealous girl? Didn't these girls have any faith in themselves?

We all sat in silence and watched the dancers jiving about. One couple were especially good and people stopped to watch them after a while.

'Wish I could dance like that,' I said.

'I'll have to teach you. Come on,' and Tom grabbed me by the hand and pulled me onto the floor.

'But I don't know how to do it!' I wailed.

'It's easy, look. I push you and you twirl and then come round ...' and somehow, after lots of hesitations and bumping into him, I suddenly got the idea and laughed at the joyful, energetic, physical pleasure of it.

'See, little country girl, it's fun. Told you.'

It was fun and I returned to the table flushed and exhilarated. Gill and Kev had also taken to the dance floor and were still out there.

'I thought you were going to be hard work,' Tom said, eagerly quaffing his new pint of beer. 'But you're warming up okay. Takes a bit of time to get used to new things but it's all great fun. It's about liberty, Bridie, about freedom. That's what it's about for us young folk now. We can do what we like. No parents, no churches, no outdated moral attitudes, no one to bother us at all. We can do just as we like.'

'Is that a good thing?' I mused, 'Is it really freedom to do what one likes without anyone else to care about? I don't really feel at all free here in London, not in the way I do back home. And I doubt you do either. It seems to me that you think you *have* to do all this ... put on a show, be part of the "scene", be "cool", as you put it. Is it really what you want? Does it really make you happy?'

He regarded me with some disquiet for a moment or two.

'Are you always so bloody serious or just winding me up? Don't you ever let your hair down where you come from?'

I laughed at this. 'We have different ideas of fun, Tom. That's all.'

'Well, let's hope they coincide soon,' he said, 'I'm not into skittles on a Sunday afternoon. I'm off for another drink, get you a gin.'

'To "loosen me up", I suppose'.

'Something like that.'

He returned with a straight whisky and a glass of gin and orange.

'Whisky already, Tom?' I said with some disquiet.

'Yes, and whiskey with an 'e'. Like you I'm Irish by descent and yes, I love a whiskey, missie.'

'But you'll get very drunk like that.'

'So? I like getting drunk as well.'

'Why do you need to be drunk, why do you need to dull your senses? Isn't it better to be conscious and enjoy everything properly?'

'No. It's better to be drunk and forget everything properly.'

I stared at him and he laughed. 'You've a deal too many prissy likes and dislikes, Miss Bridie O'Neill. But I suspect, by the time the evening is out, I'll teach you to like a lot of things you haven't tried yet.'

'I doubt that.' I was angry at being called "prissy" when, in my opinion, I was being wise.

'Do you … we'll see, eh?' He tossed back the shot of whiskey far too soon and pointed enquiringly at my glass from which I had taken a sip or two. By now Gill and Kev had returned, flushed and panting from their dance. 'Come with us, Kev, we'll get some more all round.'

Kev looked at Tom's empty glass. 'Bloody hell, you on chasers already? I'm having another brown and mild. This dancing brings you out in a right sweat. Come on, let's get over to the bar.'

The two men pushed off into the crowd. I knew Tom hoped

to get me drunk and out of control. I felt less and less sanguine about the situation and wondered how to get out of it.

'You two going steady then?' asked Gill, lighting up another cigarette.

'No, we've just met. Just a date.'

'Well, you watch that Tom Shanklin. I used to go out with him for a bit way back and he can be a right bastard when he's put a bit of drink away. He got bored with me and palmed me off on his friend Kev, but it was the best thing he ever did. Kev's a good bloke. A kind one. Rather have him any day. Just watch it with Tom, that's all I say.'

'Don't worry, I intend to,' I replied, 'Anyway, I don't want to be his girlfriend. It's just a night out.'

'Oh yeah. Not with him it isn't. He'll expect payment in kind even if he treats to you to nothing more'n a coffee.'

Kev and Tom returned after what seemed a long time during which I suspected they'd knocked back a few more drinks. On the way over, Tom stopped to chat to a girl and they laughed together as if they were friends. He pointed over to me and she looked over also and gave me a withering look. I felt upset and wondered what they were saying about me. Tom waved at us and then steered his way through the raucous, swaying crowd, balancing the full glasses like an expert. 'Just talking to a girl I know,' he grinned.

'I gathered as much. You seem to know a lot of girls.'

'Oh, we went out together a couple of times. I split up from her ages ago. We're still friends though. I'm a friendly sort of chap as you'll have gathered.' He leant towards me and looked as if he meant to kiss me but I turned my head away. He laughed and took my hand and kissed it instead then stared at me for a while as if trying to sum me up.

'I suppose you *could* be fun ... when you've loosened up. I know your sort. Passion lurking beneath a cool exterior. Play hard to get and work a fellow up to fever pitch. Makes for a good time.'

'You know nothing about me at all,' I retorted, drawing my

hand away. 'I don't like to behave like that. Teasing a man. You've got me wrong. If I love someone, I love with all my heart. Look, Tom, I'm out with you tonight just for a drink, a bit of music, okay? I don't want you to get ideas in your head that I'll fall in love with you or anything.'

'Who the hell said anything about love? What are you talking about? Don't you ever want to have some sex? What are you saving yourself up for then? Some nice bloke, a terrace house and four kids? Don't be stupid.'

I began to get angry. My eyes flashed and he grinned back.

'You're getting mad. I love it when you get mad … you look so sexy.'

'Listen,' I hissed, 'I'm not saving myself up as you call it, nor am I looking for anyone at the moment. I'm not interested in men just now. Seems they're all the same to me. Plus, I don't like what you call fun. I know what I like in life.'

'And what's that, may I ask?'

'You wouldn't understand, would you? Not cars and houses and clothes and all that rubbish. The sea, the wind, the fresh air. That's what I love.'

Tom snorted, ' And so you end up in Archway. Lots of sea and fresh air round there, don't you think?'

I shrugged. 'I won't be there for ever. It's just temporary.'

'I should bloody well hope not. Why'd Jim leave you in a dump like that?'

'He found me the place, it's cheap rent. I'm grateful for his help.'

Tom gazed at me for a while. His eyes narrowed. 'Surprised Jim didn't move you in with *him*. I bet he'd have liked that.'

'He's my brother and I don't want to be beholden to him or anyone,' I snapped.

'Your brother, eh? Ha! But I kinda like your spirit. You're quite something under that twee, buttoned-up exterior. How about another drink?'

'*No* thanks.'

'Come on … I'll get you one. Loosen up, kiddo.'

He took a little more time with the next round of drinks and we remained silent for a while listening to the music. It was pleasant enough for a while but the gins I'd consumed were beginning to make me feel giddy and light. The music jangled now. Why did I feel as if it was all so sham, so unreal and meaningless? The people around me were drinking, laughing, dancing and canoodling. But it all looked like forced gaiety to me. They didn't really look happy at all. It wasn't the cheerful look I saw on faces as they walked along sea paths and felt the breeze in their hair. Good, clean air, real joy and happiness.

I felt Tom was as much at a loss as I was. I wasn't his usual sort of date, the sleek, fashionable, urbane young women, the girls out for nothing more than a good time, plenty to drink … and then … I didn't want to know about the 'and then' … not with this man or any other. It was Ryan and Ryan alone who aroused me that way. And Ryan didn't belong in a place like this anymore than I did.

'How about another dance? Smoochy one, this time.'

I rose reluctantly and Tom steered me through the crush onto the crowded little dance floor where hot, sweaty bodies seemed to be supporting one another in slow, pointless gyrations. The lights and the drink were beginning to make me feel disorientated. I had only eaten a cheese sandwich before coming out and began to feel faint. However, Tom held me tight against him and we moved about in a peculiar shuffle, weaving in and out of the other couples.

'You're sexy,' he murmured in my ear, 'fucking sexy. I fancy you like mad, you know that?'

I made no reply and tried not to let him too close. He burrowed his face into my hair and tried to nibble my ear. His breath stank of whiskey and I turned my head away. After a while his hands began to wander down towards my bottom.

'Keep your hands higher,' I shouted in his ear. He chuckled at this and pressed me closer.

'Ooh, little Miss Prick Tease, you love playing hard to get, don't you?'

I eventually pleaded exhaustion. Tom could have circled about forever, his whiskey-laden breath in my face, his groping hands all over me. By now he had consumed several drinks and I knew he was not a safe person to be with. He seemed to lose all sense of control and propriety ... and he had little enough to begin with. Now he suddenly grabbed my hand under the table, guided me to his trousers, which he had calmly unzipped, and tried to place my fingers round his hardened cock. I screamed and jumped up.

'What's up?' he muttered, looking astonished. 'Never felt a dick before? God, you're a little innocent, aren't you?'

'I need to ... to go to the Ladies,' I said. I went off trembling with rage and left him to zip himself up and nurse his drink, looking amused.

I stood for a while before the mirror in the Ladies. Other girls pushed and shoved around me as I stood there looking and feeling sick. Gill followed me in and whispered in my ear, 'I told you so, didn't I?' But she also looked amused as if she was really rather pleased at the shock I'd received. I felt myself trembling still. I'd had enough of this lewd, coarse fellow. His posh voice and education hid a nasty, despicable nature. He was trying to treat me like a tart. Who did he think I was! I had to go back for my jacket and then I would tell him that I wasn't going to stay. As I slowly threaded my way back to the table, I heard him mention my name to Kev. They didn't notice me and I dodged behind a pillar.

'Where'd you find her?' Kev was asking. Tom laughed.

'Neat, isn't she? A real little country cutie, supposed to be Jim's sister. So he says. I reckon he's grooming her for other uses. Just thought I'd beat him to it.'

'She's pretty, I'll give you that. Nice tits.'

'*Very* nice tits. And I swear she's a virgin. Can you believe that? But I swear she is. She nearly shot through the air when I gave her a feel of my dick. Boy, I've always wanted to try a virgin. I'm looking forward to it. '

'Good luck. Trouble is she'll only be a virgin once.'

The two men laughed at this joke. I blanched at the mere thought.

'Maybe you can pass her on to me when you're fed up with her.'

'Oh, I'll soon be fed up. She's too bloody serious all the time. No go in her. No class. But worth the occasional fuck.'

I walked up to them. Picking up Kev's glass, still full of beer, I threw it in Tom's face.

'You bloody cow!' he gasped, starting to his feet.

'For a start, I *don't* like the word "tits",' I yelled. 'And I don't like crude, coarse men either. Find yourself some other *country* virgin to seduce. We're not all stupid and ignorant, you know!'

People behind me laughed and one girl clapped with delight. Tom looked furious, beer dripping from his face and shirt. I seized my jacket, turned on my heel and left the place, seething with fury.

He didn't follow me, much to my relief. I never heard from Tom again. He got the hint and obviously didn't think I was worth the waste of any more brown and mild.

Chapter 23

It took me a week before I managed to find a job at the Nags Head, Holloway, just along from the big store, Jones Brothers. It was almost my last port of call. I'd considered asking if they needed a shop assistant in Jones Brothers but a little café caught my eye and I decided to try my luck there first. There was just one person serving and she seemed to be rushing around like a maniac trying to do everything. Not that there was that much to do as only one disconsolate customer was there, sipping a cup of dark brown tea and staring at a congealed plate of beans on toast.

The manager/waitress/owner, a small, sharp looking woman, looked me up and down for a bit and then announced that I'd do.

'Can't afford much in the way of wages,' she said, 'but you'll help me wash up, serve and all that. I'm on my own. It'll be hard work.'

'I don't mind hard work,' I said. 'If you like I can help cook as well.'

'We'll see how you go, first. I don't serve much here that's fancy. Chips, baked beans, eggs and such. I do a shepherd's pie now and then or a steak pie. The blokes love that. It's just a workmen's caff. Nothing fancy.'

She seemed a bit dubious as if she felt I ought to be looking for something better but I was delighted to have found even this low paid job and made up my mind to do my best even in a 'not so fancy' caff. I turned up for work next day looking tidy and neat. I wasn't going to appear a mess just because the owner, whose name was Mo Simpson, looked as if she'd been dragged through a hedge backwards. I was going to make her raise her standards, not lower mine.

My first job was to clean the cooker. I shone that stove as it had never shone before. Bob Cranshaw and Sid Waterman would have been proud of me. Mo came and watched me in fascination as if she'd never seen anyone work that hard in her life. She said nothing but I know she was impressed.

Next, I peeled a mound of potatoes for chips which I put in a big tub of water. Then mopped the floor that was covered in grease stains and slippery and dangerous. Once the customers came in, I went out to serve. I wrote things down then tried to remember them. It was only a tiny place and not exactly overrun with clientele, so it wasn't hard. Coffee, egg, ham, beans or peas and chips seemed to be the universal food here. I wondered how Queenie managed the complicated Italian menu at De Marco's. During the day I kept up with washing dishes while Mo cooked chips and eggs till the place stank of sour oil. When the day was done, I opened the back door to let out the smells, finished the last of the washing up, cleaned the tops of the tomato ketchup and brown sauce bottles, wiped the tables down and mopped over the floor again. Mo looked at the place in wonder and said, 'Nice job, dear. Guess, you'll do.' Which was, I suppose, praise indeed.

I was very tired and glad to go home, almost falling asleep in the bus on the journey back. After a hot, soothing bath, I went to my room, sank into the armchair and breathed a sigh of relief. God, it was hard work but I'd done worse. At least I'd started somewhere, was independent and would earn a week's wages by my own efforts. That cheered me up.

Betty came up half an hour later to say my boyfriend was on the phone. She didn't seem to believe me when I said he was my brother. I went downstairs most unwillingly.

'I'll come for you tonight,' he informed me, his voice as always cheerful and confident. 'A friend's having a party in Bayswater. It's a super place. You'll have a great time.'

'Jim,' I said wearily, 'I've got to be up at six tomorrow and at work by eight.'

'Work, what work? Thought you said you hadn't got anything.'

'Well, I have now. A job working in a café at Nag's Head. Started today and I'm shattered. I am definitely not going to any party.'

He was silent for a moment.

'Why are you doing this to me, Bridie?'

'What are you on about? I'm not doing anything to you. This is *my* life, Jim. Get that in your head. I didn't come here to party and drink and waste my life aimlessly. It may be your idea of fun but it isn't mine. I need to make my living somehow. I'm going to bed early. See you another time.'

I slammed the phone down, feeling very cross with him. He really was the limit. He'd been kind, yes, but this was too much and I wanted to be left alone. Dropping into bed, I slept like a log out of sheer exhaustion.

The next day a delivery arrived while I was out and was awaiting my inspection in the hallway. Someone had taken it in, probably Betty or Dixie Dean. It was a magnificent carved stone sundial for the garden. I knew it must be from Jim, a token of remorse for being so pushy, and I was right. A sweet little note begged my pardon and said *for your few leisure moments!* He was wrong to send me such gifts and I knew I ought not to accept. But it was so lovely and, anyway, how did one send back a stone sundial?

With the help of Betty's husband, Ted, I carted it into the garden and set it in the middle of the paved circle. It did look good and everyone admired it.

'Got a nice boyfriend, eh, Bridie?' said Betty giving me a nudge with her arm. 'You're onto a good thing there, gel. Generous bloke.'

'He's my foster-brother, not a boyfriend,' I explained again but she just grinned and winked at me.

'Won't last two minutes,' Dixie said sourly as we crowded round to admire the new embellishment to the garden.

'Shut up, you miserable sod,' said Betty. 'Looks smart, don't it? All we need is a bench now, like Bridie said. We can do a whip round between us and get one.'

'I ain't givin' nuffin' for no bleedin' bench,' said Dixie. 'Can't afford it.'

'You ole misery! I'll bet you've got a heap of dosh stashed under your mattress,' said Ted, glaring at him.

'Fuckin' 'aven't!' whined the old man. 'Don't you get them ideas in yer 'ead. You'll be knockin' me off next minnit and all fer nuffin', that'll be the next thing.'

And he scarpered indoors as if the hounds of hell were after him and bolted his door.

I worked like a beaver all week at Mo's Café. She seldom said much to me but she always gave me a free lunch, said I deserved it. She was a silent, strange woman who looked as if she was in pain a lot of the time; I wondered about her and her life but she never gossiped or talked about herself nor did she ask questions. She simply accepted my existence and seemed glad of the help.

'Did you run this all alone, Mo? Before I came?' I asked one day as I turned the notice from OPEN to CLOSED and pulled the shutter down over the door. Mo had taken the mop to the floor herself today. My efforts at making her take more care with the place seemed to be paying off.

I took the mop from her. She looked too tired to manage any more. She sat down in a plastic chair and sipped at a cold cup of tea.

'Me old man left me,' she said, 'we ran it together then he upped and went.'

She said no more than that but I felt sorry for her.

'Poor Mo. It's a lot of work,' I said.

'It is,' she sighed. 'I'm glad you come to help me, Bridie. Don't know what I'd do wivout you. I'd have had to shut. Just managing as it is.'

I was pleased at this and said, 'Mo, we could maybe earn more if we made the place look nicer. I can come and give it a coat of paint this weekend if you like. And if we bought some nice tablecloths, it would cheer it all up a bit, don't you think so?'

Mo looked around at the yellow, dingy paintwork and sighed. 'It's a bit of a mess. Sam was always going to do somethin' but he never did. Too busy down at the pub chatting up the barmaid, he was.'

'I'll do it then if you want.'

'Can't offer you no more money.'

'You don't need to, just pay for the paint. I don't mind. If we get more customers then we'll both gain from it, won't we?'

She looked grateful. 'You're a good girl,' she said, 'I liked your face first off but thought you'd be too posh and leave in a day or two when you saw how hard it all was. But you ain't gone, after all, and you've already made the place look better. I'm too tired most nights to do more than shut the door and go upstairs and sleep.'

'I like to help. You don't look well, Mo. It's too much for you on your own.'

'Got bad arthritis. It's gettin' worse an' all.'

I patted her arm in sympathy and she looked pleased. I hated to see that poor, tired face crumpled in pain.

Jim rang as usual from work and asked if I liked the sundial.

'I love it and so does everybody else. Thanks, it'll make our lives much nicer. You're so thoughtful, Jim. And it must have set you back a bit. I'll pay you when I can.'

'You will not! It's a gift. Accept something in life, Bridie. It's a form of false pride and vanity never to accept, never to allow someone else to enjoy the pleasure of giving.'

'Okay, I accept.'

Jim couldn't believe his ears when I told him I was going to paint the shop that weekend instead of joining him and his mates on a jaunt on the river.

'Why? Why should you do such a thing?'

'I want to help poor old Mo. She's a tired soul and her old man has left her. She needs help. I'm young and capable. It's nothing to me and I'll enjoy making that place look nice. Maybe I can help her run it and make something of it for us both. It's a great idea.'

'You'll end up looking old,' he said. 'You'll smell of chip oil.'
'I will not!'
''Fraid so.'

I ignored him and his jibes and went to the café that weekend, painting it a lovely bright green with yellow round the pay desk. It looked so much cleaner and more cheerful. This way, the less attractive customers might be frightened off and better ones drawn in. That was my hope anyway.

Mo was delighted with the results. After a month, we found that the clientele did indeed seem to pick up as I had predicted. To my surprise, Jim came in one afternoon just as I was shutting up the place.

'So this is the glorious Nag's Head café,' he said, looking around.

'Have you come to make fun, Jim, because if so, you can go away. Mo and I are proud of our café.'

He smiled suddenly, disarming me as he always did with sudden charm.

'No, I'm not mocking at all, Bridie – it's admirable what you've done. The place looks nice and cheerful. Won't you introduce me to your boss?'

In my mind I regarded Mo as more of a partner these days. I introduced Jim as my brother and Mo smiled at him and shook hands very solemnly. She seemed a bit in awe of this posh brother.

'Jim's studying for the law,' I added.

A worried look came over her face though I had no idea why. I think in her mind the Law and the Police went together and she seemed to have some reason for being afraid of Jim because he represented the long arm of authority. I couldn't help wondering if all her dealings were above board. I had a suspicion she dodged her taxes somehow or other and made up my mind to take a look at her books, if she possessed such things, and check up that all was right. It wouldn't do to enter into business with her if she had something to hide.

I never got a chance to look at the books because we were

simply too busy. Running a café with just two people wasn't easy. I told Mo we really ought to get someone to help with the dishes and cleaning at least but she was reluctant.

'Can't really afford it,' she said. 'I'm just about managing to pay you even though things is lookin' up.'

I said no more but had to admit to myself it was making me very tired. Jim was right, I would get old and worn, and end up looking like Mo if I kept up this relentless pace.

I'd managed to get the little garden neater, put in a few shrubs and pots. It looked so nice and restful and was somewhere I could go and find a little serenity now and then. Jim came along one evening to admire his sundial and to see what I'd done.

'It all looks very nice,' he said. 'You're a real homemaker, aren't you, Bridie?'

Everyone had contributed to buying the new bench. Luke McGraw had given the most, to my surprise.

'It's wonderful to have a little space, a little oasis in this place,' he said. 'May I join you down here sometimes?'

'Of course you may. It's for us all to share and enjoy. I'd love you to join me.'

He had looked very pleased at this as if he didn't often get such invitations. However, the one time he did join me on the bench, that nasty piece of work Ted had opened his window upstairs and yelled out, 'That seat ain't for niggers. Get orf it.'

Luke had looked at me and risen but I pulled him back and said loudly, 'Don't listen to that stupid, ignorant fool, Luke. You gave more than anyone else towards this. It's your seat too.'

I glared at Ted and told him to bugger off. It wasn't often that I said such things but he really riled me. Yet another of life's interminable weaklings who liked to bully others. I wasn't standing for it any more.

Ted scowled at me but said no more because he knew Betty liked me a lot and strange as it may seem, stood in awe of his diminutive little wife. Betty was no mean adversary and looked as if she could wield a rolling pin very nicely.

Jim and I sat down on the new bench together and he smoked a cigarette as we watched the sun setting behind the rooftops. He regarded me keenly.

'You're looking tired, Bridie.'

'I am,' I sighed. 'It's hard work. But it's okay. I like to feel I'm helping Mo. She's a worried little soul. Always looking over her shoulder.'

'Sounds like she's got something to hide.'

'I think she has. I feel her accounts aren't all they should be and keep meaning to look at them before someone catches her out.'

Jim smiled thoughtfully. 'We all have something to hide.' He lit another cigarette and leant back, gazing up at the windows for a while. We both fell silent, lost in private thoughts.

'I've bought myself a second-hand cello,' he said, at last, 'Alice's brother was selling his and I managed to get it for a bargain price. I'm practising like mad and mean to get you round to listen one evening. Would you like that?'

He looked at me pleadingly and I nodded my head. 'That would be nice, Jim. Don't worry about being a good cellist, I haven't a clue what's good and what isn't as long as it sounds nice to me. You know what a philistine I am!'

'I'll help you to appreciate the finer things of life,' he said. 'I want you to enjoy Mozart and Haydn and Bach and not just pop songs. You're a bright, intelligent girl, Bridie. I want to make something of you for your own sake. You're wasted in a greasy spoon café.'

He was in earnest. But it's all a matter of opinion, isn't it? Finer taste, I mean. I was beginning to have a real appreciation for music because of Jim's explanations and his introducing me to work I'd never heard before. Yet I still hankered after the sounds of Mother Nature, the finest music of all.

Jim still expressed regret that I'd chosen to wear myself out in Mo's café and not come to work in Grantham's chambers. But I felt no such regret. Jim would have been around all the time and that would have been too much of a good thing. I liked Mo. She was *real* where in many ways Jim always tried to be something he was not, always putting on a show. Mo was a good person and nice to me in her own way. She'd had a hard life and I felt for her. I knew all about a hard life.

I had been in London four weeks now and written to Joe and Sheila since my last phone call telling them I was managing quite well and getting used to my new life. The truth was, I was unhappy. I missed Ryan more than I dared admit even to myself. When his letter arrived, I ran upstairs with it, flung everything down on the floor, fell into the armchair and opened it with a trembling hand.

Darling Bridie ...

I paused here and felt my heart open with joy. He still thought of me with love despite my having hurt and rejected him. I really didn't deserve it, I knew that. It was comforting to know he didn't hate me.

... I'm sitting writing this during first watch. Up here on the light at this late hour, when all's dark and you know the world's fast asleep, it's a strange, quiet, empty feeling. Like a man's all alone in the world, Bridie. But I know I'm not alone when I think of you. I see your face so plain and it's like you're here with me sometimes. I long for you so much. You know the other night I woke up and swear I felt your arms around me, smelt your sweet smell. It was so real. It made me all mixed up inside, all longing. Bridie, come home soon, don't make me wait a year ...

He went on to say the weather was very bad on Wolf Rock and it would be ages before he could get away. Did I want him to come and visit on leave or had I banned him altogether? Tears came to my eyes as I read this. I wanted him so much, longed to see his face and hear his slow, quiet voice, feel the peace he always brought me with his gentle presence. Yet my foolish pride prevented me from telling him so; I didn't want him to see the pitiful life I was leading here. I wrote back telling him I was doing well and wanted to stay for the year if I could and it would soon pass by and be good for us both. I didn't want him to come, I said, I wanted it to be a real test.

The only good thing was I was earning some money at last. Paltry as my wages were they paid for the rent, fares and a Spartan existence. Then there was the fifty pounds from Joe.

The notes were still in an envelope hidden behind a picture. I knew I ought to put them in a savings bank but was always too tired when I came home at night to do anything about it. In my heart, perhaps I just wanted to know the cash was available in case I should suddenly want to run back home and leave all this.

I felt very dispirited of late and wondered as always what I was doing here. I felt as if I was slowly dying away in this existence. It couldn't go on.

It was a Friday evening when the first of the disasters began.

Chapter 24

I arrived at Mo's café on Friday morning to be greeted by a very distraught looking Mo.

'I've had the inspector round,' she said, 'came and asked about my books and that.'

'Which inspector? When?'

'Came after you'd gone last night. Said he'd had a tip off that my books wasn't okay and he wanted to see them. So he took them with him. I'm scared, Bridie. Sam never paid no tax or anything – he was against tax, he was. Never did anything right. He'll get me into trouble now. The inspector said I'd go to prison if things wasn't right.'

'You won't go to prison! It's not your fault Sam didn't do things properly. I don't believe in this tax man,' I added, puzzled by it all. 'They don't call on people in the evening like that, I'm sure of it. They'd write or summons you or something. What was this man like?'

'Dunno. Big man, official-looking geezer. I know their sort. He was real, all right. Said he'd send the health inspector along too and I might get closed down if I didn't do something about the dirt.'

'But it's fine now. We cleaned up, we painted the place. It sounds like some sort of intimidation to me, Mo. Don't let it get to you. You should have refused to give him the books.'

'I was scared,' she said, tears in her eyes, 'he was a nasty man.'

We worked as hard as ever both Friday and Saturday. Mo turned the notice on the door and shut the shutters at the end of the day. She seemed even more tired and dispirited than usual.

'Ain't got the energy for all this, Bridie,' she said suddenly. 'I've been thinkin'. I'm going to shut up the caff and go off to my sister in Ealing for a bit. I need a rest, me health's just not good. I feel a strain in me heart. Sorry, love, you've done so much and been a good mate. But I'll have to lay you off. I'll give you an extra week's wages. That's all I can manage.'

I stared at her aghast. 'Don't give in, Mo – we'll manage somehow.'

'Sorry, love,' she said again. 'You'll find another job easy. You're very good.'

I sat in the garden when I got home and tried to get my ideas together. The blackbirds sang around me but I was deaf to their sweet warbling because my heart was full of misery. I understood how Mo felt and knew it was probably the right thing as far as she was concerned. It was all too much for her and in some ways for me too. Maybe it would work out for the best.

Luke stopped by when he saw me sitting out in the garden and came over to look at the sundial.

'Six o'clock on the dot. Tells the time well,' he smiled. Then he saw my sad face and said, 'You okay, Bridie? Look like you got bad news.'

'Lost my job, Luke.'

'That is bad news. If you need any help ask me. I can lend you a bit if you're desperate.'

'I've got a bit of cash put by,' I said. 'I'll manage till I find another place. But thanks anyway.'

Looking up, I saw the fleeting shadow behind the downstairs window; prying, miserable old Dixie. Upstairs Ted, in his string vest as always, was leaning out of the window smoking like a chimney, glaring down at us. I felt surrounded by unkind, malevolent people ... except for poor Luke. He was as much an alien as I was in this place.

Luke patted me on the shoulder in sympathy, his manner tentative. I looked up again and saw Ted's face. He looked back at me as if I was filth and slammed his window down,

241

muttering loudly about 'girls what consorted with blacks'. I wanted to run up and hit him but wouldn't have dared. He was a big, beefy bully of a man and looked as if he could be very violent.

Luke just shrugged and said, 'Best to ignore it. I do.'

Jim had promised to pop round later that evening and in a way I was glad to see him.

'I've lost my job,' I said mournfully as he pecked me on the cheek.

He looked at me speculatively. 'Why, what have you done?'

'I haven't done anything. But someone put the wind up Mo and pretended to be a tax inspector – threatened her really. She's not well and she got scared by it all. I suppose I saw it coming. She kept saying how it was all getting too much for her. The least problem was likely to put her off.'

'Well, I'm not sorry, Bridie,' Jim said. 'I think it was getting too much for you as well. Can I help you find something new? I feel I know what's better for you than you do, you know.'

'Maybe you're right,' I replied glumly.

'I know I'm right. I'll lend you some cash. You'll be penniless now; you won't be able to manage the rent, Bridie.'

'Thanks, but I can manage for a bit longer,' I said. 'Joe gave me fifty pounds to keep me going in case it takes a bit of time to find a job. Though I hoped to save that.'

'That was very generous of Dad.'

'He's always been really good to me,' I said, 'I'm so lucky.'

'Now I'll be good to you in his place,' said Jim with a look that got me worried.

'You're always good to me but you know me by now, Jim. I want to manage by myself.'

'Ever independent, eh? Well, we'll wait and see. One day you will need me, Bridie, you can count on it. I presume your money from Joe is in a bank and safe from these thieving characters here?'

'Well, no,' I admitted. 'I keep meaning to open an account, just not got round to it. But it is safe. I've hidden it well.'

'Nothing's safe from a thief.'

'I'll put it in a bank on Monday. I know I should.'

'You do that. Meanwhile I'll take a day off tomorrow and take you out for a day on the river. You can put all these worries behind you and enjoy yourself.'

'You are kind to me, Jim.' I looked at him and felt grateful. What would it have been like if I was all alone in this awful city without his help? He was as good as gold these days and I decided that I had over-reacted at first.

We had a lovely time the next day taking a pleasure boat from the Tower down the river to Greenwich. Being on the water, being in a boat made me think of Ryan I sighed.

'Aren't you enjoying yourself, Bridie?'

'Of course I am. Just feeling a little sad.'

'That's natural. But things will soon be right again, things will work out for the best. Wait and see.'

Putting aside my sad thoughts and longings, I let him charm and amuse me with his witty remarks. Jim was good company, it had to be admitted, though as far as I was concerned best only in small doses.

When I returned home that night, I glanced out of the window at the garden as I walked up the stairs. I stopped, horrified at what I saw. Someone had had a spree of destruction out there and the sundial had been smashed to pieces, the flower pots broken and flowers uprooted. It was as if a hurricane had chosen this spot to vent its furious energy. I ran back down and went out to survey the mess and stood and wept and wailed.

Dixie Dean came to the door and said, 'Told you, din' I? Said it wouldn't last long – not round 'ere.'

'Did you do this, you old bastard!' I said in fury.

'No, I didn't. Not me. Wouldn't 'ave the strength, would I?'

'No, but you're pleased, aren't you?' I was so furious, I almost choked.

'Too bleedin' right. Daft idea. Everyone starin' in my window. No blinkin' privacy these days with that darkie an' all out there. You wimmen is all the same.'

He went back indoors, his eyes gleaming with delight at my discomfort.

It could only be one other person. I looked up ready to scream abuse but there was no sign of Ted leaning out of the window today.

Chapter 25

I rang Jim at the chambers from the pay phone next morning. I had cried all night and wanted to die. For once I needed Jim just as he had said I would and it was annoying to admit he was right.

'Shall I call the police?' he asked.

'I can't prove anything and they'll never know who did it. Dixie Dean swears it was louts came in through the back fences and did it. He says they're always vandalising things but I'm not so sure of it. Fact is, I don't know. '

'Why don't you come over to me, Bridie, come and I'll find you a place over here.'

'How can I afford the rent round your way, Jim? You said it was too expensive yourself. I'm going out now to look for another job.'

'You never give up, do you?'

'No, I don't,' I cried with passion, 'and I never will. I won't let things beat me! I never have yet.'

'Bridie, Bridie ... why don't you just let go of this fierce independence of yours!'

'I can't. I've given up home and Ryan and everything to come here, to prove something to myself. Don't you understand, don't you see, Jim? It seems foolish to you, it seems foolish to Ryan. But something in me urges me on. I don't know why, either.'

Jim sighed. 'I don't understand. I really don't. You're beautiful, so beautiful. Any man would want to take care of you if you would let him. Yet it seems you'll never let a man near you. Not me, not Ryan. You're going to be fierce and Amazonian and much good may it do you, Bridie O'Neill. Anyway, I'm here if you do need me. You know that.'

'I do know that, Jim. I am grateful, forgive me. I can't help being the person I am.'

'You can no more help it than a bird can help wanting to fly. And I wouldn't want you to be anything else. Look, I'll come round tonight and take you out for a meal. It'll cheer you a little. Let me do that, at least. If I know you, you'll be out all day looking for work. Am I right?'

'You are right. And I *will* find something.'

'Well, do your best, my little trooper. You'll be shattered after a day looking for work. Expect me after six.'

'All right. Thanks, Jim,' I sighed and put the phone down.

I spent the day trudging around again, looking for work. I even called again at De Marco's but Queenie regretfully said the girls were proving very good and there were no vacancies as yet. She said Mr De Marco paid good wages and so they stuck it out even though he was a demanding boss.

'Good luck, dearie,' she said as I went my way, feeling like orphan Annie.

It was a fruitless day. Perhaps my confidence had eroded and it showed to prospective employers and no one wanted me. I would have to think of something else. But what?

My feet were tired when I got back to Portdown Road and I climbed the narrow flights slowly. When I went to put the key in the door of my room, I realised I'd left it unlocked. Oh God! I was so careless. A puzzled frown came to my face. I was so sure I had locked it. It really was time they put Yale locks on these doors, then they would close automatically. Maybe I'd get one put on myself when I had some cash to spare. Nervously I opened the door but all was quiet and looked as I had left it. I breathed a sigh of relief.

As I made a cup of tea for myself, I kept glancing around. There was a funny feeling in the pit of my stomach that I couldn't account for. I had looked forward to the cup of tea but it now tasted of nothing. I felt so tired that all I wanted to do was go to bed early but Jim was coming. Damn Jim! I was really too tired to be with anyone. I just wanted to be left alone, to curl up and die.

The breakfast things still sat on the table so I cleared them away and washed them up, my mind full of worries and misery. Some instinct made me go to the picture on the back of which I'd taped my envelope with Joe's money in it. It wasn't there. My heart lurched.

At that moment, Jim knocked and I let him in. My face must have looked stricken for he said at once, 'What's up, Bridie? You look white as a sheet.'

I bit my lip. 'I can't find my envelope, the one with the money Joe gave me.'

'Where do you normally keep it?'

'I always keep it taped behind a picture. It should have been safe. Jim, oh, Jim … what shall I do!'

He desisted from saying 'I told you so,' though he must have felt like it. I was a fool and naïve. I knew it and felt ashamed of myself. I was too trusting. This place was a thieves' den.

'Let's have a good search,' he said. 'Maybe it fell on the floor or something, it can't have just disappeared.'

We both searched high and low, even in the little waste bin. I was beginning to feel desperate. My self-control gave way and I sat down and sobbed.

Jim came and knelt in front of me, giving me his handkerchief to dry my eyes. I took it with a silly, nervous laugh, trying to pretend I was really okay but the sobs returned as I thought that I had only two weeks' money in my purse, only enough to pay the rent. I was tired, beaten down and felt a failure. Nothing worked for me, everything conspired to make me a passive, pathetic creature who could do very little and had no hope of making anything of herself at all. Self pity rolled over me in waves.

'Rubbish!' said Jim as I wailed these thoughts aloud. 'You're tired and upset. Naturally, you're upset. Bridie, maybe we should call the police, maybe your money has been stolen. Do you think that weird old fellow downstairs might have anything to do with it? Was there any sign of forced entry?'

That shut me up. I stared at Jim and said slowly, 'No, Jim, the door was unlocked when I got back yet I'm so sure I locked it. I must have got confused – I left in such an awful hurry this morning, my mind on everything that's happened. Usually I'm really careful, make sure the gas is off and all that sort of thing.'

'You *must* have forgotten to lock it if you say there was no sign of its being forced open. The police won't help you much if that's the case, they'll say it's your own fault. They really ought to have Yale locks; it's a disgrace. No good having a Yale on the front door when the inmates aren't to be trusted. I'm going to have a word with Mrs Townsend about it.'

'That's a fat lot of good when I've had my money stolen. I've never had that much money in my life and it's been taken from me. It's so cruel. Who did it, Jim – who could have taken it?'

I knew it wasn't Luke or Betty. I wasn't sure about Ted. I didn't really know the other couple of people in the house except by sight. However, I had mentioned having money to that old scoundrel Dixie Dean. I began to feel certain it was him.

'Maybe we should call the police. I think he should be arrested,' said Jim angrily when I told him this.

'We don't know if it's him for sure, we just don't know. If we call the police I suppose they'll search everyone's rooms and that would be so horrid. They'll all hate me. I can't stay here after this. In fact, I don't want to stay here at all. Oh, Jim, what can I do?'

I seemed to have lost all power of action. Jim went downstairs in a fury saying he would confront the old bastard and see if it was him. I heard raised voices; Dixie, Jim and their shouts were soon joined by the other tenants who came out of their rooms to witness the goings on with relish. I went out onto the landing and saw old Dixie Dean cowering in a corner of the hall with several people standing about him looking threatening.

'If you've pinched the gel's money, you miserable old sod, then you're in for it!' yelled Betty. 'And I bet you did pinch it.

You're always snoopin' and pryin' and it's bleedin' time you was locked up! Bet you smashed up our garden an' all.'

'I never did, I never touched no soddin' money!' said Dixie. His old face was a crumpled mess of fear as Ted, still in his vest and with muscles like a navvie, came close to his face, grasping the tattered shirt and almost lifting the old man from the floor.

'Well then, let's 'ave a look in your room, eh? That can't 'urt, can it?'

'I ain't got no money, I tell you,' whined the old man. 'I ain't.'

He turned as if to escape back into his room. Betty suddenly swooped upon him. 'Wot's this, then?' she demanded grabbing his shirt which gave in with the ripping sound of rotting material. An envelope was sticking half out of the old fellow's back pocket. She pulled it out and sickeningly I knew it was mine. Opening it, she revealed the five crisp tenners.

'So you never took it, eh?'

Ted picked up Dixie like a rag doll. He looked as if he was going to strike his head against the wall but I screamed and ran downstairs as fast as I could.

'It's okay, it's okay – you've found the money. Don't hit him!'

The big fellow was reluctant to give up his sport but I insisted that they let him go.

'Tell them, Jim!' I shrieked. 'Tell them he's an old man and they can't treat him like this.'

Jim was leaning against a wall taking no part in it now, just allowing things to unroll. He almost seemed to be enjoying the furore he had begun.

'She's right. We ought to turn him over to the police,' he reprimanded Ted, 'not take the law into our own hands. You'll get into trouble yourself if you do that.'

Ted considered this and Betty grabbed his arm and tried to pull him away from the scene.

'Aw, leave the bloody old fool alone, Ted. You'll be 'ad for GBH again'

Ted shrugged and said to the pale and cowering Dixie, 'You

better watch it, mate, that's all. Any more of your crap and I won't be responsible for what 'appens. Got it?'

'I never took it, 'onest,' was all Dixie could say. There was a look in his eyes of pathetic bewilderment.

Jim went to the phone. I seized his arm and stopped him just as he began dialling 999.

'No, no, let him alone, I don't want the police.'

'But justice must be done.'

'Oh Jim, shut up about justice. You're worse than bloody Shylock! I don't think he did take it.'

'What do you mean? It was in his pocket; everyone saw that.'

'I know, but ... I don't think he could even walk up all those stairs, not with his false leg. Everyone was crowding around him; anyone might have shoved it in his pocket. Look, we've got the money back, let's leave it alone. It could be any of these awful people and they're all trying to blame him. This place is a hornet's nest. I don't want to stay another night here.'

'It weren't me,' said Dixie again, looking at me hopefully. 'Don't get the rozzers in, mister.'

I looked at the poor, pathetic old fool and my heart turned over. It was time to leave this place and go. Anywhere. I ran back upstairs and Jim followed me.

I began to pack my cases, flinging things in.

'Where will you go, Bridie? You're acting like a fool. Stop for a moment and let's think it out.'

'I'm going back home.'

'And where is home?'

I stopped packing and sat down wearliy on the bed. Where indeed was home? Not with Joe and Sheila, not with Ethel in Bournemouth and my pride forbade me trying to find Ryan. 'I don't know. I have no home, Jim. I've never had a home,'

Jim came over to me then and put his arms about me, pulling me up to face him. He simply hugged me and stroked back my hair so gently that tears came to my eyes again.

'Oh Jim, I feel so unhappy. I don't know what to do, where to turn.'

'Turn to me,' he urged. 'I care about you, Bridie. You know I love you. I always have. I've tried, I've really tried to do the sister-brother thing but it won't work. You're a brave soul and a strong one and I love you for it – but just now and then lean on someone else, don't refuse help. It's foolish. Learn to take as well as to give.'

I leant on his chest and felt the strength and warmth of his body. He held me tight and let me rest there. It felt good and my sobs subsided.

'Come to my place tonight,' said Jim. 'Where else can you go? To a hotel? No, come to me, Bridie, come home to me. We'll think of something else tomorrow.'

I sighed and moved away from him. I felt utterly defeated and nodded my head. We packed the cases and he bundled them in the car and taking my keys went back upstairs to lock up the door to my room before taking me off to his flat in Finchley. As I sat waiting in the car, I saw Luke coming up the road, presumably on his way back from work. He looked tired and thoughtful. I was regretful that we would never get to know one another better. He was a good man. I popped my head out of the car window and called him.

'There's been some trouble, Luke,' I said. 'My brother's taking me away for a bit. I thought I'd better let you know you're on your own again up there.'

'Oh, Miss Bridie, I'm sorry about that,' he said coming over to speak to me. He sounded really upset. 'I'm sorry you're going. It's not on account of me, I hope.'

'No, no, Luke, nothing to do with you. Someone stole my money. It's all right, it's been recovered and I don't want to involve the police. I'm just going away. I probably won't be back.'

'I wish you luck, whatever you do,' he said and put out his hand for me to shake.

Jim came back down at this point and glared at Luke who smiled at him affably and said, 'Good evening, sir.'

Jim made no reply, just got in the car.

'Goodbye, Luke,' I said and waved as we set off.

'Who the hell was that fellow? Really, Bridie, you'd talk to anyone.'

'He has the room next to mine,' I said. 'He a really good man.'

'He's coloured,' said Jim firmly. 'I'm surprised it wasn't him who stole your cash.'

'He's just come home from work,' I said. 'Of course he didn't. Why are you men always so suspicious of one another?'

'It's the stag instinct in us,' said Jim with a smile. 'We can't abide rivals on our territory.'

I eyed him curiously. 'Stags collect a harem of does. Not a very good example. I hope you don't think I'm going to be a part of your doe collection.'

He looked genuinely shocked. 'Heaven forbid, Bridie! You're the only girl I've ever been interested in.'

'You could have fooled me. Well, don't think of me as your territory, Jim. It's bad enough with Ryan.'

'But Ryan isn't around to defend his territory any more,' said Jim with a malicious grin.

'No, he's not.' I fell silent at this and felt a pang of remorse. Ryan would have a fit if he knew I was going to Jim's place for the night. He'd think the worst. I was determined not to let the worst happen.

As we drove to his place, Jim chattering away in his usual fashion, I let myself relax at last and felt a sense of peace. It seemed as if it was all inevitable. At least tonight I wouldn't be afraid of Millie's ghost. It had all been my imagination and even if it wasn't, she wouldn't haunt me with Jim there to protect me.

Chapter 26

Jim's place was on the top floor of a block of maisonettes in North Finchley. There were four flats in the little block, and a small front garden round it with a close cut lawn and neat privet hedges. The secluded road curved round and Jim said that they led to some playing fields and allotments.

'Not a bad little place,' he commented as I stood and looked about me, savouring the contrast of this peaceful leafy suburb to Portdown Rd and all its noisy traffic and varied humanity.

'It's wonderful,' I sighed.

'You'll be nice and comfy here.'

He led me round to his front door which was situated at the side of the flats. The door was made of solid oak with a thin panel of bubbly glass down the centre.

'Burglar proof, I reckon,' Jim nodded, 'not that we get too much trouble round here. It's a quiet area with a lot of old folks and a few families. I don't really know my neighbours much, don't want to get too involved. I hope I'll be leaving here soon and off to something a lot better.'

'Where would you go?'

'I'd like a smart house in Hampstead some time, like Alice's mum, Mrs Townsend. It'll be a while before I can afford that sort of luxury, though.'

'But you mean to get there someday,' I smiled.

His face was serious. 'I *will* get there someday.'

We went upstairs to his flat. Apart from a tiny kitchen and bathroom, there were two sizeable main rooms, a sitting room and a bedroom. Looking around, I realised that Jim had surprisingly good taste for a man. Two or three large paintings graced the wall; one especially caught my eye. It was a painting of a Chinese lady with a strange green face by someone called Tretchikoff. I rather liked it. She had a mysterious look about her, exotic and intriguing. I was later to find copies of this picture all over the place, even at the dentists. But I'd never seen it till then and found it arresting. The room was in cream with alcoves round the fireplace painted a dark green and there were dark green armchairs and a sofa to match. A gilt framed mirror was hung over the fireplace, which had the effect of making the room look larger and brighter.

'You like it here?' asked Jim, seeing me look round.

'I do. You've got really good taste, Jim. It's not something you inherited from Millie. Or Joe, for that matter.'

Dad Joe had never been a bit interested in décor. He liked comfort and all our homes were arranged to suit this idea. As for Millie, hers had been the most pedestrian and suburban of tastes. Jim's artistic flair was a surprise.

He smiled. 'You see, Bridie, you don't really know me as well as you think. I'm full of hidden talents.'

'You are, Jim.'

'We should eat something. Bet you haven't eaten all day.'

'I had a sandwich. And I'm just too tired and upset to go out now, Jim.'

'We'll get some fish and chips, then. You just relax. I'll toddle off round the corner and get them. Make yourself at home. Relax, rest, you've come home, Bridie.'

I was too weary to make any comment on this last remark. Jim went out and got in some cod and chips and though half an hour ago I would have said I couldn't eat a thing, the appetising smell of the vinegar-soaked chips and battered fish made me realise how very hungry I was. He served the food up on plates and we tucked in with a will.

'There,' he said, looking pleased to see me wolfing it all down. 'I knew that would do the trick. You'll feel a lot less tired now. Uncle Jim's the doctor! Put your feet up tonight. I'll wash up.'

He had an air of pleasure about him as if he was truly glad to see me there and I did relax. For the first time I felt comfortable, wanted, in a pleasant place. I sat in an armchair, let my head fall back and sighed deeply. For once, I was able to let go and it was good to do so. We passed the evening chatting about varied topics. I mostly listened while Jim told me amusing stories about Cambridge and his office. I even laughed now and then. Slowly I began to feel better than I had in a long while.

'Right, you take the bedroom. I'll sleep on the sofa. It turns into a bed at night so don't feel bothered on my account, it's a very comfy bed. I've slept on it before when friends have stayed over.'

'Oh, Jim, I can't take your bed. I'll have the sofa. I won't be here for long, anyway.'

He gave me a funny look when I said that. Coming over to me he put his arms round me again and I stiffened just a little. But he made no attempt to kiss me, just held me. I clung to him and we stood together for a long time, his hand slowly rubbing my back in a comforting, almost maternal gesture.

'I love you, Bridie,' he whispered in my ear. 'I love you so much. I'm hoping that eventually I'll persuade you to stay.'

At that moment it didn't seem such a far-fetched idea. Ryan was far away from me now. I hadn't heard from him since my reply to his last letter. He was happy in his solitary splendour on some rock light out in the ocean while Jim was here, warm, human and loving. He really cared and showed it. My steely heart began to soften with his warmth. Jim was growing on me.

He seemed to sense some change for he drew away and held me at arm's length, looking deeply and seriously into my eyes.

'I'm not rushing you,' he said. 'I'm just so glad you're here. We can discover each other again. You can stay as long as you like. Stay forever, Bridie.'

'People will think we're lovers,' I objected. 'I can't stay, Jim. I'll have to live somewhere else.'

'Is being lovers so bad an idea?' he murmured and drew me to him again. I thought he *was* going to kiss me this time but he didn't and after a while he let me go. I was glad and yet not glad with all the perversity of a woman.

So the bedroom was mine to use and Jim cleared a space in the wardrobe and one of the drawers for me.

'Soon as I can I'm treating you to some nice clothes,' he said.

He left me, sensing my exhaustion. I was tired but lay on the bed thinking things over and wondering about the strange turn of events. Jim seemed to have got his way somehow but I still hoped to go out and find a job and a flat of my own. I didn't want to owe him anything. I already owed him far too much and it weighed the gratitude scales too much in his direction. I'd try and do something for him tomorrow.

With this thought in mind, I fell into a peaceful, sound and dreamless sleep.

Waking the next day without the incessant sound of traffic in my ears was a delightful sensation. I had slept more soundly here than in a long time. I could hear the rattling of cups in the small kitchen and it felt comforting to know a friend was out there and not the uncertain and unfamiliar.

Jim knocked on the door after a bit and brought me in a cup of tea.

'I'm off to chambers now,' he said, 'but you lie in, Bridie, have a relaxing day. Don't go dashing off anywhere and exhausting yourself. Everything in good time. There's no hurry to find a job or a flat. I'll be going back to Uni soon and then you can stay here and look after the place for me. You're safe with me. I'll take care of you.'

'That's good of you, Jim,' I said, feeling truly grateful for the chance of some respite from my own compulsions as much as anything else. After all, why not accept his hospitality and generosity? It would be wonderful to use this flat while he was at Cambridge. Why was I so bull-headed and determined to make myself miserable?

I drank the tea, ran a bath and enjoyed a good long soak. It was such a relief to be out of that awful house in Archway. I thought now and then of Luke McGraw and wondered why he was there and what he was doing. He didn't sound or look like someone on the buses or working in the sewers or wherever such people usually ended up. I'd never see him again, which was a shame as I felt he was a man I could trust. But I put him out of my mind and revelled in my new found sense of freedom and comfort.

I looked around the flat. Jim had few possessions but what he did have were tasteful; a marble bust on a stand in a corner, a strange, heavy but attractive piece of modern art on a shelf and a few interesting paintings and prints. He had a shelf full of books, mainly law and psychology but also quite a lot of crime novels. The old favourites were there: Raymond Chandler, Agatha Christie, Ngaio Marsh, Dashiell Hammett. There was a book on Auto-Suggestion which looked interesting but it was in French which was rather daunting. I thought I'd have a stab at it sometime and hopefully improve my knowledge. Languages had never been my forte. Jim, I decided, was really clever.

In his bedroom I saw a cello propped up in its case in a corner. He'd promised he would play for me some time. Was there no end to his talents? I sighed. It made me feel ill-educated and inadequate and I remembered my silly boast that I knew more than he did. I meant to take my education even further, acquire more knowledge through evening classes and the like. It was true that I was better read than Jim but he had a broader field of knowledge and understanding. Life was the real education, as Joe always used to say – and he was right. He always said Jim would turn into a penniless Professor while Andy would make the millions and live in style.

With nothing else to do, I routed out a duster, a vacuum and other cleaning items and began a thorough tidy-up of the flat. When I had finished that task, I contemplated what I might cook us for dinner that night. There was precious little in Jim's fridge except necessities. I would have to go out and explore and find a butcher, get a nice steak perhaps. Or make a casserole. He'd enjoy that. Just as I got myself ready to go forth, I remembered that Jim hadn't thought to leave a spare key to his flat and I wouldn't be able to get back in. Plus the fact that Jim had taken my money envelope last night and said he'd look after it as I was so careless. I hadn't been too pleased about that but he said he would come along with me when I opened a bank account as I'd probably need a reference anyway and he could provide one via his beloved Sir Simeon.

'After all,' he said, 'he is one of the best barristers in London. You could hardly have a better reference than that!'

'But he doesn't know me,' I objected.

'Oh, we'll fix it somehow,' was the reply. 'I'm sure he'll do it for a friend of his son's.'

I wasn't convinced about it but London ways were beyond me; they seemed to have rules of their own here. Jim always sounded so positive about everything it was hard to resist him. So I agreed and handed over the envelope. Looking in my purse now, I found I still had some change from a fiver. That would be plenty enough for the meat and there were potatoes and carrots mouldering in his cupboard which I could use up. However, I could hardly go out and leave the door on the latch. Jim had said it was a quiet, crime-free area but I didn't like to risk it. He had some nice stuff in his flat.

This was a frustrating dilemma. I so wanted to please him and do something for him in return but I couldn't. I wondered if he kept any spare keys anywhere. It wouldn't be right to hunt through his things. I did have his number at work but on looking around I realised that he hadn't had a phone connected yet. Strange for someone as efficient and up to date as Jim but maybe it was to save money. Despite all his boasts, Millie hadn't exactly left a fortune to her boys. What there was from the house sale and her savings (augmented by the fact that she had inherited her own parents' place) had been shared with Andy. It had been enough to buy the flat and the car and that was probably about it.

I went to the window and looked out at the quiet scene below. Plane trees lined the street, giving it a pleasant, green appearance. It was nice here, a leafy suburb, yet suddenly it felt a bit like a prison. There was nothing I could do and nowhere I could go until Jim returned and a feeling of panic arose in me. I told myself I was being silly. It just had not occurred to Jim I would be stuck in here and we hadn't had the sense to sort it out before he left for work. I would tackle him about it tonight and ask him to get a set of keys cut for me. I also decided I'd ask for my cash back and open a Post Office account instead. They didn't need references for that and it was a lot simpler. I preferred not to be beholden to anyone, Jim's marvellous boss or anyone else.

Making that decision made me feel better and more in control. I made myself a simple lunch of bread and cheese with a glass of milk and began to read one of the crime books on the shelf. After a while, I rose and paced about and stared again out of the window. There was scarcely ever a passer-by here. It was an odd thing that the loneliness in London troubled me a lot whereas being out in the open with only the rolling sound of the waves and the cries of the sea birds for company never worried me at all. I loved to feel alone with just the vast expanses of land and sea, the sense of communing with something greater than myself. Here I felt hemmed in and trapped and the empty streets seemed to symbolise my empty life.

Surely there must be some spare keys somewhere. This flat door had plenty of locks: both a Yale and a mortise lock. I assumed that spares were usually left with a neighbour or under a plant pot or something. Oh, well. To pass time I decided to forgo my sense of nicety and have a look around anyway so I searched the kitchen drawers and then peered into the bathroom cabinet full of male shaving equipment. Jim didn't stint himself on things like aftershave; he liked the expensive stuff, Christian Dior and the like. I smiled. And they thought only women were vain! I thought of Ryan who wouldn't touch such stuff, said it was for queers. That, of course, was going to the other extreme but then these two men were so different in nature. They couldn't be more different.

Thinking of Ryan gave me a sudden lurch and I longed to be with him. I was beginning to get a funny feeling about being here with Jim. It all felt wrong. He was pleasant and charming and when he was with me I always fell under his spell but when he was absent something niggled me about him.

There was nothing very personal in his flat but in one of his bedside drawers I found a cache of my letters and a photo of the four of us taken some years ago when I lived at Millie's. The body language in that photo said it all. I stood there shrinking away from Millie and Andy and leaning my body towards Jim. It was subtle but noticeable. I looked thinner and my face had a sad, wistful look about it. Jim had an arm about my shoulders and was smiling into the camera with his usual boyish charm.

I was touched that he kept my letters. I hadn't done the same; his had all been destroyed almost as soon as I read them. I wasn't the least bit sentimental about them. A picture of Millie and Andy and one of Joe and Sheila at their wedding stood on the mantelpiece. There didn't seem any signs of any other love interest in his life. I didn't like to look in the little desk in the corner. It was rude enough of me to pry into his things and only desperation and boredom had driven me to do so.

In the little hallway was a rack with a couple of jackets and a mackintosh. I felt in the pockets. In the mac, I discovered a set of keys and for a moment felt delighted. But they didn't look right. In fact they looked very like the keys to Portdown Rd; one yale key for the front door and a big old key for the room upstairs. He'd locked up last night, so of course that was why they were here. He hadn't worn this mac last night but probably slipped them in there on the way in, meaning to return them to the landlady.

No, that was wrong. I frowned. Searching for my handbag, I looked inside and found the identical keys still there. Yes, he'd handed these to me when he got back in the car and I'd put them in my bag. So why the other set of keys as well? Why keep spares to my room?

Oh, he was just well organised, I thought; that's what it was. He probably thought to keep spares in case I lost mine. How sensible of him. But what a pity it hadn't occurred to him to give me a spare set to his own flat.

When at last he came back home, I ran to greet him.

'Jim, I've been so miserable and bored! I couldn't go anywhere.'

He looked taken aback then flung off his jacket and gave me a hug and a kiss.

'I thought you'd just want to rest today,' he said. 'Sorry,

Bridie, I didn't think. That was stupid of me.'

'I would have rung you at work but you don't have a phone in the flat.'

He was apologetic. 'No, I keep meaning to get one put in but as I'm only here over the summer and then back to Cambridge and my student digs, it didn't seem worth it. The car is more useful to me and it costs a packet to run. Once I'm living here on a permanent basis and working full time, I'll sort it out, make this place nicer. Have to take things a bit carefully until then. However, that doesn't mean we can't go out and have a nice meal tonight.'

'I wanted to cook for you, to thank you for your kindness.'

I sounded so disconsolate that he smiled and looking around remarked, 'Why, Bridie, you've already done wonders. The place has never been so clean and tidy. Thank you for that. It's more than enough. I don't expect you to be my slave, you know. I'm not my mum.'

'Thank God for that!'

'No, I'm not at all like her,' he went on, 'I love you and I want to make amends to you for all you've suffered. I want you to be happy, Bridie. I'm so sorry you've been stuck in all day. We'll go out now to make up for it so go and put on your pretty blue dress. On Saturday when I'm free we can shop for some nicer things for you.'

'With what?' I said. 'Neither of us is exactly flush. Which reminds me – I think I'll have my money back, Jim. I've decided to put it in the Post Office after all.'

'Oh, sure. I haven't got it here just now though. I put it in the office safe. We don't want anyone pinching it again.'

I was annoyed by this but said nothing. He really did take things into his hands that were no business of his. However, I didn't want to spoil the evening and was determined to look my best so I dressed with care, put on some powder and lipstick and came out of the bathroom to be greeted with an admiring look.

'You look like Maureen O'Hara,' he said, 'with that lovely coppery hair of yours and those green eyes. You're a beautiful girl, Bridie. You ought to be a film star or a model.'

'Oh, shush!' I said but felt a bit flattered.

'I mean it.'

'You are a charming old flatterer, Jim Bosworth.'

We both laughed and set off in his car to a nearby restaurant. We ordered a meal and while we waited Jim chattered away as he always did. He had lots of funny anecdotes. He was clever, interesting and enjoyable company. We had some wine that night and unused to drinking anything but tea and lemon barley I found myself mellowing and becoming decidedly woozy too. It was a nice feeling – as if all the cells in my body were expanding and relaxing and I felt happy and beautiful and special. It really made up for the lonely, frustrating day.

'You look so much happier and at ease now. Not the wild-eyed lassie who greeted me earlier. You had the air of a bird in a cage busting to get out. Hope you feel better,' smiled Jim. 'You're not mad at me, are you?'

'Of course not. You're right, it forced me to rest. I'm never like this as a rule. It's something about being in London. There's this restless energy everywhere and it makes me feel bothered and rushed. I want to be on the go, busy. It's not a peaceful place, Jim.'

'It's a city, the Metropolis, it's bound to have that sort of energy. You get used to it after a while. You won't be a country lass forever and believe me, you won't want to go back to that slow, quiet pace of life after this. London's the place to get your blood pumping a bit more, gets you going. It's active, exciting. Isn't that much better than being stuck on some old cottage by a lighthouse?'

I was dubious. 'I suppose so. I suppose I will get used to it.'

'I've asked for another day off, Bridie, made up a good excuse. Fact is I want to take you sightseeing, really show you the London sights. I haven't taken you anywhere yet what with one thing and another. It's time to do so, don't you agree? You'll be thrilled. I don't want you to think living in London is all bad, you know. You've just had a difficult experience. And we must do some shopping.'

'Yes, we must do some shopping tomorrow but not clothes,

Jim. Food shopping is what we need then I can cook. We can't eat out all the time, can we? I can't afford to and neither can you by all accounts. As for a new dress, I'll get something nice with my next wages. As you know I mean to find work and then I may use Joe's money as key money and look about for another place to live. It's nice of you to ask me to stay in your place but I've been thinking it over and don't feel right about it. I really don't. If I found a couple of rooms round here, I can still keep an eye on your flat. You think I might find some lodgings in this area?'

'As we've already said it'll be a lot pricier here than Archway. You'll have to get a decent job to afford it, Bridie, not your scumbag cafes. We'll discuss all that in good time. Don't rush things, Bridie. Promise me.'

With reluctance I agreed. 'By the way, Jim,' I asked as the thought struck me, 'why do you have a spare set of keys to my room in Portdown Rd?'

He looked slightly shocked and said nothing for a moment. 'Have I? Where did you find them?'

'In your mac.' I blushed a little but said quickly, 'I was looking for a spare set of your own keys, Jim, sorry. Didn't mean to be prying in your pockets or anything but I felt a bit desperate stuck indoors like that.'

'Yes, yes, of course,' he said in an absent-minded sort of way. 'I understand. I forgot I had those spare keys. Mrs Townsend must have given me two lots. You may as well give me the other ones and I'll give them back to her agent tomorrow. I told you, didn't I, that she was my friend Alice's mother?'

'You've told me a dozen times. Was Alice really your girlfriend?' I asked to tease him.

'For a bit,' he said, 'but it was never anything serious. Alice is a useful contact, that's all. She lives with her mother in their Hampstead house. Mrs Townsend is a divorcee and a pretty astute business woman – reckon she's making a mint. She has property all over London and lets it out. She buys up in cheap places like Islington and Archway where she can pack loads of people into one house. It doesn't bother her that they're African,

Irish or Greek as long as she can pack them in.'

'She sounds awful and very greedy.'

'She is. You're right. Put that awful place behind you, Bridie. I'm sorry I found you such dismal lodgings; it just seemed so reasonable a rent and a nice enough room at the time. I thought it would be fine to start with.'

I looked at him thoughtfully. 'Well, it *would* have been all right. But things just seemed to go wrong. Maybe I was silly to rush off like that. After all, it was my fault I left the door unlocked like that. I suppose it *was* a temptation to someone.'

'You were probably in a hurry that day, you said you woke early and became a tad disorientated.'

'I was. The whole thing was odd.'

'And don't forget the damage to your nice little garden. You couldn't have stayed there.'

'I know. That upset me more than nearly losing my money,' I sighed. 'Well, never mind, it's over now.'

I ate my dessert in silence. Then as if in a dream, in my mind's eye, I had a flash of Jim opening the door for me when we first went to Portdown Road. He'd been wearing a jacket that day and had handed those keys over to me. Then the next day he had *almost* taken some other keys out of his pocket and that day he had been wearing the mackintosh. Then there was the strange gut feeling that someone had been in my room when I had been out and it had felt as if Millie had been there. Well, of course she hadn't – but Jim might have been – and he always carried an aura of Millie for me. I was absolutely sure I hadn't left the door unlocked that day I went out. Who else could have got in but Jim? He had the keys. And then there was the photo of Ryan … and the strange visit of the tax inspector after I'd mentioned looking at Mo's books to Jim …

Jim was staring at me. 'What is it, Bridie?'

I mustered myself and forced a smile. 'Nothing.'

But inside my gut churned with a sense of fear. Had Jim sabotaged my job with Mo's café? Had he stolen the money and planted it on poor old Dixie Dean? If so, why on earth would he do such a thing?

Chapter 27

When we got back to his flat, I pleaded to feeling tired and a bit headachy.

'I'm just not used to wine, Jim,' I said, 'I really need to sleep. This day of inactivity has been more tiring than walking about and being busy.'

'I know the feeling,' he agreed. 'As I said, I'm taking a day off tomorrow. We can lie in and then go and enjoy ourselves. It'll cheer you up a little. Things have been rotten for you lately. We'll have fun.'

I lay awake for hours and tossed all these things in my mind. I decided in the end that I was being unreasonable and getting all confused. Jim wasn't the sort of person to break in and steal my money, mess up my life like this. He was so sweet and kind to me. What possible reason would he have to do such a thing? I was becoming irrational. He has simply forgotten the spare keys in his pocket. It hadn't rained much of late and he probably hadn't worn that mac for ages.

The next day we rose together and had breakfast curled up on the sofa. The plan was to go and shop for food, bring it back, then get the Underground into the heart of London and see the sights.

Jim pored over his London A-Z . 'We'll start with Trafalgar Square, walk up the Mall to Buckingham Palace and relax a bit in St James's Park.'

'Heavens! We'll be exhausted.'

'Not a bit, you'll love it all. We'll take some sandwiches and a bottle of wine and eat lunch in the park.'

'No more wine. Not at that time of day. You'd have to cart

me back home on your shoulder.'

'Nonsense; the more you drink wine, the quicker you'll get used to it.'

'But why *should* one drink wine? It's hardly a life necessity.'

'Oh, but it is – a life*style* necessity. You have to get used to it. It's the done thing. You're still so old-fashioned, Bridie.'

'Well, I am then and I mean to stay that way. I'm not sure I want to be a part of this London lifestyle as you call it. It strikes me as false and trivial. Ryan hated it.'

'Now why doesn't that surprise me?' Jim's voice was heavy with sarcasm.

'Why do you hate Ryan so much? He's a good man, Jim.'

'Maybe that's *why* I hate him.' He fell silent for a while. 'You know the real reason,' he added.

I didn't want to know. It was all becoming too complicated for me. I refused to take the bait, rose and went to the bedroom and got myself dressed. It wouldn't do to carry on this conversation.

As it happened the day passed most pleasantly. It was lovely to feel free of worries and just become sightseers and tourists. I enjoyed all the places we visited and the sun shone bright for a change. Our picnic in St. James's Park was my happiest experience. It felt so open there and the gleaming grey of the Serpentine winding its way through the park cheered me. Standing on the bridge in Kensington Gardens, I watched the swallows skimming over the lake and realised then my overwhelming need to be near water in some way. Maybe one day I might afford a house by the sea or at least by a big river. There *had* to be water somewhere for me to be happy and content.

'You see,' Jim smiled and looked over at me. 'London has such beautiful places as well as ugly ones. Admit it's lovely here, Bridie.'

'I do admit it, Jim. But I know I shall never be a city person.'

'You'll get used to it in time.'

That evening I cooked a delicious meal and we sat contented and replete. I made sure I took the armchair. The sofa was too intimate and I was determined to keep Jim from getting amorous. However, he behaved perfectly, making no lovey-dovey comments or any giving any other indication other than that of a friend and brother. I began to relax again. It had to be said he was good company and we passed time that evening playing cards and cribbage, laughing and joking, just as we used to do when we were young.

'Isn't this nice?' he said as the evening drew to a close. 'We get on so well, don't we, Bridie? We always have, haven't we?'

'We have, Jim. You've cheeered me up and I'm grateful for it.'

'Better than being on your own in that dismal room in Archway with all those rough people for company, isn't it?'

'Much better. The only nice person there was Luke McGraw. He was educated and gentlemanly.'

'The coloured bloke? People complain that they're a lazy lot.'

'Jim! That isn't true. And it's definitely not true of Luke.'

'Maybe he's an exception. But they're not like us. They're a different culture altogether. Anyway, why are we talking about that fellow? You do let your mind wander, Bridie. I'll begin to think you a regular flirt.'

'That's silly, Jim. God, you sound like Millie sometimes. Can't a man and woman like one another and talk together without it having flirty overtones?'

'In my book it's impossible for men and women to be "just friends". But then you are so unromantic at times.'

'Okay, I'm unromantic, Jim, I'm not a sentimental person but a realist. Life knocks anything like that out of one.'

'For me romance is essential food for the heart. Don't you like nice gestures, flowers, chocolates and all that? I wish you were a bit less down to earth at times.'

'Well, I am,' I said flatly. 'It's called survival, Jim.'

'Look, if you let me take care of you, you wouldn't have to put on this tough front,' he said softly. 'I suspect something a lot gentler and more feminine lurks beneath all this hard talk of yours. If you felt safe and cared for you could let that sweeter side of you come out and blossom. I want to help you to do that. Being with Ryan will just make you tougher and harder. You'll need to be tough to survive the sort of lonely existence he offers. It's all right for him. His nature is solitary. He's not the marrying sort, Bridie. Why can't you forget him?'

I had a sudden vision of a lighthouse against the dusky sky, its beams rotating slowly, piercing the oncoming darkness and lighting up the vast deeps that surrounded its fragile form. I saw the loneliness and grandeur of the sea and the huge empty cliffs and could almost hear the slapping and roaring of the engulfing waves against the sides of the rock-light on a tempestuous stormy night, waves sometimes sixty foot high. I could feel the spray on my face and hear the mourning of the sea birds as they wheeled about the light at night, round and round, enamoured and half-crazed by it. And there was this light, tended day and night by these amazing, dedicated men in order to help people navigate their way safely to land. There was the lighthouse keeper, a friendly, kindly, noble human being who was willing to set out and rescue anyone in distress if the need arose.

'You don't understand, Jim,' I said simply, 'you're a town person. Ryan and I am not.'

His face darkened at that and he looked angry and disappointed. In that moment I saw Millie all over again. I knew then that he wasn't the man for me. It wasn't his fault but he would always remind me of her and she was the one person in this world I hated with all my heart and soul and whom I would never be able to forgive. He was a part of her and I wanted none of him – not as a lover anyway.

Jim rang in and said he was sick the next day.

'I just want to be with you again,' he explained when I looked surprised at this deception. 'We had such a marvellous evening yesterday, didn't we, Bridie? I want to have a bit of holiday myself. Like you, I've just been working away. All work and no play … you know the old adage …'

We spent the day visiting St. Paul's and the City and Jim took me to see Temple Bar and the Inns of Court, which marked the edge of the City of London and Westminster. I had to agree with Jim that it was beautiful round there with a sense of being suspended in time, part of another age when life moved in slower rhythms. He explained all abut the four Inns, Inner Temple, Middle Temple, Gray's Inn and Lincoln's Inn and how these Inns had the right to be called to the Bar.

'What is the Bar?' I asked. 'What does it mean?'

'It's literally the bar that separates the gallery from the court.' He looked around him as he said this. 'I mean to join one of these Inns and be called to the Bar one day. I mean to be a great barrister, take silk and be Queen's Counsel like Simeon Grantham. I may even be knighted like him one day.' His eyes had fire in them and I believed him. With his ambition and his talents he would do it.

'I'll be so proud of you, Jim.' I nodded. 'I really believe you *will* do it.'

'Do you?' he said eagerly. 'Yes, I will. And you *will* be proud of me and I of you. You'll have the smartest clothes then, swan about looking lovely, have the best house and the most fascinating company. You won't need to clean or cook any more. Just think of the life we could have.'

I ignored this remark, smiled and changed the subject.

Later that evening, I cooked a delicious chicken roast and Jim plied me with wine. I didn't like to be a spoil sport and keep refusing so I drank a glass or two. It was heavy red stuff and made me very thick headed though deliciously warm and light in the body.

'I am going to play you some music,' said Jim after a while. 'You've never heard me play the cello, have you? No? So there's a treat in store for you. At least I hope you'll think it a treat – my playing isn't that good. Not as perfect as I'd like.'

'You want everything perfect, Jim. I'm sure you play divinely. You do everything so well.'

'I wish. But I'll do my best, *ma donna*.'

'I told you, I know so little about music that just getting a tune from an instrument is a marvel in itself to me. What will you play for me?'

Jim rose and went into the bedroom to fetch the instrument. He brought it back, took it from its case and regarded it lovingly.

'This is the most expensive thing I possess,' he said. 'I've had it specially insured. It's a good instrument and it means a lot to me. Music is very important to me. It's the one thing that truly relaxes me.'

'Besides a bottle of wine?' I joked.

'Oh, the two together, even better!' He propped up the instrument and held it between his knees.

'Shall I hold you like this, between my knees?' he asked with a sly grin.

These words made me jump rather delightfully inside. 'Jim, just play some music.' I scolded.

'I'm going to play you the start of Haydn's Cello Concerto in C Major. One of my favourites.'

He began to play, drawing the bow across his instrument with a look of intense concentration, shades of feeling passing over his mobile face that I had never seen before. His arm moved the bow swiftly and almost fiercely across the instrument and music spilled forth and filled the room with its melody. It was stately and measured and yet at the same time cheerful, lilting, happy and energetic. I knew so little about classical music as Millie wasn't keen at all and Dad Joe preferred silence or the shipping forecasts. These waves of glorious sound lifted my heart and enraptured me.

'Oh, Jim, that was so beautiful.'

'I didn't play well, did I?' He looked discontented.

'You played beautifully. I didn't realise how wonderful music could sound.' I regarded him with a new feeling at this moment. 'You played beautifully,' I repeated and put a hand on his arm to reassure him.

He took my hand and raised it to his lips.

'We need some more wine,' he said.

'Please, no more wine, Jim, I've had enough.'

'Oh, have some more,' he said refilling my glass despite my protests. 'We haven't got to stagger home from anywhere, have we?'

Jim had poured out a large and liberal glass for us both and we quaffed this in silence. He refilled our glasses again after that till we finished the bottle, all the while keeping his eyes on me in a way that made me begin to feel uncomfortable. It was as if he was waiting for something.

The wine mingled with my bloodstream; it warmed me, made nerves and muscles relax till I felt strange and limp, a rag doll, incapable of movement. The warm feeling seemed to trickle down to my genitals, stirring me in a way I'd never experienced before. It was as if I wanted to open my legs wide and be touched down there. This frightened me, the sensation no longer pleasant. I shook myself and tried to stand. I needed to get away from these unwelcome sensations, needed to escape Jim's unrelenting stare. He moved closer to me on the sofa but I stood up, a little dizzy and smiled vaguely, saying 'I ... I think I'll turn in now, Jim. I feel ... a bit peculiar.'

Jim rose too and said thickly, 'You're just a little tipsy, my love. And what's more, you want what I want, don't you? I can see it in your eyes, hear you breathing faster. Come on ...let's turn in together.'

He came towards me and took me in his arms. This time there was no pretence. His polite barriers melted with the wine and he kissed me, his tongue entering my mouth, his hands moving over my body with an insistence I had never experienced with Ryan who had always managed to keep himself under a kind of savage control. I struggled to free myself but Jim held on tight. The liberating effect of the wine coursed through my blood again. I began to return the kiss and the heat between us was palpable. He was nothing like that lewd, disgusting Tom Shanklyn. He understood women and had obviously made love before. There was something experienced and determined about his manner. His hands slid under my thin blouse and took a firm hold of my breasts. I felt myself losing control, ready to lose everything.

'Bridie, Bridie, I've wanted you so long!' he panted.

Then in that dangerous moment I swear I heard Ryan's slow, deep voice, as if he stood behind me putting out a hand to restrain me. It was terrifyingly real. I tore myself away from Jim's fervent grasp and looked around in terror. But no one was there.

'Oh, God! Ryan!' I burst into tears. 'I can't, Jim. Stop, stop. I can't do this!'

His face was flushed with wine and rage. The man who had a moment or so ago played me such beautiful music, who had been so warm, attentive and delightful, had changed into a fierce, lupine being. In that moment I was very much afraid of him.

He seized my arm as I turned to flee and began to drag me towards him. I screamed but, setting his arm across my neck and choking the noise, he began pulling me towards the sofa. I tried to kick back at him and caught his shin hard. This made him pause for a moment but then he tightened his grip on my neck even more. I felt sure he would strangle me. The thought flashed through my mind that he was really dangerous, this man I had trusted so long. He might well kill me in his drunken, frustrated rage. Maybe it was easier simply to give in and let him have his way.

But to hell with that. Here I was cornered by Millie again in the form of her precious son who was determined to make me bend to his will, defile my body, make me betray the man I loved. Well, he bloody well wouldn't! Somehow I would stop him. For a moment his grip loosened. I dug my elbows into his ribs with all the fear-laden, fury-driven force I could muster and cursing me, he let go at last. I ran towards the front door. Jim gave a shout and following me, seized me again, dragging me back and flinging me on the sofa.

'You won't get away, damn you! You'll never get away, d'you hear me! Never!' he yelled.

The tears were running down my face but they were as much tears of rage as fright.

'And you won't get me, Jim. I'll die rather than let you rape me!' I sobbed, 'You won't get me, you won't!'

There was a piece of carved stone on the shelf near me and I grabbed it in my desperation, determined to use it as a weapon if he tried to force himself upon me. At that moment I didn't care if I killed him. He deserved it.

Jim saw the wild look in my eye and the stone in my hand and knew then that I was as ready to be as violent as he was. The fight seemed to stream out of him like air from a hot balloon. He breathed deeply and flung himself into a chair.

'You were all ready for it, damn you!' was all he said, his face turned away from me. I believe he was actually weeping with frustration and rage. 'What the hell happened?'

'I'm as good as engaged, Jim.' My breath still came in laboured panting gasps. 'You know...you know I love Ryan and no one else. It's really wicked of you to get me drunk and try to rape me. It's really wicked.'

'Oh, fuck your prissy morals,' he said angrily. Then he calmed down a bit and said pleadingly, back again to his smooth, charming, winning tone. 'Bridie, Bridie – I adore you, I need you – I want to marry you. I'm not out to seduce or rape, as you put it. Good God, I couldn't do that, not really. It's the wine made me lose control and it's you, Bridie. I just can't help it; you're so beautiful and desirable. I acted badly. Look, I apologise.'

I regarded him with something akin to contempt. 'You apologise, do you? Well, that's not enough. You frightened me, Jim. How can I ever trust you now? And *is* it just the wine? Or are you your mother in another form? Jim, I'm sorry but I could never marry you. It would be like marrying Millie.'

'I'm not like Mum, Bridie, you're so wrong. You *know* I'm not like her. We get on so well, us two, we've known each other so long. I have a prior claim to you, for heaven's sake. It's only right I should care for you after all you've gone through.'

'You're obsessed with that idea. I don't *need* you to care for me. I've learnt to cope alone and that's how it will be from now on. Ryan suits me and gives me space to breathe in and be myself. I thank you for one thing. You've made me realise the fact that I want him and no one else. I'm going home, Jim. I'm going to go back to Ryan, if he still wants me.'

His anger flared up again. 'After all I've done for you? After I've defended you in the past, helped you in so many ways. I'm willing to give you everything. This is your gratitude, you bitch!'

'Don't give me this rubbish, Jim. You did these things yourself, I didn't ask you,' I retorted. 'Thanks for showing me what you're really like. It *was* you who came to my room and took my money, wasn't it? All a part of your mad scheme to get me to come and live with you. God, I can't believe you've fooled me like this. Ryan was so right, you aren't to be trusted. He always said so.'

'Ryan, Ryan – *fuck* Ryan! Don't even mention his name. Get to bed and think things through, Bridie. You're mine, do you hear? I'll make sure that bastard never gets you if I have to kill you.'

With this threat ringing in my ears, I moved round him warily, ran into the bedroom and locked the door behind me, then pushed the chest of drawers against the door. I didn't even undress but began to pack my cases and was deeply thankful that he would be going in to work in the morning and I would be able to leave. Eventually I lay down on the bed and fell into a deep wine and stress-fuelled sleep.

Chapter 28

When I woke up the morning was well advanced. To my astonishment the clock said nine-thirty. I listened with care but there wasn't a sound to be heard. Please God, he had decided to go to work today and leave me alone. I felt frightened of his last words. What had he meant by them? My hope was that he had spoken in a drunken rage and his words were just so much hot air. I didn't truly believe that he was as violent as Millie; not her sort of in-your-face violence. No, his violence was far more subtle and frankly a lot more frightening because he was intelligent and cunning.

I lay there and told myself that never, ever would I let myself get drunk again. My head was hammering and pounding, stomach heaving with nausea. What induced people to get drunk as if it was some kind of pleasure when this was the result the morning after? Plus that terrifying effect, the libidinous longing that it had aroused. Though I loved Ryan so much and often thought of how beautiful it would be to have sex with him, I had never before experienced quite the kind of unthinking lust of the night before when for a moment any man might have taken me, I wouldn't have cared, so desperate was my desire to appease the raging need of the moment. Ryan had saved me, miraculously saved me. It was like Jane Eyre being saved by Rochester from the cold, hateful St John Rivers. I'd never have believed such a thing could happen – but it really had.

Pushing back the chest of drawers, I called Jim's name but there was no response. I unlocked the door and peered out, glad to see the flat empty. He had gone to work – what a relief!

I washed and dressed, had a drink of water, then got my bags together. I wanted to get out as fast as I could. I didn't have a lot of cash, that was my worry. How far could I go on what little was in my purse? I sat down for a moment to think about it. I didn't have enough for the fare to Bournemouth. My plan was to go to Ethel's place first and from there get in touch with Ryan and ask him to come and meet me when he next was ashore. Then we could decide what to do from there. Suppose Ryan didn't want me any more! I had been so selfish, proud and unkind to him. The thought was too awful to contemplate.

Obviously keeping me short of cash like this was all part of Jim's plan. I felt anger as well as fear rising in me at his scheming. Thank God, I'd kept the keys to the room in Portdown Rd and not given those to him as he had requested. I could go back there and wait for Luke McGraw to come home and ask for his help. I felt sure he would aid me. Jim wouldn't think of looking for me there.

My mind relieved by this decision, I went to the front door. To my dismay I couldn't open it. The bastard! He'd locked the mortise lock on going out and I was a prisoner. There was I locking him out and he'd turned the tables nicely and locked me in. I stood and screamed in panic but there was no one to hear me or if they did they ignored it. Did anyone live downstairs? And if someone did, how could they open the door without a key?

I sat down and wailed. He meant to keep me a prisoner. That was madness. He couldn't keep me here forever. Maybe he just wanted to punish me, maybe he wanted to make me his sex slave. My mind reeled round a dozen different notions and none of them were pleasant. I felt truly frightened. Pulling myself together, I washed my face and told myself to stop bawling and work something out.

I looked around. There had to be a way to escape. Call someone in the street and get them to bring the police? I looked out of the window but the solitary passer-by with his dog was well down the road by now. It was such a tiny, quiet street, a cul-de-sac perhaps. I had no idea, hadn't really taken much notice of where the street went as it wended in an arc and round the corner. Jim had mentioned playing fields but no one would be out there at this time of the morning. Someone must come by eventually but I dare not wait in case Jim was coming back. Anyway, they might think me mad if I said I was a prisoner and please fetch the police. It sounded like some bad B movie.

At the back of the flats the window overlooked a sort of lean-to affair which belonged to the people downstairs. It was intended to be a little sun-room and had corrugated plastic sheets on top to form a roof. It didn't look very safe but I reckoned I could lower myself onto it somehow and at least it would break my fall. Sheets, that was the thing. I'd tie sheets together and get out that way.

I decided not to take all my luggage, just the essentials. Putting all these into a smaller bag that I found in the wardrobe, I knotted together as many sheets as I could find, slid them through the handle and lowered the bag onto the ground, letting one end go so that the bag fell the rest of the way but landed intact on the grass. Then tying the sheets tight to the leg of the bed, I began to lower myself down the side of the wall till I reached the lean-to and gingerly let myself onto it and from thence jumped the remaining six feet to the ground, rolling over on the grass and breaking half a dozen gladioli with my fall.

I expected some irate house owner to come charging out asking me what the hell I was doing, but no one appeared. Picking up my bag, I crept round to the gate that led out of the garden. In the kitchen I saw an elderly lady busy at the table, her back turned to me. She was obviously deaf as a post.

I took the bus to the Underground and from there to Archway. It made me feel strange to be back at Portdown Road, yet just now it seemed a lot safer than the flat I had escaped from. Letting myself into the house, I looked to see if Dixie Dean was around. I knocked at his door. His frightened old face appeared in the crack and I saw he kept the chain on now. Poor old man! I felt so sorry to have been the cause of making him miserable and afraid.

'Wot you want?' he quavered. 'Ain't you caused enough trouble?'

'I just wanted to say how sorry I am you got accused of robbing me. I know who it was now, Dixie. I know it wasn't you.'

'I fuckin' got framed,' he said, 'they should 'ang the bastard.'

'I'm sorry, anyway.'

'Fuck off,' he said ungraciously and slammed the door.

I sighed but felt I'd cleared my conscience anyway. Clambering up the narrow stairs, I knocked on Luke's door but there was no reply. Naturally, he was at work, one of the few people in the house with a regular job. I'd have to wait till he returned. I just prayed that Jim wouldn't put two and two together and come here looking for me. He knew I had very little cash and couldn't get too far. If only he hadn't met Luke and I hadn't kept going on about how nice he was. That might make him suspicious.

I left my bag in the room, made sure the door was locked, then thought with regret that I should have taken the spare keys in Jim's mackintosh as well. Damn! On the other hand it would have been a real giveaway where I'd gone, so it was a risk all round. I went out for a walk and had some lunch at DeMarco's. Queenie remembered me and smiled and asked how things were going.

'I'm going home, Queenie,' I said sadly.

She looked at me with sympathy. 'You're just a kid,' she said, 'shouldn't be runnin' about on your own. What's your dad up to lettin' you run about on your tod? I left home your age and wished I hadn't. I'd have done better stayin' in Bromley. Home's best place for you, dearie.'

When she brought my meal she slipped me an extra roll and butter with a bit of ham in it. 'Might be useful if you've a long journey ahead of you,' she whispered. I felt tears come to my eyes again.

Returning to my room, I opened the door with some trepidation, my heart hammering in case Jim might already be here – but he wasn't. I sat down and waited. At last I heard a step out in the corridor and peeped carefully round the door. It was Luke and my relief at seeing him was unbounded. I ran out to meet him.

He was astonished. 'Miss Bridie!'

'Oh, Luke ... please help me, please say you'll help me!'

He took a look at my distraught face and ushered me into his room.

Leaving the door partly open for propriety's sake, a touch I found most old fashioned and reassuring, he told me to sit down.

'What is it, what's happened?'

I poured the story out to him, at least some of it. The details and background were not important. All he needed to know was that Jim had wangled it so I'd end up at his flat and tried to rape me and make me a prisoner.

Luke listened gravely.

'This is a frightful story,' he said. 'I'll be glad to help you, Miss Bridie. But how? If I try defending you, it'll be his word against mine and you know who'll win.'

'No, Luke, I don't want any heroics, believe me. I just want to get away from here, go back to my home in Bournemouth and find my fiancé. I just want to borrow enough for the fares. I'll send you the money as soon as I get home or ... ' I broke off and removing the silver bracelet I always wore, a present from Ryan, I offered it to him. 'Or you can keep this as collateral, if you prefer.'

He waved the bracelet away. 'I will *give* you the money,' he said. 'I hate to see you in trouble. You're a very nice girl and I'm honoured to think you came to me in a time of need.'

He gave me a ten pound note. Probably his week's wages.

'I can't take all that.'

'Take it. Who knows, maybe you'll help me out some day.'

'I hope I can, Luke. You're a real gent. Tell me, what sort of work do you do? I keep wondering ... you seem so... so well educated.'

'I was trained as an accountant back home in Jamaica,' he said, 'I came here thinking, man, I'll do really well here in Mother England. They promised all these good jobs. But they didn't take account of how the people here would react to us "darkies". One look at my face and my qualifications don't mean a thing. So, I'm a bus conductor and that's likely where I'll stay.'

'Don't you ever want to go home?'

He looked wistful. 'Don't I just? You know, first time I saw fog I thought maybe this is the end of the world and started praying! Stupid but that's how it was. I thought I'd come to a place clean, smart, rich and cultured. That's how white people appear to us over in Jamaica, that's how they all seem to be when they're over there. But the reality is very different here in England. Poor white people look unhappy, scared and miserable here and I see my black friends getting that same look on their faces – pinched, dead like ghostly critters. But I have my pride, Miss Bridie. Back home they think I'm living in clover. I can't disappoint them. And I still earn more than I would back there. There's the old folks to think of and relations all looking forward to what I send them. Maybe some day … '

We parted and I thanked him from the bottom of my heart.

'I won't forget you, Luke.' I said. 'I hope I can do you a good turn some day. I'll write to you.'

'I'd like that. Good luck, Bridie O'Neill. Be careful and keep away from London and seducers!'

'Believe me, I'll never come back again to the Big Smoke. I can't wait to see the sea again. And my darling Ryan.'

I gave him a peck on the cheek and waving goodbye, left that house forever.

At Waterloo, I boarded the train to take me home to Bournemouth and leant back on the seat with the utmost gladness and relief in my heart. It had been mad of me to come. I was determined that I'd never have anything more to do with Jim Bosworth again in my life. I didn't care if he lived or died.

Chapter 29

Ethel didn't exactly welcome me with open arms.

'You soon changed *your* mind, then,' she said scathingly when I arrived on her doorstep, penniless, emotionally exhausted and feeling a complete failure.

'It's a long story,' I said wearily. 'I won't stop long, Ethel, just till I hear from Ryan.'

'Running back to our boy, are you?' she said but her tone changed a little when she saw the tears welling in my eyes. She wasn't an unkind woman, just a bit tetchy like all older folks who hate having their routines disturbed by emotional young women.

'If he'll have me.'

'Oh, he'll have you. He's right taken up with *you*. Been that miserable since you went off. Glad you've come to your senses, running off to London like that. Knew it was a waste of time. You young girls are all the same, don't know what's good for you.' She paused in her scolding, surveyed me for a bit, then added in a milder tone, 'Anyway, sit down and let me make you a cup of tea. You look all done in. What made you come home in this state? Run into a spot of bother, did you?'

'A lot of bother,' I said but refused to answer any more questions despite Ethel's curious probing. I didn't want to say anything that might reach Joe's ears. Jim was his son, after all, and he was more likely to believe his son's version than mine. Now that I was safely away from London, it all seemed a mad, silly business. Jim had turned out to be as strange and obsessive as his mother and for the moment made me the source of his attention. He would be furious at my escape and would know that I had gone back home to Joe or Ethel but wouldn't dare to follow me here. After a bit, thankfully, he would forget me and transfer his attentions to some other hapless female. I was safe now. It was such a relief to have shaken him off. That family were the bane of my life.

Yet there were times when he came to my mind very clear and sharp; times when he was being charming, affectionate and loving towards me and I regretted losing his attention and care. Nobody else had ever treated me in that thoughtful manner before, Ryan least of all. I also missed his accomplished and interesting mind and the things he had to say, the way he said them, his ease with words. If only Jim had treated me as a sister, not got his feelings of love for me all mixed up with the sex bit, then we could have been good friends forever. I regretted that. But I knew one thing. I didn't love Jim and never would. He could never commune with my innermost soul in the way Ryan did without words or need for elaborate, urbane, clever ways. Ryan knew me and Jim did not. Jim was fun to be with but he never gave me the peace and containment that I felt when I was with Ryan. Ryan allowed me to be who I was while Jim wanted to make me into something he was looking for in his ideal woman. I would never have lived up to his exacting requirements, no one could. It was like being passed through a fine mesh of his expectations … who could possibly get through that mesh?

I went for a long walk over the Chines the next morning. It was time for inner communion, a time to find some peace within myself. Waves of longing for Ryan swept over me and I felt the love welling up from the deepest sources of my being like a stream of light. Looking down over the cliffs, I saw two children playing on the vast empty seashore. They could be mine; children like this could be mine one day, playing at the water's edge. Just now they seemed so far away and I a long way from them as if looking down into another world. I spent the day wandering about like this, unable to make any efforts towards writing or communicating with anyone. I needed to be alone.

In the evening, I found myself back at the seashore. It had

been a mixed day with bursts of sunshine soon expelled by a high wind that pulled dark clouds in its wake. The summer crowds had dispersed to their hotels, boarding houses, pubs and other places of evening entertainment. People were still out on the strand, taking dogs for walks and playing a last game with their Frisbees. The barking of dogs as they dashed into the waves and sporadic shouts of cheerful laughter came drifting over on the wind, giving me a sense of comfort in my self-imposed loneliness. For a long while I stood and watched the wild waves pitching and swelling against the jetty, splashing up in frothing, surging fury, water drops spraying everywhere – what a tremendous sight, what energy pounded and heaved there! The skies were louring and sad but the greyness and the wildness of the day with its fine soft mist of rain suited my mood. I felt a delight in solitude; a bliss in my own self. God seemed with me in that time spent alone. This inner communion with Nature helped to heal my wounded spirit.

Ryan became something more than a mere man to me in those moments – he became like a god. Yet I knew that I must not allow myself to slip into such dangerous thinking. I had to find my own centre, not live through him or anyone else. But not by running away.

I wrote a letter to Ryan and posted it with some trepidation. It was hard to admit defeat – my pride, my ego rebelled. He was still stuck out on Wolf Rock with his father, so I resigned myself to the fact that it would be a long time before the post was able to reach the rock especially in these high seas. And even longer before he could send a reply or come and see me if he came at all.

Now, quite easily and without any problem, I found myself a job serving in a café in the town. All of a sudden it seemed different as if the wind was blowing my way for a change and not against me. This new ease of accomplishment after all the frustrations and upsets of the last few weeks seemed symbolic that I had made the right choice. The wages in Mary's Pantry were poor but adequate and I was able to pay Ethel for my board and lodging. I also helped her clean the house and cook the Sunday roast. She was getting on and grateful for the help.

'You're a sight more use than Susan, she's no use at all,' Ethel complained. 'All she can think of is dressing up and going out with that boyfriend of hers. She's far too young still for that sort of thing but she takes no notice of me. Don't know what Sheila will say. No good talking to youngsters these days, they've all the cheek in the world. Would never have talked to my mum and dad like that.'

The days turned into weeks. There was no reply from Ryan, not a word. My heart grew heavy and sank within me. Had I lost his love with my foolishness?

One Thursday afternoon I finished my stint at Mary's Pantry, took my cardigan from the peg and went out into a cool autumnal day, the wind fresh and skittish. Russet and golden leaves blew around me and I watched them idly as I made my way to the bus stop. Then I heard my name being called and stopped stock still, my heart thumping in my chest.

'Bridie! Wait for me!'

Running up the road towards me was Ryan Waterman, his jacket flying open, his cap almost ready to take off and join the leaves skeltering along the street. I stood and stared at him as if he was an apparition, afraid that I was dreaming. He soon caught up with me and putting out his arms, caught me in them and we hugged one another for ages, speechless with joy.

'Nan told me you worked here,' he said, sliding my arm in his as we walked together to the bus stop. 'I couldn't wait for you to come home so got myself here quick – even then I almost missed you.'

'When did you get here? How long can you stay?'

'Got here about an hour ago, the bloody train was late in. I'm on shore leave now for a month. Nan said she'll put me up on the sofa. Bridie, oh, Bridie, thank God you've come back to me!'

'You never wrote back. I was so scared you'd forgotten me, Ryan.'

'I was due leave so there was no point in hanging around. Once I got your letter all I could do was wait for the relief to come and make it here as fast as I could. Like I told you in my last letter, it's been pretty stormy up at Wolf Rock and the relief was delayed about a week. I was on tenterhooks, dying to get off and come to you. You've no idea how happy your news made me feel.'

Ignoring the interested looks of others in the bus queue, we kissed and smiled and grinned at one another like idiots. Love makes one daft but it's a marvellous feeling. There's no other happiness like it when all goes well.

Back at Ethel's place we sat down in the front parlour while Ethel discreetly left us to ourselves and busied herself in the kitchen. Susan had been thrilled to see her brother and almost cancelled her date with Tony on his behalf but a word in her ear from Ethel made her stare at us both and then quietly collect her handbag and go out.

'I reckon you two had better sort things out properly,' she remarked as she sallied forth. 'Time you made up your minds. I want good news when I get back, d'you hear?'

'Out of the mouths of babes ...' sighed Ryan, 'but she's right, Bridie.'

We sat on the sofa in the parlour by a cheerful, roaring fire and spent a good deal of time kissing and staring speechlessly at one another. Eventually, Ryan broke away, lit a cigarette and gazed at me in that slow, thoughtful way, just as he used to. I felt myself quail a little under his honest, searching look. Lowering my eyes from his, I sat and stared into the fire.

'Bridie, you've got so thin. Your face has changed too. The eyes ... you've a sadness I've not seen there before for all you went through as a kid. What made you change your mind so suddenly? You were like all blazin' to go and in no time you're back home. Don't get me wrong, I couldn't be happier and more relieved. But I can't help wondering what happened to you, darling? You're different somehow.'

'Am I?' I sighed. 'I suppose it was a brief but ... educational experience. Being apart from you, being in a huge city like London

– oh, Ryan, it was the most awful place in the world! It was just as awful as you'd said. I didn't have the courage to keep at it.'

'It's probably a great place for those who like urban life,' he said, 'but it's not for the likes of us, Bridie, not for you and me. We like the big spaces, the open air, the sea. I may sit in a lighthouse day in and day out but I've only to go out on the rock for some fishing or out on the gallery and there I am in the midst of vast space and beauty, in touch with the elements. It's what's real. Cities aren't real; they're man-made and divorced from nature. People crowded together like rats in a box. They reckon rats start killin' and eatin' one another when they're all packed in like that. No wonder the people in cities are sick. Sick in the head and in the body too.'

He fell silent after this speech and I nodded in agreement, full of sadness at human plight. He was so right. But a great many people chose to live in cities, loved the crowded, action-filled, busy, crazy life they led.

'Maybe you met some of those mad folks,' said Ryan softly. 'Somethin' upset you. I know you, Bridie.'

I stared at the fire. Did Ryan suspect something?

'It was the sea like you said – that's what I missed so much apart from you.'

He smiled his slow tender smile and took my hand in his.

'Missed you too, Bridie. I thought how the hell will I survive a whole year without my girl? And what if she fancies some other bloke and comes back married? I would have gone nuts.'

'What would you have done if I had?'

'Dunno, topped myself.'

'Oh, Ryan, you would not! Don't even joke that way.'

'It's no joke, Bridie. You know how I feel.'

'Promise me you won't ever say such a thing again.' I felt a shudder pass over me at his words. 'You once said you'd never do that for love of a mere woman.'

'I was a fool then and I didn't know what love was like,' he said softly.

We both fell silent for a little while. Ryan looked at me keenly.

'You are different,' he said again. 'Why do I get the feeling you're not telling me everything?'

'I haven't really told you *any*thing,' I said with a sigh. 'It was all an unpleasant experience. The Labour Exchange was the nastiest place and I couldn't find work. When I did it was just exhausting and the lady I worked for was a pathetic, scared, little soul who left me in the lurch. I had my money stolen and the people in the place I was renting were mostly all horrible and weird. I didn't eat well, slept badly and felt frightened most of the time. In the end I couldn't abide another minute especially as what money I had was almost gone and it would have meant going on the dole and that I couldn't bear. I realise now that I should have stayed in Bournemouth and looked for a job. Trying to run before I could walk, wasn't I?'

'Bloody hell! You did have a rough time. My poor darling. You did rather choose to jump in at the deep end. What made you want to go to London?' His eyes narrowed. 'Wouldn't be nothing to do with Jim Bosworth, would it? Joe says he's bought himself a pad in North London for when he's not poncing about at Cambridge.'

I lowered my eyes. 'Yes, he did suggest London to me, said it would be great.'

Ryan looked angry, 'Is he behind all this, Bridie? Has he been making passes at you?'

Passes! He didn't know the half of it. I tried to pour oil on troubled waters.

'He was nice to me, Ryan, took me out for a couple of meals, found me a room and all that. It just all went wrong. I was upset because I couldn't find decent work. He offered a job in some place he was working in during his vacation. But I didn't want an office job so I said no.'

'Hope you said no to any other ideas he might have had an' all.'

I sighed. 'Look, Ryan, I left London. I'm back with you now. Are you giving me the third degree about it? I'm sick to death of jealous blokes.'

'Are you now? Sounds like there's more to this than you're

saying, Bridie, but I'll leave it at that. Sweetheart, I can tell you've been in trouble, I can sense it. You never had that sad look in your eyes before. I've told you I know you better'n you know yourself. If that Jim Bosworth laid a finger on you with or without your consent, I'll kill him. He'd better not come near us again, the bastard.'

'Ryan! Do stop it. Forget Jim. It's about us, about our loving one another and being together. But you know – you still have to do it.'

'Do what?'

'Propose to me properly or I swear I'll show you the door.'

Ryan smiled. 'I'll pick the right moment.'

'When will that ever be?'

'Wait and see.'

It was when we were both out walking along Alum Chine beach one evening. It was getting late and the brightly coloured beach huts were all deserted and locked up for the night. In some cases their owners had long packed up and gone to their homes, leaving summer activities behind them. The sun was setting over the sea and the golden light spilled out from behind a dark cloud on the horizon.

'It's like the beam of the lighthouse,' I said, 'look at those rays of light, like a halo on a saint. It's so beautiful and I feel so happy we're together. I'm sorry we parted the way we did but I think it was a good thing, really.'

'How come?'

'It made us both realise what life might be like without one another.'

'A meaningless, miserable existence,' Ryan said softly. He suddenly knelt in the damp sand and took my hand. 'Will you marry me, Bridie O'Neill? Will you promise to stay with me forever, no more going your way and me going mine? Our ways together forever.'

'Yes, I do, I do, Ryan. I'll marry you and follow you wherever you go.'

He rose and took me in his arms. 'And will you be content

and happy as a lighthouse-keeper's wife, accept her lot? I wouldn't want you to feel lonely like Mum. I promise in turn, I will never let you be unhappy like that. If you are, I'll leave the service and find summat else to do.'

'That's a fair promise,' I said. We kissed one another standing there on the shore till the incoming tide began to lap around our feet and laughing, holding hands, we ran back up into the Chine woods and all the way home to tell Susan and Ethel the good news.

Chapter 30

Ryan had to go back after his month's leave was up but we had already made plans to marry early next spring. I rang Joe at the harbour master's office and told him our happy news.

'Best thing I've heard in ages,' he said. 'Sheila will be delighted. We got really worried when you went haring off to London like that and are glad you're back, sweetheart, back with your family. You can get so lost in London, I can tell you from my own experience. You become part of the faceless and the lonely. We might have lost you forever.'

'I'm glad I'm back too,' I replied, 'and more than happy, Joe. Still, sometimes we have to do these things, distance ourselves a little, get a different view of things before making up our minds. It was all for the best.'

'You're getting to be quite the philosopher, Bridie. Oh, I understand completely. We'll make it a grand wedding.'

'No, no, Joe – not a grand one, a simple quiet one. That's what we both want. Just you, Sheila, Ethel and Susan at the registry office here in Bournemouth. And a nice meal after in a hotel.'

'Not the boys?' He was puzzled.

'No, I'm sorry, Joe, definitely not the boys. You and the Watermans are my family now. I don't feel they ever have been.'

'I thought Jim was a bit of a favourite.'

'You thought wrong,' was my decisive reply. 'I don't want the boys.'

'Fair enough.' But I could tell he was a bit disappointed.

After our wedding we honeymooned for two weeks down at

Falmouth in Cornwall. We both loved the Cornish coast most of all, a reminder of our happy days spent when we were in our teens. We visited Sennen again, then St. Michael's Mount and Arthur's Seat and St. Just in Roseland, played on the beach together or walked along the sands when the sun set, arms about each other. But most of all we spent time in our hotel bed making love, exploring and discovering one other. A deep sense of shame still rankled in my soul because of those lustful feelings aroused by the wine when I was with Jim but I reminded myself that nothing had really happened. It was all over now, never to be repeated.

We had a blissful week together. How right to call it a honey moon … the sweetest moments of one's life. I wanted to weep when Ryan had to go back to Wolf Rock again. He looked pretty miserable too.

'I've asked Master at Trinity House if I can put in for a land light as soon as one comes up,' he said. 'Though I reckon it won't be for a while, maybe not till we have kids. I told them we wanted to start a family so we'll have to see how it goes.'

'I feel a bit scared when you're on that rock out there,' I said, 'Dad says it's a dangerous station to be at.'

'No more than any other rock, Bridie. They're mostly all in dangerous spots, that's the whole point of 'em isn't it? Wolf's got a great history, especially during the two wars when they could only shine at half power to help Allied convoys through the Channel. Remember Longships? The Germans used to use it for target practice in the war! I mean to study all the different stories and histories of the Lights, maybe write about it all someday. You can help me do that. You're a lot cleverer than me with words.'

It was to be a long while before Ryan was sent to a new light and meanwhile I missed him so much. He came over every four weeks and then we had a whole month together. There wasn't much privacy at Ethel's place even though she'd had a regular shuffle round, bless her, giving me and Ryan the best bedroom – and she would have taken the box room but in a fit of surprising generosity, Susan offered to do so instead.

'I may well be leaving myself soon,' she explained. 'Tony and I want to get engaged when I'm seventeen. He's hoping to get a promotion as manager at another branch. When he does, we'll put a deposit down for a flat. I've saved up loads already.'

I was impressed by her shrewdness and felt I too should save up and maybe get a permanent place somewhere rather than move about from light to light with Ryan. If we had children, it would be so much better to have a secure home. Plus I still had the notion of starting up a restaurant or even a boarding house by the coast some day. However, for the moment, I would follow him wherever he was posted and see how things went.

I buried myself in work, saving money hard and trying not to think too much about Ryan. I started doing evening classes in book-keeping. No real reason, just thought it might be useful, especially as I'd always been such a duffer doing maths at school. It was surprising how easy it was to learn and understand when there seemed to be a purpose behind it. Working out how long it took a tap to drip enough water to fill a bath or how many workmen it took to lay seventeen bricks an hour had never really inspired me in my schooldays.

Ryan was right when he said that the constant separation actually made us enjoy one another the more. Every time he came onshore, it was a new honeymoon. We couldn't wait to get to bed together. Ethel and Susan knew what we were up to and left us alone the first few days though we got plenty of ribbing when we did at last emerge.

I'd never known sex could be so good. It was very good. And Ryan and I were constant lovers in heart and soul and couldn't wait to see one another. Nothing could be less like the marriage of either Sidney and Sheila Waterman or Joe and Millie Bosworth. And we meant to keep it like that.

At the end of the year, the news came that Ryan was to be sent to a land light situated way out on a bare, chalky headland on the North East coast where the keeper's cottages were attached to the station. The loneliness and isolation didn't trouble us a bit. We would be living together in our own place at last. I said my goodbyes to Ethel and Susan, who said they would miss us no end, left Mary's Pantry without too much dismay and set off to my next home on the Yorkshire coast. I decided that this was my fate. I would always be upping sticks and going off somewhere new and that was how it would be. In some ways, it was exciting. It meant I would never be bored with life but always starting again, re-inventing myself.

The headland at Flamborough was a beautiful location looking out over the North Sea. The lighthouse was a strong, squat, whitewashed structure with the keepers' houses attached. The usual high white wall enclosed the area in order to shelter them from the wind that blew relentlessly along the cliff tops, strong enough at times to blow a child away. The larger of the two houses in the enclosure belonged to the PK, Martin Whitworth, and his wife and child. We had one of the smaller ones, while the tiniest over the tower entrance, a mere two rooms, was occupied by a young man acting as SAK. It was small but I loved my little home and made it as cosy and pretty as I could. It felt good to be settled for a bit and above all to be able to see Ryan more often. No more long waits and silences.

These particular cliffs were a haunt for sea birds and day and night we heard their noisy clamour as they swirled overhead and veered into the wind or nested and chattered amongst themselves on the rocks and caves below. Standing at the edge of the cliffs on the right, one looked down a sheer drop to a surging, boiling sea that never seemed to be still. Used as I was to the sea and cliffs, that particular view often gave me vertigo. It made me feel dizzy, as if I wanted to throw myself over into that maelstrom below, so strong was the pull of the foaming sea. I kept well away from it. It was a dangerous area and there were tales of rocks being swept from the cliffs in the wind and how one keeper had been killed by a flying boulder when climbing back up the steps from the rocky coves below.

Despite these tales, I often walked down these steps carved out of the rock-face, down to the little cove beneath the light. Here there were smooth pure-white pebbles of limestone chalk when tide was out. Ryan and one of the other keepers had painstakingly brought back sacks of topsoil every time they went to the farm nearby and made a raised bed where we could all grow some vegetables. I brought back some of the white pebbles to decorate the edges of the garden and the tops of the flower pots.

The grassy slopes of the cliff side were covered in a riot of wildflowers in spring and summer. Little streams flowed down the grooves along the cliffs and joined the sea, always the sound of running water to join the incessant crashing and pounding of the waves. I loved it best when a mist rolled in … they called it a sea-fret in those parts. It would stay around for days at a time, even in the height of summer. Then I would stand on the empty shore and look out onto that grey nothingness where once the sea had been, listen to the mournful boom of the fog horn and the shrieking of the birds flying in and out of the rocks that stood like pillars in the sea. The grey nothingness was never still but like a living creature that shifted and swayed in the wind, coyly revealing more ocean and cliffs then moving back again, obscuring all. When I wended my way back up the steps, I would look up and see the huge white pillar of the lighthouse looming out of the fine, damp swirling mist and it gave me a peculiar sense of comfort.

In London, I had felt lonely and sad. Here, despite the isolation, I never felt lonely and certainly not sad. There was time to do things with care, time for the essentials in life. I thought of the constant rush and grinding hard work when I was at Mo's café. I worked just as hard here, cleaning, cooking, doing all the household chores but it was so different. This was my home, I cooked for the man I loved and I cooked what I liked, good healthy food, not those incessant fry-ups that stank the place with rancid oil.

Ryan was watching me one day as I sat by the window, humming a song and sewing tiny pieces of material from old floral patterned dresses round octagonal pieces of paper. Later all these little octagonal shapes would be set together to make a huge quilt.

'That's just what my Ma used to do,' he observed.

I smiled and looked up at him. He had taken to smoking a pipe and the sweet scent of tobacco drifted over towards me.

'That's just what my Dad used to do.'

'Reckon we're turning into our Mum and Dad?'

'I think everyone does, don't you? That's how the world keeps going in circles. Nothing ever really changes, does it? Just goes round in circles all the time. I like making these quilts; it's a soothing pastime. I can listen to music or plays on the radio while I'm busy with it all – or just hear the birds and the wind whistling outside.'

'Oh, aye, that sort of sound is *real* music,' said Ryan with a nod, 'none of your fancy orchestral stuff for me.'

For a moment I though of Jim playing his cello. That had been beautiful too, but I agreed with Ryan. The sounds of Nature would always be the sweetest sounds in the world as far as I was concerned. Everything made by man was contrived and artificial in some way, poor imitations of Nature. Even this counterpane I was stitching could never be like the flowers in a summer meadow.

Ryan looked at me and a slight anxiety came to his face. He often seemed to sense any shift in my thoughts in that uncanny way of his.

'Bridie, you don't get bored here? You don't feel like you miss London life?'

'Miss London? Are you joking? Bored? My darling, I never get bored. I don't understand how people *can* be when there's so much to do. I'm going to do a first aid course in Scarborough in a few weeks because I though it could be useful to have another person around who knows some First Aid. I know all the keepers have to learn about it but you might all be busy when someone falls and hurts themselves, one of the kiddies maybe. I want to be able to help and be useful, you know. Then there's all the work in the house and the vegetable garden and trips into Scarborough to shop and all that. I love this simple, quiet life more than anything.'

'You do a lot already,' he said admiringly, 'You know what, the blokes all call you Bridie Nightingale because you sing all the time when you work. Now they'll call you that because you'll be able to do up their hurts and care for 'em. You always love to help folks, don't you, Bridie? You're the best and sweetest girl.'

I would often see Ryan up on the lantern, cleaning all those panes and prisms of glass, a job that had to be done all the time as the birds were especially attracted to the light at night, sometimes bumping into it in their flight and leaving their mess all over it.

'Still, it's better'n being at Dungeness where the migrating birds smash into the light of the lantern and even the windows as they pass by at night,' Ryan told me. 'They're attracted to the light like moths and come surging towards it, all crushing up against each other. It's the queerest sound, the tapping and scratching and beating of their heads and wings against the windows. Poor things just pile up dead or injured at the bottom of the chamber and round the bottom of the light and you have to spend hours clearing up. That's a nasty experience, that is.'

In order to make some more money, I began to bake cakes, scones and sausage rolls which I sold to the keepers' wives and the rest I took in to Scarborough and sold to a couple of bakers there. This operation proved so successful that I eventually made enough to buy myself an old banger. It needed constant attention but luckily we had an SAK at the time who knew a lot about cars and enjoyed fiddling about with it when it went wrong. The use of a car was a great freedom. I could take days out and go exploring different parts of the area as well as find new venues for my baking activities. It felt good to be able to make a contribution to our finances and slowly but surely put some aside for when we might buy a place of our own.

In all this time, I hadn't heard a word from Jim. That was a relief. Somewhere deep inside I was always that bit afraid he would cause me some harm. I hoped he had put me out of his head in disgust and that I would never see him again and yet, in a strange way, I missed him. He was the nearest I had ever known to family apart from Joe. I gathered from Joe that he was doing well, had found a tenancy in a prominent barrister's chambers and recently taken on a few minor briefs of his own. Andy had, as anticipated, forged ahead in his varied business ventures, made a mint of money and married early in the year. He never kept in touch with me at all for which I was supremely grateful.

'Andy and June have a really fine house in Portsmouth now, five bedrooms and all mod con.' Joe was clearly impressed by his two sons and their achievements. He showed me Andy's wedding photos. The bride was small, blonde and pretty. Not the blonde I'd seen him with before who looked as if she could take care of herself. This girl looked a lot more timid and soft. He'd bully her all right, just like his mum used to bully me. He'd had good training. I pitied her with all my heart. It wasn't worth the nice house and the diamond earrings I saw in her ears to have the life she was likely to lead.

Joe and Sheila declined coming over to Flamborough to see us. It all was too much of a hassle getting to that remote place and Sheila's legs weren't up to walking so much any more, she'd got a bit arthritic, poor soul. My feeling was she never wanted to see a lighthouse ever again. So instead we went over to them in the summer and stayed at the little harbour master's house. It was nice to be in a busy harbour town but Ryan and I were becoming so used to the seclusion and quiet of our isolated lifestyle that we were always glad to get back to it again and relax into our varied routines. Joe reckoned we were getting old before our time. Sheila said having a baby or two would sort things out.

Just before we left, Joe said, 'Oh, by the way, Bridie, last time Jim was here he said he'd come over and visit you. Said he hadn't heard from you in a bit and wanted to catch up with your news. I told him you were in a really out of the way place now but he said he didn't mind. In fact, when I told him where you were he said he was keen on bird-watching these days and the cliffs round your way are famous for their bird colonies. He might come and stay for a bit. That would be nice, wouldn't it?'

I was busy washing dishes at the sink as he said this and that was a blessing as he didn't see the fact that my face went white with shock. I wanted to scream out *why did you tell him where we are, Joe, why!*

But I couldn't say that as he'd need to know why I wanted to stay away from Jim and then the whole thing would come out – and Ryan might well go and thump Jim and there'd be trouble all round.

I paused in mopping a dish and then put it carefully in the rack while I composed myself. To say I was disturbed by this news was putting it mildly.

Joe was surprised by my silence.

'You'd like to see him, wouldn't you, Bridie?'

'Yes, sure,' I said as casually as I could. 'If he really thinks he'd enjoy coming to see us.' Bird-watching! That was a good one. Jim was the last person in the world to have a hobby like that unless it meant watching the sort of female birds he liked so much. Joe hadn't really swallowed that story, had he? More likely Jim wanted to come and stir up trouble with Ryan and me. The news depressed me a lot but I said nothing to Ryan. Maybe it was just all talk and Jim, who had now moved to Hampstead, would never dream of leaving the comforts of London to scramble over cliffs and gaze at a load of noisy, smelly sea birds.

Chapter 31

For a long time I felt fearful that Jim might turn up out of the blue, but time passed and he did not appear. The old anxiety lurked once more beneath the surface and I was angry about it. I thought I had put all that behind me and felt safe and happy in my new life with Ryan. Now it was as if Millie, in the form of her hateful son, had risen once more from the grave to haunt me. Would I never be free of them both?

However, thinking this way was nonsense. I forced myself to be rational and put it all out of my mind. So what if Jim did come, he wouldn't get anywhere and as like as not Ryan would make it very clear that he was most unwelcome. I breathed again. Ryan would protect me.

I was busy hanging out the washing one morning when I saw him coming. My heart stood still and I almost fled back into the cottage and barred the door. I could hide, pretend I was out and he'd have to turn back again. But it was too late. He'd seen me now and waved to me.

'God, Bridie,' he puffed as he came over to me, 'you need to be fit to live in this darned place.'

I went on pegging up the clothes and said in a low voice, 'No one invited you to come, Jim Bosworth. You can bugger off.'

'Don't be like that,' he said, 'aren't you going to welcome your long-lost brother? I've wanted to come for a while but haven't been able to get time off. You know I've taken tenancy with Sir Jonas Radcliffe now, don't you?' he added with pride.

'I haven't a clue who you're with, these names mean nothing to me. And what's more I don't care.'

'Bridie,' he said winningly, 'why are you being so unkind? Can't we let bygones be bygones, bury the hatchet and all that?'

I remained silent and he came closer, bent and peered up into my face making me smile a bit. He could be so charming, damn him!

'There, that's better. Can't you forgive me for acting like a fool? I know I did and that's why I'm here. To apologise to you and make amends.'

'You can *never* apologise enough,' I said, cold again and turning my back on him.

One of the other wives came out at this point, curious to see who the visitor was. We had few enough visitors between us and tended to appropriate one another's as if the visitor was a parcel to be shared out. I had no desire to explain to Tina Anderson about my past so I hastily told Jim to follow me indoors, much to my neighbour's chagrin.

Once inside I closed the door. Jim stood in the middle of the room and watched me. He had grown taller and broader since I last saw him but he was still as good looking as ever – if not more so. His face had a mature look about it now and appeared serious and gentle. He kept his hands in his pockets as if to prevent himself touching me and assumed a remorseful air.

'I apologise again, Bridie,' he said. 'If you want I'll go down on my knees and beg your forgiveness. My behaviour was reprehensible and ungentlemanly. Do you believe me when I say I'm really sorry to have frightened and upset you? It was all for the sake of love.'

'You've come all this way to say that?'

'My penance. Walking all the way from the village to this remote headland was true penance – how the hell do you do that every day? I would have driven over but the car's being looked at just now, got some problem with the steering. I wanted to write many a time but knew if I wrote you'd chuck the letter in the bin. I had to face you and say sorry.'

'You're right. I would have chucked a letter in the bin.'

'But do you accept my apology now I'm here?'

'It all depends, Jim.'

'On what?'

'On how genuine you are or whether you just came to cause trouble.'

He lowered his eyes and sighed. 'I don't want to cause trouble, Bridie. I suppose Ryan knows all about your London experience. If he hits me in the eye, I know I'll deserve it.'

I stared, astonished at this apparent humility. Somehow, I still didn't trust him. If I said that Ryan did not know, Jim might use this information against me.

Skirting with care around the truth, I said, 'He knows about my London experience, as you put it, and he *won't* be pleased to see you. You've come, you've apologised. All right, I accept that but now, go.'

Jim smiled and came towards me. I backed away.

'Hey, steady, I'm not going to touch you. You're like a cat on a hot tin roof. I just wanted to give you a grateful hug. Look, I've come a long way. You might at least offer me a drink.'

'All right,' I said begrudgingly. 'I'll put the kettle on.'

'Haven't anything stronger, I suppose? No, I thought not. Okay, I'll have a cup of tea then.'

He wandered about the cottage as I got things ready and looked at my books and pictures with interest.

'This your mum and dad?' he asked as he came to the photos of Bill and Maureen on top of the sideboard.

'You know perfectly well they are.'

'You're the image of your mum, aren't you? Dad always said she was a beauty.'

'And you're the image of yours,' I replied, handing him a cup of tea.

Jim took the cup from me and sat down, stirring in a lump of sugar. He looked thoughtful.

'I know I am, Bridie, but only in looks. Not in nature.'

'You could have fooled me.'

'Come on, I didn't harm you, Bridie. I wouldn't lift a finger against you to hurt you again. Be assured of that.'

'Thank you for that assurance,' I said dryly.

We fell silent for a little while. I refused to be pally with him;

there was nothing I wanted to say. However, Jim was never easy to stop once he felt in a chatty mood.

'You know, I've got a steady girlfriend,' he said after a while. I was pleased to hear this; it sounded as if he really had got over me. In that case, perhaps his reason for coming was genuine. I looked up with interest.

'Thought that would grab you,' he grinned. 'You've met her, haven't you? It's still the clinging Alice Townsend. Thanks to her connections I was able to get this tenancy in Jonas Radcliffe's chambers at Lincoln's Inn. He was one of her mother's lovers apparently and they're still good friends. Alice and I are living together in her mum's house in Hampstead. Mrs Townsend has toddled off to the south of France with her latest boyfriend of twenty-five so we've got the place to ourselves. I always wanted to live in Hampstead, as you know. Remember I told you about the Townsends?'

I nodded. 'The woman who owned the house in Portdown Road.'

'The very same.'

'Well, I'm glad to hear you've settled. Why do I get the feeling you don't intend to marry poor Alice.'

'Not likely, nor ever will. She thinks I will, of course, but then she's not that bright. I've got other plans. Luckily her mother isn't fussed about such conventions, not being the world's best example of matrimonial fidelity herself. She's been married three times and can't be bothered any more. She's made a mint from the men in her life and has no need for more husbands. As for Alice, she's pretty and useful, that's all.'

'I'm glad you've got a "useful" girlfriend. That's certainly the sort that would most appeal to you. I sometimes wonder if you have a heart, Jim.'

Jim ignored my irony. 'Mmm ... Alice is a randy little beggar. Not as coy as you, Bridie; a shame as I rather like a bit of a fight. She'll open her legs for anyone so I don't feel unduly flattered by her attentions. Plus she wasn't a virgin as you were. I suppose you meant to hang on to your maidenhead for Ryan's sake.'

'If you're going to talk like that, you can go,' I said angrily.

'Pax,' he said, moving his hands apart in a conciliatory gesture. 'I'm being stupid again and yes, Bridie, I do have a heart. You should know that.'

'I know nothing of the sort. You tried to ruin my life.'

'But I didn't, did I?' he said, looking around. 'Maybe I helped you make up your mind and drove you into the arms of the very man I least wanted to see you with. Maybe I ruined my own life. I was a fool. Went about things like a fool.'

'It's all in the past. That's where it should stay. You should never have come, Jim. Why did you come?'

'To see you, Bridie,' he said simply.

I fell silent. He stood and watched me closely. A shudder of fear ran over me.

'Look, Jim, Ryan's due home soon, I'm going to start his dinner.'

'Aren't you asking me to stay the night? It's a hell of a long way back.'

'How can I, Jim? Ryan would have a blue fit. You can find rooms in the village or at the farm.'

'Ryan's a decent bloke – he'll accept my apology, won't he, like a man?'

I was horrified at the thought. Ryan would then question me when Jim left and assume that more had gone on that I had admitted.

'Please don't. Don't say anything to Ryan. Don't stir things up. It's me you had to apologise to. You've done that. I'd rather you went.'

But it was already too late. I saw Ryan coming along the path from the land light, a little early as bad luck would have it. I swore under my breath, resigned myself to whatever would happen and went off to the kitchen to get the potatoes on the boil. There was nothing more I could do

Ryan opened the door and as he came in, said, 'What's the door shut for, Bridie, it's not cold today.'

We all tended to leave our doors open at Flamborough Light. Outsiders seldom made their way here and certainly not at night. It was as safe as could be, so different to London. Yet, at that moment, I felt as if it was no longer the safe haven I had grown accustomed to. A snake had wound its way into the Garden of Eden.

Then Ryan saw Jim and stopped in his tracks. I regretted shutting the door now. It looked suspicious. Was I to be damned for whatever action I took?

'Hello, darling,' I said as cheerfully as I could. 'As you see, we have a surprise visitor.'

'A very big surprise,' said Ryan, standing there, his arms folded across his chest, 'what makes you want to visit us in this part o' the world then, Jim Bosworth? Aren't the London sights exciting enough for you any more?'

Jim rose and came over, hand extended. 'Nice to see you, Ryan, and congratulations on your marriage to our Bridie,' he said with ease. As always, he oozed charm and sophistication. Even for this adventure, he had the latest gear on: smart Levi jeans and a thick Arran pullover. He'd laid his new hooded donkey jacket over a chair along with a small overnight bag. It was obvious he meant to stay.

To my surprise, Ryan took the offered hand and shook it.

'Thanks,' he said gruffly. He looked at the overnight bag and said, 'You planning to stay here with us then?'

'If that's convenient,' said Jim, 'Just a day or so. I was hoping to get in a little bird-watching. I've taken it up as a hobby. Being stuck in an office or in court all day takes it out of you. It's good to get off somewhere open, wild and different. Good exercise too.'

'Might have been an idea if you'd let us know you planned to come. Hard getting extra supplies over here.'

'I'm sorry, I ought to have written. It was a bit of a last minute thing. I didn't appreciate quite how out in the wilds you were.'

'It's a fuckin' lighthouse, isn't it? What d'you expect?'

'Point taken,' smiled Jim. He was so smooth, so urbane. In contrast Ryan seemed rough and almost rude in his bluntness.

'Don't swear, Ryan,' I said automatically. I knew the men all swore like troopers when they were alone together on the light but Ryan seldom did so at home. It showed he was feeling angry.

Ryan seemed to consider. 'All right, just a couple of nights then. Can hardly send you off now. It's getting dark and it won't be safe to get back to the village. You townies are likely to go driving over the cliff edge in the dark. Where's your car?'

'I didn't bring the car. Train to Scarborough, then a taxi. The fellow dropped me off at the village and told me to keep on walking until I got here. Gave me a bit of a shock when I saw how steep it was. But it's a lovely spot. In many ways I envy you.'

'Do you? I'm surprised to hear that.' Ryan divested himself of his thick sweater and poured out a glass of beer.

'Want one?' he offered.

'Thanks.' Jim in turn offered a cigarette from his packet and the two men sat down comfortably in the armchairs and regarded one another with cautious interest.

'So you're into birds. What do you hope to see?'

'Whatever's here. I've heard there are guillemots and razorbills this time of year.'

'You heard right. You missed the sea puffins; they come April to July. Funny little critters they are, nesting in old rabbit burrows at the top of the cliffs. You can almost go up and touch them. Pity you missed out on that. But there's fulmars, kittiwakes. The cliffs are limestone further along, a sheer drop and you'll certainly get to see and hear and smell the ruddy birds as well. You're right to come here. It's a great place for bird-watching. If you're lucky you might even get to see a dolphin or porpoise down in the waters.'

Once Ryan got onto a favourite subject there was no stopping him. Jim seemed genuinely interested.

'That would be great. I've brought a decent camera.'

'Well, you'll have to get about on your own, I'm afraid. I'm on during the day tomorrow so I won't be able to show you where to look.'

'That's fine. I don't want to put either of you out. I'll find my way around.'

'Just mind where you go, that's all,' said Ryan gruffly, 'dangerous cliffs round here and you're a novice by all accounts. Just stick to the pathways. You'll see plenty enough that way. Bridie'll maybe take you if she's not busy baking.'

I laid the table and called them over to eat. Listening to them talk like this beggared belief. I could see that Ryan was really trying to put his dislike of Jim aside for my sake. He was married to me now so as far as he was concerned he had won the game. It made me feel such love for him and his honest and honourable nature. It did seem as if Jim too was sincerely trying to make amends. I decided to follow Ryan's example, put aside my doubts and fears.

We had a pleasant evening after that. Jim was in great form, told us stories about his work and the cases he'd dealt with, making us laugh over some of the odd goings on at the Old Bailey. Ryan seemed to mellow towards Jim and told him lighthouse stories in turn. I made coffee and sat and listened to them, relieved that it was all taking a turn for the better.

Just before bedtime, Jim suddenly produced an envelope from his jacket pocket.

'I forgot – this is yours, Bridie,' he said, 'I should have sent it back long ago but didn't know where you'd gone.'

I opened the packet and there were the five crisp tenners that Joe had given me so long ago.

'Thanks,' I mumbled. Ryan was watching me keenly.

'What's that for then?' he asked.

'I was going to put it in the bank for Bridie – but she left suddenly. I didn't know where she'd gone so I just held on to it,' Jim explained with an amused look at me. I turned my gaze away and stared at the floor.

'You could have given it to Joe, couldn't you?' I said sulkily.

Jim looked surprised, 'Why so I could. But I kept thinking I'd come over some time and deliver it to you myself,'

'I thought your money got stolen?' said Ryan narrowing his eyes and still watching me in that intense manner he always had. I felt guilty when I had done nothing. Ryan should have been the lawyer, not Jim.

'It was,' I said, 'Jim helped me get it back from Dixie. We found it on this old man in the house I was living in. Then Jim took care of it.'

'Funny, you never mentioned any of that. Seems there's a lot of untold stories of your London life. You'll have to tell me them all some day,' Ryan said.

'Nothing else to tell, Ryan.'

While Ryan was washing his teeth in the bathroom, Jim followed me into the little guest bedroom. I was making up the bed and he took the other side of the sheet and helped me.

'So, Ryan doesn't know everything,' he murmured. 'I thought it odd his being so affable – for him. How wise of you not to spill the beans, Bridie.'

I paused and looked at him but said nothing, finished the bed-making and left the room looking stormy just as Ryan came out of the bathroom.

Later, in bed, Ryan took a hold of me, turned me over and made fierce and passionate love as noisily as he could. I reckoned he was making a point and felt humiliated and angry. Just a doe in the middle of them, watching while the stags locked antlers.

I made out I was very busy next day and in truth I did have a great deal of baking to do. Ryan set off for his next watch early that morning and, taking Jim out before breakfast, pointed out some of the best walks along the cliffs before he went.

'Stick to the paths,' he said again.

'I will,' said Jim.

After breakfast, when Ryan had gone, Jim asked in his usual winning, half-pleading tone, 'Won't you come with me, Bridie? Do you always have to be cooking? Have a break.'

I was quite tempted to do that, go and look at the birds and get some fresh air rather than slave over the hot stove. But it was cash we needed and I'd promised to deliver that morning.

'This is my work, Jim,' I explained. 'I've promised Mr Griffiths a whole batch of cakes and pork pies. It takes me an age to get to Scarborough in my old banger. So I need to start early as I can and get off. You just carry on with your bird-watching. You should have let me know you were coming, shouldn't you?'

My tone was ironic. I still didn't believe that this supposed interest was genuine. Just a clever excuse to come over to see us. However, he had all the gear: the field glasses, the camera, the book on sea birds and obviously had thought it all through. I gave him a flask of coffee and some sandwiches and he set out resolutely along the path Ryan had indicated.

I shrugged. Well, wonders would never cease. Maybe I was all wrong about Jim. He really had grown up and changed his attitude. I was just being suspicious and paranoid as usual. It was time I grew up too.

Finishing the batch of pies and cakes, I packed them in boxes and then put these into large square canvas bags. As I lugged the bags to the car, I saw Jim standing on the headland, glasses to his face looking out to sea intently. I smiled. I still couldn't get over hedonistic Jim turned bird-watcher.

Later that evening, I prepared a really nice meal, having stocked up a bit while in the town. It was pork chops, potatoes and plenty of the home-grown vegetables which we'd managed to cultivate in our little raised garden. I made a delicious apple crumble too. I knew it was Jim's favourite and I wanted to make him feel more at home now he was proving to be genuine. He had come back looking pretty exhausted with all that clambering about on the rocks.

He and Ryan exchanged bird notes and they seemed to be getting along a whole lot better. Ryan was not so terse and snappy but chatted away amicably. To be honest, I had never known him so chatty before. All in all, it was a revelatory visit. Jim behaved with perfect propriety and when he left, there were smiles and handshakes and Ryan said not a thing when Jim came and gave me a hug and kissed me on the cheek.

'Thank you both. It's been a great visit.'

'You're welcome,' said Ryan.

Ryan had offered to give Jim a lift to the station in Scarborough but he'd refused, saying he didn't want to be a bother, and called a taxi instead. After we'd waved him off down the lane, Ryan took me by the arm and steered me roughly inside.

'I want to know the truth, Bridie,' he said, 'the whole truth.'

'What do you mean?' My heart beat wildly with the shock of this assault.

'You're holding back on me. I can tell. Don't I know you inside out? What actually happened in London? What made you turn tail and run like that? You've never been faint-hearted and I always wondered at your giving in so easy. It's not like you.'

'I told you about it, Ryan, there's no more to say.'

'Oh, but there is, my girl. I sense something between you and Jim. My guess is he tried it on with you and you ran away from him. And now he's come back to try and see where the land lies and if he can get you back again.'

I fell silent. Ryan was always able to spot the truth; he had an uncanny instinct for it. He took me by the shoulders and shook me a little. 'The truth, Bridie.'

'All right,' I said wearily. 'Jim did make a pass or two at me and I did get a bit scared. But it was a combination of everything made me give up. Mostly because I missed *you*, you great oaf.'

He softened his expression at that and gathered me closer and kissed me.

'And that's all, Bridie?' he murmured in my ear. 'You didn't sleep with the bastard?'

I shook him off at that.

'Ryan, just leave it alone. No, I did *not* sleep with him and I would never, *ever* want to. Are you satisfied now? He's always been a big brother in my mind and I think he's genuinely sorry I got upset and came over to apologise. He *is* a gentleman, you know.'

'Oh, aye, a poncey gentleman from a nice boarding school. You like that sort don't you? Better'n rough, old Ryan, eh?'

'Not better at all. But I do wish you wouldn't always be so taciturn with everyone.'

'Yes, I know I could learn a lot from your Jim, couldn't I? Nice manners, very nice – and always dressed up like a bloody model, even to come so-called bird-watching. He doesn't know the first thing about birds, it's all crap. Didn't even know puffins are from the auk family. Don't think he'd ever heard of an auk.'

'You don't think his interest is genuine then?'

Ryan gave a scornful snort.

Suddenly I laughed and laughed. The whole thing tickled my sense of humour and in the end Ryan joined me and we both rolled about.

'Silly bastard,' said Ryan.

The he sobered up again and added, 'But I don't think we've seen the last of him, Bridie. He's got somethin' on his mind, he has.'

And, as always, Ryan was right.

Chapter 32

It was bleak on that headland in the winter but we made our cottages snug and cosy with log and coal fires. It was almost impossible to scale the cliffs in the snow or when it was wet or icy. I missed my little trips down the path to the seashore. It was wonderful to be right down there by the water's edge but it was just too dangerous. However, we none of us felt cut off despite the awful weather and the constant sea-frets that meant the fog horn went off day and night. In the end one simply ignored the noise. In fact, I rather liked that muffled boom in the background. At least one knew it kept the ships safe from crashing onto the rocks. It was a regular graveyard in the ocean out there, and the eerie echoes in the wind sometimes sounded like the ghostly cries of long dead men.

We all shared and shared alike. The camaraderie between the keepers and their wives was cheerful. There were few of the squabbles and petty quarrels that sometimes occurred when people lived in such close proximity. It was more like one big family with merry evenings playing whist, watching telly or chatting round the coal fires, knitting or doing other useful pastimes together. I know that the men were also comrades. They spent so much intimate time in one another's company on the Light and even off it. Sometimes if the weather improved the women would bundle into my car and we'd go off to Scarborough or Bridlington for the day for tea and shopping. On the whole, everyone seemed content to pass time together, not asking for more. It was a close, happy little community.

Spring arrived at last and the weather was magnificent but despite the sunny days and blue skies the sea never stopped raging and hurling itself at the cliffs. It was like a bubbling witches' cauldron down there, one of those steady sounds in the background like the mournful cries of the birds. The sea puffins arrived for their breeding season, returning to old burrows they had made in the vegetation on the cliff. I loved to watch them diving deep into the sea and returning with their catch to feed the raucous chicks. The razorbills came in from the sea where they passed most of the winter and one could see them now on the cliffs where they would lay their eggs in May. Watching them fling themselves off the cliffside and into the turbulence made one wish to be a bird and ride the waves with ease the way they did. It all looked so easy. Why couldn't human beings fly like that?

Just like his father, Ryan always liked to be on Middle Watch.

'I love just standing there, looking up at the stars and watching the light as it beams over the lonely seas. Sometimes I see a light far off and know a ship is passing a long way out at sea. Everyone is asleep. It's like I'm the only person alive at a time like that, a God watching a universe. That fills me with awe, Bridie.'

One night as I sat up late while Ryan was up there on the light, I felt an urge to go and join him. It wasn't the thing to do but I always felt a fascination for the lighthouse and enjoyed clambering up to the very top. On the spur of the moment. I put a thick coat over my nightdress and went over the yard towards the tower. It was well past midnight and all the keepers' wives and their children were in bed. Not a light shone from any of the cottages and the darkness seemed impenetrable. The wind was cold but felt delightfully fresh for it was a clear night and there was no mist to obscure the glimmer of the sea as the beam from the lighthouse swept its radiant furrow over the choppy waters.

I stood for a little while, listening to the pounding and thundering of the waves on the sea shore below and felt a wild sense of ecstasy. A crescent Moon shone fitfully through a few clouds that moved across her as if she was a shy maiden drawing a veil across her face. I walked up to the heavy door of the lighthouse and tried it. It opened on well-oiled hinges and I entered the large hallway beyond, shutting the door quietly behind me. The lights were all full on and I climbed the steep stone stairs till I reached the first landing. On one side of this were the sleeping quarters where the assistant keeper slept when on duty. The door was shut and I knew Alan Freedman was in there snoring peacefully and awaiting his turn before dawn arose. I walked past the room, slow and careful in slippered feet, and clambered the narrow iron stairs to the lantern room. Here I came across Ryan busy with the radio, sending out messages to the next light on his rota. He looked up as I came in and stared in astonishment. Finishing his call, he turned and said, 'Well, well, you decided to join me on Middle Watch then, my lassie? You'll catch your death of cold, still in your nightie. Come over here and let me warm you.'

I went over to him and he sat me on his lap and hugged me to him.

'Good to have you here,' he said after we had kissed a good deal.

'I thought you might be angry.'

'Why would I be angry?'

'Because you love to be alone on this watch, you love your peace and quiet.'

He smiled and kissed my cheek. '*You* are my peace, Bridie; my rest, my meditation, my everything. I would never not want you with me.'

Setting me down again, he rose and taking my hand, said, 'Come, let's go look at the stars, shall we? But then you must go back, dear heart. You know you shouldn't be here, don't you?'

'I know. But it's such a magical night and I wanted to be with you so much.'

He regarded me with that long, level look and gave me his most endearing smile.

'I'm glad you want that. I'm glad. Come with me, Bridie.'

We climbed up the little iron staircase that led out onto the gallery and Ryan helped me through the little door. We stood close, his arm about me, our bodies melding together. I shivered a little in the cold night air but was entranced by the deep velvet darkness of the night sky. The clouds had floated on and the moon shone brightly. I couldn't have chosen a better night to join him. The stars shimmered with a brilliance that amazed me – in particular one large bright one. I pointed to it.

'Look at that star, Ryan.'

'Now is that a star or isn't it a star? It's a planet, that is. That's Jupiter, Bridie, biggest planet in our solar system. Beautiful as can be. And see there, the Milky Way. I used to think I could fly up there as a kid and walk along the Way. Sounded so romantic. Makes you feel small doesn't it, when you think of them planets so far away that all we can see is a twinkle of reflected light in the sky.'

'Does it make you feel small, Ryan? It just fills me with a sort of hugeness, as if I could encompass everything looking out there.'

'I know what you mean. Let's say it makes the Ryan bit of me feel insignificant. He's just a stupid fella who thinks he knows a lot of things. But it makes some other part of me feel great and vast and belonging to it all.'

'How lucky we are to be here,' I said. 'This is the loveliest place in the world.'

'And the loveliest time. Don't you feel the loneliness, the space, the deeps of the night?'

'I do. I understand why you love it, Ryan. What sort of things do you think of when you're alone up here?'

'All sorts. I think of you, I think of life and God and all sorts. It's the turning inwards, it's like being a sort of monk for a bit, contemplating and wondering and feeling awestruck by the beauty of it all.'

'I hope you will always have lovely thoughts like that then,' I said, turning my face up to gaze at him. 'Never have ugly or horrible thoughts.'

He bent down and kissed me and said, 'Ah, well, there's no saying there mayn't be bad thoughts now and then as well, Bridie. We're human, aren't we? We all know how to love and how to hate. Just now, though, I'd like to make love to you like anything. But it's neither the time nor place, so off you go and I'll creep into bed with you in the morning and wake you with a kiss, that I will. So off you go and dream of me. Tonight I'll be thinking of that! But not too much or it'll be like I got a lighthouse in my trousers! I'll not be keeping an eye on things properly.'

I laughed and kissing him again, went quietly back down the stairs and off to bed to dream of my beloved and to await eagerly his passionate return in the early hours of the morning.

To be honest, we had forgotten Jim by the spring. I didn't feel he'd bother to come again. As Ryan said, he wasn't a genuine birdwatcher and the experience of clambering about on the cliffs had exhausted him. He had seen for himself that Ryan and I were very happy, made his apologies and returned the money. I was grateful he hadn't returned the clothes I'd left at his flat when I ran away. That would have been a dead giveaway. I didn't want them anyway. They would have felt contaminated by that experience. It still made me shudder to think of it. I wasn't sure I really had forgiven him for all the trickery he had played, the violence and misery he'd subjected me to.

I was busy that week with my usual batch of baking and had just put a fresh load of pies in the oven. It was a pleasant, mild morning though as always a fine mist was still hanging over the sea and the feel of rain was in the air. Hearing a bark from Sandra's collie, I looked up and saw Jim coming towards the open door.

'Smells good as always,' he announced. He stood there smiling at me for all the world as if he'd never gone anywhere but been here all the time.

I put down my rolling pin and wiped my hands on a tea towel.

'I didn't think you'd be back.'

'I like it here,' he said. 'And Ryan said I could come back even if you didn't. Still, I know you're a good girl and always do as you're told.'

'Do I? And what if I send you packing?'

He came in, dropped his bag on a chair and came up to me, giving me a peck on the cheek before I could back away.

'Ever welcoming, aren't you, Bridie?' he grinned. 'The Prodigal Son would have been sent off with a flea in his ear if you'd been about. Maybe that's what I love about you. It's the chase that appeals. Men never like easy women. We're hunters at heart.'

I picked up the rolling pin and looked ready to lash out in his direction but he ducked and laughed at me and caught my arm in flight.

'You're still so utterly desirable, Bridie. Did you know that? All the more exciting when you belong to another.'

'If you're going to go on like this, I really will send you packing.'

'I'm joking! You used to have a great sense of humour. What happened to it? Guess it's living in this out of the way place that's makes you so ill-tempered. How do you bear it here? It must be so lonely, so boring.'

'Well, it isn't. We have a great community life and we're all very happy here. You know I love the sea and the wild spaces. It's how you bear living in that smoky, over-populated city beats me. *That* is sheer madness.'

'Ah, but I'm beginning to get a taste for this country life,' he said laughing. 'It has indubitable areas of fascination and maybe someday I'll buy a cottage somewhere charming like Devon. A country retreat.'

'You'll be a typical weekender,' I said. 'Not a clue about the country, just liking it all pretty and nice and not even beginning to see the cruelty and the dark side of it. I see it and yet I still love it. It's not the prettiness that appeals to me but the whole grandeur of it all. The cycles of life and death, the beauty, ugliness, storm and calm. The contradictions that are a part of life. We're all part of it and it has a nobility and a majesty that takes one out of one's petty existence.'

I expected him to laugh and mock me for this little speech, said from my heart. But he didn't; he looked at me as if trying to understand something.

'That's nice, Bridie,' he said, his tone sincere. 'I like what you just said. You've put me in my place and you're good at that, bless your little heart. Teach me about the grandeur of it all then.'

'I'll teach you, if you like,' said a voice and Ryan walked in, smiling and extending his hand to Jim.

I was dumbstruck at this show of friendship from my normally taciturn husband and watched open-mouthed as the two men shook hands like long lost mates.

'So, how long you stayin' this time?' asked Ryan almost as if he had been expecting Jim and was not at all surprised at his sudden, and as usual, unannounced, appearance.

'Three days will be enough for you to put up with me, I'm sure,' smiled Jim. 'I thought I'd come over in late spring this time and see the nesting birds and hopefully the puffins, which they say are about this time of year.'

'Aye, they've arrived in early this year as the weather's been good. There's quite few of them nesting on the cliff ledges up there. Didn't you hear the racket they made as you came over?'

'I certainly heard a great deal of noise, like an old radio full of static.'

'Sure enough, that'll be them. You can hear them over to Bridlington, I reckon! Noisy little beggars. But they're great fun to watch, they're comic little characters.'

'I really look forward to seeing them,' said Jim and he sounded as if he meant it.

Ryan had some time off the next day and took Jim on an exploratory trek across the cliff tops nearby. Apparently they saw scores of razorbills, guillemots and Atlantic puffins. The two men came back later and Jim looked very tired with all the unaccustomed exercise. Ryan, of course, was perfectly used to it and sat smoking his pipe after dinner watching Jim and I play a game of chess.

'It was most interesting and enjoyable to see all those birds,' said Jim, 'What a racket they make. But they are amazing, they really are. I never realised how fascinating it might be to study them so close. I'm becoming quite hooked by the experience.'

'Seems we'll be seeing a lot more of you then,' said Ryan.

His voice was calm but his eyes narrowed as he gazed at Jim. For a moment, Jim shifted uncomfortably in his chair as if he sensed something beneath the quiet remark. He looked up at Ryan and smiled in his winning manner.

'Well, only if you are happy to have me as a guest now and then.'

'All depends on Bridie, don't it?' said Ryan. He knocked his pipe out in a huge ashtray. 'It's her what has to cook and care for us blokes, isn't it? It's up to her.'

Jim looked at me with his charming smile. 'Do you object to all that, Bridie? You always love caring for others, always have.'

'I never mind caring for people, Jim,' I said, my eyes lowered.

'Good. How about you take a walk with me tomorrow then? I'd like to see more of the seashore and explore the area a little. No pork pies to cook tomorrow?'

I laughed a little at this. 'No, no pork pies. All right. We'll walk along the cliffs a bit and you can come down to the seashore with me. It's a bit of a clamber. Are you up to it, Mr Townie?'

'I am. Getting tougher by the day. I think I'll try getting myself in trim next time I come though. It's certainly hard work for a desk man. But I feel the better for it, feel the old limbs loosening up. There's no denying yours is a healthy life.'

'It is,' said Ryan. 'It's a man's life. Working outdoors, feeling the wind and rain and spray on one's face. That's real life. That's what we was born to do, be out amongst nature, part of the whole thing, not separated by walls, staring at paper all day, talking rubbish most of the time.'

'I agree but few people now could live like this, Ryan,' Jim said thoughtfully. 'It's different, this life, it's solitary and cut off. I understand that you feel passionate about it. The closeness to the elements ... but we've moved along since those days when men were always at the mercy of nature and her whims and ways. It is a simple life but also a hard life. It's natural to want things easier though things have maybe become more complicated as a result and someone has to do the paperwork.'

'Oh, someone has to,' agreed Ryan. 'I leave it all to you. Anyways, I've had a hard day so I'm off to bed now. You two finish your game then come to bed, Bridie.'

'All right, Ryan.'

It was hard to concentrate on the game when he had gone. I felt Jim watching me closely and sensed something in Ryan that troubled me.

'Oh, let's leave it ... you've almost won anyway,' I said after a while.

Jim smiled at this. 'Have I, Bridie?' he murmured and took my queen and moved it around the board.

'You see, you *can* be the winner if you want. You give up too soon. But I don't, Bridie, there's the difference in us. I never give up. What I want, I get.'

His hand closed on mine and he tried to pull me towards him as if to kiss me. I rose quickly, almost knocking over the little table and the chessboard. The queen fell on the floor and I picked the piece up and set her back in the box.

'Stop it, Jim!' I whispered fiercely, 'Go to bed. You can stay another couple of days and then I don't want you to come back again. Neither of us do, can't you see that. You're not going to win this game at all, don't kid yourself.'

Jim smiled but said no more and took himself off to bed. I took my time getting to mine, feeling too upset to sleep. Thankfully by the time I got there, Ryan was sound asleep and snoring sweetly.

The next day, after breakfast, Jim asked, 'You will come with me today, won't you, Bridie?'

By now, I rather regretted having said I would but could think of no real excuse not to go along. 'All right.' I said reluctantly. His face lit with pleasure and I felt, *after all what's the harm in it? It's daytime and there's folk about.*

I decided to take Jim down the steep steps that led to the little cove at the bottom of the Dane's Dyke, the one they called the North Landing. Looking up, we could see the lighthouse towering against the sky, a white pillar, beautiful and strong. We could be seen by anyone up in the lantern and this made me feel more comfortable. Jim walked silently behind me as we slipped and slithered down muddy steps amongst the damp grasses and wildflowers that grew in profusion all around us. The wind rippled across the grasses and tugged at our clothes as we descended.

'It must have poured last night.'

'It did,' I replied, 'so take care. I slipped badly once and was lucky not to break an ankle.'

'But you're always a tough one, aren't you, Bridie? Always a survivor.' He stopped and looked upwards at the lighthouse, stark and white against the pearl grey sky. Last night's rain had stopped at last but clouds still blanketed the sun. We could see one of the men out on the gallery, polishing up all the lenses.

'Do they have to do that all the time?'

'All the time. The birds keep smashing into the light at night and sometimes, it's a most unpleasant sight in the morning.'

'Poor things. They are, like all creatures, attracted to the light.'

'Yes, and they die for their pains.'

He continued to look upwards as if fascinated.

'I shall have to go up there sometime. Right to the top there. Think Ryan'll take me up?'

'I suppose he might. If you're really interested.'

'Oh, I'm interested, all right.'

I don't know what it was in these words or the manner in which he said them that made me feel apprehensive. I looked at him as he stood there, his fair hair blowing out from his face with the strong wind. He lowered his gaze and smiled at me.

'You look beautiful this morning,' he remarked, 'the breeze is making your cheeks rosy and your eyes bright. I love you, Bridie. I have to say that to you while our dear Ryan is out of earshot. I have to say it whether you like it or not. I can't help it, I love you.'

I turned my gaze away from him, my eyes drawn upwards towards the lighthouse.

'I wish you wouldn't say it, Jim.'

'Why? Why are you afraid of my feelings for you? Is it because you feel the same deep down? Is it, Bridie?'

'Stop it, Jim!'

'I'll never stop it. Never!' He had to shout above the crashing of waves coming into the shore as the wind began to whip up again. I looked up at the light again uneasily. It was foolish, –no one could hear, thank goodness. Heaven knows what Ryan would do if he heard all this.

'Then you must never come back again!' I shouted back and the words were whipped away from my mouth and tossed across the sea. But he heard them and gave me a sudden strange smile that chilled me.

We walked together in silence up the shore. A little way out to sea was a tall, up-thrusting column of rock and several gulls and razorbills were swooping, diving and then settling back on it. Jim got out his glasses and studied their movements, a little smile of amusement curling round his lips.

'Foolish creatures in some ways,' he said, 'they just eat and eat. Nature does nothing but eat; one creature made to eat another and all trying hard not to be eaten so that their miserable little species can survive. And they have to survive simply so as to provide food for the next predator up. It's all so peculiarly pointless.'

'It isn't pointless at all, Jim. All these creatures survive and develop and are beautiful to watch.'

'But *we* watch them. *We* are aware of them; we observe and are conscious of their existence. They aren't. They are purely instinctual, totally unaware of what they are. Is that why humanity was created to be conscious? So that God could watch all these things through our eyes? Or are we the gods?'

I stared at him, nonplussed by the strange bitter sound in his voice.

'Are *we* the gods?' he shouted out, tossing his arms towards the sea in a violent gesture. 'Are we, like Adam, in charge of all the living creatures or is someone pulling our strings, making us dance in turn like monkeys with a barrel organ? No, I won't be pulled around, I'll make my life as I want it. Have the woman I want! Take note, ye gods!'

'You're crazy, Jim!' I couldn't help feeling caught up in his madness, laughing at the power of the wind whipping the waves and slapping my face, pushing and buffeting our bodies as we stood there on the chalky pebbles of the beach.

'You see …you're mad too!' he exulted. I sobered down and said 'Better get back, it's going to rain again in a short while.'

I turned and began to make my way back up the cliff and Jim followed unwillingly. Something about the wildness of the elements had moved him in a way that it always moved Ryan and myself. But we were used to these things all our lives, knew how to read and respect nature's wildness and wilfulness. Jim did not. His hubris made him look wild and foolish. He reminded me of King Canute, ordering the tide to stop rolling in. He seemed to forget at that moment that he was a mere human being and that the elements would always be greater than we puny mortals.

I reached the top of the cliff and Jim was still some way behind me, puffing a little with the exertion. I watched him with some contempt. How fine and strong a man Ryan was in comparison! At that very moment, a huge boulder became dislodged halfway up the cliff face and came crashing down.

'Jim, watch out!'

It narrowly missed him by a few inches. He stared after it in sheer amazement and shook his head. Then he scrambled all the faster till he joined me at the top.

'Are you all right, Jim?' I asked, my voice shaking a little.

'I'm fine,' he said shortly.

When Ryan came back for lunch, I recounted the incident of the boulder. Jim looked cross as if he would have preferred that I didn't mention it.

Ryan looked at Jim and said, 'You were bloody lucky. I've heard tell of such accidents before. Bird-watching has its dangers, you know.'

'Life has dangers everywhere,' Jim responded. 'Crossing

Piccadilly Circus is a fraught business. Just different dangers. One has to keep one's wits about one all the time. That's life. I don't believe in wrapping myself in cotton wool any more than you do, Ryan.'

Ryan smiled, 'Good words! I'd sooner die young doing something interesting and daring than live forever, me feet on a fender, a paper in my hand reading of other's exploits. Good for you, Jim!'

He took out his pipe and filled it and puffed for a while. Jim in turn lit a cigarette and the two men stared into the air and remained silent. I looked from one to the other and then cleared away the plates and went about my household tasks in equal silence.

'I'll take a wee snooze now as I've three watches on the trot today,' said Ryan after a while. 'It's Middle Watch for me tonight. My favourite.'

'Why your favourite?' Jim asked curiously.

'I like the darkness and the silence; I like the sense of being alone in the world. I prefer to work through till four in the morning rather than be woken up and have to stagger over there half asleep.'

'Not for me, not the silence and the loneliness,' said Jim.' I couldn't live like that, not all the time.'

'No, you're a townie,' I said scathingly, 'we know that, Jim. And you know that.'

So why come at all, I felt like adding and I could see a similar question on Ryan's face as well. Jim wasn't looking at us but out of the window.

'I suppose I am,' he said slowly, 'I suppose I will always be that. But I also understand why you both love it here. I felt it this morning on the seashore and even the narrow miss with the boulder seemed to be a part of it all. You do feel alive here. Really alive.'

'So,' he turned and looked at Ryan, 'so you'll be up there tonight while we are all asleep. It's a curious notion. I wonder what sort of thoughts will be in your mind as you sit up there and look out to sea? I wonder.'

'Maybe best no one knows,' said Ryan with a smile.

'You're probably right.'

Listening to them both I felt, as I often did, undercurrents of unspoken feeling running beneath these apparently innocuous conversations. I longed for Jim to go away and leave us but I knew he planned to stay one more day and that Ryan had promised to take him right down onto Flamborough cliffs later tomorrow morning to see the nesting birds and their eggs.

Ryan got himself ready to go to the lighthouse after tea. He looked out at the skies and smiled. The wind had died down a little and the sky looked a lot bluer and brighter than it had this morning.

'Hope it stays clear tonight,' he said as he left. 'I mean to get the telescope out and do a spot of stargazing. They reckon Venus'll be brilliant tonight.'

When he had gone I cleared away the supper dishes. Jim helped me wash and dry them then stack them away. We sat and watched *Coronation Street* on the telly. Jim found it distinctly boring as he made very clear by yawning all the way through, eventually getting up to fetch a bottle of wine he'd brought with him, there never being anything stronger than beer, sherry and an odd bottle of whisky left over from Christmas in our house.

'Have a glass, Bridie?'

I declined. 'No thanks. You know that stuff goes to my head.'

He smiled but made no comment and settled himself down with his claret and his book while I followed the goings on at the Rovers Return.

'I really don't know how you can watch that rubbish,' he commented after a while when some raucous episode distracted him from his reading.

'I don't know how you can drink all that wine,' I retorted. 'It's all a matter of taste and one isn't better than the other for all you think you're so posh just because you know your vintages. It's all show and nonsense. At least *Coronation Street* is about ordinary people and their funny little lives.'

'Have it your way,' he said affably.

I rather enjoyed an argument with Jim and was disappointed by this tame reply. It was obvious he had no wish to get himself drawn into one of my debates on life so I let it go and we said little to one another that evening. Now and then, I found him looking up from his book and regarding me with a curious look in his eye that made me feel uncomfortable. I hated that sense of being watched as much as Ryan did.

'Why are you staring at me?' I demanded.

'I'm not staring, just admiring you. You have the most beautiful green eyes,' was the reply.

'Well, don't, Jim. It makes me feel nervous.'

'You've no need to be nervous,' he said, 'you're very jumpy, aren't you?'

'We're on our own, Jim,' I pointed out, 'and I'm still not sure I can trust you.'

He made no reply to this, just smiled, then gathered his books and said, 'Well, I'm off to bed now. I've a lot of climbing to do tomorrow. Ryan said he'd take me on the steep cliffs nearby to see some nesting birds close to.'

'It's dangerous on those cliffs,' I said, 'and the birds don't like being disturbed. What's Ryan think he's up to, taking you up there? You'd think they were his private property at times. He really loves them and guards the eggs like a daddy. So do the other keepers; they keep a watch for people scrambling about the cliffs in case they're poachers after the eggs. Most of the birds only lay one egg a time and if it's stolen or the nest spoiled, that's it for the season.'

'I'm hardly going to steal any eggs,' said Jim. 'What d'you take me for?'

'Sorry, I know you wouldn't. You're right, I am getting jumpy and it's mean of me.'

'I've been a good boy, so far, haven't I?'

I smiled at his winsome tone. 'Yes, more or less – and you'll carry on being a good boy, won't you? You and Ryan seem to be getting on a lot better. I'm glad of that at least.'

'We fellows are getting on famously. It's you I need to win round. But I will. I always win everyone round in the end, don't

I? Well, goodnight, Bridie.' He pecked me on the cheek.

'Goodnight, Jim.'

I went to the front door and looked out into the night. It was still only eleven o'clock and Ryan would be sitting in the service room or chatting to the relief keeper in the little kitchen. I debated taking him over a cup of coffee but in the end, felt too sleepy to bother. The white beam was flashing every few seconds, lighting the courtyard, turning trees and shrubbery into ghostly and fearful night objects. I looked up at the dark tower looming overhead and pictured Ryan later on, while we were all fast asleep, writing out his weather reports or sending radio messages to one of the other lights in the area. He might even be out on the gallery, gazing up at the stars through his telescope. A lone man awake while all around him slept.

'I love you, darling,' I whispered and blew a kiss in the direction of the tower before turning in for the night.

I awoke and felt him in bed beside me. A hard urgent cock was pushing itself against my back and I turned over sleepily and put my arms out to hug the man beside me.

'Ryan?' I murmured and then as I felt the naked flesh, I knew at once that it was not my husband. Ryan had firm, muscular, taut flesh; this man was firm but somehow soft and smooth. I was immediately awake and began to scream.

A hand clamped down over my mouth. The darkness was intense but the occasional flash of light from the lighthouse lit the room and I could see Jim bending over me.

'Don't scream, Bridie,' he said, 'don't dare scream. You do so and I'll tell Ryan that I still have your clothes at my place which you left there on purpose. And that it wasn't you running away from me, but me kicking you out because you were getting too much to handle. I'll tell him we were lovers all the time and that you've always been up for it.'

I fell still, horrified at such a thought.

'You 'll keep quiet?'

I nodded, my mind racing. How was I to get out of this situation? There were no handy objects here that I could hit him with. If I screamed he would tell Ryan a pack of lies and Ryan was more than likely to believe him, such was Jim's charm and smoothness. He always said he could win anyone round and it was true. He had won Ryan round – or so it seemed. Ryan, I felt sure, was already suspicious of me.

'That's better,' Jim murmured, slowly retracting his hand. He began to pull my nightie up my body and above my breasts. He still had me pinned down beneath him with one arm and struggle as I might, couldn't push him off. He was not as wiry as Ryan but he was heavier and every bit as strong. I could scarcely breathe with his dead weight upon me. However, he moved his body up and, pushing my knees open, began to enter me.

'Jim, please don't, please don't,' I sobbed.

'You want me, Bridie, don't pretend. I know you do.'

His movements were slow and sweet and not at all fierce or painful. It was as if he wanted me to enjoy the experience and he murmured soothing things in my ear as he slid in and out, his hands moving expertly around my breasts, his lips kissing me tenderly and gently. That was when I realised that he was right. I wanted him. I didn't love him as I loved Ryan but I did desire him and this realisation made me angry and ashamed of myself. I hated myself for it.

'Let me go, please,' I begged him.

But his lips clamped down again on mine and I suddenly pulled him towards me fiercely and raising my hips into his movements gave in to the darkness and the shame and the delight of it all.

A long while later I opened my eyes and looked towards the open door of the bedroom. I had a terrifying feeling someone was there in the shadows, watching us.

'Ryan!'

I tried to sit up but Jim pushed me down.

'Don't try that old trick,' he said, but he also looked over his shoulder. There was nothing but stillness and darkness but I felt sure that for a brief second I had heard a stirring in the shadows beyond.

'Don't be ridiculous, Ryan's on his precious lighthouse and

he's not going to leave that alone, is he?' said Jim, but he sounded rattled.

No, Ryan wouldn't do that. He would never abandon the light even for a moment. He knew full well if he did such a thing and was caught, he'd be thrown out of the service. I sank back on the bed.

'You've had your way – leave me alone now,' I said.

'You enjoyed it in the end, didn't you?' I could hear the triumph in his voice. 'Didn't you? Oh, Bridie, you know I love you, it's not to hurt you. It's just I need you so much. You've no idea how glad I felt when you responded, when you returned my kisses. Bridie, I've dreamt of it, longed for it till I could think of nothing else.'

'What about your Alice? Don't you feel anything for her?'

'*My* Alice! She's just a silly bitch. I use her to get on in my career. I won't need her much longer, that's for sure. She's convenient and good in bed. Not such hard work to capture as you – but you're a prize worth fighting for, worth winning.'

'Jim, I don't understand. I'm not sophisticated and clever like these women who further your career. I'm dull and boring and simple in my ways. What do you love about me, why do you pursue me like this?'

He was silent for a while then he said slowly, 'I know you're not the usual sort of girl I'd take out. But you're not dull and boring at all. You excite me somehow; I can't explain it. Who can explain sexual attraction? And you're far more lovely than any of the peroxide blondes I've made love to. I wouldn't want to marry you, Bridie, any more than you'd want me. But I need you desperately. Something about you, some quality you have is the only thing in life that can satisfy me. And I have a feeling you feel the same. You need me too.'

I shook my head fiercely. 'No, Jim. I don't need you. I have everything I want. Promise you won't come back, Jim. Don't come back again.'

He caressed my face with his hand and bent to kiss my lips once more.

'But I will come back, Bridie,' was the quiet, calm reply.

'And we'll be lovers again. A taste of honey, that's what this is. And next time round I want you to come to *me*, giving and willing. I want you to let yourself go and enjoy me. I'm a good lover, I know I am. Look, it won't be often and Ryan need never know. You can meet me anywhere you want. I can afford to get a room somewhere in a nice hotel in Scarborough, say, or anywhere you fancy. Just now and then, that's all I ask. We're bonded you and I, we always have been. I think we'll be bonded till the end of time. I need you in a way I can't describe.'

'And if I refuse?'

'I'll tell Ryan you lured me to your bed, that it was your idea I should come over here. I have no shame, Bridie. I'll do anything.'

'I know you would.'

I was weary now and looking at the luminous dial of the bedside clock said, 'You *must* go. Ryan might decide to come home after his watch. He may be back any minute.'

Thankfully that had the desired effect and Jim slid out of the bed and returned to his room. I got up, went to the bathroom and washed the smell of sex from me but it lingered in the air and I felt afraid. Drawing the bedclothes about me, I lay in the dark until dawn began to creep in through the curtains. Ryan didn't come back early and for once I was relieved. My heart and mind were churning with dismay and misery. I didn't want to be Jim's lover and yet a part of me wanted him again. It had been a taste of honey, as Jim had said. It was Ryan that I loved more than my life but it didn't stop my lustful desire for Jim. How terrible that Jim had woken me to this realisation!

He would make sure he kept me to it, bind me to him more and more. Ryan would discover it in the end and all would be lost. The future spent in this way unfolded before me and filled me with horror. I was so happy with Ryan and now all was ruined. I no longer felt clean inside, my pure love for Ryan tainted – but what was I to do? I dared not tell Ryan … yet in the end I would have to do so, whatever the consequences. It would be better to face his fury than to betray him for the rest of my life. And I knew Jim wasn't going to give up on me. Not ever.

Chapter 33

Jim rose early and was sitting outside on the bench with Ryan when I at last staggered up. I had overslept badly which wasn't surprising given the lack of sleep and all the worrying thoughts and emotions tumbling inside me like washing in a dryer. My head felt stuffed with cotton wool, my mouth dry and furry.

'Not like you to sleep in,' said Ryan turning round as I came to the door, still half asleep, looking as if I'd washed up with the tide. There they both sat looking perfectly at peace as if nothing had happened at all. For a peculiar moment, I even began to wonder if it had all been some nasty dream. I stood staring at them both.

Ryan's face was unsmiling, his expression unfathomable. I must have looked a picture of guilty anxiety but he made no comment nor did he seem a bit surprised. In that moment my heart failed me. He knew. I could tell somehow and I was terrified of what he would say to me once Jim had gone. At the same time I couldn't understand why he was sitting there smoking a cigarette as if nothing had happened. He always swore he would do for Jim if he laid a finger on me. With or without my consent, had been his words.

'I don't feel too well,' I mumbled and went back indoors. Making myself a cup of tea, I sat cradling it over the kitchen table. It was not a dream at all. I wanted Jim to go away. I wanted him to go away and never, ever return. It was just like Millie all over again. I didn't want this person in my life, frightening me, trying to take me over. He would never leave me alone but make me be his lover like it or not and a part of me *did* like it. That was the worst of it. What could I do? I decided I must make a clean breast of it all when Jim left and ask Ryan to make sure he never came back, throw him out if he tried. Hopefully, Ryan wouldn't throw me out along with him. There was no knowing what he would do or say. I prayed his love for me would win through. My love for him was fiercer and stronger than ever. I didn't want to lose Ryan, I didn't!

I remembered telling Ryan a long time ago that Eve must take a bite of the apple, that it was her fate. Well, I'd taken my bite, let the serpent into the Garden. I was now cast out of Eden and the way truly barred. I could almost see those angels with their fiery swords barring the way. I would never be able to go back; there's no way back when you've lost your innocence. Things would never be the same between any of us ever again. A sob escaped me; everything seemed so lost, so hopeless and I wanted to run out and throw myself off the cliff. However, I swallowed my misery down along with the tea and began to sort the washing, make the beds as if all was normal.

Ryan came in and collected his binoculars. He looked at me as he did so and noted my red-rimmed eyes. He held my gaze for a long moment but again he said nothing at all and this made me feel frightened. What was happening inside him? What was going on his head?

Looking out of the window, I saw how a fine rain had begun and said, 'Don't go on Bempton cliffs today, Ryan. It's going to be slippery and dangerous.'

'It's fine, don't worry,' he replied, his voice calm and quiet.

I came out of the house and saw Jim was ready and waiting, his rain coat with its attached hood drawn up over his head. The rain was getting stronger and steadier.

'The birds won't come inland if the weather turns rough,' I said. 'It's pointless going now. Please don't go, both of you. I feel worried about it. Leave it till tomorrow or another time.'

'Worried your Jim will come to some harm, then?' said Ryan. He spoke lightly but I saw a strange, fierce look in his eyes.

'I'm worried you'll both come to harm,' I said, taking his hand and looking at him beseechingly. *Whatever's in your mind, don't do it, Ryan ... .*

He held my hand for a moment or two then withdrew it and stared out at the cliffs and then the sea where a solid plate of stratus clouds was gathered, a minute band of blue showing right on the horizon. Over the cliffs however, the skies looked bleak, grey and dreary. There was a long silence in which I felt my heart beating hard and painfully. I was very afraid in that moment.

'It's right enough,' he said at last, 'there's not much point in going now.'

Jim looked from one to the other of us and a slow frown gathered on his face. I wondered what he was thinking and if he, like myself, got a sudden sense of danger in the air.

'That's a shame,' he remarked. 'But you're right, Bridie. There's some massive dark clouds out there. I'm not a good climber and it does seem madness to go out when it's wet and slippery, even with an expert like Ryan.'

This latter comment bore a hint of sarcasm.

'Not much point in you stayin' really,' said Ryan in his slow, measured tones. 'Weather looks due to be stormy and this is one of the worst places to be when it turns bad. Years back one of the keepers fell over the cliffs, another 'un died when a loose rock hit his head as he was coming up the cliff steps in a Force Eight gale. That near happened to you, didn't it? It's not safe for you, Jim. Not safe at all. Reckon you might as well call it a day. Not much bird-watchin' to do when the weather's bad – as Bridie rightly says.'

Jim looked from one to the other of us. A slight flush was on his cheeks. The tension between us all was palpable, quivering like an electric storm.

'Fair enough,' he nodded. 'I'll pack my bits and get the train from Scarborough this afternoon after lunch if that suits you – if you don't mind giving me a lift to the station, Bridie?' He paused as an idea appeared to strike him. 'Maybe just to pass time – and as you're free a bit this morning – why not show me round the lighthouse, Ryan? You're allowed to do that, aren't you?'

Ryan considered.

'Okay,' he said doubtfully. 'I'll show you round if you're really interested.'

'Oh, I'm interested all right.'

I breathed a sigh of relief. It seemed a good idea and would pass time until lunch, then Jim would go and I would be left to face the music. I knew I would have to have it out with Ryan, I couldn't bear this terrible silence between us. Better to have a row and clear the air. Ryan wasn't the type to have rows, he was like his dad in that respect, preferred to turn his back on things. He might end up running off to his beloved light just as Sidney Waterman had done and I would be ignored and neglected just like Sheila. I would make him talk about it whether he liked it or not. It had to be faced and dealt with whatever the consequences.

The two men set off along the path towards the lighthouse door. I watched them and then with a sigh went inside to begin the lunch. My mind wasn't really on cooking but I shoved a few potatoes in the oven to bake, picked over the remnants of some boned ham then shelled a few peas and put them in water. Sitting down, I began to sew some pieces of the quilted bedspread together, anything to take my mind off things. Flashes of last night's encounter kept coming up before my eye; Jim's handsome face as he bent over me, my disgusting enjoyment of it all despite my fear and shame. No, things could never be the same between Ryan and me – yet strange as it might seem my love and need for Ryan had deepened. What I felt for Jim was inexplicable and I loathed myself for it. If he was sent away, never allowed to return, all would be well. The lustful desire would go away. Ryan seemed to be keeping his temper with Jim and that troubled me. It seemed out of character, somehow.

I dozed off a little, exhausted by these events. Drifting away, I kept seeing Mean Millie's face mocking and laughing as if she'd got her way somehow and had me enthralled, her slave and servant forever. Struggling to wake through this was horrible, like drowning and trying to rise to the surface, knowing I was asleep and dreaming of waking up but unable to move, like a paralytic case. I woke at last and put my hand to my mouth to stifle a scream. Something terrible had happened. I knew it.

I grabbed my cardigan and threw it over my shoulders and ran out of the gate towards the lighthouse. It stood silhouetted against a grey blankness, thrusting upwards into the sky, a huge stone structure which, in my confused state of mind, now appeared alarming and sinister. The door was open but no one was about in the yard. My breath came in little gasps as I ran, my limbs felt odd as if they were unreal and no longer belonged to the rest of me. Was this real or was I still trying to wake up from some nightmare?

As I went up the steps and entered the small hallway I heard a sudden shout and, looking up, saw Ryan and Jim struggling on the small landing at the top of the stairs. In the mêlée of arms and flailing fists, it was hard to see who was attacking whom or what exactly they were trying to do – but the intention was obvious. They were both fighting for their lives.

'Ryan!' I screamed. 'Ryan, what's happening? Stop it, stop it, both of you!' It was as if I was asking two boys to stop a play fight. But this was no play. I glimpsed Jim's face in that moment and it was filled with a ferocious fury as he twisted round in Ryan's gripping embrace and hit out with all his force. In so doing he lost his precarious footing on the narrow stone steps which descended straight from the landing to the floor level of the main entrance to the lighthouse. With a terrified yell, he fell at an odd angle as he tried to seize Ryan in his flight, perhaps hoping to pull his assailant along with him. Instead he banged his head on the wall with a crunch, his body twisted and bounced along the steps, slithering down the last few till he lay at the bottom a motionless heap. Before my eyes flashed the memory of the day that I fell down the stairs at Millie's home and how it had felt as if it would never end.

'Oh, Jim! Oh my *God*!'

I ran to him as he lay there crumpled at the bottom of the stairs, his head twisted to the left and a trickle of blood oozing from his mouth and took his limp hand in mine to feel for a pulse. By this time the commotion had brought the assistant keeper running out of the kitchen and he stood for a shocked moment behind Ryan at the top of the steps.

'What's going on here? What the hell …'

Ryan had not come down the steps to see if Jim was all right. He sat at the top, his face buried in his hands, but he moved his body a little to let Alan Freedman pass by. Alan came racing down.

'I'll go and get the medical kit,' I said, my voice trembling now.

Alan looked at Jim and put his fingers to his neck. Jim lay so still, so white, his eyes wide open and a look of such terror on his face that I shuddered. I almost dared not breathe for I knew the answer. Alan looked up at me with troubled eyes.

'No use, my dear. Poor lad's gone. Broke his neck. We'll have to radio for help.'

I covered my mouth with my hands again, wanting to retch, and began to weep. Jim looked so still and pale. I knelt beside him, sobbing, unable to speak and touched his face briefly, a sad, lingering touch and then I closed his eyes. I couldn't bear to see that look there, that terrible look. Jim Bosworth – that handsome, charming, greedy, ambitious man; he wanted to take silk, be a QC. Now he was nothing but a broken body. In a moment it was all gone and had been for nothing because he had pursued the one thing he couldn't obtain for all his looks and charm, the one thing he wanted to try and possess. And that was me – Bridie O'Neill – a nobody. Was I worth this man's death? I looked up at Ryan, still seated on the stairs and watching us. My eyes burned with the question … *did you do this?* … .

Ryan shook his head imperceptibly …*no, I didn't* …

In that moment we both knew that we were glad Jim was no more.

Later, Ryan explained it all to me.

'We'd looked round the lantern and Jim was coming down the stairs behind me. We came to the landing which led to the relief keeper's room and the kitchen before going down that last lot o' stairs that lead down to the entrance hall. I'd been explaining a point about the optics and then I got this funny feeling of a sudden. Like an animal does, this sense of fear. So I looked round at Jim as he stood at the top of the stone steps. And there he stood, his arm stretched out, his face downright evil and I knew he meant to shove me down them stairs with all his force and intention. I made a grab for him, the bastard, and he leapt back up on the landing and we grappled for what seemed a long while and of a sudden, as I twisted him round and punched him in the face, he tried to hit back but went off careerin' down those stone stairs. He tried to pull me after him, you saw that …and that's the truth of it, Bridie.'

'Yes, I saw that. I saw what happened then, Ryan.'

Again I remembered my own fall down the stairs when Millie had frightened and threatened me all those years ago. I recalled her callous indifference to my pain and suffering and Jim's look of compassion as he helped me to the sofa. My heart ached.

Oh, Jim, I did love you in a way. You were the only one who cared about me in those dreadful days. Why, oh, why did this have to happen? I would have always loved you as a brother, always …

There had to be an inquest into the death. There were no witnesses besides myself – the other keepers were busy in the kitchen at that time and heard nothing except Jim's shout as he fell. I begged Ryan to stick to the fact that Jim had lost his footing and fallen and not say anything about a fight on the stairs. It was the truth, after all, and needed no embroidering. There was no reason in anyone's minds why anything different might have occurred. They knew nothing of our personal drama, nor did they inquire. Accidents happened in difficult, dangerous places like lighthouses. Keepers were known to trip and fall and they were used to difficult stairs. Ryan, being that sort, wanted to tell the whole unvarnished truth but I told him it would look bad. I didn't want Jim's name sullied either; it would have been awful for Joe, he was so proud of his eldest son and his death was bad enough without knowing he'd had murder in his heart.

In the end Ryan agreed. A verdict of accidental death was returned.

I tried to bring up the subject of Jim again after the inquest. Up till then we hadn't said a thing about it to one another. I wanted to make a clean breast of it. I stood for a while looking out of the window over the bleak landscape and tried to picture my life without Ryan. Tears came to my eyes. I wouldn't be able to bear it but I had to speak.

He came over and stood beside me. As always he caught my mood and putting an arm about me, said, 'What's up, love?'

'Ryan,' I said my voice faltering with fear, 'I feel I ought to try and explain about things.'

He looked at the floor and said nothing, got out a cigarette from a packet and lit it.

'Not sure there's anything you need to tell me,' he said quietly.

'I never told you Jim tried to rape me in London.'

'I guessed it, anyhow.'

'And on the night you were on middle watch. The night before he died. He came in the night … .he … we … ' Tears began to course down my cheeks.

Again he said nothing but the hand holding the cigarette shook a little.

'Bridie,' he said at last. 'What's done's done. I guess he loved you. I love you – who wouldn't? I've no hard feelings any more. I wanted to do the same to him, throw him off the cliff, I mean. I'm ashamed to say I'm no better'n him at heart, we were both the same deep inside. It's been a hard lesson to know one's own evil. But now I know. If I don't forgive him, I won't forgive myself. And there's no place to go if you don't know how to forgive yourself.'

'But do you forgive *me*, Ryan?'

Putting his cigarette down, he put his arms about me and made me face him. Tears were streaming down my cheeks and he wiped them away with his hand before kissing me.

'Isn't your fault men love you. You're beautiful and kind. You're that sort of woman. Men can't help but be attracted to you. It's some inner thing you have, some vulnerability and yet strength too, brings them to their knees. Brought me to mine minute I saw you, long ago when your dad brought you to us at Longships. I've always loved you, Bridie, you know that.'

'And I love you, Ryan,' I said simply. 'And always have. I never loved Jim.'

It wasn't strictly true but my love for Jim was quite different, something twined inside my psyche since childhood. Even Ryan wouldn't understand that. I didn't understand it myself.

When I had asked for forgiveness, I had meant did he forgive me for making love to Jim. His answer was not what I had expected to hear. Did he forgive me or not? He knew I'd succumbed to Jim in the end. He had been there in the shadows, I felt sure of it. Or was I? Had it been a trick of my imagination and my own sense of guilt? I would never know any more than I would ever know if Ryan had pushed Jim down the stairs himself. Perhaps it was better that way, better we didn't know or admit the truth and have to face those demons head on. They always said you should only look at the Gorgon in a mirror, see her reflection and never stare her in the face.

I would wonder about it all my life long.

Trinity House moved us shortly after this. The Elder Brethren could be very kind when they chose to be and realised we couldn't work and live where such a tragedy had affected us. It meant Ryan had to go to another rock light but rather than follow him there I decided that I would go and live in Bournemouth and find us a house and a secure base. I was expecting a baby and felt it would be better for our kids to have some sense of permanency in their lives. To be honest I was tired of wandering here and there and never feeling settled. So we bought a nice little semi near Ethel Alcott, soon to be a great grandma and very proud of it.

I haven't forgotten my wish to run a nice little restaurant some day. But time will come when we'll all move to Cornwall. Joe and Sheila say that's where they'll go when they retire and Ethel wants to join them. Susan has married now and lives in Manchester and says she loves it there; she was never a one for the wild seascapes and romance of Cornwall. Much more of a pragmatic turn of mind, a city dweller is Susan. I still cook for the local cake shops and caffs and keep my hand in catering for little dinner parties and birthdays now and then. Some day I'll get round to starting something up on my own but life's a bit busy at the moment. I'm not in a hurry. For the first time in years, I feel at peace and contented, all the old anxieties have gone. I've got others to think about now, not just myself.

Remember Luke McGraw? I returned the money he lent me years ago with interest and we've kept up a correspondence every now and then. In the end, he moved back to Jamaica, took up a teaching job and met a lovely girl there. They have two kids now. They've invited us over for a holiday some time and we may well take them up on it. It'll be the first time in an aeroplane for Ryan and me and that will be really exciting. Jamaica! It sounds so exotic. Sunshine and sea together, all very idyllic. Not that I'm tired of stormy weather and grey skies but it will make a nice change.

Andy Bosworth went on from rich to super rich. He's outside our league and has nothing to do with us and we have nothing to do with him. I have news of him from Joe occasionally but frankly, I'm really not interested in the man. He's a stranger in my eyes, an unpleasant one at that, for all his urbane charm. Last time we met was at Jim's funeral and he hardly spoke to us. Maybe he held Ryan responsible in some way and hinted as much. His little blonde wife looked scared most of the time and I had no trouble guessing what sort of life she led with that bully. It was the price she had accepted in exchange for all that wealth.

We called our fair, blue-eyed little girl Bella. She is so adorable, sweet natured and pretty, the apple of our eye. After a year, I had a dark-haired, brown-eyed little boy and he's called Mark, the image of his dad, a proper lively little terror. They are the loveliest children in the world as far as I'm concerned but then I'm a proud mum. All the same, when Bella was about two years old, I caught a fleeting expression on her face when she was mad at something that made me realise with wry amusement how much she looked like Mean Millie.

It seemed that Millie and Jim would always be a part of my life one way or another.